BLO

BRUNNER SMASHED THE flat of his sword at the grinning mouth, knocking the goblin away, and leaving it to choke on its broken teeth. Another goblin crawled its way to the top of the rock pile, its red eyes gleaming with sadistic intent. Brunner roared at the little creature, causing it to flinch and slide away back down the rock pile.

More goblins were rounding the barrier. Brunner drew the short hatchet from his belt, turning his body from side to side to favour all his foes with his cold stare.

'Come on!' the bounty hunter snarled. 'Which of you vermin is tired of living?'

More Warhammer from the Black Library

· WARHAMMER NOVELS ·

GOTREK & FELIX by William King

THE VAMPIRE GENEVIEVE NOVELS
by Jack Yeovil

THE TALES OF ORFEO by Brian Craig

THE KONRAD TRILOGY by David Ferring

A WARHAMMER NOVEL

BLOOD AND STEEL

C. L. WERNER

For Ma. Now maybe she'll start speaking to me again.

A BLACK LIBRARY PUBLICATION

First published in Great Britain in 2003
by BL Publishing,
Games Workshop Ltd.,
Willow Road, Nottingham,
NG7 2WS, UK.

10 9 8 7 6 5 4 3 2 1

Cover illustration by Martin Hanford

A CIP record for this book
is available from the British Library

ISBN 1 84416 009 2

Set in ITC Giovanni

Printed and bound in Great Britain by
Cox & Wyman Ltd, Reading, Berks.

See the Black Library on the Internet at
www.blacklibrary.com

Find out more about Games Workshop
and the world of Warhammer at
www.games-workshop.com

THIS IS A DARK age, a bloody age, an age of daemons
and of sorcery. It is an age of battle and death, and of the
world's ending. Amidst all of the fire, flame and fury
it is a time, too, of mighty heroes, of bold deeds
and great courage.

AT THE HEART of the Old World sprawls the Empire, the
largest and most powerful of the human realms. Known
for its engineers, sorcerers, traders and soldiers, it is
a land of great mountains, mighty rivers, dark forests
and vast cities. And from his throne in Altdorf reigns
the Emperor Karl-Franz, sacred descendent of the
founder of these lands, Sigmar, and wielder
of his magical warhammer.

BUT THESE ARE far from civilised times. Across the
length and breadth of the Old World, from the knightly
palaces of Bretonnia to ice-bound Kislev in the far north,
come rumblings of war. In the towering World's Edge
Mountains, the orc tribes are gathering for another assault.
Bandits and renegades harry the wild southern lands of
the Border Princes. There are rumours of rat-things, the
skaven, emerging from the sewers and swamps across the
land. And from the northern wildernesses there is the
ever-present threat of Chaos, of daemons and beastmen
corrupted by the foul powers of the Dark Gods.
As the time of battle draws ever near,
the Empire needs heroes
like never before.

The Old Worlde

PROLOGUE

THE WORLD IS beset on all sides by great and terrible perils, creatures of the Old Night, things far beyond the imaginings of those safe in their beds within the sturdy walls of Altdorf. Evils, both mortal and supernatural, stalk the lands of men, from the green pastureland of Bretonnia to the swarming cities of the Empire. From the harsh deserts of Estalia to the crumbling strongholds of the dwarfs, dread forces move and dark deeds are consecrated to the most abominable of powers.

My chosen vocation is as a chronicler of such things, for I have ever been drawn to the workings of evil, as a moth is drawn to a flame. Indeed, it was my notorious work, *A True History of Vlad von Carstein*, and the unwanted attention it gathered, which caused me to flee my native Altdorf. For I discovered that supernatural monsters lurk even in the very shadow of the Emperor's palace and hunt in the very streets of his capital.

But even in exile, a man is still who he is. I continued to write tales of mystery and adventure, drawing upon the life experiences of sometimes less than reputable sources.

Sometimes, far too rarely, I would uncover some valiant and noble heart who had stood defiant before the forces of ruin and Chaos, who had heroically challenged the powers of darkness and driven them back into the shadows. More often, however, I learned the depths of greed and avarice to which a human soul can sink. Gold, I discovered, had stirred more men to action than any righteous cause. For the promise of gold, a man might stand his ground against the most terrible of monsters, the most debased and degenerate parodies of humanity, and thank steel rather than the gods that he emerged triumphant.

I had good cause to consider such things as I sat within a small tavern in the Bretonnian city of Parravon. It was to here that I had migrated after my hasty departure from the Tilean city of Miragliano in the south, and it was to here that I had returned after my brief flirtation with adventure, chronicled in my pamphlet *The Fall of the Black Prince*. Many months had passed since I had parted ways with my companion on that enterprise. Occasionally I would hear a rumour of his activities, a tale of murder and mayhem from some desolate corner of the realm. But of the man himself, there was no sign until the first thunderheads began to slip down from the looming heights of the Grey Mountains.

It was a dreary, chill evening and the sun was just beginning to forsake the sky. Overhead, thunder rumbled, echoing through the streets of the narrow Bretonnian township. I stood just outside the door of the tavern, watching the play of lightning in the distance. I was minded of old stories of storm gods and their capricious battles amongst one another. The flash of lightning was said to be the gleam of their swords as they struck one another's blades, the boom of the thunder was their raised voices as they contested in the sky above the storm. It was a fabulous display, each blue flash of light cast by the weather making the craggy heights of the mountains manifest from the deepening shadows like some spectral apparition.

For many long minutes I lost myself, fascinated by the awesome display of elemental might unfolding before me. It reminded me that there are things so much greater than fragile mankind, and that all his works, all his advances in civilisation, in science and wizardry, must seem as small and worthless as an ant hill beside them. What was man beside such forces as those that assailed him? The borders of his lands were ever threatened by the howling hosts of orc and goblin; the forests within his domains were the refuge of twisted, horrible things: mutants and beastmen, the children of dark gods and perverse corruption. Fiendish predators stalked the streets of even the greatest of his cities, fearsome monsters who had long ago forsaken their humanity for a loathsome parody of immortality. Beneath those same streets, other things lurked – the foul skaven, warped rat-like creatures of Chaos, working their foul intrigues below while the people living above discounted their very existence as spurious myth and superstition.

More loathsome than any of these, however, were the still human degenerates who had willingly betrayed all that was decent and good and bowed instead before the altars of the Ruinous Powers in hidden covens, forsaking their very souls in exchange for unspeakable promises. Evil was everywhere, lurking, waiting, biding its time until the hour of doom should arrive, and too few were those who might stand against it.

I looked away from the storm, distressed by the course my thoughts had wandered on. The sky was fast growing dark and I turned to go indoors. Even in Parravon, with its gardens and cobbled streets, its high walls and guarding cliffs, even here did the reach of evil extend. For generations some nameless thing had prowled the city after dark, so that none would willingly risk travelling the narrow lanes after the sun had forsaken its post. I had learned that it is often wise to heed such customs, as past experiences had taught me that many legends are more real than we would like to believe.

As I turned to re-enter the tavern, I noticed a figure striding through the gloom. There was something familiar about that walk, and I hesitated.

The man who approached was tall, his build lean, betraying a quality of muscle and power. He wore a suit of brigandine armour about his frame, over which a breastplate of gromril encased his chest. At some point, that fabulously hard metal had been scratched by a tremendous blow. Steel vambraces, darkened black to prevent any betraying shine, enclosed the man's forearms, while mismatched shoulder guards protected his upper arms. Hard leather boots with steel toes rose to meet the steel leg greaves that protected his thighs.

The man was a walking arsenal, a small crossbow pistol dangled from a clamp set upon one of his vambraces and a belt of knives crossed his chest. An expensive-looking pistol sheltered in a holster set across his belly while a thick-bladed hatchet swung from his belt just above his right leg. A massive, cruel knife nestled beside the hatchet, a blade with a serrated edge that its owner had morbidly named the 'Headsman'. A scabbard on the man's left side held a longsword, its pommel and guard shaped in the form of a golden dragon with outspread wings. Its name was 'Drakesmalice', a sword with some history and reputation in the lands formerly owned by the house of von Drakenburg, and now claimed by the Viscount de Chegney.

The warrior continued to stride towards me out of the darkening twilight. His face was largely concealed by the mask of a rounded sallet helm, of the sort favoured by the militia and soldiery of Reikland. It was of black steel and a dent in its surface gave evidence to some past service it had performed for its wearer. Cold blue eyes regarded me through the visor.

'Stoecker,' the man addressed me in a hard voice.

'It has been a long time, Brunner,' I said. 'Over half a year.'

'I've been busy,' Brunner replied.

'No rest for the wicked?'

'Not until they put me in the ground,' was his response. 'And you? I should have thought you would have left a back-water like Parravon a long time ago.'

'I keep myself busy,' I lied. In truth, the tedium of the place, the unending chore of transcribing the Duc of Parravon's grossly enriched family history, had been working on me and I had begun to consider moving on. 'The climate here agrees with me,' I elaborated. Actually, the climate had become fairly hostile ever since Yvette had forsaken my company for that of a dashing young guardsman, who seemed unable to cope with the presence of a former paramour of his beloved.

'Perhaps we might repair indoors,' I said, noting with alarm the rapid onset of night. Brunner inclined his head, motioning for me to lead the way. It was a short walk back to the tavern, and I soon secured a table and two tankards of mead, for they had long since run dry of anything approaching beer. Brunner sat at the table, leaning back against the wall, his eyes canvassing the room, studying each face with a practiced gaze.

Brunner was a bounty hunter, one of the most notorious in the Old World. From the bandit strongholds of the Forest of Shadows, to the lowliest thieves' nest in Gisoreux, his name alone was enough to make outlaws shudder with fear. His reputation was something of a legend in and of itself, and it was said that he never failed to bring in his prey once he was on their trail. Death was the only escape from this relentless hunter, and even then there was no guarantee that he would not yet bring his catch back. The 'Headsman' was not so named casually, that gruesome instrument had earned its name. I had often seen the evidence of this for myself.

I had met Brunner in the south, during my years of exile in Miragliano. At the time, I had been penning adventure pamphlets for a spurious publisher named Ernesto, and the bloody career of the bounty hunter had formed the basis for some of these schilling dreadfuls. There was something at once terrible and fascinating about the man, repulsive and compelling at the same time. I should have never had anything to do with him after the events that led to my hasty flight from the Tilean city, yet when he had arrived in Parravon on the trail of the infamous Black Prince, I had not only renewed our association, but even accompanied him on his perilous hunt. Now I found myself once again sitting over drinks with the remorseless killer.

'I unearthed one of your books in Gisoreux,' Brunner said after he had sipped at his mead. 'Amazing how far those things have travelled.'

'Everyone appreciates a hero,' I said. 'It gives them an escape from the hardships of everyday life.'

Brunner leaned forward over the table. 'You should try writing the truth sometime. Write about what really happened. Not some tripe about a noble warrior on a white horse, riding off to right wrongs and champion the weak and punish the wicked.'

'Indeed,' I shot back, 'you would prefer me to write about a heartless bastard who would put his sword through Sigmar reborn if he saw gold in such a deed!' The bounty hunter glared at me for a moment, then laughed grimly.

'Perhaps you have the right of it,' he said. 'Nobody wants to face the way things really are. They like their lies and fables.' He sipped again at his drink. 'I don't think many people would appreciate some of the things I've seen and done.'

It is one of the failings of my personality that I have a morbid fascination with tales of horror and the macabre, but I must also admit to a profound interest in the less than stalwart deeds of men such as Brunner. Their very existence on the fringes of society, their ability to kill without question or pity, their amazing knack for surviving against even the greatest odds has become a compelling mystery to me. As I heard the haunted tone in Brunner's voice, my ears picked up and I set about trying to draw the story out of him. At last, he relented.

Brunner finished off his mead, wiping the sleeve of his tunic across his lips. Then he settled back and began to speak.

'As you know, some time passed between your departure from Miragliano and my coming to Parravon,' Brunner rumbled. 'There are a great many things that happened to me while you were away...'

BENEATH THE VAULTS

NICOLETTA SLOWLY MADE her way from the raucous commotion of the large common room that dominated the lower floor of the Purple Kitten. It was a busy night for the notorious Miragliano brothel. No less than seven merchant vessels had docked in the harbour during the day, each having just returned from a long and dangerous voyage to the northern port of Marienburg. But the eagerness of the sailors and mercenary marines to squander their wealth was not attractive to Nicoletta this night. Her mind was troubled, making it difficult for her to abide the crude gaiety of the common room, much less the physical aspects of her trade. Though the hour was not very late, Nicoletta had given her sisters of the night her share of the custom and was now making her way to her small room on the upper floor of the bordello.

Of course, such a dereliction of her duties was not without its hazards. If Madame Livia were to discover her absence, the best she could expect would be a beating. More likely, the wizened hag would detail Nicoletta to entertain some of the brothel's more curious customers, and their less than common tastes. Normally, the least appealing of the girls was given such duties, but Madame Livia never failed to threaten her prettier workers with the detail when they were not compliant with her wishes and the demands of business.

The woman paused before her door. She could hear sounds coming from the other rooms and a part of her mind chided her for her foolishness, for throwing away all the silver and gold she might earn if she would just forget about things. There was nothing she could do, and worrying would solve nothing. She was risking the wrath of her madame by not working. All it would take would be for one of the other girls to discover that she had slipped away and inform the madame and she would have even more problems to occupy her mind. It was no good – the softer, less practical instincts were too strong to wish away with common sense. Nicoletta could not help worrying about her beloved, nor could she distance herself enough from him to ply her trade.

She had met him years ago, right here in the Purple Kitten. He had cut a dashing figure, a handsome rogue sailor, an adventurer who had travelled to nearly every port Nicoletta had ever heard of. He'd seen the great statues of all the old emperors in Altdorf's Konigplatz. He'd sailed his ship beneath Marienburg's high bridge and passed within view of the craggy coasts of the fabled and dreaded Norsca. She'd at once warmed to his rakish charm, aided in no small way by the gold and jewels he had lavished upon her. He'd promised to take her away from the Purple Kitten when he had amassed enough wealth to provide her with a home in whatever city she chose. Unlike the many other infatuated sailors and mercenaries she had entertained, she'd believed Bruno Brega. The small treasures he presented her every time he made port in Miragliano convinced her of his sincerity. One day, Bruno Brega would indeed take her away from Madame Livia and her customers. And, Nicoletta decided, living with the good looking smuggler wouldn't be such a bad price to pay for her liberty.

She opened the door and stepped into the darkened room. At once a foul animal reek struck her. She clutched her nose against the smell, her powdered face twisting into a grimace of disgust. It was as if every dog on the Strada dei

Cento Peccati had rolled around the overflowing gutters and then pranced about in her room. Nicoletta snarled a curse and stamped across the small room, past the large bed and toward the sole window to lift the shutter and allow the disgusting smell an avenue of escape.

As the trull made her way through the shadowy room, a patch of darkness detached itself from the wall. Before the woman could react, the apparition had placed itself between her and the door. An arm, wrapped in leather bindings, extended from the shadow; its hand fastened upon the door, and slammed it closed.

Nicoletta opened her mouth to yell – possibly to gain the attention of the burly toughs that protected Madame Livia's girls – as she backed away toward one of the walls. But the sound died on her lips as the feeble light from the window illuminated the hand. It was not human at all, but something clawed and twisted and horrible.

The shadow advanced upon her, and as it came forward, the animal stench filled her lungs. She could only just make out the basic outline of the sinister figure: it was a tall, lean creature, shrouded in a hooded cloak that fell to its thighs. The legs seemed wrong in some way. As the interloper came forward, it seemed as if its knees folded backward and forward at the same time. Hard boots that reflected the dim light from the street encased its feet.

Nicoletta retreated before the fearsome presence, cringing into some tiny corner of her soul, sobbing like a child. The animal stench grew and Nicoletta could see the visage that observed her from beneath the shadowy hood. The lower face was wrapped in a thick, heavy scarf of rough material, but above the scarf the skin was coarse and swarthy, hirsute and weathered. Eyes gleamed from the masked face – eyes that burned and glowed with an orange light in the darkness.

Nicoletta trembled, fumbling at the pocket of her dress for the small knife she kept hidden there. The shadow laughed, and then it spoke.

'Ah, my mangy dove,' the shadow's voice rasped. It was like a foul wind blowing across a dank bog, bubbling with corruption and decay. 'I have waited so very long for you to return to your roost.'

Nicoletta lifted the knife, and held it between herself and the horrible spectre. A scratchy bark-like sound rumbled from below the scarf and with a slow, deliberate gesture the malformed hand gently pulled the knife from the woman's grasp, dropping the weapon casually upon the floor.

'Do not worry, my mangy dove,' the shadow laughed. 'Your dubious honour is safe with me.' Nicoletta wept a tear of terror as the malformed hand caressed her cheek and slowly slid down her face, lingering on her chin for a moment, before falling to her chest. 'I have pressing concerns this night, and no time to squander.' The hand on her chest knocked Nicoletta backwards, causing her to crash on the floor beside her bed. 'More's the pity,' the shadow hissed with a touch of regret.

Nicoletta started to pick herself up from the floor when the intruder closed upon her once more, pulling her head upwards by the long locks of dark hair. His fingers twisted inside bunches of Nicoletta's hair, forcing her to stare into the ghastly eyes.

'Tell me what I need to know, my mangy dove, and I shall be about my business.' The hand gave a hard yank, bringing a sharp gasp of pain from Nicoletta. 'You do want to be a good little whore and tell me all I want to know, don't you?' The shadow paused, relaxing his grip so the girl could nod her head.

'Good,' the shadow hissed and bubbled. 'That will save us much unpleasantness. You do, of course, know a man named Bruno Brega?' Nicoletta's eyes widened with fear when she heard the gruesome creature speak the name of her beloved, the very man whose well-being had so discomfited her. 'I need to find him. There are people very interested in his whereabouts. People with very deep purses. Tell me, my mangy dove, where is your admirer?'

Nicoletta felt a surge of dread welling up inside her – not for herself, but for the man she loved. This greater fear coursed through her, steeling her and providing her with a paltry simulacrum of courage. She croaked a response to the pitiless deeps of the stranger's cat-like eyes.

'I... I do n–not know... any such man!' The hand in her hair pulled back hard. She cried out in pain.

'So,' the shadow's loathsome voice rasped with mock regret. 'I see we must do this in a more time-consuming manner.' Her captor reached beneath the folds of his cloak and drew out a small metal tube, no larger than her knife. One end of the tube was angled and sharp, like the point of a scribe's pen. The entire implement was hollow like a flute.

The intruder crouched over Nicoletta, twisting her head around so far it almost snapped her neck. He stared into the woman's terrified orbs. Her mouth opened again, but the hand clutching the metal tube pressed itself against her lips, stifling her words. A trio of short sounds issued from the shadow, like the gentle reprimand of a disappointed parent.

'I lied, of course, my mangy dove,' the shadow rasped. 'No matter what lies you chose to tell me, we would have come to this. Perhaps you even have a mind to tell me the truth, now.' He laughed once more. 'I shall know soon enough what there is in that pretty little head.'

With a swift motion, the intruder stabbed the metal tube into Nicoletta's skull. There was a dull crunch as the implement broke through bone. The woman's body spasmed in the shadow's grasp, but the iron grip held her firm. The shadow's distorted hand pawed at its face for a moment, pulling the scarf away.

Its lips hovered over the metal tube and then the shadow began to drink the dying woman's memories.

ON THE LANDWARD side of Miragliano vast marshlands stretched for many leagues – shallow lakes of tall marsh grass interrupted by small islands of more stable ground. Scows and barges were the means of transport here. Enterprising merchants collected the fresh water of the marsh to sell to the thirsty citizens of the city. Beyond the many leagues of the marshlands were gently sloping hills and meadows, vast cultivated fields of grains and vegetables, orchards of fruit trees, rambling vineyards and great spreads of pasture for cattle and sheep. This was Miragliano's breadbasket, protected by forts garrisoned by the soldiers of Prince Borgio himself, who was strategist enough to understand that a hungry army would win none of Miragliano's many wars.

But soon after the last fort had been passed, the cultivated lands faded. Here the landscape grew more desolate, stands of thin-boled trees grew in unmanaged, confused clusters, brush crept ever nearer to the few roads and paths, threatening to consume them. The rolling hills sheltered deep shadowy hollows, places where the hot Tilean sun could not reach. This ungoverned region was home only to a few hardy trappers and woodsmen, hunters and foresters who wrenched their livelihood from the wilds. Packs of beastmen roamed these places; small tribes of orcs and goblins eked out a miserable and tenuous existence preying upon the weakest of the merchant caravans that dared to brave the ill-kept roads. Bands of human predators lurked alongside the monsters – outlaws and deserters from the numerous mercenary companies employed by the many merchant princes. Wise was the traveller who trusted no man he encountered in these lonely wilds.

Five men stood in a small circle before the ruins of an old, ramshackle hunter's cabin. On the ground between them, a sixth man lay, arms and legs spread to either side of his body. He was secured to wooden stakes by thick loops of rope. The standing men all sported similar dark clothing, piecemeal armour and a motley array of weapons. They each wore an expression of cruelty and avarice.

The darkly handsome Tilean features of the man on the ground were ashen with fear. He knew these men, and he knew he had every reason to be afraid.

'Come now, Bruno,' a giant of a man grunted through his thick black beard. 'Tell us where you hid the gold, so we can just kill you and have done with it.' The huge man's dirty hand fell to one of the dozen knives criss-crossing his massive belly on a worn leather bandoleer. 'Otherwise I'll have to cut you some. I'd like that, but I can guarantee you won't enjoy it!'

'I told you before,' the man stretched between the stakes spoke from his bruised face. 'He didn't pay me! The bastard tried to kill me after I delivered it to him!'

'Don't lie to us!' spat a thin man whose nose was scarred with a knife wound. 'You should have played square with us, Brega!' He kicked the prostrate man in the ribs, bringing forth a groan of pain. 'Not so smart after all, eh? Cheatin' us is the last thing you shoulda done!'

'I should have let them hang you in Tobaro when I had the chance, Sollima!' snarled Brega, struggling against his bonds. The thin Sollima rewarded the captive's efforts with another boot into his ribs.

'Are we gonna beat him to death or find out where he hid the gold?' growled another of the men – a tall man wearing a studded leather tunic and an old battered helmet.

'You heard him, Bruno,' said the giant with the collection of knives. 'Do you tell us where the gold is, or do we beat you to death?'

'The Dark Gods rot your flesh, Nuccio! There *is* no gold!' Brega lifted his head from the ground to roar at his captors.

'As you like, Bruno,' the hulking Nuccio replied, drawing a knife from his bandoleer. 'Two of you hold him down. It takes a steady hand to peel flesh from bone.'

Two of the men descended upon Brega, grabbing hold of his body and forcing him to lie still. Brega spat a glob of phlegm into the face of Nuccio as the butcher leaned over him. The giant paused a moment, wiping the spit from his beard, then a grim smile grew across his features. This was going to be fun.

'Ranald's cloak, who is that?' exclaimed the thin Sollima in a whiny tone. Nuccio looked up, the knife now inches from Brega's face.

An armoured shape strode into the clearing, its chest encased in metal, and its face hidden by the blackened steel of an Imperial-style sallet helm. A cloak of grey cloth was draped about the man's right arm. His left arm rested casually against the hilt of the sword sheathed at his side.

The five ruffians glared at the lone warrior.

'I hate to intrude upon your entertainment,' the warrior said in a voice as cold as steel, 'but I need your playmate.'

'A poor jest,' grunted Nuccio, as he rose to tower above his fellow smugglers. Each of the men was now fingering the hilts of their weapons. The prisoner was momentarily forgotten. 'And one that is going to cost you.' Nuccio nodded to two of his comrades who began to stalk away to the right, while the others began to circle to the left. 'If you have a god, pray to him.' Nuccio took a step forward, drawing a fat-bladed sword.

The warrior did not wait for the man to close in on him, nor did he wait for the other ruffians who were tightening the circle around him. Throwing back his cloak, he revealed the curious crossbow gripped in his gloved hand. It was a strange device of inhuman construction, with a box-like mechanism set on top of it. Before Nuccio could more than register the fact that the interloper held a weapon in his hand, the steel bow string had snapped three times in rapid succession. The first bolt smashed into the large man's breastbone. The second tore through his windpipe. The third broke his teeth before burying itself in the rear of his mouth. The brutish thug silently toppled backward, like a felled tree.

Brunner turned from the slain Nuccio, and trained the skaven-made weapon on the rogues to his left. The men were staring in open-mouthed horror at the carnage the bounty hunter had delivered upon their leader. As soon as they realised that Brunner's weapon was now trained on them, the two thieves turned and ran. Brunner could hear their comrades to his right already crashing through the brush and brambles.

The bounty hunter cradled his weapon in his arms. The murderous bow was indeed a fair payment for his infiltration of the dungeons of Karl-Franz. He was grateful to the sinister little rat-man he had met in the Dancing Fox.

Brega emitted a muffled groan. Brunner strode forward, and stared down at the man pinned beneath the giant Nuccio. He coughed, the dead weight of Nuccio crushing the air from his lungs. Brunner smiled down at the trapped man, then rolled the hulking body to one side.

'The grace of all the gods be yours, stranger,' gasped Brega after he had recovered his breath. 'I thought I was carrion for certain.' Brega tugged at the bindings lashed about his left arm, as if to alert his saviour to his predicament. But his saviour had other matters to attend to. The bounty hunter turned from the prisoner and crouched over Nuccio's corpse.

Brega craned his neck as far as he could to see what the killer was doing. He soon wished that he hadn't. Brunner was leaning on the slain ruffian's chest, a flat wedge-like device gripped in his gloved hand. Brega watched in horror as the man quickly pried the three crossbow bolts from Nuccio's body. He raised each bolt to his visor as he pried them from the corpse. The one dug out of Nuccio's chest was discarded into the dust. The others he put back into the box-like magazine of the crossbow. Then the bounty hunter's hand fell upon the pommel of the massive knife sheathed between pistol and sword on his belt. Brunner freed the blade, its serrated edge gleaming in the light, then he leaned back over Nuccio's body.

Eventually the bounty hunter rose, dropping his dripping trophy into a small sack. Then he turned and strode over to Brega's bound figure once more.

'My name is Brunner, and this is your unlucky day,' his icy voice rasped. Brega cried out just as the man's gloved hand smashed into his face, but the smuggler was unconscious before the sound could fully be uttered.

BRUNO BREGA AWOKE slowly, moaning in pain. His first thought was infuriation that he should be feeling pain. The priests always said that there was no suffering in Morr's realm, only eternal rest and silence. He tried to raise a hand to feel the lump he sensed bulging from his forehead where the bounty hunter had smashed him, but the bindings prevented him from doing so. For a moment, the smuggler was puzzled – he was clearly no longer stretched out on the ground between the stakes. As he opened his eyes, Brega realised that he was lying across the back of a horse, his wrists and ankles bound together underneath the animal's belly. The motion he had sensed was now clear to him: he was being carried like a sack of goods by a pack animal. He tried to twist his wrists inside his bindings, but they were held securely.

Brega wondered if his luck could desert him any more completely. Everything had gone wrong for him since he had stolen the old clay pot from Altdorf. It was clearly an artefact of immense antiquity, some relic from the vast deserts of Araby. Even Brega had heard the old legends brought back by the crusaders about the daemons of the desert, the mythical djinn, who were imprisoned in sorcerous vessels long ago, so that they might be enslaved by the most reckless and power-mad of Araby's mystics. When he had first seen the old clay pot, he had sensed its disturbing air of unnaturalness, and wondered what might lie within it. One of his fellow smugglers, well versed in antiquities, had claimed that the picture writing on the pot was older than the scratch-script of Araby, from before the birth of the Empire even. He had seen such picture writing before, in the curio shops of Luccini and Miragliano, where relics looted from the Land of the Dead sometimes found their way.

Other hands had stolen the jar from a private collection, but Brega and his band of smugglers had been given the duty of getting the ancient artefact out of the Empire. There was a man in the Tilean city-state of Remas who was prepared to pay a small fortune for the object. The agent of the Tilean had given Brega and his men a most handsome advance.

The journey, however, had gone badly. On the Reik, as they were making their way towards Marienburg, the smugglers had been attacked by river pirates of a most despicable cast. They were led by a bearded madman, a devotee of the terrible Blood God. Several of Brega's mob died before their vessel finally eluded the pirates. Ironically they had taken protection from the imposing cannon of the infamous Reiksfang prison as the running battle drew close to its walls.

Further along the River Reik, a winged thing – some nightmare horror – had fallen upon their decks, wantonly slaughtering men before it was disposed of, and its foul corpse pushed overboard. In Marienburg, Brega's ship had joined a small flotilla that was making its way to the southern ports of Tilea. This was the first good omen since leaving Altdorf, but it did not take long for the tide of ill fortune to catch up with them again. Norse raiders struck the fleet shortly after it left Marienburg, and seven ships were left burning as the fleet fled the fury of the Northmen. Off the shores of Bretonnia, some ghastly sea beast had plucked seven crewmen from the deck of the ship nearest Brega's. Rounding the horn of Estalia, a thick fog had enshrouded the fleet. When the fog eventually lifted, the leading ship began to sail back towards the west, and its deck was not manned by human shapes...

Brega was certain that they would never reach Remas. He had even considered tossing the pot into the sea, certain that it was accursed. But the prospect of the gold awaiting him at the end of the journey stayed him. In the end, they did reach Remas, and Brega immediately set about meeting their mysterious employer. They met in a darkened back room of a dockside tavern. Brega could not get a decent look at the Tilean, such were the shadows in the chamber. He had presented the man with the clay jar, at which the Tilean had laughed – an unnerving, insane sound. Brega rose from the table, shocked by the mad laughter, just as the Tilean leapt to his feet, drawing a sword. Brega drew his own sword then, prepared to teach the cackling madman to honour his contracts.

The villain had rounded the table, emerging into the feeble light that filtered into the room from the gaps between the planks of the door. Brega could see that the man was dressed well, a fashionable black cloak fell from his shoulders and a gaudy gold buckle gleamed from his belt. Of the man's face, however, he could see nothing, for it was covered by a glistening red mask, such as might be worn to a masque ball, shaped like a fang-mouthed skull. From the deep pits of the grotesque mask's sockets, crazed eyes blazed with maniacal emotion – exhilaration mixed with bloodlust to form a psychopathic frenzy. Brega had not seen such insanity, even in the eyes of Chaos-worshipping pirates.

For a brief second Brega was able to study his duplicitous employer. But as he rounded the table, the man had brought

his sword slashing toward Brega who barely managed to
turn it aside with his own weapon. The madman's stroke
had not been skilful; it was too wild and bloodthirsty to
belong to any school of swordsmanship. But what it lacked
in skill, it made up for in strength. As Brega met the man's
blow, his body shuddered with the force. The madman's
sabre deflected toward the table, and crunched through it
like a hot knife through cheese. As the table fell apart, and
his attacker recovered from his failed strike, Brega brought
his own sword upward to a guarding position. It was then
that he saw how deeply the lunatic's hit had bitten into his
own blade. There was a deep notch in the smuggler's sword,
so deep that barely an inch of steel held the two halves
together.

Dread bubbled up within the smuggler. Even a madman
should not have such strength; no mere human foe could
call upon such immense power. Brega cast his ruined sword
into the face of the ruby mask and turned, fleeing from the
tiny dark room and the bloodthirsty horror that lusted after
his life.

For what seemed like hours, the smuggler fled through the
streets of Remas, trying to lose his maniacal pursuer. There
was something evil in that jar, he was sure, and he had
unwittingly delivered it to someone who would put it to
some dreadful purpose.

In a heroic tale, Brega would have tried to find and undo
the terrible evil he had unwittingly brought to the city, but
he was too sensible to be a hero. He stole a horse and fled
Remas at the first opportunity. He had ridden first for
Miragliano and the company of his mistress, retrieving a
small cache of money he had left in her care. Then he had
ridden for this old hideout, to recover still more loot. But he
had been too slow. Nuccio and some of his former comrades
had been waiting for him, mistaking the reason for his flight
from Remas. They were determined to get their share of the
money that Brega had never collected.

Now he was free of his murderous comrades, but he had
traded them for someone worse. Brega had never set eyes
upon the bounty killer called Brunner, but he had heard

enough tales whispered about him in thieves' dens across the Old World to know that he did not want to.

BREGA LOOKED ABOUT him. He could see the grim figure of the bounty hunter, mounted upon a massive bay horse, scabbards dangling from the steed's harness. Behind the bay was a smaller grey packhorse, laden down with numerous sacks and equipment, and a few small wooden kegs. A rope connected the packhorse's bridle to the bounty hunter's steed, and another rope connected Brega's mount to the packhorse.

Not only had Brega's situation changed, his surroundings had as well. The cabin and its clearing, indeed the entire forest, were no small distance behind them. Brega could see the monstrous slopes of the Vaults towering before him. The terrain was hilly and rocky, the path upon which their animals marched little more than a game trail. Brega could see traces of worked stone lying toppled among the raw boulders scattered along the side of the trail. They were half-formed columns and unfinished faces, abandoned long ago to the mercy of rain and wind.

The bounty hunter turned his head and stared at his prisoner. The black steel of his helmet nodded in satisfaction.

'Good to see you're coming around,' the cold voice said. 'I was afraid that I might have hit you too hard. You're no good to me dead.'

The chill manner in which the bounty hunter voiced this twisted parody of concern caused Brega's heart to skip a beat. The smuggler mumbled a feeble prayer to Ranald under his breath. More loudly he said: 'I have done nothing! I was set upon by bandits and thought you to be my rescuer! My family is poor, they cannot afford to pay you a ransom.'

Brunner laughed, a dry chuckle that was as menacing as the snarl of a rabid wolf. 'Perhaps, but Judge Vaulkberg has deep pockets. Deep enough to satisfy me.'

The bounty hunter's words caused Brega to moan with despair. Judge Vaulkberg! The most notorious magistrate in the Empire, infamous for his harsh judgements and wanton cruelty. There was a tale that he had once ordered that a priestess of Verena's lips be branded with a heated iron for speaking out against the execution of a man who failed to doff his cap in Vaulkberg's courtroom. And that had been one of Vaulkberg's more lenient judgements. More often he set his ogre executioner to cause limbs to bend in unusual ways.

'You are mistaken!' Brega declared.

The bounty hunter twisted about in his saddle, fixing him with a cold stare.

'I don't make mistakes,' Brunner said. 'You are Bruno Brega, a petty smuggler. You usually operate moving black lotus on the Upper Reik, when you are not sneaking grain past the Emperor's excise men in Altdorf.'

The smuggler's head sagged back down against the side of his horse. He knew that any feeble attempt to convince the bounty hunter that he had the wrong man would not work. Ahead of him, the hired killer chuckled.

'I know all about you, Brega,' Brunner stated. 'I came all the way from Altdorf to look for you.' The bounty hunter laughed again. 'Ordinarily I wouldn't cross a county for a reptile like you, but Vaulkberg's put a very pretty price on your head, a very pretty price. It seems that last cargo of beef you smuggled into the capital was tainted, corrupt. It also seems that Vaulkberg's mistress ate some of it and died. The judge has spent quite a few lonely nights thinking about what he wants to do to you.'

Brega stifled a sob of horror. Judge Vaulkberg was a cruel, sadistic fiend when he was in good humour. The smuggler didn't even want to think what he would be like angry.

'I have hidden quite a bit of money,' Brega let the words hastily slip from his lips. 'I can pay you well!' The bounty hunter shot the smuggler a withering glare from behind his visor.

'When I accept a commission, I see it through,' he snarled. 'If you offer me money again before we get to the Reikland, I'll stuff a gag in that scheming mouth of yours. And that might make eating a bit difficult.'

Brega bit down any reply. He didn't really want to find out whether the bounty hunter was bluffing. Instead he looked past Brunner, casting his gaze toward the towering peaks of the Vaults. Unlike most of the teeming masses of humanity, Brega could read a map, and had seen them on many occasions. Knowing where one was and where one was going was vital for a smuggler. But that knowledge brought home a frightening realisation. Brunner meant to take him back to the Empire, to the Reikland. There was only one problem with that, and Brega was looking at it.

The Old World was divided by a series of mighty mountain ranges. The Apuccinis formed the eastern boundary of Tilea, separating the merchant princes and their holdings from the lawless Borderlands. The Irranas, marking the northern limit of Tilea, acted as a barrier between the city states and the kingdom of Bretonnia. Running northward, the legend-haunted Grey Mountains, the fence between the Empire and Bretonnia.

The Black Mountains formed the southern border of the domain of Karl-Franz; it was the Empire's rocky wall that kept out the orcs of the Bad Lands. Each of these ranges stretched for hundreds of miles, uncrossable save for a handful of closely guarded passes.

All four of these massive formations met in the north-east corner of Tilea, crashing together in a vast, titanic upland known as the Vaults. It was an impenetrable region of towering rock larger than the entire Plain of Luccini. Some of the Irranas and the Apuccinis reached heights of ten thousand feet and more. Amidst the Black and Grey Mountains, there were peaks that exceeded fifteen thousand feet. Even the tallest of these was a mere hill compared to the peaks of the Vaults. They loomed above the converging ranges like giants, the smallest of their number near the twenty thousand foot mark. The tallest were nearly five thousand feet higher still. Only the World's Edge range could boast loftier heights in all the Old World.

The peaks of the Vaults were perpetually shrouded in snow. Even in the most sweltering Tilean summer, the ice held its grip upon the uppermost slopes. The mountains were steep, jagged and twisted like the fangs of some gargantuan rock daemon. Deep crevices wormed their way amongst them, their depths unknown and unknowable.

Even the most reckless of mountain explorers had not dared the inner reaches of the Vaults, for they understood that the giant formations of stone and earth did not offer adventure and discovery, only the promise of a lonely death.

'You're taking me to the Reikland?' Brega asked, a new tone of horror creeping into his voice.

'Worked that out on your own, did you?' Brunner replied, without turning to look at his prisoner.

'But the Vaults!' exclaimed the smuggler. 'Surely you can't mean to cross the Vaults?' The bounty killer did not reply. Terror welled up within Brega. 'You can't cross the mountains! Even if we don't get eaten by beasts or orcs, there isn't a path through them! We'd freeze on the high slopes, or plummet into a crevasse! You can't go over the mountains!'

Brunner twisted around in the saddle. 'Who said that we are going *over* them?'

Four GRIMY MEN sat in the darkened interior of a long unused cabin. Two of them pulled heavy cloaks tighter about their bodies as the cold night wind slithered between the gaps in the log walls. One of them despondently tended the small fire that had been made in the shallow pit at the centre of the cabin.

'Such valiant scum I keep company with,' snorted Sollima. He cast a surly look at his comrades. 'Let that vermin just swoop in and steal Brega right out from under us!' He placed a finger against his gruesome nose. 'From right under our very noses!'

'I didn't see you standing your ground after he killed Nuccio!' snarled the man tending the fire.

'I was too busy chasing the coat tails of my very brave friends!' spat Sollima.

'Call me a coward again, you rat, and I'll take the rest of your nose!' grumbled the fire-stoker, his grimy hand falling to the sword at his side.

The other two smugglers shrugged free of their cloaks to draw their swords. The older of the two, whose head was encased in a steel helmet, moved between the arguing men.

'Settle down, both of you!' he ordered. 'We should be thinking how to get Brega back, not trying to kill one another!'

'And who elected you boss?' snapped Sollima. The smuggler beside the fire pulled his sword free from its sheath.

'I've had my fill of the lot of you!' the fire-stoker growled through his beard. 'I'll get him on my own, and I can guarantee Brega will spill what he knows when I get my hands on him!'

'And you think you'll be able to kill that bounty hunter on your own, do you?' scoffed the helmeted smuggler. 'Think a bit of slink and strike will work on his sort?'

The companion of the helmeted smuggler worked his grimy hand toward the hilt of the dagger on his belt, prepared to back whatever play for leadership his friend was about to make. As he did so, he noticed a peculiar and foul odour. He glanced toward the open doorway of the cabin, grimacing at the thick animal stench coming from that direction. He wondered what sort of animal had slunk its way past the thin curtain of hide covering the doorway, and hoped that it was not a rat or some equally noxious creature. The growing ire of the other smugglers, however, quickly drew his attention from the vile smell and whatever bore it.

'I suppose you have a better idea?' hissed Sollima.

'As a matter of fact–' the smuggler began to reply. But his words trailed off into a dry rasp as a shaft of wood blossomed from his breast, red feathers turning a deeper shade of crimson as the smuggler's life-blood engulfed them. The man fell, dropping his sword from nerveless fingers. His helmet rolled away as his body struck the earthen floor.

The other rogues sprang into action. The smuggler at the fire sprang away from the pit, seeking the safety of the shadows. Sollima dived for his gear, hastily retrieving a small wooden shield. No sooner had he gained the shield than an arrow thudded into it, the force of the impact causing him to fall onto his back.

The last smuggler ran for the door of the cabin, sparing no thought for his comrades. All he wanted was to put as much distance as he could between himself and the thing that had set upon them. His cowardice marked him as the second to die. As he ran for the door, a figure rose from the shadows near the portal. It was indistinct, with only a vague suggestion of a human form. The smuggler could see a bow gripped in one of its hands. The other struck out at him. He had a moment to feel fingers of steel close about his throat. His remaining seconds of life were nothing but pain.

The stricken smuggler stumbled back into the centre of the cabin, hands clamped about the gory weeping hole beneath his jaw, torn tissue trying to give voice to his silent scream. The dying man stumbled into the pit, toppling into the flames. For a moment, he tried to pull himself out, but didn't have enough strength to do so. His clutching fingers finally grew still as the life faded from his body.

Sollima and the bearded smuggler watched their comrade's demise. Both men gave a yelp of fright as a gory object was tossed into the area illuminated by the fire. It landed beside the dead smuggler's arm. It was his throat.

Their attacker strode forward, its movements peculiar and inhuman. An animal reek overwhelmed even the stink of burning flesh rising from the fire pit.

Eerie eyes stared from the black shadow of its head, reflecting the flickering light of the fire with an orange luminosity. It was roughly human in shape, shrouded in a hooded garment cast about its shoulders. As the two smugglers watched, their shadowy attacker drew a curved sword from a scabbard on its belt.

'I have questions,' the shadow spoke in a terrifying rasping croak. 'You will answer them for me.' The thing stepped further into the light, allowing the two men to see its twisted form. Its head swept from side to side, fixing each of the men with its ghastly gaze, despite the darkness. 'You will tell me everything,' the rasping voice gurgled, 'before you die.'

With a snarl of his own, the bearded smuggler fired his crossbow at the monster. The shape dropped to a crouch with impossible speed and the bolt whistled over its cowled head. Before the man could reload, the shape sprang up and leapt forward like a pouncing tiger. Sollima could not see the creature any longer, as it disappeared into the patch of darkness the other smuggler was hiding in. But he could hear what ensued. The sound of screams. The sound of tearing cloth. The sound of flesh being ripped from bone.

Orange eyes gleamed at Sollima from the shadows. The smuggler watched as the creature walked back into the light. Blood covered its arms and dripped from its hands. It gestured toward Sollima with its unbloodied sword. The smuggler cringed backwards, his back crushed against the timber wall.

'You are dead,' the creature hissed. 'Slow or long, it is your choice how you die. Choose quickly.'

Sollima gave a shriek of fright, throwing his sword and shield away. He scrambled forward, dropping to his hands and knees as he entered the circle of light. Tears of terror dripped from his eyes, and inarticulate sobs escaped from his chest.

'Please,' he gasped between sobbing breaths. 'I'll tell you whatever you want! Don't kill me!'

The shadow bent down over the weeping smuggler. One of its malformed hands closed about the man's chin, forcing his face upward. The other wiped away the man's tears, leaving smears of blood as it removed the watery trails. The orange eyes burned from the shadows of the hood.

'Tell me, little rabbit,' the rasping gurgle croaked. 'Where is Bruno Brega?'

The shadow was as immobile as a statue. Between choking sobs, Sollima related what had befallen them, how they had captured their former leader only to lose him to the armoured bounty hunter. When the smuggler had finished his story, the shadow made a strange, dry sound like the yapping of a parched jackal.

'Brunner,' the shape chuckled. 'You think to take my merchandise to market.' Another bestial laugh hissed from the grim shadow. 'I think not. I've followed your scent before.' Orange eyes fixed their gaze upon the cringeing, pitiful man at the shadow's feet.

'You've done well to tell me this,' the shadow croaked. 'But it is best that I ensure the truth of your words.' Sollima gave another squeal of fright as the hand on his chin closed about his lower jaw, crushing the bone with a grasp as strong as steel. He squirmed in agony, batting ineffectually at the hand that held him. His thrashings became still more desperate as he saw the shadow remove a small hollow tube of metal from its clothing.

'You've been deceived, little rabbit,' the shadow hissed, firming its grip upon the metal implement. 'You have no choice in how you die.'

'UNDER THE MOUNTAINS,' Brega mumbled to himself for the hundredth time as Brunner led the horses along a narrow deer run that wove its way through the tall, imposing pines that had surrounded them for the past two days. Since they had resumed their journey after their camp on the first night, the bounty hunter had at least allowed him to sit upright on his horse. It was some small comfort not to be lugged about like a sack of grain. The smuggler straightened himself up in the saddle, and sneered down at the bounty hunter as he walked ahead of his mount, the massive bay, Fiend. 'You know, you have quite a reputation,' he said. 'But I had never heard that you were mad!'

Brunner did not deign to reply, he was intent upon the meagre trail ahead. Suddenly, the bounty hunter turned his head, staring off into the woods. Behind him, Brega stiffened – cold fear ran through his body. What had the killer heard, he wondered? Bound as he was, Brega would be defenceless if they were attacked. And in the wild and forsaken foothills at the base of the Vaults, anything could be stalking the forest. 'What is it?' Brega demanded, his voice somewhat shrill. 'What did you hear?'

'Nothing,' replied the bounty hunter, stalking back to Brega's steed. Brunner grabbed the smuggler about the waist and roughly shoved him from the saddle. Brega crashed to earth, landing hard in a patch of ferns. Groans of pain emanated from the man. Brunner ignored them. He strode over to the fallen thief and pulled him to his feet.

'What are you doing?' Brega groaned. Suddenly a vile odour, like an army's privy, washed over them both.

'Hunting,' the bounty hunter responded, drawing a black powder pistol from its belly holster. With his other hand, he grabbed the rope binding Brega's hands together. 'You're going to help me.'

Without another word, Brunner strode from the trail, dragging the protesting smuggler behind him.

THE FOUL STINK grew as Brunner led Brega deeper into the forest. Brega corrected himself: it was more like the stench of an enormous army privy. He was amazed that anything could grow in such an atmosphere, that the leaves on the ferns and bushes hadn't curled up and died from being immersed in such a vile miasma. His fear increased as the bounty hunter continued onwards. There could be no question, he was heading toward the source of the smell. Brega trembled as he contemplated the manner of hideous charnel that might be the source of the reek. Worse, he wondered what sort of beings might dwell in such a place? Nightmare tales of undead horrors and the twisted perversions of Chaos gathered in his mind.

At last, when the smell had grown strong enough to bring tears to Brega's eyes, the trees parted into a slight clearing. A massive old oak tree dominated the far side of the clearing. It was ancient, its bulk as wide as a house. It was also dying: half of its branches were bare and twisted as the claws of a skeleton, many others sported sickly yellow leaves. The huge, serpent-like roots of the tree bulged from the dirt. And beneath them, the ground had been undermined, small holes angled downward into the earth. Only a few yards from the holes lay a huge pile of greasy black and green matter. Black horseflies buzzed about the reeking pile. The sight of the dung mound made Brega retch.

Small figures prowled about the openings of the holes. They were slight, thin-limbed creatures, somewhat like malnourished children in overall shape. Their heads were large, with long sharp noses, and pointed dog-like ears. Their grinning mouths were filled with sharp teeth. None of them was more than twenty inches high, and none wore more than a grimy scrap of cloth or fur about its waist. The pallid green skin of the creatures was hairless and glistened like the hide of a salamander.

The miserable things turned as the two men entered the clearing. Scores of tiny red eyes considered the bounty hunter and his prisoner.

Brunner did not meet their confused, idiot gazes, but carefully sighted his pistol on the largest of the snotlings, whose arms were cradled about a rusty kitchen knife as though it were a great sword.

Brunner fired the pistol. The shot pulverised the tiny goblinoid, shattering its head and shoulders, and spraying its fellows with a greasy green paste. The other snotlings mewled pathetically as the roar of the pistol echoed about the clearing. They dropped whatever they were carrying and scrambled back into their holes.

Brunner holstered his pistol and pulled a leather bag from his belt.

'That will keep their heads down until their tiny brains forget why they are hiding,' Brunner declared. He thrust the bag into Brega's hands.

'What do you want me to do with this?' the smuggler demanded. Brunner pointed a gloved finger at the pile of snotling shit.

Brega blanched. 'Shoot me now! I'm not touching that!' Brunner shrugged his shoulders and began to draw the Headsman from its sheath.

'Why do you want snotling manure?' Brega asked as he stepped toward the offensive heap. Brunner slid the partially drawn knife back into its sheath.

'Where we are going, it will be beneficial for us to stink like a snotling set,' the bounty hunter explained. 'Anything that catches wind of us will think we are snotlings.' Brunner gestured at the exploded snotling carcass. 'Not much meat on those. Not many creatures can stomach eating something that wallows in its own dung. The things that do put snotling on their menu are small, and easily dealt with.' Brunner gestured for Brega to get to work.

'Can I at least have something to shovel with?' Brega complained as he crouched beside the mound, face wrinkled in disgust.

'No,' Brunner answered. 'And make sure you fill the bag.'

THE BOUNTY HUNTER'S destination came into view a half-day's ride from the snotling set. From the rise of a low hill, Brunner stared down, his keen gaze focused upon the great gaping hole in the side of the mountain.

It was a colossal, imposing portal that put the great city gates of Altdorf to shame. Nearly fifty feet wide, and just as tall, the massive doorway was supported by gigantic granite columns that were twenty feet broad at their base. The entire length of the columns was engraved and sculpted. Scrolling and runes had been carved with consummate skill into the tough, ancient stone. Several figures had once been carved into the sides of the columns, ordered in ranks like a silent company of guardsmen, but they had all been defaced and vandalised. Shards of their stone faces peered upward from the rubble that had collected beneath the archway between the columns. Crude symbols in blood and other rude pigments had been daubed over the figures, robbing them further of their silent dignity.

Between the hill and the doorway, the land was littered with boulders and heaps of stone, their sprawl quietly suggesting the outlines of long-collapsed buildings, of forgotten walls and ruined towers. From a small grassy knoll, part of a grim, bearded marble head glowered at the two riders, as though it were angered at this additional violation of the dead settlement. Brunner did not spare a second glance at the giant stone head. He did not honour his own gods, and he would not honour those of another race.

'Ranald's cloak!' exclaimed Brega. 'Where are we?' There was awe in his voice. He had visited some of the greatest cities of the Empire such as Altdorf and Marienburg but the ponderous mass here belittled the walls and fortresses of men.

'It is our road through the mountains,' explained Brunner, eyes still prowling the wasted piles of rubble. His gaze sought to penetrate the dark, shadowy cavern between the columns. 'I learned of this road years ago, from a dwarf who once plied my trade. In ages past it was a great stronghold of the Ever-Kingdom. But it fell, like so many of the great dwarf cities. To fire and earthquake and goblin, it fell, nearly a thousand years ago.' Brunner's voice had dropped into a strange, sombre tone, as if the age of the ruins, and the weight of their history, had forced a measure of respect into his tones. 'Only a few of the dwarfs still use this road, for it is long and perilous. Even among their kind, there are not many brave enough to enter the darkness beneath the Vaults. Among men, there are even fewer.'

Brunner favoured Brega with a cold, icy smile. 'After the shadows of Karag-dar, you may find even the Reiksfang prison a comforting sight.'

The bounty hunter nudged Fiend with his spurs and the horse began to walk slowly down the hill, pulling his grey packhorse Paychest and Brega's steed after it.

'There are things in dark, forgotten places more fearsome than pain and agony and the red ruin of Judge Vaulkberg's mercy,' the bounty hunter said in a low voice.

Ahead, the great cavern-like door of Karag-dar yawned like the mouth of a giant beast, eager to consume them.

BEYOND THE GAPING doorway of Karag-dar, all was darkness and silence. The brooding antiquity seemed tangible; even the horses were ill at ease. Brega swallowed the lump in his throat, his breath turning to laboured gulps, as though the pressure of the weight of the Vaults was seeping into the tunnel and making even the air heavy. Ahead of him, Brunner dismounted, and made his way back to Paychest to remove a lantern and some oil from a pack fastened to the animal's back.

The light of the lantern revealed a gigantic chamber just beyond the great doorway. Tall rectangular columns reached up into the mountain, each of which was topped by a bearded dwarf whose outspread arms and arched back supported the ceiling high above. Each of the twenty pillars was thus adorned. But no two of the giant statues were alike; each one was meticulously sculpted to preserve the likeness of some ancestor lord who had died before Karag-dar was founded.

The bounty hunter played the light of the lantern across the length of the chamber. Once this had been a sort of trading post, where the dwarfs had swapped weapons of steel for grain and meat with the primitive tribes who would one day become the Tilean people. Great doors of steel had once towered within the doorway, protecting this hall from any outside invader. But those doors were now broken and dismantled, their steel scavenged by goblins and orcs to craft crude implements of slaughter. Brunner considered the empty doorway for a moment, the light of the sun streaming between the columns, past the ranks of defaced stone sentinels. Then he trained the light towards the interior of the mountain.

The stalls of the dwarf merchants were long gone, the stone cast down and carried away, the wood rotted and decayed into dust. Only the great flute of the canal that had run from deep within the stronghold to this chamber broke the emptiness of the hall. A thin trickle of water still flowed along it, feeding into a simple granite cistern, the fish and cave frogs carved upon it broken and defaced, and covered with a spongy yellow mould.

Playing the light of the lantern still further into the hall, Brunner could see the far wall, flanked by columns just as ponderous and elaborate as those at the entrance to the mountain. There, he knew, was the true beginning of the stronghold, the true entrance to the night world that had once been Karag-dar. He stared for some time at the dark, gaping opening between the columns where a second set of steel doors had once stood. At last, he was content that there was no furtive shape lingering in the darkness. Nevertheless he listened for a moment more, then turned his attention back to Paychest. He removed a bundle from the packhorse and strode back towards Brega.

'You're mad,' the smuggler gasped. 'We'll die! You can't take me in there!'

The bounty hunter ignored him and removed the foul-smelling sack tied behind Brega's saddle. Then he strode back toward Fiend. Undoing the first bundle, Brunner removed some crude hide leggings, slit along their backs. He tied four of these to Fiend's legs. Then he dipped his hand into the bag of snotling filth. Fiend snorted in protest as the bounty hunter lifted the dung from the sack. Brunner patted the animal's flank by way of apology, then began to smear the muck on the hide leggings.

'I've used this road before,' Brunner commented as he rose from his task and repeated his labour on Paychest. 'And come out alive.' The bounty hunter looked over at his prisoner. 'Keep your head, and you will too.' Brega found the chuckle that accompanied Brunner's remark almost as unsettling as the tunnel itself.

'Look, I have quite a bit of gold stashed away...' Brega pleaded. Brunner strode toward the smuggler's horse. He looked at the man for a moment, as though considering his proposal. Then, without warning, he pushed Brega from the saddle. The bound man struck the floor hard, crying out as he landed. Brunner ignored the man's painful moans and tied the remaining hide leggings to Brega's steed.

'I warned you once before that I would gag you if you made that offer to me again,' the bounty hunter said, not looking at his prisoner. 'I have a mind to fill your mouth with this before I shut it,' he added as he rubbed a handful of snotling dung into the hide leggings. Brega whined in terror as Brunner rose from his task and stalked toward him. He began to scramble away on his hands and knees, but the bounty hunter's foot pinned down the end of the rope that bound his hands together, causing him to fall and crash his chin against the unyielding floor. Brega rolled onto his back, yelling in protest as Brunner loomed over him, his gloved hand filled with reeking filth. The bounty hunter smiled and rubbed the excrement on Brega's tunic.

'Can't have some critter down here thinking that you are for eating, can I?' Brunner laughed. He bent down, picked up the rope and began to walk off. Brega scrambled on his knees after the bounty hunter, trying to keep from being dragged by his captor.

Brunner fastened the rope to the saddle on Fiend's back, then calmly checked the magazine of his repeating crossbow as he drew it from its holster on the saddle.

'The gun's not loaded,' he said, indicating the weapon sheathed on the other side of the horse. 'And I thought it best if I kept hold of this.'

'You can't take me in there without any protection!' cried Brega.

'I'm your protection,' the bounty hunter replied. 'You're worth a lot to me... alive. I don't intend to let anything happen to you.' Brunner smiled at his prisoner. 'Not until I'm paid, anyway.'

The bounty hunter turned away, narrowing the beam of the lantern to a slender dagger of light. Taking hold of Fiend's reins, he began to walk both the animals and Brega toward the deeper darkness beyond the inner doorway.

'The dwarf tunnels run clean through the mountain,' the bounty hunter said. 'It will take us a week to reach the far side. Keep quiet. Keep alert. Listen for the slightest noise.' Brunner cast a final look back at Brega.

'Remember,' he warned, 'if I die, you're goblin food.'

IT WAS SOME time before the bounty hunter at last found a place for them to rest. They had trudged for long hours through the darkness. Brega had been impressed by the mammoth size of the main tunnel while they had remained within it. It seemed to grow even more massive as they journeyed deeper into the mountain; rising into the very heights above. A few stretches had crumbled and collapsed, leaving giant boulders and huge chunks of worked stone strewn about the tunnel floor. For a time, Brunner had navigated a path through the debris, relying more upon the light of his lantern than the feeble sunlight that trickled downward from cracks in the ceiling.

Brega noted the mouths of other tunnels branching off from the main hall, but the bounty hunter had ignored them, never pausing to look at the intricate carvings, nor the often defaced statues that loomed beside them.

All was silence save for the muffled sound of the horses' hooves. Brunner had fastened fur boots around the feet of the animals to soften the sound. Only the gentle babble of the faint stream of water flowing along the old channel added to the noise of their progress.

Brunner paused but once, stopping to examine more closely a crude banner wedged into a pile of rock. He stared at it for some time, so Brega had a chance to look as well. It was a homely thing, a length of poorly cured hide stretched between two braces fashioned from the bones of some creature.

The glyph upon it was a simple representation of a snarling mouth, with black fanged teeth bared for violence and battle. Soon after, Brunner had diverted their route into a side tunnel. The ceiling in the second passage dropped alarmingly – from the towering height of the main hall to only fifteen or twenty feet. It was only then that Brega became aware once more of the heavy brooding pressure of the mountain above.

Brunner had explained the detour after Brega had pestered him for some time about it. 'This area was controlled by the Sharp Nose clan the last time I passed through these halls. Over the years, I've come to a sort of understanding with the Sharp Nose goblins. They leave me alone and I don't kill them.'

'Then why the detour?' Brega asked.

'Because that totem we found was from the Black Fangs. Nasty bastards, even by goblin standards. I'd prefer to steer clear of them. We've never come to any sort of understanding, you see.'

They had continued on along the side tunnel, taking several turns until Brega could not be certain if they were running parallel to the main hall or were now working their way back toward the entrance. They passed numerous rooms and chambers, the bounty hunter pausing to make sure the rooms were empty as they passed. Once, Brega heard something huge moving in the darkness. Brunner had grown tense, creeping forward to investigate the sound. He had soon returned, wiping sweat from his brow, before replacing the helmet.

'Only a stone troll,' he said with relief. 'We'll wait here until it moves on.'

'What did you think it was?' Brega asked nervously. The bounty hunter just shook his head.

'Something that should be very far from here, a thing the dwarfs named Arijogk.' Brunner uttered a nervous laugh. 'In Khazalid, as I understand, it means "Slaughter". A Chaos troll, from the Wastes themselves. Come down during the Great War Against Chaos, or so the dwarfs say.'

'Have you ever seen it?' Brega wondered, fear creeping into his voice.

'I've seen what it can do,' Brunner replied. 'That was enough for me.'

At length, when the bounty hunter decided that the stone troll had moved on, he began to lead the way onward into the blackness.

THEY MADE CAMP at last in a small room that branched off from the tunnel. Brunner chose the site because it had two entrances, which would make it more easy to defend and would give them an escape route if they were set upon by enemies or wild beasts. There was also the fact that he heard water running in the room and a quick examination revealed an old cistern fed by iron pipes. Brunner tasted the water, deciding that it was relatively pure, so the thirsty horses could drink.

The bounty hunter slipped Brega's rope from Fiend's saddle. Keeping the smuggler's hands tied, he let his captive drink at the cistern while he retrieved a coarse blanket from Paychest's load and settled himself on the floor.

Brega greedily drank the water. It had a stale, metallic taste to it, but it was welcome just the same. The smuggler rose from the cistern and began to move about the room, inspecting his surroundings.

'Don't go wandering off,' Brunner advised, not rising from the blanket. 'Something might find you before I do.'

Brega ignored the threat, and gazed at the carvings cut into the walls. He was struck by the craftsmanship of even the smallest details, the gently whirling scrollwork at the base of the walls, the savage, flowing cuts of the dwarf runes. If any of it was portable, it could probably fetch a tidy sum in Altdorf or Marienburg. The smuggler walked the length of the room, stopping when he encountered a small statue in the corner opposite the cistern.

'The dwarfs certainly do good work,' Brega declared. He reached forward, his hand sliding along the smooth surface of the small statue. 'I doubt if any sculptor in Tilea could match this statue. It almost seems alive.' Brunner did not pay the smuggler any attention. He was busy cleaning his sword.

'Why, you can even see the folds in the statue's cloak, the chips in its teeth,' Brega continued his observations. 'Such detail. And on a statue of a goblin, of all things.'

Brunner leapt from his seat on the floor, advancing swiftly toward Brega, his longsword, an ancient blade named Drakesmalice, gripped tightly in his hand. The bounty hunter placed great value on the sword, and never removed it from its sheath without good reason. Brega cringed back from the bounty hunter's fearsome advance, but Brunner had his eyes focused upon the stone goblin.

'It's alright,' the smuggler muttered weakly. 'It's only a statue.'

Brunner pointed at the goblin. 'More details you didn't notice. See these shiny things along its nose? They are steel spikes, mark of the Sharp Nose clan. That knife thrust through its belt is steel as well. How do you imagine a sculptor managed that?' Brega stared in a mix of wonder and horror at the goblin, pondering the bounty hunter's question. The bounty hunter nodded. There might be some risk in examining the statue, but it was slight compared to the possibility of running into its creator. Brunner pulled a hatchet from his belt and smashed its blunt end against the statue. The statue rocked in place, then crumbled apart with a second blow of the hatchet. The sound of the stone breaking echoed from the chamber walls. The smuggler winced at the sound, wondering what sort of things might be drawn to the din.

Brega smelled the foul odour of rotten meat even over the stench of the snotling dung. Brunner replaced his hatchet and drew a knife. On the floor, the broken pieces of the goblin lay in a heap. The seemingly solid statue had been revealed to be hollow, its interior filled with grey, decayed flesh. Brunner stabbed the meat with the tip of his knife.

'Dead a few weeks, at least,' he said, rising from the petrified corpse. 'Hopefully what did this is far away by now.'

Brega cringed from the gruesome remains, now understanding that the statue had once been a real goblin, a creature of flesh changed to stone by some hideous sorcery. The skin on the back of his neck began to crawl as he considered the horror of such an unnatural death.

'Like I said,' Brunner called out to his prisoner as he sat back down, moving his crossbow to a more readily available position beside him. 'Don't wander off.'

A FEW HOURS later the bounty hunter was back on the march, making his way through the darkness of the abandoned dwarf stronghold. Brega was at a loss to understand how the man was able to navigate with nothing but the slender beam of light emanating from the lantern. It seemed an almost unnatural skill, as if some sixth sense was guiding Brunner through the forgotten passages, showing him a path through the vacant halls and silent chambers.

Brunner stopped abruptly. Crouching, he examined something on the floor and nodded his armoured head. He trained his lantern on the walls, and examined them closely. Then he turned, stalking past Brega to the packs and sacks lashed to Paychest's back. The bounty hunter removed a long pole of about four feet in length. He moved back to the fore of his little train and slowly urged Fiend to back up. When he had made the animals retreat a satisfactory distance, he returned his attention to the object he had spotted on the floor.

Brega watched in silence as Brunner carefully worked the tip of the pole underneath a tripwire – a length of tough sinew – stretched across the corridor. The bounty hunter slowly lifted the wire until at last it snapped. There was a flash and a large crude blade of steel fell from a crack in the wall, scything across the corridor just in front of Brunner like an Estalian pendulum. The pole snapped with a loud crack as the blade struck it. The murderous length of steel ended its fatal swing by crashing against the other wall, the metal trembling from the force of the impact.

'We're lucky you saw it!' Brega exclaimed. By way of response the bounty hunter readied his crossbow.

'I've been expecting something like that,' he said, eyes scanning the darkness.

'Expecting it?' Brega asked, his voice nervous.

'It explains why they've been waiting,' Brunner said. 'We've been followed for the last mile,' he added.

Before Brega could ask his captor what he was talking about, shapes launched themselves from the shadows, shrieking and snarling with shrill, gibbering voices. The bounty hunter aimed back along the length of the horses and fired. There was a meaty sound of steel punching into flesh and a high-pitched scream. Brega heard a body fall and something metal clatter along the stone floor.

Brunner turned and faced the passage before them. Red eyes gleamed in the darkness, and small shadowy shapes raced forward. The bounty hunter did not wait – he fired two more bolts into the oncoming creatures. Two sets of red eyes pitched to the floor, whining in pain. Brunner turned once more, firing another bolt into one of the creatures closing upon the horses. There was another shriek of pain as the bolt found its mark. The horses were agitated now, snorting and moving about the narrow corridor. Brega braced himself, certain that the bounty hunter's huge steed was going to crush him against the wall.

Brunner drew his sword as the first of their attackers began to close upon him. With his other hand, he threw open the lantern, allowing its light to engulf the corridor. The light revealed their attackers. There were at least a dozen of them, each no larger than a small child. The creatures wore dark hooded cloaks, ropes of dried animal gut tied about their waists. They had short, bandy legs and long, spidery arms. The faces that grinned from beneath the hoods were twisted and malicious. Each of the goblins' long noses was marked by a set of small steel spikes driven into the spongy flesh.

As the light of the lantern was released, the goblins drew short their charge, raising their arms to their faces to protect their eyes from the sudden light. Brunner did not hesitate, for that might give the greenskins a chance to recover, an opportunity to decide if they would use the axes and clubs gripped in their hands or turn tail and flee before the light. The bounty hunter's sword slashed through the face of the first goblin he closed upon. The creature was flung aside by the force of the blow and crumpled into a shrieking heap against the wall.

A second goblin was disembowelled, its green-black blood spraying the walls. A third was decapitated, the head still mouthing a shriek as it sailed from its shoulders. A fourth goblin found Brunner's steel crunching through its chest. The bounty hunter kicked his foot against the mutilated goblin, tearing its body from his blade.

Still blinded by the unexpected brilliance of the lantern, the other goblins could hear the rapid and brutal demise of their fellows, their deaths all the more horrible because they couldn't be seen. The remaining goblins dropped their weapons, crying and wailing in piteous, simpering tones as they began to retreat. Blinded, the goblins crashed into one another in their reckless haste to escape the fearsome man they had hoped to claim as their prey. To speed them on their way, Brunner grabbed hold of the slowest by its hood and smashed its skull against the murderous steel pendulum.

Brunner turned from the carnage he had wrought, and stooped to clean his blade with the cloak of a slain goblin.

Brega stared in awe at the scattered goblin bodies. The entire fight had taken perhaps two minutes, yet the bounty hunter had managed to kill nine of the creatures in that time.

'Sharp Noses,' Brunner declared as he stepped forward to take Fiend's reins. 'Fortunately they don't have any skill with a bow, otherwise they might have given me some trouble. That probably explains why their clan is so small.'

Brega fixed an angry glare at the bounty hunter. 'I thought you said you had an understanding with the Sharp Noses!' he accused.

'I do,' Brunner said. 'But sometimes you have to kill a few of the young ones. Remind them why they should listen to their elders.'

FOR LONG HOURS they continued on, through the endless night of Karag-dar. Brega could tell that the area they were now travelling in was derelict even by the standards of the former dwarf stronghold. There was no sign of activity in this area, though the walls were pitted in places by the rude tunnels and caves that he had come to understand were the work of goblins. Yet unlike the rest of the tunnels and halls they had walked, there was a sense of an even longer neglect here, as though even the savage inheritors of Karag-dar had forsaken this place. Cobwebs were everywhere, dust lay thick upon the floor. As they moved onward, there was a scratching sound. Brega looked up. With some horror he discovered the source of the sound. A thin trickle of dust fell from overhead. That was the reason these tunnels were abandoned, the smuggler realised with dread. Goblins were not great miners, like the dwarfs, but even they could recognise when a tunnel was ready to collapse!

Brega cleared his throat of the lump that had risen there and opened his mouth to speak. The bounty hunter turned on him, a gloved finger upon his lips.

'Be quiet,' Brunner whispered. 'Make any noise here and you may just bring the entire mountain down on us.' The killer smiled coldly. 'Before you go thinking that would be a nice death, consider that you might not die outright in the collapse. You might be trapped, trapped under tons of stone and rock, where even the gods won't be able to find you. Buried alive in the shadows of Karag-dar. Starving, suffocating, spending long miserable hours waiting for the end. Or perhaps the rats of Karag-dar might find you first and hasten your passing.'

Brega shuddered as the bounty hunter detailed such a terrible death. Brunner smiled as he watched his prisoner recoil from the image he had painted for him. He turned once more, leading the horses still deeper into the silent, brooding dark.

'Mind the cobwebs,' Brunner warned. 'The spiders grow quite large down here.' The bounty hunter's last whispers drifted back to Brega as a disembodied sigh. 'They need to.'

IT SEEMED LIKE days later before the bounty hunter called a stop, though Brega knew that so much time could not possibly have been spent on the march. The lengthy periods of tedium had been interspersed with moments of absolute horror as dust drifted down or rocks shifted overhead. Once, Brega had been certain the entire tunnel was going to collapse when he saw the numerous goblin holes that had been cut into the walls, weakening the ancient surety of the dwarf construction. But in the end, he and the horses had received only a bath of dust and a few bruises from small stones that rained down upon them.

At last the unstable section was behind them. Brunner trained his lantern frequently on the ceiling, studying it and peered into the rooms and side passages that they passed. Finally he smiled, nodding for Brega to come forward and see what he had discovered.

'Bats?' the smuggler asked as he saw the squeaking shapes clutching to the ceiling of the room.

'They don't settle in areas that are weak,' the bounty hunter explained. 'Like rats on ships, they have a certain sense for such things. It means we can finally take a rest.' The bounty hunter pushed Brega back into the corridor. 'I'm sure the horses would appreciate a bit of a break.'

Quickly the bounty hunter examined a side passage beyond the room where the bats had made their nest. After a keen study of the floor, Brunner began to unburden the horses. Brega stood aside, letting him work. He had learned not to get in Brunner's way, and his hand still pained him from the last time he had drawn too close to one of the bounty hunter's many weapons.

He sat on a rock and watched as Brunner removed the saddles and harnesses from his animals. When he had finished watering and feeding the horses, Brunner removed a blanket from the unloaded packs and sat down, his back against the rough wall, crossbow at his side.

Brega watched Brunner dig a piece of dried meat from a pouch on his belt. His mouth watered as he watched the bounty hunter eat, his stomach groaning in protest at the sight.

'Don't I get anything?' he asked. Brunner looked over at his prisoner.

'You ate yesterday,' the cold voice of the killer stated between bites.

'I thought you wanted to bring me to Vaulkberg alive,' protested Brega.

Brunner stared at his prisoner. 'Alive doesn't mean well-fed,' he said. 'I keep you hungry, I keep you weak. I keep you weak, and there is less chance of you getting into any mischief. You'll eat tomorrow.' Brunner tore another bite from the salted beef. 'If you behave. Maybe.'

Brega slumped, gazing at the floor, trying to ignore the sounds of Brunner chewing. He was allright when it came to fighting the Emperor's customs men, or fleeing the city guards through midnight streets, but this perpetual, unremitting ordeal was more than his courage could endure. The reality of his situation suddenly smashed him flat as the last, foolish shred of hope deserted him. He had held out hope that somehow, by some trick of fate or stroke of fortune, he would escape this hideous situation. He had thought that, despite everything, he might be able to outwit his captor. But now he faced the cruel, harsh reality. There was no escape. In a dozen ways, his captor had seen to it, a hundred measures to crush the very thought from his mind.

'What… what do you think… he will do to me?' Brega asked, his voice hollow, broken.

Brunner stopped eating, stuffing the rest of the meat back into its pouch. He paused for a moment, as if to consider the question.

'I've seen Vaulkberg's ogre pull limbs out of their sockets,' Brunner said, his voice emotionless. 'He's quite good at it. Of course, the judge also keeps an entire staff of professional torturers at the Reiksfang. Perhaps he'll let them have a go at you for a while. I've heard they can keep a man at the edge of death for weeks.'

Brega broke out into a cold sweat, his swarthy skin paling beneath its dusky tones, as the bounty hunter's casual description of his end stabbed into his mind like a hot knife.

'Of course, perhaps he'll just make you face Raubfalke, Vaulkberg's champion. I've heard that even Ludwig Schwarzhelm lost a fencing match to him. But somehow I think that Vaulkberg will have something more inventive in store for you than simple trial by combat.' Brunner suddenly looked away, pulling the helmet from his head. A look of intense concentration marked his weathered features. Brega began to mumble a half-coherent offer of wealth and fortune for the bounty hunter to consider. Brunner fixed the man with an angry glare.

'Be quiet,' he hissed. 'We have company.'

The bounty hunter's words brought Brega instantly from his mournful state. A new and more immediate fear stiffened his frame. Brega stared into the dark of the tunnel, his eyes trying to detect a trace of motion in the dark. The bounty hunter was silent beside him, his body tense, waiting.

By degrees, a sound began to manifest itself. It was a strange, curious noise, like the clacking of wooden shoes across a cobblestone lane, or the sound of a fisherman cracking open a lobster's shell. It was a strange, indecipherable sound, and it made Brega slink back towards the bounty hunter, taking refuge in the evil he knew.

The sound grew louder and louder. The horses reacted as it drew closer, stomping their booted hooves and tugging at the ropes that bound them to iron spikes set into the floor. The bounty hunter remained vigilant, the strange repeating crossbow held at the ready, the lantern burning brightly. There was still no sign of whatever was making the sound, but it was growing louder, definitely advancing towards the camp.

At last, the light from the lantern revealed something large, shiny and black in the dark. Brunner fired the instant he saw the reflected light. The sound of the bolt punching through a solid mass was punctuated by a liquid, popping sound. But whatever it was did not cry out in pain; it merely advanced more quickly. Brega gave a shriek of fright, and leapt to his feet making to run past the frightened horses. Brunner spared a glance at him, stamping his foot down on the dangling length of rope that bound the man's hands together. Brega's flight was brought short, and he crashed to the cold stone floor. It seemed he had not learned his lesson the last time he had tried to flee.

Brunner fired again as the shape scuttled forward. Once more the bolt found its mark, punching into the oncoming mass. Once again the creature did not seem to notice the injury it had been dealt. As it charged more fully into the light, its form was revealed: it was an immense black beetle, a mammoth insect as large as a pony, huge rending mandibles spread before its armoured head. Multi-faceted blue eyes gleamed weirdly in the feeble light. Brunner's bolts had impacted against the insect's thorax, and from each wound, pulpy green paste bubbled and oozed, like rancid porridge boiling from a pot.

Brunner sighted at the monster and fired again, the bolt smashing into the insect's eye. The eye broke apart under the impact, and a burst of pulpy material spewed from the wound.

The insect kept coming, the long antennae before its head weaving about, the mandibles clacking together like the jaws of a bear trap. Brunner fired again, the bolt smashing through a leg segment. A thin fluid drooled from the injury and the insect's pace slowed a fraction. Yet still it came.

Brega wailed in horror as he saw the seemingly unkillable monster scuttle forward. The horses echoed the man's fear. Brunner drew his sword, glaring at the monster. The insect did not meet his gaze. Its antennae were twitching before its damaged head, seemingly intent on the struggling horses. Brunner turned around, severing the rope holding Brega's horse with one clean stroke. The horse turned and galloped away as soon as it was freed. The beetle, antennae still twitching, scurried after the fleeing animal. Brunner shook his head and sheathed his sword.

'Damn things are like orcs,' he commented. 'They don't know when to lie down and die.' He looked at Brega. The man was still curled up on the ground, his head hidden within his hands. Brunner kicked the man with the toe of his boot.

'Rest time is over,' he said. 'We're moving on.'

Brega looked around, turning his head to try and find the monster. 'Where did it go?' he asked.

'It must hunt by something other than sight down here, in all this dark,' Brunner replied, lifting a heavy blanket to Paychest's back. 'Movement, if my guess is right. I just gave it something a bit more lively than us to occupy it.' Brega looked around again, noting for the first time that his horse was gone.

'Hope you like walking,' the bounty hunter commented as he tied a bundle to the back of his packhorse. 'You'll have a fair amount to do even when we get out of here.'

A FEW HOURS later the passages they had been following emptied out into a vast, cavernous main hall. The hall was hundreds of feet tall, the upper limits of the pillars supporting it disappearing into darkness overhead. The columns were vast, like giant trees, so wide that six men would be hard pressed to link hands around their bases. The far ends of the hall stretched beyond the vision of the two men, vanishing perhaps half a mile away where the inky darkness became absolute. At first, Brega thought that they had emerged outside, so bright was the vista, so immediately did the sense of pressure lessen. But the smuggler's elation soon dissipated as he saw that they were still in the subterranean world of Karag-dar.

This section of the main hall was lit by some means that Brega could not fathom. He could not have guessed that he was seeing distilled sunlight, captured and reflected a dozen times over by crystal lenses scattered like a series of sentinels between the main hall and the side of the mountain far

52 C. L. Werner

above. The light came down as a grey filmy thing, reflected
from the white columns and pillars that supported the ceiling. Arches spread between the pillars, ornamental supports
from which had once hung tapestries and banners depicting
the triumphs and glories of the Ever-Kingdom. But such glories had long since rotted away, claimed by the ages. The
sombre, silent statues of bearded dwarf warriors loomed
from the walls, each scarred by axe and hammer and defaced
by crude goblin glyphs.

In the centre of the hall, the shallow water channel emptied into a wide pool before diverting north and south to
bear its life-giving waters to deeper halls within the mountain. The light gleamed and danced upon the waters, casting
weird shadows upon the forest of pillars and the rubble piles
where some had fallen. A low gallery and an upper walkway
wound among the pillars, leading toward chambers and
tunnels even higher in the mountain.

Brunner observed these carefully before leading the way
into the hall, his keen gaze constantly alert for goblins. He
was not certain how far the Black Fangs' territory extended,
but it would be in keeping with their vile and craven nature
to lurk upon the upper walkways and pepper an enemy
with arrows rather than trading sword strokes.

At last, satisfied that no goblin waited upon the upper
floors, and that the piles of rubble were likewise clear,
Brunner began to lead the way into the main hall. It would
only take a day or so now to reach the Reikland side of
Karag-dar, but the bounty hunter was intent on remaining
wary every step of the way.

The arrow nearly placed itself squarely in Brunner's face.
Had the bounty hunter not hesitated, warned by some sudden feeling of unease, it would have struck him down.
Instead, as Brunner's step faltered, the arrow swept past the
visor of his helm. Brunner dropped into a crouch at once,
taking cover behind Paychest, pulling Brega down with a
savage tug on the man's leg.

In the darkness, something hissed its displeasure, sending
another arrow screaming from the blackness to sink itself in

the large salt-filled keg lashed to the packhorse. Brunner snarled an oath, moving his animals toward the sparse safety of a pile of rubble. A third arrow nearly caught the bounty hunter once more, striking the vambrace encasing his left arm. Brunner could feel the impact rattle his bones as the arrow was deflected by the armour. He dropped down into the cover of the rubble, pushing Brega down onto his face.

'Stay low,' Brunner ordered, hefting his repeating crossbow. 'There is only one of them, but it will only take one arrow to make you worthless to me.' The bounty hunter looked over the edge of the rock pile, trying to see where the attacker was firing from. Another arrow smacked into the stone, missing Brunner's head by a matter of inches.

'Give up the smuggler!' a rasping, bubbling voice called out from the darkness. 'You'll never leave here with him, Brunner.' The voice trailed off for a moment into a deep, grunting laugh. 'Not alive, anyway.'

Brunner crouched low behind the rubble, cursing under his breath. He knew that voice – it had the nightmare tone that stayed with a man to the end of his days. He had hoped to never hear it again, but at the same time, he had known that their paths would inevitably cross again.

'Think it will be that easy?' Brunner called back. 'Krogh!'

Krogh. An ugly name for an ugly thing. It had been human, once. It had been a soldier, though where and when, Brunner had never known. But something had happened to Krogh, something terrible. Something had slowly, insidiously and completely consumed his humanity. Most men would have destroyed themselves. Others would have run into the wilds, to become the beasts their bodies had come to resemble. Still others would have quietly waited for the witch hunters to cleanse them with scourge and flame. But Krogh had found another path. He had abandoned his homeland, turned to the city states, to Tilea, where decadent, corrupt men would hire the unspeakable to perform the unthinkable. He had not embraced the kiss of Chaos, but neither had he denied it. Whatever Krogh had once been, he was now only a hunter. A hunter of men.

'We can make a deal,' the rotting voice of Krogh hissed. Brunner tried to follow the sound, but it seemed to dance and echo from every crack and flaw in the walls.

'What kind of deal?' Brunner called back. He caught the look of absolute horror that had found its way onto Brega's face. It seemed he was more afraid of being handed over to the source of that ghastly voice than remaining with Brunner.

The bounty hunter smiled. Brega had good reason to be afraid.

Brunner gestured with his crossbow, making it clear that Brega would not get far if he decided to make a break for it.

'If you hand over Brega, I'll let you live,' Krogh's voice croaked. Another arrow struck the pile of rocks, just to lend a little weight to the offer.

Brunner smiled. He had a fairly good idea where his enemy was now. If he could just keep him talking, he might get a better fix. 'I'll kill him myself before I hand him over to you!' Brunner snarled. Brega's eyes grew even wider and more alarmed. The smuggler couldn't understand how things could keep getting worse.

An inhuman, bestial laughter hissed its way from the shadows. 'Kill him then! I don't need him alive to collect my bounty!' The mutant laughed again, the sound becoming a daemonic chorus as it bounced from pillar and stone.

'Hand him over, Brunner!' Krogh ordered. 'Give him up, and I spare your life. Walk away, Brunner. Cut your losses.'

Brunner risked another look over the edge of the rubble pile. He was certain now that Krogh was slowly circling in the shadows. He had slipped into a pattern. Brunner was pretty sure where the mutant's steps would bring him.

'Don't insult us both!' Brunner called back as he ducked down behind the rocks. 'I know as sure as a toad has warts that as soon as I walk out, you'll put a shaft through my face. And you know that if you let me walk away, I'll get Brega back before you can slink back to the entrance!'

Krogh laughed again. 'I'm being paid seven hundred gold ducats for the smuggler,' he boasted. 'But I'll kill you for free!'

'I'm glad you feel that way,' Brunner muttered to himself. The bounty hunter leapt from his cover, firing the repeating crossbow in a quick series of shots. The bolts hammered into the darkness behind a tall column beneath one of the causeways. Brunner was certain that he heard the shots impact against something solid, but did not hedge his bets. He rolled back into cover behind the rocks. He waited for some time, ears straining for any suggestion of sound.

'Did you get him?' whispered Brega, his voice filled with nervous terror. Brunner threw his prisoner a sour look. He flipped his crossbow around, then removed his helm, placing it over the stock. Gripping the weapon by its front, he slowly edged the stock over the top of the rocks. Almost instantly, something struck the helmet, ricocheting off into the dark.

'Apparently not,' Brunner sighed, recovering the crossbow. He stared for a moment at the new dent in his blackened helm, before replacing it on his head.

'Hand him over now,' Krogh's rasping voice commanded. 'I'll not ask again!'

AWARENESS SLOWLY ROUSED the monster from its slumber. Heavy, leathery lids snapped open. Crescent-shaped pupils narrowed and expanded as they adjusted to the meagre light. The monster shifted its weight, working stiffness from its muscles. After a moment, its tiny mind considered what had disturbed its slumber.

For many thousands of years had the monster's kind prowled the darkness of Karag-dar. Even in the time when the halls had been ruled by the dwarfs, had they been there, slinking through the shadows. The monsters had some slight intelligence: over the centuries, they had learned to equate the slightest vibration in the rock with the presence of prey – lone miners and craftsmen toiling in the darkness.

It did not concern the monster that its lengthy tail was already fat and bloated with so much digested nourishment that it could safely sleep for months without needing to hunt. Indeed, the world was very simple for the monster; it was reacted by only two stimuli: danger and food.

The monster began to creep through the dark tunnels, drawn by the slight vibration its incredible senses detected: the impact of an arrow upon a pile of stone.

BRUNNER CONSIDERED HIS situation. In his previous encounters with the mutant bounty killer he'd been lucky to escape with his life, and it seemed luck would have to play a part in his survival this time. Krogh had him pinned down, and his attempt to shoot the mutant with his crossbow had been his best chance of outsmarting his rival. Now, he knew, Krogh would be twice as wary, his inhumanly keen senses and reflexes ready for Brunner to try again. That would be a mistake, and Brunner knew that he had already used up his quota of mistakes in this deadly game. No, if he was to regain control of this situation, Krogh would have to make the first mistake.

Brunner looked over at the cowering Brega. The bounty hunter drew a deep breath. He was reluctant to do what he was now considering, but it had become a matter of his own life, and no matter how much gold Judge Vaulkberg was offering, it would do him no good if he could not collect it.

The bounty hunter removed his helm. His cold eyes met his prisoner's. Brunner held the helm before his gaze for a moment, then looked back at Brega.

'Ever thought about becoming a bounty hunter?' Brunner's icy voice asked.

Brega wailed in horror as he realised what Brunner was planning. The smuggler began to scramble away, crawling from his captor. Brunner pounced upon the man, rolling the struggling Tilean onto his back. The bounty hunter smashed a fist under Brega's ribs, knocking the wind out of him. The smuggler's struggle became a boneless pained twitch. Brunner did not give the man time to recover. He held the helmet over Brega's head, and slowly lowered it.

A sudden noise caused him to stop. His head whipped about, eyes seeking out the source of the sound. It came again, a sickly, hollow trumpet note. Brunner replaced the helm on his own head, rising from his groaning captive.

'Change of plan,' Brunner said in the same frigid tone.

KROGH SPUN ABOUT in the shadows, a bestial snarl rumbling from his twisted frame. He sprang away from the column he had been hiding behind, lest Brunner heard the sound and trained his crossbow on him. Krogh had been taken by surprise by the other bounty hunter's earlier attack – one of the hastily fired bolts had skinned his leg. Krogh had no desire to tempt Brunner's aim a second time.

Now the situation had become decidedly more complicated. Sullen rage built up within Krogh as he heard the horn sound again. Given enough time, he could have worked his way around to Brunner's position and come upon him from behind. When the need arose, Krogh could move so quietly that even an elf would be hard pressed to hear him. But such stealth would take time, and time was something Krogh no longer had.

The mutant bounty hunter hissed again, a soft, angry sound, and crouched behind the toppled head of some forgotten dwarf king. The interlopers would pay dearly for intruding upon his business this day. The beast would slake its thirst for blood on these foolish things. Then it would be Brunner's turn to die.

THE HORN SOUNDED again. Brunner risked a glance around the edge of the rubble. He swore as he saw what was slowly making its way out of the shadows. He had hoped for something to distract Krogh, but not something that put him in jeopardy as well. The bounty hunter turned his head – shapes were also stealing out from the mouth of the northward tunnel. Looking upward, he saw more diminutive figures stealthily slinking across the causeways, descending towards the main hall from the upper corridors.

They were little more than indistinct shadows, but Brunner knew all too well what they were. Each of the tiny shapes was the height of a child, and wore a black hooded robe about its scrawny frame. Brunner knew that those garments would

carry the red eye of the night goblin tribes, and that, unlike
the Sharp Noses, these goblins would bear no ritual scarring.
Instead, they would sport mouths filled with teeth blackened
by fungus-distilled pigments. Krogh had chosen to set up his
ambush within the territory of the Black Fangs.

Several of the tiny figures gathered upon the causeways,
facing towards the pool. They unslung small short bows and
nocked arrows to the weapons. One goblin, slightly larger
than the others, lifted a horn crafted from the dried and hol-
lowed stem of a gigantic mushroom and blew out another
whiny, diseased note. In reply, more goblins began to slink
forward, with spears and a motley arrangement of weapons
held at the ready. Brunner could hear the monsters whispering in their thin voices, presumably relishing the prospect of
adding more trophies to the halls of the Black Fangs.

Brunner took aim, deciding that the archers were his most
pressing concern. He fired his crossbow, smashing a bolt
into one of the robed creatures. The goblin uttered a shrill
shriek as it fell from the causeway. The goblins below abandoned their caution, and began squealing like enraged
swine as they charged. The goblins above let loose their
arrows. Most of the missiles fell well short of Brunner's position, many more were ill-aimed, striking into shadowy spots
far removed from the bounty hunter. Only a very few
bounced from the rubble pile.

Brunner took no satisfaction in the erratic aim of the goblins. He knew that the Black Fangs often coated their arrows
in vile poisons, and that only one of them would need to
find its mark to finish him.

The bounty hunter rose from his cover once more. There
were perhaps twenty goblins below, cackling and gibbering
as they ran towards him. There were at least another twenty
above. He weighed up his chances. Among the Black Fangs,
the more capable warriors became bowmen, preferring to
kill an enemy from a distance than to risk their own neck at
close quarters.

The goblins below were closer, but far less dangerous than
those above. Brunner made his decision and fired again.
Once more a black-garbed creature howled in horror as the

bolt found its mark and the archer fell from his lofty height. Brunner smiled as he heard a second crossbow, somewhere to his left, hit another goblin archer. It seemed that Krogh had reached the same decision. Abandoning stealth, the mutant had turned to the stopping power of his own crossbow rather than the quiet of his longbow.

Brunner emptied the remaining bolts in the repeater, hitting two more of the goblins, though one was only wounded by his shot. Another goblin fell as Krogh's weapon punched a hole in its head. Its body fell within Brunner's line of sight, and he watched as it exploded in a bright burst of green blood upon striking the unyielding stone floor. The bounty hunter drew his pistol and sword, bracing himself for the melee of armed goblins.

Twenty to one were poor odds, but Brunner was determined that the greenskins would pay a heavy toll before they got him. The odds became better, however, when half the goblins broke off to charge towards Krogh's hiding place. Above him, the archers had been maintaining sporadic fire. The arrows were more concentrated now, aimed either at Brunner's position or that of his rival. As their kindred charged forward, a goblin arrow smashed into the back of a spear-wielding wretch. The creature gave a yelp of pain and surprise, then fell on its face. The goblin beside it snarled a curse in its own whispery tongue, and hurled its own spear back at the distant archers. The weapon fell short of its mark, but the archers replied in kind. Both the spear-thrower and a goblin bearing a spiked mace fell, shrieking and whining as black-fletched arrows sank into their bodies.

The first goblin to reach Brunner screamed a savage war cry. Brunner blew its head apart in a spectacular discharge of his pistol. The goblin scrambling up behind it screamed in horror as the greasy brain matter of its comrade splashed across its face. The bounty hunter's sword lashed out, cleaving the goblin's head from its shoulders before the creature could recover.

A third goblin rounded the rock pile, snarling angrily. It held a great hatchet in its thin hands. Brunner struck the weapon with his sword, knocking it from the goblin's

grasp. A look of amused embarrassment overcame the
goblin's grinning face as the hatchet skidded across the
floor. Brunner smashed the flat of his sword at the grinning mouth, knocking the creature away, and leaving it to
choke on its broken teeth. Another goblin crawled its way
to the top of the rock pile, its red eyes gleaming with sadistic merriment. Brunner roared at the little creature,
causing the goblin to flinch and slide away back down the
rock pile.

More goblins were rounding the barrier. Brunner drew
the short hatchet from his belt, turning his body from side
to side to favour all of his wretched foes with his cold
stare.

'Come on!' Brunner snarled. 'Which of you little vermin is
tired of living!'

KROGH'S SWORD FLASHED downwards in a murderous arc. The
goblin did not even have time to scream as its body was cut
cleanly in two. The two goblins to either side of the brutally
slain creature gave simultaneous squeaks of fright, fleeing as
fast as their tiny legs could move them. The beast within
Krogh wanted to pounce, and chase after them, but the
mind subdued it. To chase after them would be to forsake
his cover, to tempt the goblin archers above. Krogh darted
aside as another group of goblins closed upon him. The
mutant's hand whipped out, grabbing the haft of the spear
the foremost goblin thrust at him. The wood splintered
under Krogh's iron strength. The goblin tried to pull the
weapon back, but Krogh's hand had already released it, and
was darting for the goblin's throat.

With a loud snap, Krogh cracked the goblin's neck. He
lifted the still-twitching body and threw it into the other
goblins.

They fell in a tangle of limbs and curses, three pairs of
hands trying to push aside the weight of their dead comrade.
But even as they struggled, Krogh pounced, landing amid
them, his bare hands ripping and tearing. The whiny sounds
the goblins made as they died rose from the blackness, and
unsettled the archers on the causeway above. They were not

sure what sort of intruders they were fighting. And the little monsters wondered if they really wanted to know.

BRUNNER PULLED HIS hatchet from a black-cloaked body, watching as his last adversary turned and ran. He had added four more goblins to his tally. Drakesmalice was slick with green blood and pulpy bits of goblin flesh. The bounty hunter spat, wiping his weapons clean on the cloak of the last goblin he had slain. The sickly mushroom horn sounded again. Brunner looked over the rock pile, trying to see what new mischief the goblins were planning. He snarled a curse on the heads of any gods that happened to be listening.

A strangely clad goblin had appeared on the causeway next to another fifteen archers who were still sporadically firing their weapons downwards. A new mob of black-robed archers scurried after it, bows held in their scrawny fists, adding another score to the ranks of his adversaries. This new goblin was taller and thinner than the others, its black robes picked out by crude embroidery that looked like yellow flames. He watched the thin goblin exchange words with the horn-bearing chief, then saw the creature draw a large white object from a big leather bag. The chieftain nodded his head, his shrill laughter inciting merriment among the archers. Brunner picked up the skaven crossbow and began to quickly reload it.

The Black Fangs had earned a fearsome reputation among the few who dared the forsaken passages of Karag-dar. It was not their skill as warriors that made them fearsome, nor some uncanny expertise with the bow. It was their knowledge and use of all manner of poisons and venoms that earned them their sinister infamy.

The masters of that despicable art were their shamans, twisted, depraved, maniacal creatures, hated as much as they were feared. The shamans drew their sorcery from the spirit force of their tribesmen, and turned their aggressive energies into murderous spells. The goblin gods were known for their fickleness, however, and the shamans had long ago learned not to rely solely upon their sorcery. These shaman were

masters of more than magic. They cultivated deadly strains
of noxious fungi unknown to even the chieftains of the
Black Fangs, and cemented their power by offering death in
innumerable sinister guises should their divine edicts be
questioned.

The tall goblin held the white ball in front of it and began
to chant in a low, scratchy voice. The chieftain slunk away,
putting ten feet between himself and the chanting shaman.
Brunner fumbled to get the bolt into the crossbow's magazine, knowing that time was running short. But even as he
did so the chieftain blew on his horn again. Brunner turned
his gaze to the tunnels. He was not surprised to see more
black-garbed shapes pouring into the main hall. But a sick
sensation gripped his stomach as he saw what was with
them.

Amongst the rabble of armed night goblins there were
four hulking shapes, great greenskinned giants, crude
armour lashed about their bodies, massive blades clutched
in their monstrous paws. These new monsters squinted
beneath their helms as their eyes adjusted to the light, their
massive, tusked faces snarling. Beside them, a goblin with its
hood drawn back capered, gripping a small staff with jawbones dangling from its tip. Like the teeth of the goblins, the
jawbones had been dyed black, and the symbol of the Black
Fangs was carried on in the large tattoo that covered the goblin's bare scalp.

It tittered wickedly, gesturing with its staff. The lumbering
monsters beside it snorted in contempt, but strode forward
just the same. Brunner shook his head, his eyes straying to
the shaman above. The tall goblin had finished its chant and
Brunner could see that the round white ball had turned yellow – whatever magical preservation the shaman had
worked upon the puffball was dispelled. The fungus was
active now, a lethal spore bomb.

Taking courage from the four orc mercenaries in their
midst, the goblins were charging forward, twenty strong.
Brunner swore again. They would be on him far too soon,
and orcs, he knew, would not go down as easily as their
smaller kin. Against four orcs, the bounty hunter did not

favour his chances. But they would still be better than the certain death the shaman held in its claws.

THE MONSTER SCUTTLED forward. It was not able to detect sounds very well, but it could sense the impact of running feet; it could see the warm bodies racing about in the darkness ahead. Warmth, like the gentle vibration in the rock, was also a sign of food. The monster increased its pace.

Its heat-based gaze settled upon the nearest warm body. The monster prepared to attack.

THE GOBLIN SHAMAN cackled, a dry rattling sound. It was enjoying the fear and awe of its fellows on the causeway. The creature paused for an instant to let the terror of its fellows, and the absolute dread of the terrible weapon invigorate its black heart. Suddenly, the warm feeling coursing through the shaman's veins was interrupted by a powerful force that smashed into its ribs. The shaman twisted about, spun by the force of the impact. Even wounded, with a death-dealing bolt in its lungs, the monster maintained a careful hold of the spore bomb, its own fear of the weapon greater than that of its impending death.

The shaman's thin shriek caused the orcs to look upward. The goblin mystic was lost in a cloud of white gas as a red-fletched arrow pierced the puffball. The white explosion engulfed ten of the nearest archers, their shrill screams echoing across the great hall. The dust drifted outwards, catching a dozen other archers. The goblins shrieked as the caustic spores dissolved their flesh, ate away their eyes and liquefied their bones. Still screaming and pawing at their crumbling forms, the archers collapsed into their black cloaks, the garments filthy with the lethal white powder.

Two more goblins leapt from the causeway, preferring to topple to their deaths than brave the deadly spores. The other archers scrambled to race back into the upper tunnels.

The horn-bearing chieftain blew furiously on his instrument, trying to stem the rout. But even as he tried to assert his authority, a well-aimed shot from one of the archers silenced him. An arrow transfixed his throat.

SOME OF THE goblins were charging toward the rubble where Krogh had fired his deadly shot. The black fanged creatures tittered frenziedly as they advanced, spears held before them, swords and clubs waving wildly above their heads. The goblins were trying to incite a maniacal courage in their craven hearts, trying to convince themselves that they would overcome their foe and take long, bloody pleasure in avenging their fallen shaman.

A black shape lunged out of the shadows, landing on the foremost goblin, and crushing the creature beneath its feet. The broken warrior squealed in agony as green blood exploded from its mouth. Krogh did not spare a thought for the writhing form beneath him; he lashed out with his sword, cutting the arm from another of the startled would-be attackers. The goblin went down, thin screams replacing its earlier howl of retribution. Krogh turned from the maimed greenskin and lashed out at another of his adversaries, opening the neck of a club-bearing goblin. Only the cloth of the creature's hood prevented the head from flying from its body.

The tattooed goblin noticed that the attack on Krogh had begun to falter. Snarling at the top of its voice, the goblin gestured at the tattered figure of the bounty hunter, and shook his staff at his enemy. The biggest of the orcs favoured the goblin with another sneer, then barked a brutal string of grunts at one of his fellows. The orc broke off and charged toward Krogh. The others, still supported by a dozen goblins, sprinted toward the other adversary.

Brunner spat on the floor, shaking his head angrily. 'Sure, send only one of those bastards for Krogh,' he hissed. Raising his crossbow, he sighted at the oncoming brutes. The bounty hunter fired, and the bolt smashed into the helm of one of the orcs. The bolt bit into the metal, and Brunner could see a thin trickle of green ooze running into the orc's face. But the bolt had not punched its way deep enough into the brute's skull; it had not ruined the orc's tiny brain. The orc kept coming, barely affected by a shot that would have instantly slain a human foe.

Brunner swore. Noticing the laughing goblin boss dancing about behind its orc mercenaries, Brunner fired again. The laughter was silenced as the bolt smashed through the goblin's forehead and the tattooed monster was thrown across the floor. The bounty hunter knew that he should have at least tried to bring one of the orcs down. But knowing that the snivelling vermin that had led them to battle was carrion made Brunner feel a great sense of satisfaction.

He lifted the crossbow again, sighting on the biggest of the orcs. The brute was at least six feet tall, built like a brick privy. It wore a necklace of teeth about its thick neck, fangs and molars dug from the mouths of past victims. In its massive paws was a crude axe, like a great butcher's cleaver. It was pitted and rusted, crumbly flakes of dried blood crusting its edge.

If he could kill their leader, it might make the orcs forget their bloodlust and flee. Brunner knew that the goblins would have no stomach for the fight if the orcs were to break. Disdaining to offer a prayer to any god, he took aim.

THE GOBLIN STARED for a moment at the splattered remains of the archer. It was one of the night goblins that had decided to jump rather than face gruesome death by the shaman's ruptured spore bomb. The goblin was not bothered by the ugly sight – its red beady eyes were focused on the weapon still clutched in the paws of its dead fellow. It reached down, and pulled the bow from the rigid fingers. Cackling happily, it tested the string, then reached down once more to remove the quiver of arrows from the corpse. With a bow of its own, the goblin would be one of the great warriors of its clan. The goblin had been close enough to the shrouded mutant to know that it never wanted to be near such an enemy again.

The goblin looked upward as its keen ears caught a sound. Its first thought was that the archers had returned to the causeway and were going to strike down the shrouded beast with their deadly arrows. But it froze in terror as it realised its mistake. The sound had come from *beneath* the causeway.

A monstrous creature was gripping the underside of the causeway. It was larger than a bull; its body covered in shiny brown and black scales where its skin was not pale and peeling. The upside down monster maintained its hold on the causeway with eight powerful legs – the sharp black claws of each foot sunk deep into the stone. A bloated, fat tail drooped from the monster's body.

As the horrified goblin watched, the creature's horned, reptilian head turned towards it. A membrane snapped into place over the monster's eerie yellow eyes as it focussed on its prey. As the goblin tried to run, a bright flash of searing energy passed from the eyes of the basilisk to those of the goblin. In an instant the transforming Chaos energies spread from the goblin's eyes to the rest of its body. The goblin's terrified paralysis became permanent as its skin was turned to stone. The basilisk's scaly jaws opened in a hungry yawn.

THE BRIGHT FLASH of light spoiled Brunner's shot. The bolt went wide, speeding off into the dark of the hall. But his misfire was not noticed by his enemies, for their attention was drawn to the source of the unnatural light. The orcs and goblins gawped at the stone goblin, with Chaos energies steaming from its body. A huge shape dropped from the underside of the causeway, falling to the ground with a meaty thud. The basilisk righted itself with a quick roll, then lumbered toward the stone goblin. A powerful blow from its long, fat tail shattered the statue, casting fragments about the hall. Steam rose from the super-heated meat within the stone shell. Once again the giant lizard monster smacked its scaly jaws, and a jagged, barbed tongue flitted from its mouth. It closed upon the nearest of the fragments and began to scrape the steaming meat from the stone shell with its barbed tongue.

The goblins whined amongst themselves as the predator fed, but the snarls and curses of the orcs stilled their fear. With a great roar, the orcs charged the feeding monster, the brutes thinking what a mighty trophy the fangs of such a beast might make. The basilisk seemed indifferent; it was intent upon its food. Only when a goblin spear was thrown into its side did the reptile look up.

Brunner continued to feed bolts into his crossbow as he watched the basilisk react to its attackers. Whichever way the fight went, he knew that he would have more killing to do.

BRUNO BREGA COULD hear the shouts and snarls of the battle. He did not know what was going on, nor did he have any great desire to find out. For the moment, Brunner was nowhere to be seen, and that was enough for Brega. The smuggler pulled himself to his feet, gripping a fallen boulder with his bound hands. Brega tested the lashings once again. There was no give in the ropes. He looked around him, sighting Paychest, and the numerous bundles strapped to the animal's back.

Brega was sure he would find a blade somewhere amongst the bounty hunter's gear. He needed something to cut through his ropes. He paused for a moment, gathered his courage, then decided upon his course of action. Swiftly, he moved toward the bounty hunter's animals. As he did so, a dark shape rounded the pile of rubble that Brunner had employed as cover.

The goblin snarled wickedly as it ran towards Brega. The smuggler stopped, eyes wide with fright as the goblin slashed at him with its sword. In dodging the attack, Brega fell, and landed on his back. The goblin's malicious laughter seethed through its fanged mouth as it noticed its enemy was bound. The vile creature scrambled forward.

Finding the conflict with the bounty hunters and the basilisk too perilous, the goblin was eager to slake its thirst for blood on a defenceless prisoner. The leering visage of the goblin's malevolent face filled Brega's vision as the greenskin lifted its sword for a murderous downward stroke.

THE BASILISK ROUNDED on its attackers, hissing as it drew a deep breath. The goblin that had thrown the spear squeaked in fright, turning and fleeing as fast as its legs could carry it. Two other goblins hesitated, uncertain whether to press the assault or flee as well. Their hesitation made the decision for them. Angered by the wound in its left rear leg, the reptile scuttled forward at great speed. Powerful jaws snapped closed on the foremost goblin while a swipe from one of the reptile's legs tore open the other. The basilisk crushed the maimed goblin under its foot, breaking those parts of the goblin its claws had not ripped apart. The giant lizard lifted its head, swallowing the still struggling form of its enemy whole. Then the monster was among the rest of its foes.

The basilisk's movements were swift and brutal. The powerful tail lashed from side to side in battering blows that broke bones whenever it struck. As the enraged lizard lumbered amidst the greenskins, its claws slashed and ripped, its fanged jaws closing on green flesh as often as empty air. Mangled goblins were hurled about like rag dolls, their screaming bodies landing in tattered heaps to moan and whine in agony, and to painfully crawl from the rage of their monstrous foe.

The reptile's rampage carried it through the goblins and their orc allies. Brunner readied himself as the maddened beast came near. He fired the repeating crossbow, and the bolt crunched into the thick bone just above the creature's eye. The lizard reared back from the painful injury, its tree-like tail lashing the ground. Brunner fired again, this time putting a bolt into the monster's cheek. The basilisk's frenzied motion became even more agitated and it worked its injured jaw to try and remove the hurtful bolt embedded in its flesh.

The basilisk began to bob its body up and down in an angry, threatening display, its breath hissing loudly, wrathfully. Brunner fired again, the shot once more narrowly missing the monster's eye. This time it sank into the flesh of the reptile's neck. The bounty killer swore as he saw the membranes snap close over the lizard's yellow eyes. The terrible Chaos energies were building up within the reptile. Brunner hastily averted his eyes, knowing as he did so that he left himself open to the rending claws and snapping jaws of the beast.

A thick, powerful axe-blow severed one of the basilisk's rear legs. It spun about, its small brain too angry now to take any great notice of this new wound. The basilisk's attacker lifted his axe for another cleaving stroke, but his piggish red eyes found themselves transfixed by the petrifying gaze of the monster. The orc did not emit any sound as the transforming energies flowed into his body, hardening his scarred hide into a shell of stone, as the Chaos power cooked his innards.

The necklace-wearing orc was charging the monster even as his comrade was turned to stone. The goblins were dead or running, the other orc lying somewhere, broken by the basilisk's tail. Now the brute's last ally had been slain. The orc roared a throaty challenge through his tusked mouth and ran at the giant reptile. The orc's great weight slammed into the stone carcass of his comrade, toppling its body onto the head of the lizard. The statue broke apart as it smashed into the basilisk's skull, dashing its head against the hard floor.

The orc did not hesitate, but leaped onto the back of the stunned reptile. The greenskin's sword rose and fell, gouging great cuts into the basilisk's body. The lizard shook its body from side to side, trying to dislodge the clinging orc straddling its back. As the lizard's neck craned about to try and fix its foe with the petrifying gaze, a steel bolt shot out of the darkness, exploding the basilisk's left eye. The lizard rolled onto its back, crushing the orc beneath it as it writhed in agony.

Brunner watched as the basilisk rolled across the floor and smashed against the archway of a tunnel, its mass dislodging the remaining dwarf warrior that stood against the wall. The massive statue broke apart at the waist, crashing downward. A sound like a hundred thunderbolts roared about the hall as blocks of stone cascaded onto the floor. The massive pillars trembled with the violent impact, and swayed slightly in their positions, like mighty oaks disturbed by a raging hurricane. In the darkness, the echoes of the collapse boomed like cannon fire, carrying the message of destruction through the length of Karag-dar. It reverberated through every chamber and goblin-hole within the ancient dwarf stronghold. The world disintegrated into a grey mist as dust exploded from the destruction, and billowed outward in a gritty cloud.

When the dust had cleared, the tunnel was lost to sight, now buried beneath tons of rubble. The basilisk had been caught in the rockfall; now the only sign of the reptile was a twitching leg sticking up from the broken stonework.

Brunner gazed about the hall. Dozens of black-cloaked bodies lay strewn about the ground – some were moving, many more were still. The bounty hunter looked over towards where Krogh had made his stand. A great number of goblin bodies had been thrown about the area, many torn limb from limb. Amid the carnage, Brunner could see a single orc, its jaw ripped from its head, a gaping hole at the centre of its chest. Of the mutant, there was no sign.

A movement nearby made Brunner draw Drakesmalice from its sheath. Brunner cast his cold eyes on the shape of the orc champion. Most of its bones had been crushed under the basilisk's weight, there was dark green blood bubbling from its mouth, and still the brute struggled to stand. The bounty hunter walked toward the dying orc.

'Thanks for the help,' Brunner said as he met the angry creature's eyes. The bounty hunter swung Drakesmalice in a decapitating blow. 'I appreciate it,' he added as the head bounced across the floor.

BRUNNER RETURNED TO his horses, thankful to find them unharmed, then looked around for Brega. Near to the horses, he found the smuggler's bindings, and beside them the body of a goblin. Brunner examined the goblin for a moment, noting the marks about its neck, the way its tongue protruded from its face. A man without a sword has few options left to him. Strangulation was one.

Brunner followed faint traces in the dust. He cursed when he saw where Brega had run. The tunnel through which the smuggler had made his escape was blocked by the massive rockfall caused by the basilisk. Worse, it was one of the ones from where the goblins had emerged. Brega had escaped his captor all right – by running even deeper into the territory of the Black Fangs.

With a sigh, Brunner returned to his animals. The corridors and halls of Karag-dar were a near-endless maze. It would take days, perhaps weeks, to find Brega's trail. The bounty hunter knew that others would find the scoundrel first. Smarting with the slaughter wrought in the great hall by the bounty hunters and the basilisk, Brega could expect a very nasty reception from the Black Fangs.

The bounty hunter shook his head and started to lead his animals back the way they had come. The reward Judge Vaulkberg was offering was only good if Brega was delivered to him alive. It was a stipulation that Brunner always found tiresome, but, under the present circumstances, it had become impossible. Since first taking up his bloody and violent trade seven years ago, Brunner could count on one hand the number of times he had failed to collect his prey. But he was also pragmatic enough to know when it was pointless to continue the hunt. His only comforting thought was that Brega wouldn't be boasting of his escape to anyone… at least anyone that wasn't green.

BRUNO BREGA COULD see the brazier just beyond the circle of grinning, leering green faces. The barbed, hook-like irons were slowly beginning to glow. The large goblin standing beside the brazier licked his black-dyed fangs eagerly.

Brega moaned again, struggling against the ropes that held him against the top of the crude stone altar. He was, he admitted, in virtually the same position as when he had been discovered by the bounty hunter. But whatever Nuccio and his other former comrades had planned for him would have been quick and clean compared to whatever his present captors were intending. Once again, Brega wondered what he had done to so offend Ranald for his fortunes to continually spiral downward. At least, the smuggler thought, things have finally struck rock bottom.

The night goblin crept away from the brazier, a glowing iron gripped in its thin-fingered hand. The other goblins cackled and snickered as the torturer moved toward Brega.

The goblin leaned over the prisoner's body and Brega could feel the heat of the iron as the goblin held it over his chest.

'Make pretty sound,' the goblin's whispery voice hissed. Brega let loose with a scream that echoed from the walls of the dingy cave-like room. The goblins laughed and snickered once more.

'Want better,' the torturer commented as his own laughter died away. Brega tensed his body, waiting for the iron to sear his flesh.

The loud *thok* of a crossbow firing echoed in the room. The goblin torturer was thrown back as a bolt smashed into his throat. Brega wept tears of relief as the other goblins began to scramble away, shoving and punching one another in their haste to escape. The smuggler had not dared to hope that Brunner might still find him, that the bounty hunter would search the halls of Karag-dar to track him down. Whatever horror Judge Vaulkberg intended for him, it would be pleasant compared to the attentions of the goblins.

Brega craned his neck upward to stare over the altar as he heard his rescuer draw near. The colour faded from his face as the shabby, cowled figure strode towards him. Orange eyes glowed from the hooded face of the shadow.

An animal stink filled Brega's lungs as Krogh leaned over him. The mutant bounty hunter reached into the folds of his tunic with a twisted hand and drew a hollow steel tube from a pocket.

'For you,' the rasping, bubbling voice of Krogh hissed from beneath the folds of the scarf covering his face, 'this is a very unlucky day.'

DEATHMARK

THE BOUNTY KILLER sat in the shadows at the back of the Black Boar, slowly sipping at his stein of beer. Normally, the transplanted Reikland beer hall would be almost deserted at such an early hour. But today the hot Tilean sun had punished the city of Miragliano with a vengeance, baking the streets with the fury of a raging kiln. Many were those who had retreated from the oppressive temperature and the foul stink of sweating unwashed bodies for the cool innards of the many taverns on La Strada dei Cento Peccati. The Black Boar, with its clientele from the cooler northern climes of the Empire, had swelled almost to bursting point.

Brunner watched as a mob of dwarf warriors made a game of tossing throwing axes at a wooden target that looked rather suspiciously like an orc in size and shape. A pair of dour-looking wool merchants from the Sudenland were drinking away their sorrows, and trying their best to ignore the raucous din set up by the hulking figure at the table beside them. He was a mountain of a Norse pirate named Ormgrim, and he was currently trying to discover if the beer barrels in the Black Boar's storeroom really were bottomless.

Along the counter of the bar was a group of mercenaries from across the Empire, who had recently arrived in Miragliano as part of a trade caravan from the rival city state of Remas in the south.

A dark, rail-thin man slipped into the beer hall. No displaced product of the northern lands was he – his swarthy skin betraying the harsher, punishing sun of the south. He was an older man, certainly well past his prime, but without the crushed, defeated stoop of an elderly peasant who had been abused by his overlong years. His face was pinched into a perpetual look of suspicion, his fleshless cheeks stretched tight over the bones of his jaw. He wore a dark coat of soft fabric, his feet shod in leather shoes fronted by elaborate brass buckles. The extravagantly frilled cuffs of a pristine white shirt exploded from beneath the black coat, and engulfed the man's slender hands.

Brunner watched the thin man walk across the tavern, his head glancing from side to side as though in search of someone. Several times, the thin man was jostled by glowering Northmen as they crossed his path. Twice an extended boot caused the man to stumble. The patrons of the Black Boar considered the inn a home away from home, and they viewed any Tilean setting foot in the tavern as an intruder.

At last, the man appeared to find what he was looking for. Brunner watched impassively as the man walked over to his table. Beneath the table, however, he kept a steady grip on a small pistol-sized crossbow.

'You are the man they call Brunner?' asked the thin man. Although he looked like a Tilean, his accent bore the telltale inflections of Estalia. 'You are the fearsome bounty hunter?'

'Perhaps,' Brunner said, sipping at his drink.

'I am Ortez,' the Tilean said. 'In the service of her ladyship the Contessa Carlotta de Villarias.' The man waited a moment, as if expecting Brunner to be awed by the name. When the bounty hunter's expression did not change, the Estalian hurriedly continued. 'My mistress has sent me to find you. She has a job for you.' The man paused again, then added, 'It will pay very well.'

Brunner set down his drink and rose from his seat, replacing the crossbow pistol to its place on his vambrace. The Estalian's eyes went wide as he saw the weapon appear and breathed a sigh of relief when it was put away.

'I have my own ideas of what a well paying job is,' Brunner told Ortez. 'But we'll go and see your mistress and find out what it is she wants me to do for her.' Ortez smiled and nodded his head, leading Brunner back through the tavern.

As they passed the bar and the group of mercenaries, a surly voice accosted the bounty hunter.

'You there! Thief!' the speaker growled. Brunner turned, finding himself staring into the angry countenance of a face that had been weathered and reshaped by years of hardship and battle. The man was originally from the western part of the Empire, Reikland or Altdorf to judge by his accent. But he had been long from his homeland; his once fair skin had been baked almost brown by the brutal sun of the south, his moustache and beard trimmed away into the rakish style of the Tileans. Indeed, were it not for the blond hair and piercing blue eyes, the man could quite passably present himself as a native of the city-states rather than some imported sellsword. An elaborately engraved breastplate encased the man's chest, while a rich blue shirt billowed out from beneath the armour.

Mercenary and bounty hunter stared at one another for several tense moments. Ortez was sliding away from Brunner, eager to distance himself from any conflict.

'If you are looking for trouble,' the bounty hunter's chill voice warned, 'I suggest you look elsewhere.'

The mercenary captain was not to be intimidated. Instead, he took a step closer, and curled his lip into a disdainful sneer. The bounty hunter casually slid his hand to the butt of his pistol.

'Brave words for a thief!' the mercenary snarled. He pointed his leathery hand at the golden dragon-hilt of Drakesmalice. 'I've seen that sword before,' the inebriated warrior said. 'You could not have come by it fairly!'

The tense situation erupted into violence. The drunken mercenary moved to pull his sword from its sheath, but discovered that he did not have enough room to draw it. At the same instant, Brunner surged forward, smashing his metal vambrace into the man's face, then grabbing him about the throat with his arm. The bounty hunter kicked the stunned man in the back of his knee, forcing him into a forward fall. The mercenary's head smashed into the counter. Brunner held him there, drawing his pistol and thrusting it into the face of the brutish bearded ruffian who had run forward to help his leader. Brunner turned his attention back to the man who was choking in his hold.

'You know this sword, do you?' the bounty hunter asked.

'It is the blade of the Baron von Drakenburg!' accused the mercenary between gasps.

Brunner leaned forward and hissed into the mercenary's ear. 'I don't know any von Drakenburg,' he stated. 'I took this sword from a self-styled baron a year ago. He lived in a miserable muddy hovel down in the Borderlands. Perhaps he stole it.'

'What was his name?' demanded the mercenary, despite the pressure on his throat. Brunner released his hold and stepped away.

'The scum was named Albrecht Yorck,' the bounty hunter declared. He removed the pistol from the face of the other mercenary and backtracked to the door. Behind him, the drunken mercenary sobbed into the wooden counter.

'Yorck!' the man cried, slamming his fist into the wood. 'It was Yorck who betrayed us!'

Brunner left the man to his sorrow, emerging in the sweltering, stinking street. Ortez hurried to catch up with him.

'What was that about?' the Estalian asked as he fell into step beside the bounty hunter.

'Nothing,' Brunner answered, not meeting Ortez's gaze. 'Ancient history.'

MIRAGLIANO WAS NOT the chaotic warren found within the walls of most Imperial cities. The city was formed of distinct and identifiable districts, as removed and independent from one another as individual nations. Partially, this was due to the elaborate civic improvements and planning orchestrated by the genius Leonardo da Miragliano. Under his direction, Prince Cosimo had devastated much of the old city, to replace it with a well-ordered and easily navigated metropolis. The inner reaches of the city, which were most difficult for attackers to reach, became the homes of the wealthy merchant princes and those who had earned their favour. These were also the districts of the artistically enriched temples which were showcases of the city's wealth and piety. The outer sections were given over to mercenary barracks, the taverns and brothels that served them, and to the labourers and seamen who toiled to fill the coffers of the princes. Around the entire city, thick walls guarded against invasion, and numerous towers leaned upward from their soggy foundations to protect those walls.

But it was not the genius of the engineer that kept the districts from swelling beyond their boundaries as they had in the cities of the Empire. It was the fact that much of the city was built on numerous small islands, so that in many places, canals took the place of streets, and thick walls and guarded gates maintained the inviolate boundaries between merchant and servant.

The scarecrow-like Estalian led Brunner to one of Miragliano's most prosperous districts. It was in the very heart of the old city, and was protected from the sprawl around it by its own thick stone wall. Located as it was on a separate island from the warren-like maze of warehouses, shops and taverns that catered to the merchant fleets and their crews. Brunner and the emaciated Ortez were forced to embark upon a narrow gondola. The bounty hunter pointedly waited for the thin Estalian to pay the gondolier his fee. The man quietly poled his charges away from the mercantile domain, past the scows and barges of the water sellers, towards the looming wall of the old city. A small pier jutted out from the front of the wall. The gondolier manoeuvred his craft toward the small jetty where a trio of glowering soldiers awaited them.

Brunner could see that these were not members of the mercenary watch hired by the guildhouses to protect their goods and maintain a semblance of law in the mercantile

district. These were hard-faced Tileans, scarred veterans who
had already cut their teeth as dogs of war. Over their suit of
reinforced leather armour, each man wore a tabard decorated with the scarlet field and black tower of Prince Borgio
himself.

The scowling soldiers motioned for the gondola to stop at
their post, which was set before a massive iron portcullis
that blocked the canal's progress under the wall. One of
them produced a long boat hook to facilitate the landing.
The other two soldiers fixed their stern gaze on Brunner and
his companion.

Ortez smiled back at the guards, thumbing three gold
coins from his money belt. The soldier with the boat hook
accepted the payment without a word, then nodded at his
comrades.

'Search it,' the soldier growled. Both men grabbed short
spears from a barrel resting on the jetty and began to tap the
bottom of the gondola, listening intently for any hollow
sound. Satisfied in this respect, the guards looked carefully
at the sides of the small boat, their keen eyes searching for
anything that shouldn't be there. As one of the soldiers
turned to replace the spear in its barrel, Brunner caught sight
of a small, hairy hand-like paw swinging from a leather strap
on the man's belt. It seemed that rat catching as well as gate
keeping was part of the soldiers' duties.

The soldier with the boat hook set the implement down
and strode towards the wall. He spoke into a barred grille of
a heavy iron door. Soon, the corroded portcullis that
blocked the canal was groaning its way upward. The gondolier pushed off and began to navigate his way into the
prosperous old quarter.

The canal soon narrowed beyond the wall. Looking back,
Brunner could see the creaky portcullis lowering once more.
A pair of crossbowmen in burnished bronze armour
regarded the passing gondola from the top of the wall, then
returned their attention to their duties.

The temperature was noticeably cooler here. The palazzos
of the merchants and the Tilean noble houses rose to either
side of the canal, their many balconies reaching across the

reeking water to within an arm's length of one another, casting the waterway below into shadow. Brunner studied his surroundings, noting the garish, opulent porticoes that fronted the mansions, each of the colonnaded entryways trying to outdo the next in extravagance and artistry. At times, a tired-looking footman in the livery of some merchant house could be seen leaning against one of the doorways, desperately awaiting some visitor to break the tedium and provide him with a brief escape from the stench of the canal.

The gondolier expertly navigated the confused network of canals, at last drawing his craft toward a massive grey-stoned building. Like the other palazzos, this one sported an extravagant portico, its fluted columns fashioned of black marble. Intricate carvings writhed about the mantle in a manner that suggested serpents as much as they did vines. A thick-necked, burly figure stood at the top of half a dozen steps that descended from the door to the canal. As the gondola approached, the doorman descended, accepting the rope the gondolier offered him and fastening it to an iron fixture cast in the shape of a swan.

'The house of my lady, the Contessa Carlotta de Villarias,' Ortez announced proudly as he stepped from the gondola. Brunner waited for a moment before following the scarecrow-like steward. He spared a moment to once again observe the elaborate portico. There was indeed an opulence to it, but there was also a touch of decay. Dirt had infiltrated the scroll-work, and cobwebs had gathered in the corners. It was an observation that gave him some misgiving. Was his prospective patroness the inheritor of a failing fortune? It had been the bounty hunter's experience that there were few creatures more dangerous than an expiring dynasty seeking to preserve the illusion of wealth.

'The contessa, she wait in the black room,' the massive doorman growled, his accent thick with the tones of Miragliano's most debased street thieves. Brunner took note of the brief, furtive glance between Ortez and the doorman when the thug mentioned the black room. He made a pretence of scratching at his forearm, as though the armoured vambrace were chafing at his skin. But he was actually

ensuring that the needle-sharp spring-loaded stiletto he had
relieved from the mercenary Ursio years ago was ready for
plying its murderous function.

'This way,' Ortez gestured, showing the bounty hunter the
door, as though Brunner had been ignorant of its presence.
The scrawny Estalian hovered on the threshold as the doorman pushed the portal inward. The swarthy-visaged
scarecrow looked into the room beyond for a moment, then
turned his eyes back on Brunner. He had a puzzled and
somewhat annoyed expression on his wrinkled features.

'After you,' Brunner said, his voice icy, one hand caressing
the pistol across his belly. Ortez favoured him with a nervous smile, then entered the palazzo. Brunner trained his
eyes upon the thuggish doorman, watching him for the
slightest suggestion of untoward intentions. The big Tilean
just glowered back, his expression no less unfriendly than it
had been upon their arrival. The bounty hunter smiled back,
his mind working to place a name to the hulking ruffian's
face, and a price to fit the name.

THE PALAZZO OF Contessa de Villarias was a cold, clammy
place. Despite the heat outside which slowly boiled the filth
floating in the canals, the air in the noblewoman's residence
carried a definite chill. The marble floors were dusty, and the
bounty hunter's eyes were quick to note the trails that disturbed that dust. He mentally filed away the prints,
cataloguing each distinct set, and slowly calculating how
many others had been privileged to disturb the Contessa de
Villarias's dust.

The winding corridor and stairway that Ortez had conducted him through bore all the traces of a wealthy house.
Statues of quality and antiquity adorned marble pedestals
spaced along the walls. Where the statues were absent, portraits took their place, displaying the fading features of once
powerful men. Each was the work of a master, though it was
evident no one hand had painted any two. Moreover, many
of the portraits featured men in costume dressed after the
fashion of noblemen from ages past. It was a curious collection, for it was apparent that the portraits bore no familial

connection. Perhaps the contessa was an eccentric spinster trying to fill her empty halls with a tiny trace of that which she had never claimed?

Everywhere amidst the artwork and elaborately engraved moulding that framed every doorway was the air of decay. Dust had silently gathered in the corners, in the cracks and crannies of the skirting, on the frames of portraits and on the brows of statues. Cobwebs dangled from the narrow space at the top of the vaulted ceilings. Brunner considered the paltry number of footprints he had seen. It was obvious that the contessa did not maintain a large household. It was equally obvious that what servants she did keep were tasked to duties other than maintaining the palazzo.

The man stopped before a set of double doors, massive things of dark Drakwald timber, with a pair of leering gargoyles carved into the face of each panel. Ortez placed his hands on the steel handles and pushed the doors inward. Brunner paused an instant then followed the man inside.

The black room had been named well. The floor was of onyx, the lustrous black stone shining in the flickering light cast by a hanging chandelier. The walls were draped in heavy black cloth, a slight draught making the cloth rustle with a faint motion, as though the room itself were alive. Brunner noted the walls with particular suspicion. He studied each motion of the cloth, watching for anything that might portend more than a mere draft. The room itself was almost devoid of furnishings, the only exceptions being a small claw-footed table and a tall leather-backed chair. A decanter of some dark, smoky crystal stood upon the table. In the chair sat the Contessa Carlotta de Villarias.

The noblewoman wore a soft velvet dress that had been dyed to match the floor and the walls. The neckline was cut low, in a v-shaped pattern and trimmed with intricate spider webs of lace. A great, ponderous pendant of gold hung from her neck. It was a gleaming trinket that resembled a terrible eye as much as it did the unblinking disk of the sun.

The contessa lounged in the chair, posing to accentuate every curve of her voluptuous figure. Above the pendant, the woman's face regarded the bounty hunter from within a frame of sleek black hair. Hers was a sort of timeless beauty that had been aped throughout the ages by Tilean painters and sculptors. Her delicate nose was like a small button set at the centre of her face. The full, slightly pouting lips were at once inviting and mocking. The high cheeks and slight chin were clothed in soft, pale, unblemished skin, as flawless as polished marble, as cool and inviting as the soft sands of the shores of Ulthuan. The sensual green eyes shrouded by long lashes taunted the observer to gaze into their emerald depths, and to dare unlock the secret thoughts and unspoken knowledge that rested behind them.

'I welcome you, bounty hunter,' the contessa said, her voice soft, inviting. 'I am pleased that you have accepted my commission.' As she spoke, she stroked a small, short-haired cat resting in her lap.

Brunner found himself unable to turn his eyes from the beautiful figure seated before him. Emotions long abandoned welled up within him, and the more controlled part of his mind became ever more unsettled. She was beautiful. Her voice was soft as new-fallen snow. Her eyes were the most captivating he had ever seen. The contessa Carlotta de Villarias was the most lovely woman he had ever encountered. He needed to clear his head. It had been a long time since he had succumbed to such thoughts. He was here for business, he needed to focus on that.

'Something troubles you?' the noblewoman asked, her slender hand hesitating in its stroking of the cat. The black-furred animal turned its head to face the bounty hunter. Its great eyes snapped open in its head. They were eyes of jade, dull imitations of those of its mistress.

Brunner stared back at the woman, meeting her piercing green eyes. She was indeed beautiful, but the colour of her gold would be more so. The bounty hunter considered his need for the woman's wealth, using his lust for revenge to counter the desires that had risen unbidden within him. A brief flicker of emotion crossed the contessa's face, something that conveyed amusement and annoyance almost as a single expression.

'It remains to be seen if I will accept your commission,' Brunner stated, struggling to keep his voice level. The contessa smiled back, nodding her head.

'Do not let the condition of my Miragliano house deceive you,' she said. 'It has been many long years since I last had cause to visit this palazzo in the city. As my servant has no doubt explained, I am a native of Estalia, and it is there where I make my home. Moreover, I wanted to keep my arrival in the city as unremarkable and unnoticed as possible. Bringing sufficient staff to restore this place would have been detrimental to my present concerns.' The contessa allowed herself a slight, hollow laugh. 'Rest assured, bounty hunter, I can well afford your services.'

Brunner adjusted his stance, once again eyeing the curtained walls with suspicion. 'I have not yet heard what it is you wish to hire me to do. I don't take a job until I know what it is.'

'Right to the point. All business,' the contessa observed. 'I find it is a rare thing to find men who are so, ah, professional. Very well. I wish to hire you to secure an item which was stolen from me, and to eliminate whoever is in possession of it.'

'That would depend on the nature of the item,' the bounty hunter stated, 'and who is in possession of it. I am hardly going to accept a commission to murder Borgio the Besieger because he happens to have stolen some bauble of yours.'

'Do not worry,' the contessa said. 'Those who have stolen from me are no great princes or merchant lords. They are thieves, simple robbers and nothing more. Whoever they might have traded my possessions to is also criminal scum. You won't be decorating one of Miragliano's leaning watch towers by accepting my assigment, I assure you.'

'I just wanted to make it clear to you that there are some lines which I will not cross,' Brunner explained. 'Suicide is one of them.' A slight smile of mockery and amusement tugged at the noblewoman's features.

'If you are half the man they make you out to be, then you will have little problem in reclaiming my stolen property.'

The contessa gestured with her hand, indicating a stack of small pamphlets resting beside the decanter. Brunner could see that they were a collection of Ehrhard Stoecker's adventure stories, tales that Brunner himself had related to the man.

'Alright,' the bounty hunter said, doing his best to ignore the contessa's reference to what he himself considered to be spurious fabrications diluted from his real exploits. 'Just exactly what is it you wish me to find?'

The contessa straightened herself in her seat, upsetting the cat, which cast a sullen look up at its mistress. The noblewoman paused for a moment, the tip of her tongue licking her bottom lip as she collected her thoughts. Finally, having decided where to begin, or, more likely, how much to tell, she began to relate her story.

'Several months ago, I came into possession of a map which showed the location of a previously undiscovered tomb in Nehekhara. I have always been fascinated by the ancient civilisation of the pyramid builders, and fortunately have enough wealth to indulge my penchant for such antiquities. I travelled to Araby and arranged to outfit an expedition to the tomb. I myself did not go, of course, but I did send a number of representatives along with those Arabyans I employed.

'Two months passed before my representatives returned. Some of the Arabyans I had employed had deserted the expedition, taking with them a number of priceless artefacts. My men had observed that one of the Arabyans had displayed some knowledge of Miragliano and its black market. In fact, he had been trying to convince the other men to desert with him and to bring away a greater portion of the loot. With this report, I at once made arrangements for passage to Miragliano and hoped to reclaim my property.'

'And have you?' asked Brunner.

'Only partially,' sighed the contessa. 'Many of the smaller items have been recovered by my own people, but one of the most noteworthy items has not.' She paused again, wetting her lip. 'The preserved mummy of a Nehekharan priest-king has eluded our best efforts to recover it.' When she paused again Brunner could see the first trace of life in her compelling eyes. They were wide with fear. 'The mummies of Nehekhara are valuable in themselves, but not in the same way as gold or gems or even scrolls and books. The mummies are sometimes sold to apothecaries, who chop them to bits to make powerful medicines. But there is a much darker possibility. It is possible that the mummy has been sold to a necromancer, to provide the degenerate wizard with a mighty relic for his warped experiments.' The contessa paused again, fixing Brunner with her gaze. 'It is that possibility which I fear the most.'

'You want me to recover something that may be in the hands of a necromancer?' Brunner questioned, a trace of disbelief and shock in his voice. The contessa inclined her head slightly.

'Indeed,' the contessa replied. 'Find whoever has the mummy. Kill them and destroy the mummy, lest it has absorbed some unholy sorcery while in the possession of such a fiend. I will sleep safer knowing it has been destroyed, and that by my actions no nameless horror will have been unleashed upon the world.' The noblewoman's face became softer, the fear in her eyes becoming a more desperate pleading.

'You will help me? You will destroy this thing I caused to be taken from the Land of the Dead?'

Brunner stared back. 'For two thousand gold crowns,' he replied. 'Fighting sorcerers and the living dead is not something I do on the cheap.'

He wasn't entirely convinced by the contessa's claims that she was worried what someone else might do with this mouldering relic. But if she paid him enough gold, he didn't care if she was going to grind it up herself and poison the king of Estalia with it. The colour of gold could silence many questions.

The Contessa de Villarias's face twisted into an angry glower, but it quickly faded. 'If gold is all that moves your heart,' she said at last, 'then gold you shall have. But you must act swiftly, lest my fears come to pass!'

The bounty hunter inclined his head. 'Just have the money ready,' he commented, his tone surly. 'I'll provide the bodies. Dead and even more dead.'

THE THING THAT had taken the title of Contessa Carlotta de Villarias watched the bounty hunter depart. He was an unpleasant creature, the sort of vermin whose neck she would happily snap like a twig without giving it a second thought. There was only a residue of the higher emotions within him, not even enough for her to play upon and exploit. Gold and the pursuit of wealth were the only desires that motivated the bounty killer. Even for one of her kind, dealing with such a despicable creature made Carlotta feel soiled and unclean.

Still, it had to be admitted that the villain was not without his positive attributes, particularly if a callous and ruthless nature could be considered a virtue. Brunner's reputation for getting a job done bordered on legend among the thieves of Miragliano. The merest rumour that the bounty hunter might be on their trail was enough to make many men relocate to another of Tilea's walled cities.

Carlotta had been surprised when she had discovered that the street novels of the exiled Altdorf author Ehrhard Stoecker contained more than a germ of truth in them. If anything, the writer seemed to have downplayed the fear with which the underworld of Miragliano held his subject. The bounty killer had acquired a truly formidable reputation. Carlotta had read the spurious pamphlets out of simple curiosity. After all, Stoecker was of some slight interest to members of the Aristocracy of the Night after his scandalous *True History of Vlad von Carstein*. But as she read, she had become intrigued, and saw the bounty hunter as a solution to her present troubles.

The man was no less impressive in the flesh, what she could see of him at any rate. He was well built, without the grotesque overabundance of muscle favoured by many men who depended upon violence as their trade. The wary manner in which he carried himself, the cunning, calculating light in his eyes – as though prepared for attack – had made their impression upon her. Indeed, he was a man that she might have dallied with, maybe even allowing him to cross the threshold of Morr and become one of her thralls. But he was also possessed of an arrogant and disdainful manner. He seemed to lack deference to those of a loftier station than his own. True, he might be brought to heel, but Carlotta had a feeling that breaking the man might not be so easy. His will was strong; he had even resisted her attempt to beguile him into her service. Seldom had the ancient vampire encountered a mortal who could manage to deny her ethereal charms, her mastery of the art of seduction with the merest glance. Carlotta pondered whether she might be able to transfix the man, should she be forced to deal with him herself. Might he throw off her compelling gaze? Might he even be able to raise his hand against her?

The vampiress considered the possibility. But it was just such an indomitable will that she was in need of. She needed a hero, a man who might stand against the most dire of horrors, and fight against beings that even the undead feared. He might even prevail against it.

Carlotta shuddered as she pondered the creature she had sent the bounty hunter to destroy. She had spent the better part of her existence living in fear of the day when the thing might walk again. Even among the deathless, certain names still carried an awful power. Among these was that of Nehb-ka-menthu, priest-king of the ancient city of Khareops, the city of pillars.

The memory of her first meeting with the priest-king was clearer to the ancient vampiress than any she had collected in her thousands of years of unlife. The great army of Alcadizaar the Conqueror had fallen upon Lahmia, crushing the city utterly and completely for Queen Neferata's partaking of the elixir of Nagash, the great necromancer. The vampires had fought with all the fury and wrath they could muster, but the army of Alcadizaar was driven by a religious frenzy. They had come to punish the city for adopting the heresies and blasphemies of the accursed Nagash. They had come to put to the torch all trace of the necromancer's evil work. Or so Alcadizaar had supposed. Among his army was the host of Khareops, and leading that host was the priest-king of Khareops, Nehb-ka-menthu. He did not come to wash his soul in righteous slaughter. He had come to plunder, and steal the dark knowledge Lahmia had acquired. For the priest-king harboured his own hideous ambition: he hoped to elevate himself far beyond even the eternal life and supernatural might of the vampires. The insane priest-king hoped to become something much greater. He aspired to become nothing less than a second Nagash!

So much became clear to Carlotta after she had been captured by a group of Khareopan soldiers during her attempt to flee the doomed city of Lahmia. Nor was she alone. Ten other vampires were locked in silver-lined boxes by the soldiers of Khareops, to be transported back to the city of pillars. Nehb-ka-menthu had protected his dark secret, ordering the death of all the surviving soldiers who had taken part in the siege of Lahmia as his force returned to Khareops. The hundreds-strong force had taken turns removing the heads of their comrades, the last of their number ripping open his belly with a flint knife. Then the priest-king had conducted his secret plunder into the heart of the pyramid that had been erected in preparation for his eventual death.

There are torments that can break even the will of the undead, and Nehb-ka-menthu had discovered them all. Over many years, the other vampires gave up their secrets, as the insane priest-king probed their bodies with salt and silver and hawthorn. He bled them, drinking the vampiric ichor so that he might perpetuate his own life. One by one, Carlotta's fellow captives had been used up, their remains fed to wild dogs so they might never rise again. The vampiress herself had nearly succumbed before history conspired to set her free.

The Great Ritual had struck all of Nehekhara as Nagash perpetuated his final blasphemy against his ancient homeland. The lands of Nehekhara had long been poisoned and plagued by the great necromancer, but now, the few who remained amongst the living had perished, and the ancient dead had been stirred. The Great Ritual struck the whole of the ancient kingdom, and Nagash's black magic did not spare the city of pillars. Those who still walked the streets of Khareops perished as the dark energy smothered them. In the dungeons of his pyramid, Nehb-ka-menthu had been drawing ichor once more from Carlotta's weak, withered form when the awful power of Nagash's spell struck him down. As life drained from the priest-king, Nehb-ka-menthu had not cried out in pain. Instead, he had declared, 'Such power shall be mine!'

Carlotta had fled the dead city of pillars, and crawled into the desert like some vermin in human form. From the dead things that now walked the lands of Nehekhara, she could derive no nourishment. She was reduced to preying on the thin fluids of scorpions and scarabs – the only creatures hardy enough to have survived Nagash's spell of doom.

It had taken her months to finally make her way to the mountains, and to feed on the equally rancid blood of orcs and goblins. In this way she at last found her way to the north, to the domains carved out by those who had escaped the doomed city of Lahmia. It had been centuries since she had endured such privation. The taste of such noxious provender had been expulsed from her by countless feedings on the rich warm blood of hearty men and supple women. She had left the sands of Nehekhara as a wretched, almost animal thing, but she had been reborn in the north as an elegant and lethal predator, an angry goddess of the night whose displeasure was as certain as the vengeance of any deity.

The final words of Nehb-ka-menthu still filled Carlotta with terror, a dread she had not known since she had become a vampire. She could still recall the nauseating horror that had filled her when she had been prowling the musty old museum in Magritta and seen the shard of pot bearing the glyph of Khareops. The sands of the desert had consumed the city of pillars, or so she had been told. Yet now it seemed that Khareops had been rediscovered, and that what should have remained lost had been found again. Carlotta knew fear again as she considered what might have been taken from the dead city.

It had taken years to trace the relic in the Magritta curio-house back to its source. Carlotta had learned from the now elderly tomb robber how he had found the cursed city, and what he had found within it. The city, it seemed, was largely intact despite the sand and the centuries, unspoiled by time and tomb robber. She wondered if this could be true, if Khareops and that which it held had indeed survived the ages. She decided that she could not take the risk that it had. The vampiress had indeed organised an expedition to the tomb, but she did not send them to claim lost treasures. She sent them to destroy the remains of Nehb-ka-menthu.

But her plan had backfired. Not wishing to endanger herself, Carlotta had sent a vampiric thrall with the expedition, and her surrogate had been destroyed by the faithless Arabyans. Worse, when she had finally caught up with some of the treacherous thieves in the city of Ka-Sabar, she discovered that they had found the lost city of Khareops, and had already penetrated the tomb of Nehb-ka-menthu.

As Carlotta had suspected, the undying liche priests of Khareops had mummified the remains of their slain king in the wake of the Great Ritual. The Arabyans had seen the mummy with their own eyes. Recalling her orders, several of them had decided that some potent magic must lie within the priest-king's mouldering remains. They conspired to bear the mummy away to the coast and transport it to the Tilean city of Miragliano. One of the men was certain his contacts in the black market would enable them to dispose of the carrion at great profit.

Carlotta did not like to think what the ancient priest-king might have become in death. The embalming arts of the liche priests would have prevented his spirit from abandoning his dead form. But what effect might the vampire blood he had so laboriously extracted from his Lahmian captives have had upon him? In life, it had held back the sands of time, but in death? What sort of monster had the foolish Arabyans taken from the dry wastes of Nehekhara, and what might happen if the awful thing were to stir from its centuries of slumber? Nehb-ka-menthu's mummy might be nothing more than a wasted corpse, but could she take that risk?

The black drapes parted and a pair of darkly handsome figures drifted across the onyx floor to stand beside their mistress. They were very alike in many ways, possessing the same pale skin, the same hungry cast to their lean faces and similar lustreless eyes. The vampire thralls had waited in hiding, to guard against any sudden aggression on the part of the bounty hunter. The contessa did not know whether her guest had been instructed in the detection of vampires by his literary chronicler. And she had learned that one could never be certain how the fragile living would react to the presence of the undead.

'Mistress,' spoke the vampire who had emerged from the left side of the room. He was a tall, well-built man. Two hundred years ago, before Carlotta had taken a fancy to him, he had been the premier duellist in Miragliano. He still wore his heavy duelling cloak, and still bore the light duelling rapier at his side. Carlotta reflected how even after hundreds of years, her kind were very much creatures of habit. 'Why engage the mortal? You do not need him.' The vampire's voice dropped into a conspiratorial whisper. 'I can find this carrion you so greatly fear.' He drew his sword, letting the exposed steel gleam in the candlelight. 'Time has not dulled my skills. I am still the greatest blade in all Tilea!'

'Do you think that mere swordplay is enough? It would take more than a sword to strike down anything my lady fears,' scoffed the other thrall. He was shorter than the other vampire, but no less handsome. He wore a set of elegant clothes with large frilled cuffs. His elaborately trimmed tunic resembled those that might be worn to the elaborate balls held by the wealthiest of Tilea's merchant princes when they were not making war against one another. Indeed, Torici had once been a fixture at such functions: a dashing, witty rogue who had a reputation for making even the coldest heart warm to him. Carlotta had been amused by his wit, by his clever observations on the world, and she had taken him, that he might continue to entertain her into the long night. While Relotto was her brawn, Torici was her brain. The two thralls naturally complemented each another.

Relotto scowled back at his rival, baring his elongated fangs. Torici ignored him and continued to speak. 'I must observe, with all deference my lady, that I am also at a loss to understand why you hired a vulgar bounty killer instead of sending one of us to deal with this matter.'

Carlotta fixed her slave with a withering look. 'Because I do not wish there to be any trail that might lead back to me. If what I fear is true, if he walks again, I want no chance that he might find me! If I sent you, he would know I was behind the attack, because he would taste me in the blood that courses through your carcasses. But the bounty hunter is a different matter. There is nothing in him that will lead my enemy back here.'

'Do you really think the warm-blood has any chance?' Relotto remarked. 'If the Vile One has not awoken, he might be able to destroy it, but if the Vile One walks again?'

'Yes,' replied the contessa. 'You are quite right. I must keep an eye on my bounty hunter. I must know if he succeeds or fails.' The vampiress lifted the animal nestled in her lap, and turned it so that she might whisper in its ear. She stood and gently set the animal on the floor. The cat swiftly scurried away and was soon lost in the deepening shadows of the corridor beyond the black room.

The cat shared some of Carlotta's unlife; it was itself a thing removed from the living. By concentration and exertion of her will, the vampiress could see through the feline's jade eyes. Her familiar would follow the bounty hunter. When Brunner found the hiding place of the priest-king, Carlotta would know. And if he found the mummy still locked in its ancient rest, and if he put the abomination to the torch, Carlotta would be close at hand to reward the villain for the boundless effrontery he had shown her.

Carlotta looked again at her devoted minions. 'Notify the servants that we are leaving,' she said. 'In the event that the bounty hunter does fail, I want to be ready to quit the city immediately.'

The vampiress settled back in her chair as her minions returned to the shadows to carry out her orders. She reached a slender, pale hand for the crystal decanter, poured the rich red liquor into a small glass and daintily sipped. She held the blood on her tongue, savouring its salty, vibrant taste. And as she drank, she found herself hoping that Brunner would survive his task.

She was curious to know what his blood would taste like.

THE DINGY CELLAR was dark and cool, like the hole of some rodent. Brunner strode through the darkness, dodging the wet strips of cloth dangling from the wooden supports, and heading toward the rearmost corner of the underground room below the tannery. The stink of garbage and rotten vegetables assailed his senses as he pushed aside the damp rags. A faint light beckoned from the shadows.

'Ah, my old friend!' a frail-sounding voice coughed from somewhere near the light. 'You've come to visit me once more and relieve my loneliness!'

Brunner advanced on the speaker. The man was spindly and old, his bones wrapped in wrinkled skin. The man's skull-like face bore ghastly tooth-like projections. One of the hands that protruded from the sleeve of his thin nightshirt was malformed; it resembled a set of boneless tentacles. The human wreckage lay upon a rickety cot, with a small wooden chair set before it. An old lantern hung from a hook set into the beam above his feeble figure.

'Tessari,' Brunner said, as he seated himself in the old wooden chair. The mutant smiled as he heard his name, and his large, watery eyes misted with emotion.

'It is so nice to hear my name spoken by another voice,' Tessari confessed, tears slithering down his malformed face. 'Sometimes I almost forget what it sounds like.' He closed his eyes, his wasted body heaving with dry sobs. 'Sometimes I almost forget what it is. I have to recite it to myself in the night so that I will remember.'

Brunner sighed, adjusting his position on the chair. 'If you could delay the onset of madness for a few minutes, I have some questions for you, old man.'

Tessari's eyes snapped open, the tentacles of his hand writhing and twitching. He contorted his features into a grimace of distaste. 'I was forgetting myself. Forgetting who I was talking to. Tell me, Brunner, is there even a trace of pity in that stone heart of yours?'

'None,' the bounty hunter replied. 'And since you seem so forgetful, I think I'll just take my questions somewhere else.' Brunner rose to leave. Tessari waved him to sit down again with his still-human hand.

'There are many things I still remember,' Tessari said, his tone sullen. He tapped his forehead with one of the worm-like digits of his altered hand. 'There are still a few things in this skull of mine.'

'Let's just hope that what I need is in there,' Brunner commented as he sat back down.

'Perhaps,' Tessari responded. 'But this time I want my fee paid in advance.' The mutant's tentacles clenched in a macabre parody of a closing fist. 'And no tricks this time,' he warned.

'Of course not,' assured Brunner. He lifted his helmed head to consider the hanging lantern. 'After all, I see that you put your previous fee to a good purpose.'

'Just so we understand one another,' wheezed Tessari, settling himself back into his cot. 'Who are you hunting this time?'

'Not "who",' the bounty hunter corrected. 'I am paid to find a "what" this time. A relic stolen from an expedition in Araby. My patron has reason to believe it is here in Miragliano.'

Tessari made a disgusted groaning noise. 'Stolen property in Miragliano,' the mutant laughed. 'You might as well seek an individual snowflake on the ice fields of Kislev!'

Brunner favoured Tessari with a knowing smile. 'I imagine that this particular item might be unusual enough to be remarkable. What was stolen was the mummified body of a Nehekharan priest-king.'

Tessari's wormy digits convulsed as they tried to make the signs of Shallya and Morr together. 'Gods preserve us!' he exclaimed.

'I imagine that would be most people's reaction,' Brunner stated. 'There can't be too many men in Miragliano willing to deal in such wares. Even fewer who would have ties to thieves from Araby.'

'There is only one whom I can think of,' Tessari said after a moment's consideration. 'Abdul-Qaadir bin Shereef. Normally, he deals chiefly in Crimson Shade and other narcotic herbs from the South Lands, but he is not above dabbling in slaving and the black market. He is an Arabyan, but has lived in Miragliano for the past ten years. He is a ruthless and cruel man, utterly without morals. It is said he fears neither god nor man. I should think he would be just the sort of person who would buy or sell this thing you seek.'

'This Abdul-Qaadir does indeed sound like the man I am looking for,' Brunner agreed, tossing a set of silver coins onto the edge of Tessari's cot. 'Where can I find him?'

'Abdul-Qaadir maintains a warehouse off La Strada di Falco,' Tessari answered, lifting his body so that he might retrieve the coins. 'But be warned, he keeps much of his illegal merchandise there, and the warehouse is always guarded. Abdul-Qaadir is not like Ennio Volonté. He knows when and where to spend his money. His guards won't be the usual gutter-trash.'

Brunner rose. 'Good,' he said, 'I was getting worried that this job wasn't going to be interesting.'

'It might be more interesting than you can handle,' cautioned Tessari. 'You have given thought to the possibility that Abdul-Qaadir has already sold the mummy? Ask yourself what sort of man would want such a thing? Ask yourself what he might hope to do with it?'

'I've already been warned of those possibilities, old man,' Brunner retorted, caressing the pistol holstered across his belt. Tessari shook his head.

'Once, when I was still young, the caravan I led happened upon a barrow mound just off one of the back trails to Monte Castello. Trust me when I tell you that guns and swords are no proof against the restless dead.'

Brunner stood still for a moment, considering Tessari's advice. 'What is?' he asked.

'Faith,' the old mutant replied. 'Faith in the good and noble gods, faith that they will preserve and protect you against such abominations.'

Brunner snorted contemptuously, stalking away from Tessari, and making his way back through the maze of damp rags. 'I'm afraid that my faith in anything has run pretty low, especially faith in the gods. I prefer to put my trust in steel. And in gold.'

Tessari shook his head, and listened as the bounty hunter's steps carried him from the cellar.

'Steel and gold won't help you, Brunner,' he said to himself. 'They won't help you at all.'

ABDUL-QAADIR PUSHED his swarthy hand into the wooden box, immersing it in the crisp dried leaves that filled it. The Arabyan smiled, stroking his scruffy beard with his free hand. This shipment of Crimson Shade that had been smuggled into Miragliano was the largest and freshest he had ever received. The noxious herb leaves felt like wealth, like power.

The broad shouldered black marketeer removed his hand, bringing with it a fistful of the leaves. The Tileans were fanatics for this maniac art they called the vendetta. Many of them fancied themselves masters of the sword, true artists of the duel. But a Tilean did not like to leave anything to chance. He would plot and plan, laying schemes within schemes to ensure that events would transpire toward the end he sought. It was the same with the duellists. Their skill with the blade might indeed be remarkable, but they always liked extra insurance. Some would coat their weapons in garlic or some other blood poison so that the merest scratch would finish their enemy. Others preferred to make certain that theirs would be the swifter blade. Such men were easily lured into the use of Crimson Shade, an exotic herb that would speed up their reflexes and reactions.

Abdul-Qaadir smiled again. That Crimson Shade was also dreadfully addictive was a side-effect his customers discovered for themselves. The Arabyan looked up and gestured for one of the hulking mercenary guards who stood watch in the sprawling warehouse. The hired sword walked over, his hands twitching on the grip of his halberd. Abdul-Qaadir handed him the leaves he had scooped from the crate.

'A bonus, my friend,' the black marketeer said. 'You did well in ferreting out Emir's thankless thievery.' The Arabyan shook his head sadly. 'Poor Emir, such a disappointment. He, more than anyone else, should have understood that there must be honour among thieves.' Abdul-Qaadir gave the big Tilean a knowing look. He knew that the mercenary had informed on Emir, but it was only because he had been too stupid himself to figure out a way to steal from his employer. The black marketeer dearly hoped that the mercenary would continue to be thick-headed. Smart men made poor guards.

The swarthy Arabyan looked about the warehouse. It was a broad, squat building, crowded with the crates and barrels that held the black marketeer's wares. In one corner was a massive iron cage. It was a little early yet to collect drunks from La Strada dei Cento Peccati. The Arabyan barques with their secret holds would not be in port for several months yet, and feeding prospective slaves for weeks on end would cut into Abdul-Qaadir's profit margin. Profit was the black marketeer's lifeblood. He'd sold his own mother to a caliph's harem when he was a boy for the price of a camel. No matter what leader's face graced the coin, Abdul-Qaadir knew the value of a piece of gold.

There was a furtive rapping on the heavy wooden door that opened onto La Strada di Falco. The guard nearest the door listened as the series of knocks was repeated. Abdul-Qaadir did not pay it much attention. The code had been given. It was one of the petty addicts who peddled Crimson Shade to Prince Borgio's soldiers in the many taverns and brothels scattered throughout the city. It never failed to amaze the Arabyan how the street peddlers always knew when he had a new shipment. It was almost as if they could scent the leaves like a pig with a truffle.

The mercenary opened the door, and stared down at the heavily cloaked figure beyond the portal. Abdul-Qaadir's herb-sellers often arrived in shabby disguises. The guard swore an oath and stepped through the doorway. He held his halberd in one hand and balled a fist with his other.

'The boss will send for you when he wants you,' the guard growled. 'You'd be smart to stay away from here until he does.' The guard lashed out with his fist, aiming a punishing blow to the man's belly. He was shocked when the cloaked shape dodged aside from his blow. A surprised look froze on the guard's face when a slender stiletto sprang into the figure's hand and the cloaked killer punched a needle of steel into his throat. The guard slumped into the doorway, supporting himself against the halberd, as his fingers clutched at the spurting wound in his neck.

The cloaked figure tucked the stiletto back into its place beneath the armour enclosing his forearm. Other weapons filled the bounty hunter's hands.

It had not taken Brunner long to find one of Abdul-Qaadir's Crimson Shade vendors. It had only taken a little longer to extract the information he needed from the wretch: the coded knock that would gain the man entry to the Arabyan's warehouse. Now he only hoped that Abdul-Qaadir would be as forthcoming.

Brunner checked his weapons and kicked open the door that had been left ajar. Across the street, a tiny shape observed the prelude to death and violence. It was a small black creature with jade green eyes.

ABDUL-QAADIR TURNED as the door of the warehouse slammed noisily. A ragged-looking man wearing a shabby brown cloak stood in the doorway. The Arabyan could not make out the man's face beneath the hood of the cloak; much of it was masked by the visor of a steel helm. The curious-looking crossbow and heavy blackpowder pistol gripped in the man's gloved hands, however, were menacingly identifiable.

'Jafar's rotting soul!' Abdul-Qaadir exclaimed. 'Brunner!'

Even as the Arabyan spoke, the bounty hunter had sprung into action. He sprinted across the room, closing upon the stunned black marketeer. The hulking Tilean Shade addict moved to intercept him.

Brunner's repeating crossbow sent steel bolts smashing into the guard's stomach and breastbone. He fell to the floor in a bleeding pile.

Abdul-Qaadir made to draw the curved blade from the colourful sash that crossed his midsection, but the business end of the bounty hunter's pistol made him reconsider. The remaining five guards surged towards the intruder who had killed two of their number and was now menacing their employer.

'I wouldn't,' growled the bounty hunter, as he gestured with his repeater crossbow. 'Any closer, and your boss dies.'

'You can't get us all,' snarled one of the Tileans.

'Maybe not,' agreed Brunner. 'But I can get at least two more of you before you reach me. Who's it going to be?' The bounty hunter uttered a short, mocking laugh as he saw the mercenaries falter, and doubt and indecision worked their way onto their faces. 'I should warn you, I coat my bolts in garlic. A trick I learned from you noodle-slurpers. That way if the bolt doesn't finish you, poison will.'

The mercenaries were all but cowed now, their grips on their weapons becoming lax.

'You're professionals,' Brunner said. 'You understand that no matter what, I'll splatter your boss's brains all over this place. If he dies, the paydays dry up.'

'Listen to him!' pleaded Abdul-Qaadir, staring into the yawning barrel of the gun. 'Don't try anything stupid!'

Suddenly the Arabyan was finding himself regretting hiring men who were not the greatest thinkers. A clear-headed man would understand that there was no way to help him except to obey the bounty hunter. But what lunacy might the idiots he had hired contemplate?

'All of you,' Brunner snapped. 'Outside! I have a few questions I need your boss to answer. Then you can all get back to your swindling, stealing and smuggling.'

'Do as he says!' urged Abdul-Qaadir when he noted his men were hesitating. With muttered oaths and murderous looks, the guards filed out of the warehouse, into the street.

'I thought they would never leave,' Brunner said, training his attention on the prisoner. 'I have a few questions for you,' he said in a dry, icy whisper. 'And trust me, you won't like it if I have to ask you twice.'

Abdul-Qaadir swallowed the lump in his throat. He brushed sweat from his brow. 'You could ask me for the keys to my daughters' chastity belts and they would be yours!' affirmed the Arabyan, his voice cracking with fear. He could well imagine that if Brunner were to discharge his weapon, there would be nothing left of him above his beard.

'Good,' the bounty hunter said. 'We're going to get along quite nicely.' The icy menace returned to his voice and he pressed the tip of the gun barrel against the Arabyan's hawkish nose. 'Tell me, what do you know about mummies?'

THE BLACK BOAR was even busier than it had been when Brunner was first contacted by Ortez. The bounty hunter stalked through the crowd of merchants from Marienburg, mercenaries from Reikland and sailors from Kislev. He made his way to the bar, and grabbed the sleeve of the balding barman.

'Where is Mahrun?' he asked, speaking so that he could be heard over the din of Reikspiel spoken in a dozen contrasting dialects. The barman nodded towards a door set towards the rear wall of the tavern. Brunner turned and strode toward the back room.

He did not knock before pushing the oak door aside. The room was small and dark. It smelled of beer and the unwashed. A few miserable specimens of humanity shuffled out of the bounty hunter's way as he entered. They watched him pass with furtive, frightened looks. These were wretches, the slovenly displaced Imperials who had been stranded in Miragliano when their money dried up or their luck ran out. The owner of the Black Boar allowed such men to spend what few coins they could beg or steal, but he did not want them cluttering up the main room. He also found it useful to keep a few such men on hand in case some ship's captain was looking for a few bodies to increase his crew. Men such as these would never rise again from their squalor and misery; they were marking time until they passed beyond the gates of Morr.

There was only one man among these whom the tavern keeper took genuine pity on. That man was Mahrun. Brunner found him seated on a wobbly, warped chair, staring despondently into a dented tin stein. He wore a shabby brown robe similar to the one Brunner had worn on his visit to Abdul-Qaadir. The man's blond hair was long, scraggly and filthy, his beard unkempt and matted. Brunner walked over to the wretch, staring down into the man's rheumy, drunken eyes.

'Mahrun,' the bounty hunter said. He produced a pair of copper coins from his belt, and held them tantalisingly before the drunk. 'Would you like these?' Mahrun snatched at the coins, but his clumsy reach was easily avoided by the bounty hunter. 'You have to earn them,' Brunner stated.

'What can I do?' the wretch asked, his voice cracking with emotion. 'What use am I?'

'None at all,' the bounty hunter replied. 'But maybe you have something that is worth buying? Let's get your things and have a look.'

Mahrun slunk from the back room, and crept out into the main hall. He made his way through the kitchens and into the storeroom where the taverneer was hiding his few possessions. The taverneer was trying to protect them from Mahrun's impulses, but the wretch had discovered where they had been hidden. It was not stealing, for however low he sank, there were things Mahrun would not do, even in his most drunken stupor. The things he retrieved really did belong to him; they were relics from another life.

Brunner watched the drunk return, cradling a bundle wrapped in black cloth. The man set down the bundle, and spread out his belongings like a bazaar merchant displaying his wares. The bounty hunter glanced over the objects, and nodded his head as he saw a funnel-shaped cylinder of wood resting beside the mouldy old Sigmarite prayer book.

Gotz Mahrun had once been a warrior-priest in the service of Sigmar, tasked to a band of templars that was charged with rooting out a nest of vampires from a haunted fortress in Averland. Whatever had happened in that blighted place,

Mahrun's companions had died. Apparently, the warrior-priest's courage and faith had not stood up to the unnatural horror of the undead.

Mahrun had fled, eventually ending up in Miragliano. He had become a broken shell of a man, plagued by inner daemons of guilt and self-loathing.

The more valuable of Mahrun's possessions – the silver buttons of his black priest's habit, the silver Sigmarite hammer that had once hung from a slender chain about his neck, the massive steel hammer he had been taught to wield upon the enemies of the Empire – had long ago been transformed into beer by the wretched priest. All that was left were objects that had no great material value – unless one had a specific use for them.

'The stick,' Brunner said. 'I'll buy that.' He tossed the copper coins down to Mahrun. The wretch grabbed the money, and stuffed it into the top of his tunic. Then he reverently handed the long wooden stake to Brunner.

'It is hawthorn,' Mahrun explained. His thumb twitched, brushing one of the inscriptions that had been carved into the stake. 'Blessed by the temple. Invocations to Sigmar carved into the wood. A very potent weapon,' Mahrun's voice slipped into a hollow whisper, 'against them.' The man slumped down onto the floor, tears streaming from his eyes. 'Would that I had had the courage to use it. Would that I had been worthy of serving mighty Sigmar.'

Brunner left the wretch to wallow in self-pity. He considered the weapon for a moment, then thrust it into his belt and made his way out of the den of lost humanity.

Abdul-Qaadir had been very forthcoming with information; Brunner had only been forced to cuff the man with the steel barrel of his pistol three or four times. Through his split, bleeding lip, the Arabyan had informed Brunner that he had sold the mummy to a Tilean, a man named Carandini. Another slap of the steel and Abdul-Qaadir had admitted to Brunner that Carandini was reputed to be a practitioner of the dark arts, a black magician who had turned to the black marketeer in the past to provide him with unspeakable, abominable things.

The confirmation that the mummy of Nehb-ka-menthu had indeed fallen into the hands of a necromancer did not discourage Brunner, but it did make him cautious. He knew that it was best to fight magic with magic, and while he might no longer honour the gods, he knew that they were not without their own magic. He always felt it was better to err on the side of caution. Mahrun's wooden stake would provide him with a little extra insurance.

THE HOUSE IN which the necromancer could apparently be found was in one of the easternmost districts of Miragliano. The land had begun to sink here, the entire island was slowly crumbling away to join the marshes beyond the city walls. It was a dilapidated district, abandoned, and all but deserted. The canals had become so choked with mud and overgrown with weeds, that they were no longer navigable. The network of dubiously maintained bridges had to be crossed to move about the district. Only the thick walls that surrounded the area had been kept up. Their bases had been shored up with rocks, boulders, gravel and rubble, to prevent them from sinking, and to preserve the integrity of Miragliano's outer defences.

Brunner walked through the derelict neighbourhood. Fallen tiles from rotting roofs crunched beneath his feet as he strode the broken cobblestone streets and decaying bridges. The only sign of human life he encountered was a work crew removing the heavy statue of a cavalry hero from the forlorn remains of a piazza. They were obviously salvaging the work of art before the swamp could consume it. The Tileans were rather odd when it comes to art, thought Brunner.

Although human life had forsaken the district, it was not without other denizens. A family of red-feathered shrikes had established a gruesome nest in the broken window of a dilapidated palazzo, numerous frogs and insects impaled on the broken splinters of the window's shutters. Great brown rats scuttled along the edge of the street, descendants of that plague of vermin that brought the red pox to Miragliano centuries before. A solitary vulture, its scrawny neck fringed by a circle of white down, pecked at a rotten cadaver that swayed from the only visible guard tower in the district.

The bounty hunter made his way through the silent streets. Even the sound of water lapping at the edges of the stone-lined canals was missing from this blighted area. On every side, doorways yawned, their ornately decorated panels looted long ago, like the glass that had once filled the empty windows above them.

Brunner paid the desolation scant notice. He was not interested in the lost glory of this neighbourhood, much less in the sorry abandonment it languished in. He was intent on finding the red-roofed three-storey building that Abdul-Qaadir had informed him served as the lair of the necromancer Carandini.

It was nearly an hour before Brunner found the house. The abandoned district was a confusing maze of streets, and some sections were unreachable now that the canals had become a muddy quagmire. This was a part of the old city that had never been reconstructed by Prince Cosimo to match the orderly planning of the great Leonardo da Miragliano. The bounty hunter was annoyed by the delay and determined that when the job was finished, he would be paying a visit to a certain Arabyan black marketeer and discussing his skill at giving directions.

Brunner checked his pistol, then unslung the curious skaven crossbow from his back. Examining the magazine that held the crossbow's bolts, he slid it into place on the weapon. Patting the large wooden stake thrust through his belt, Brunner set out for the warped, leaning building.

As the bounty hunter worked his way along the street, he took advantage of every shadow and doorway so that his arrival might not be detected. But he did not see the pair of green eyes watching him from the mouth of an alleyway. The lithe feline watched the bounty hunter for a while, then turned and strolled away, obeying some summons only the ears of an immortal cat could hear.

BRUNNER MOUNTED THE steps that led to the second floor of the ramshackle palazzo. It was a broad, sprawling building that leaned towards the necromancer's lair – the second floor balcony that rose above the portico almost touched the red-roofed building. The bounty hunter peered through the doorway of the room that opened onto the balcony. Seeing no sign of activity in the house across the narrow street, he swiftly made his way through the empty room and onto the balcony. A moment later, he climbed on top of the stone railing. Brunner did not even glance at the empty street below as he stepped across the gap between the two balconies. His left foot touched the wooden railing of the far balcony and he shifted his weight, letting his body fall into place after his foot. His quarry might reasonably be expected to have taken pains to guard against intrusion from the doors and windows on the street, but it had been the bounty hunter's experience that very few men took the same precautions against intrusion from above. Many were the second-storey burglars whom he had hunted down in the thieves' quarters of the Old World's cities, men who had gained entry to the supposedly well-protected domains of their victims with almost contemptuous ease.

No, the necromancer might have placed traps or spells to guard the lower floors, but it appeared he had fallen into the same trap that many a wealthy merchant had come to regret.

The bounty hunter peered into the darkened room off the balcony. It was not quite as empty as the one opposite. Piles of rubbish and heaps of mouldering clothing littered the room. Brunner kicked at one of the rubbish piles, noting with indifference the rotting head which rolled free, disturbing the enormous rat that had been gnawing at the carrion. Brunner kicked a second rubbish pile, to reveal a number of human bones. Apparently the necromancer employed this room as a repository for the refuse from his studies.

As he strode across the room, one of the piles of rubbish rose awkwardly to its feet. The shape that confronted Brunner was only partially human, made all the more hideous for its rapidly diminishing kinship to the race of man. Its skin was pallid. Ugly green boils were scattered across its flesh, and a loathsome, mouldy-looking rash covered half its face and neck. The head was misshapen, like a melon crushed out of symmetry by a strongman's grip. Scraggly scraps of hair dangled from a diseased scalp. The face was devoid of humanity, a rotten stump of nose perched atop a wide fang-filled mouth. Scraps of clothing clung to the creature's lean frame, and it was caked in filth and gore.

More horrible though was the activity Brunner had interrupted. As the monster's eyes glared at Brunner from the pits of its face, it dropped the decaying arm it had been chewing on and wiped the back of one of its clawed hands across its blood-stained mouth. The bounty hunter could hear the ghoul's wasted belly growl with hunger as it took a step towards him.

The bounty hunter had heard of such beings before, putrid corpse-eaters that were sometimes kept by necromancers as labourers and protectors. They were not truly dead, these soulless wretches, rather they were insane, morbid men whose unspeakable choice of nourishment had destroyed their own humanity. They were little more than beasts, and no more intelligent than a clever dog. But with its poison-dripping claws, a ghoul had very little need of more than animal cunning.

The ghoul took another step forward, a low moan escaping its bloodied mouth. Brunner could see the muscles tensing in the creature's emaciated frame as it prepared to pounce. The bounty hunter had no desire to test the quality of his armour on the ghoul's venomous claws, nor could he risk the commotion of a full-fledged fight. With lightning reflexes, Brunner pointed his crossbow pistol at the slavering corpse-eater and sent a bolt smashing through its left eye.

The ghoul gave a single gasp as its eye exploded, then fell to the floor, twitching for several moments as life faded from its brain. The bounty hunter replaced his weapon. He hoped that the sound of the creature's fall was no greater than the creature might make on its own, and that it would go unnoticed by its master.

Brunner stalked from the room, pausing in the open doorway. Like most of the buildings in this district, the doors had been salvaged long ago, leaving behind empty frames. He craned his helmed head around the corner, pistol at the ready. He sincerely hoped that the necromancer would not expect an intruder to set upon him from above. But with dabblers in the dark arts, Brunner had found that it paid to take nothing for granted.

He cautiously emerged into the hallway and began a systematic search of the upper rooms. Many of them were empty, but he found two that bore signs of habitation. One of these had even had a bed and a wardrobe.

Descending a rotting staircase, and testing every step before putting his weight on it, Brunner began to examine the rooms of the lower floor. He paused before a heavy wooden door to the left of the base of the stairs. He closed a gloved hand about the knob, trying to open the portal. With a scraping sound, the warped door moved, freeing itself from the equally distorted wood of the jamb.

The bounty hunter tensed, listening for any sound that suggested he had disturbed something in the house. After a moment, he pushed the door open fully, pistol held at the ready. The room was dark, lit only by a dingy light filtering through dust-choked windows. Several inches of water pooled over the floor, and the broken remains of chairs and tables lay amid the brackish, stagnant water.

A mottled orange and green salamander slid away from the dry area near the door and swam off into the dark waters.

Brunner left the room and pulled the door closed. Even a necromancer would not use rooms in such a state. He looked about him, studying the hallway. There was evidence of seepage now that he looked for it: the walls were warped and discoloured several inches above the floor. Just as he began to turn to retrace his steps and examine the third floor of the house, he noted something peculiar. The height of the water damage was noticeably less further west along the hall. Clearly the ground upon which the house had been situated had begun to shift, causing the once level ground to tilt. Not enough to be readily visible perhaps, but enough to cause the intrusive moisture to remain in the eastern section where the depression was greater.

The bounty hunter made his way along the corridor, opening the few rotting doors to inspect the rooms beyond. He knew that the subjects of a necromancer's science were bodies – heavy, fragile corpses stolen from graves and gibbets. If the villain were able, he would have set up his laboratory in one of the lower rooms, rather than hauling heavy specimens up flights of treacherous stairs. And the laboratory would be where he would find the mummy of Nehb-ka-menthu.

It was the third door Brunner opened that led to the laboratory. It was a large low-ceilinged chamber, the height of the room being further diminished by a secondary flooring of old doors, shutters and other pieces of scavenged wood – a precaution against the wetness, no doubt, as the old floor had been rotted away by the creeping damp. A number of shelves lined the walls, their upper ranks laden with scrolls, books and what looked like pieces of alchemical apparatus, while the lower ones were bare. Hanging from the support beams were a number of gruesome paintings, their subjects various necrotic bodies in assorted degrees of dissection and decay, charts to lead the necromancer in his studies. Two partially decomposed bodies rested against the north wall of the room, like a pair of logs, so stiff and rigid were their dead shapes.

Brunner looked over the room quickly, unmoved by the horror and loathsomeness of the things the necromancer had accumulated in his twisted studies. What interested the bounty hunter was the object lying upon a long wooden table in the centre of the room.

The mummy stretched nearly the entire length of the seven-foot table. Encased in mouldering funeral wrappings that had become grey-green with age and decay, the corpse was like some withered ogre. Brunner could see that in life, Nehb-ka-menthu had been a powerful man, broad of shoulder and long of limb. The bounty hunter strode closer, curious despite himself to get a better look at the long-dead priest-king of Khareops. He could see that the wrappings still bore faint traces of pigment, like oily smudge marks, presumably the last remains of the once vivid and vibrant picture writing of the liche-priests of Nehekhara.

The cloth was stretched tight about the shrivelled remains and Brunner could make out the face of the dead ruler through its mask of grey-green. The face was largely intact, displaying a dome-like brow, high cheeks and a firm jaw. There was a look of power and cruelty about the dead face that suggested an implacable will and a ruthlessness that might endure even the trial of the grave.

Brunner drew away from the mummy, pulling Mahrun's holy stake from his belt. 'I wouldn't have liked to have run into you when you were alive,' he muttered to the motionless husk. 'Let's just make sure you don't cause me any problems now that you are dead.' He lifted the stake, holding it above the sunken chest of the mummy, and placed the point against its left breast.

THE BOUNTY HUNTER found himself suddenly and violently thrown to the floor, the stake rattling across the wooden covering. He cursed his lack of caution. He should have heard someone approaching, but he had been so intent upon examining the mummy, that he had failed to hear his attacker's approach. As he began to lift himself from the floor, a powerful kick lashed into his midsection, throwing him back. The bounty hunter crashed against one of the shelves, knocking books and bones from the upper shelves and snapping one of the lower ones in half as his body smashed into it.

On his back, Brunner could see his attacker now. He was a huge man, thick cords of muscle wove about his limbs, and his chest was a great mass of meat and sinew. He wore ragged clothing, much befouled by mud and less mentionable stains. The man's head was covered only by a few patchy spots of blond hair, his features were broad, his mouth open in an idiot grin. Auburn eyes stared dimly at Brunner, fixed in a bleary dullard's gaze. In many ways, the bounty hunter was reminded of the thing he had killed in the room above. Perhaps this brute was also becoming a ghoul, sustaining himself on whatever his master did not employ in his foul experiments. The man made some inarticulate sounds with his thick, useless tongue, then shambled toward the intruder, setting down a leather sack he had been carrying.

The half-wit stooped to grab at Brunner's body, to lift him from the floor in a crushing embrace. The bounty hunter did not give him a chance. He rose to meet the muscle man, swinging around the object his questing fingers had closed on – a broken length of shelf. The splintered wood smashed into the idiot's face. Bright red blood and yellowed teeth sprayed across the wall behind him. The big man staggered back, one hand clutching at his injury, blood drooling from his ravaged mouth.

Brunner did not give the idiot a chance to recover, but was on him in an instant, smashing the board once again into the man's head. The wretch staggered with the force of the blow, and retreated from the bounty hunter, making pathetic noises with his malformed tongue. His dim eyes stared stupidly at the man who was now attacking him. Brunner swung the board around a third time, this time cracking the wood across the big man's skull. The idiot dropped like a pole-axed ox, his big body splintering the scavenged wood on the floor as he fell. Brunner closed upon the prone body, kicking the man's head with his steel-toed boot. He had felt the strength in those arms and was not about to take the chance that the dreg might get back up.

Panting with his exertions and trying to reclaim the breath the idiot's kick had forced from his lungs, Brunner knelt and retrieved the wooden stake from the floor. Pausing for a moment to collect himself, he strode back to the table and the withered corpse resting upon it.

'Where were we?' he asked as he placed the point of the stake once more over the mummy's shrivelled heart. Once again, he was kept from finishing his task.

'LEAVE THAT ALONE and get out of here!' shouted a voice from the doorway of the laboratory. Brunner spun around, dropping the stake to draw his pistol from its belt. Framed in the doorway was a thin, scraggly apparition. The man wore a loose cassock of dark blue trimmed with grey fur and tassels of hair. His brown hair was greasy and hung in ratty ropes about his unpleasant, slippery face. His skin had an unpleasant, sickly hue, as though he had bathed in pus and not dried the filth from his body.

Like his servant, the necromancer also bore a leather sack, which he dropped to the floor in alarm. From it, the butchered remains of a freshly exhumed corpse spilled onto the floor. The bounty hunter had chosen a good time to make his entrance, the necromancer had been away, securing his sickening materials from one of Miragliano's morgues. But fortune had deserted Brunner just as readily. The necromancer was home now.

The necromancer did not wait to see if the intruder would comply with his command. In one of his filthy hands, he gripped a severed hand, green with rot. Before Brunner could fire his pistol, the necromancer growled a word of loathsome power. The severed hand gave off a sickly light. The necromancer threw his free hand forward, casting a fistful of dust at the bounty hunter. Brunner dodged the particles of corruption that glowed with the same hue as the wasted extremity held by the necromancer. The dust impacted against the shelves behind Brunner, sizzling like acid as it withered the wood and corroded the leather bound tomes.

Carandini uttered a sharp hiss as Brunner rolled away from the attack. The bounty hunter fired at the necromancer, the shot passing through the loose garment and burying itself in the rotten wood of the door. Brunner swore under his breath. Either some flaw in the symmetry of the ball had thrown off his shot or some dire sorcery warded his target. He rose from his crouch, holstering the pistol and unslinging the repeater crossbow from his back.

The necromancer glared at Brunner, eerie witch-fire gathering in the hollow pits of his eyes. Carandini let the severed murderer's paw fall and clutched at the empty air with his wasted, claw-like fingers. Low, filthy sounds dribbled from the man's puffy pink lips. Brunner took aim hastily, determined to put a bolt between the necromancer's eyes before he could work his black sorcery. But before he could fire, a vice-like grip closed upon his boot, crushing his ankle with the fury of a wolf-trap.

Brunner stared down at his feet. Dull, idiot eyes stared back at him from a cracked and splintered face. There was no question that Carandini's feeble-minded assistant was dead: pulpy coils of brain hung from the ruptures in his skull. What animated the hulking brute's movements, what enabled him to reach out and grab his killer, was only a twisted perversion of life, a horrible violation of the laws of death brought into being by the necromancer.

The pressure on Brunner's foot increased until he thought the clutching fingers would crack his very bones. Clearly the strength of the already powerful dreg had been increased by this unnatural state of pseudo-life. Brunner brought the crossbow swinging low, firing into the monster at his feet. The first bolt exploded the zombie's skull, spilling brains and dark blood across the floor. A second bolt burrowed into the monster's back. The zombie grew tense as its unnatural life ebbed away, and its twice slain muscles tensed into the wooden rigidity of death. Brunner howled as the grip on his boot increased with the zombie's destruction.

Brunner had no time to extract himself from the crushing grip. The sound of shuffling feet demanded his attention. The two bodies he had noted leaning against the wall had been stirred into motion by Carandini's incantation. The zombies moved forward with stiff, awkward steps, rotting garments and flesh hanging from their wretched forms in ragged strips. Lifeless eyes were trained upon the trapped bounty hunter as they ponderously advanced upon him. The necromancer gloated from behind the long table. He was peering above the embalmed hulk of the priest-king, using the ancient body for cover. Brunner considered loosing one of his remaining crossbow bolts at the fiend, but decided that the shot would be too uncertain.

Instead, he fired his last two bolts into the oncoming zombies. The first walking corpse staggered and fell as the steel bolt punched through its rotten skull and embedded itself in the wall behind the undead automaton. As it hit the floor, a greasy putrid fluid bubbled from its wound, yellow with corruption, black with the dried remnants of the corpse's blood. Brunner fired his last bolt at the other zombie. The missile impacted in the corpse's face, sticking from its cheek like a macabre growth of bone. The zombie staggered from the force of the impact, but uttered no sound of anguish or injury. It merely swung its body around and began to shuffle relentlessly towards the bounty hunter once more.

Brunner threw the spent skaven crossbow at the approaching zombie and drew Drakesmalice from its sheath. Gripping the sword tightly, Brunner swung it downward, severing the wrist that had closed upon his ankle. He stepped away, favouring his uninjured foot. The other zombie took another shambling step forward, its wasted limbs groping toward him. Brunner leaned his body away from the necrotic thing and swung Drakesmalice at its neck. The sword clove easily through the rotted flesh and the desiccated head flew from its shoulders, bounced from the near wall and rolled across the floor. The headless body stood for a moment, devoid of motion, before toppling sidewise to the floor, rigid in its second death.

Carandini gave a yelp of fright as he watched the last zombie expire. He bounded away from the long table, scrambling toward the doorway. Brunner hobbled towards the man, murderous eyes blazing from beneath his visor. Carandini had chosen his cover only too well, for by positioning himself behind the table, he had also placed the bounty hunter between himself and the door. The necromancer hissed like a serpent, spun around and dashed toward one of the shelves. The bounty hunter paused, pulling a throwing knife from the bandoleer across his chest.

'Wait!' pleaded Carandini. The necromancer held a small glass vial he had removed from the shelf in an upraised hand. Brunner pulled back his own hand to hurl the knife into the wizard's body. 'This contains bog fire!' Carandini declared, his slippery voice at once threatening and pleading. 'If I drop this, this entire room will go up!'

Brunner hesitated. If the vial did indeed contain bog fire, the eldritch vapour might react with the air just as the necromancer threatened. The room, and everything in it would be incinerated by the volatile explosive gas. The entire house with its rotting timbers would quickly go up in flames. He might escape the room if Carandini were to drop the glass, but with his injured foot, Brunner was not sure he would escape the fire that would follow. Slowly, and reluctantly, the bounty hunter replaced his knife.

'That's right,' sneered the necromancer. 'Now put away your sword.'

'I can't do that,' commented Brunner, taking a few hopping steps forward.

'Why?' demanded Carandini, his eyes blazing with anger.

'Because I need it to remove that ugly head of yours from its neck.' Brunner took another series of shuffling steps, rounding the long table. Carandini cringed away from the killer's approach, straining to lift the glass vial still higher.

'I will drop it!' he shrieked. 'I'll destroy us both! Stop right there!'

Brunner's voice was as flat and icy as any grave-born horror. 'I have a better idea. It involves you setting that thing down. Do that, and I'll give you five minutes before I come after you.' The bounty hunter took another menacing step around the long table. 'Trust me, it's the best deal you're going to get.'

Whatever response the necromancer was going to voice died in his throat as a gasp of terror forced its way upward. Carandini's eyes grew wide with fright, his sickly finger pointing accusingly at the bounty hunter. But he was looking at something else entirely. Brunner followed his gaze and found himself leaping back from the table, injured foot or no.

Carandini's voice returned in a wheezy groan.

'I told you not to touch the mummy!'

LIGHT SLOWLY INTRUDED upon the perpetual darkness, awareness slowly returned to the mind of the ancient sleeper. A flicker of power had disturbed his dark dreams of dusty tombs and obelisk-lined necropolises. How long had he slept the sleep of the tomb? Seven centuries? Ten?

Memory stirred, recollections of a time as parched and empty as the sands of the desert. Of a great and powerful spell, a sorcerous apocalypse that had fallen upon Khareops, Numas and Khemri and all the great land of Nehekhara, which had in an instant robbed the most ancient kingdom of man of all life and vitality. It had stilled the heart and sucked the breath of every living thing in Khareops.

It had been the Great Ritual, cast by the Accursed One so that he might reclaim his throne and rule over an empire of the dead. Withered lids slid back from the dry hollows of the mummy's face, flakes of crusty decomposed skin scattering like sandy tears. Nearby, someone had drawn upon similar power, and he could feel the faintest echo of that tremendous act of evil.

More memories rose within the desiccated husk of Nehb-ka-menthu. The priest-king could recall the moment of his own death, and yet death had not been the end. His soul had not left his mortal frame. Like a spectator, he had watched as the liche-priests had prepared and embalmed his body, watched as the unliving priests, the only things in all Khareops that now walked the dead streets of the necropolis, bore his body in its golden sarcophagus to his pyramid tomb.

For some time he had remained within his tomb, detached from his body, detached from all thought, existing in the dark limbo of the dead. Was it months or aeons that he remained thus? But at last, the power had made itself felt across the Dead Lands once more. The Accursed One had awoken once more, and the power of his black resurrection made itself felt across the carrion realm of Nehekhara. The power had reached out and stirred other things from their ancient graves. So it was that Nehb-ka-menthu had emerged from his tomb, to contest with his own ancestors for the rule of Khareops.

The mummy's right arm moved, falling from its chest to the side of the table. Slowly, so slowly that it did not seem to be moving. And yet how incredibly swift must such a motion seem to a body that had lain silent and still in the cool dark of its grave for hundreds of years?

When had Nehb-ka-menthu last walked the earth? Had it been when he had mustered the dead hosts of his city, when he had set out to find the phantom tower of Nagash's disciple, the liche king Arkhan the Black, to ransack that place of darkest sorcery, to bear away its terrible secrets? Had it been when he returned in defeat from the dread city of Khemri and his attempt to force his way into the profane Black Pyramid of Nagash itself? As in life, so in death did Nehb-ka-menthu lust for the power of the dark magic. As in life, so too in death did that knowledge elude him, straying almost within his very reach then dancing away once more.

The mummy moved its other arm, letting it fall to its side. The sound of battle intruded upon the corpse's thoughts and slowly, the lingering traces of the power began to wink out around him. The sense of fading dark energy snapped the mind of Nehb-ka-menthu from his memories, from recalling ancient battles and inglorious defeats. No, he was not the match for Arkhan, who guarded the secrets of his master in his spectral Black Tower. He could not contend with the might of Settra, king of Khemri, who watched the Black Pyramid for any sign of his immortal enemy's return and prevented any from entering that place of timeless blasphemy and nameless horror. The secrets, the knowledge, the perversions that Nagash had discovered were not yet his. But they would be. The power would be his!

As Brunner disposed of the last of the zombies, the eyes of the mummy began to glow with a faint luminance, a ghostly green flame. Nehb-ka-menthu focused his will, his thoughts, his spirit back into its carriage of decayed flesh. The hands of the mummy turned over, the powerful talons within the grey-green wrappings splintering the wood of the table as they gripped it. The arms lifted and slowly the body of the mummy began to rise.

IN THE COURSE of his travels, Brunner had encountered many strange and terrible things, but never had he stood before something like this. The hulking corpse of the long-dead priest-king had been unnerving enough at rest, exuding its aura of ancient decay and loss, the faint scent of lands forgotten and ruined. It was as bittersweet as the most tenderly recalled nostalgia and as hideous as the blood-howl of an enraged orc. It was a feeling of regret and despair that clutched at the soul. The bounty hunter would have breathed easier once the thing had been destroyed and the fear creeping into his stomach had been dispelled.

How much more horrible was that withered husk now that it had been endowed with motion, now that its strong sinews and supple limbs caused it to rise from the table, to set its cloth-wrapped feet upon the rotting wood on the floor? Brunner only realised that he had been backing away from the undead abomination when his back struck the rear wall of the room. Beside him, Carandini was also gripped by terror, and did not even notice that the bounty hunter was beside him, his eyes locked upon the supernatural figure of the mummy.

The skull-like face of the mummy slowly turned from side to side with stiff, jerking motions, as it took in the room and its contents. As the head passed over Brunner and Carandini for the second time, it froze. Luminous fires of ghostly light burned in the pits of its face, regarding the two men with an inscrutable gaze.

Carandini's teeth were chattering, his muscles relaxing as he lost control of them. Suddenly the glass vial fell from his slackened fingers. Brunner caught the faint motion and watched in horror as the vial shattered against the floor. He gritted his teeth against the coming explosion, and braced himself for a quick and certain death.

A moment passed and Brunner drew another breath. He looked down at the smashed vial, and at the putrid blood it had contained seeping into the floor. Then he turned to Carandini. The necromancer had torn his eyes away from the mummy, and was glancing downward at the shattered glass. He gave Brunner a frightened, embarrassed smile; his deception had been revealed. Brunner's lip twisted into a snarl and he thrust Drakesmalice through the necromancer's belly as a reward for his bluff. Carandini groaned and slid to the floor, clutching at his punctured body, and trying to quell the flow of blood and bile spilling down his legs.

The bounty hunter did not hesitate to round on the tomb king. The mummy began to storm forward, its stride long and swift. Brunner lashed out at the undead horror, trying to pierce through the shrivelled heart in the monster's breast.

Before Drakesmalice could sink into the mummy's flesh, however, an iron grip closed about the blade, arresting his strike. Brunner tried to pull his sword free, but it was trapped as firmly as gold dust in a dwarf's fist.

The mummy tore the sword from Brunner's grasp as if the bounty hunter was a sickly child. Casually, it tossed the weapon aside. Then it reached forward to grab the man who had been presumptuous enough to attack it. The bounty hunter dodged the mummy's grasp, drawing a throwing knife and hurling it at the monster. The blade sank into the mummy's chest, causing a puff of corpse dust to rise from the wound. The monster did not pay the slightest attention to its injury, but reached out once more for its foe.

Brunner scrambled from the groping creature. Planting a hand firmly on the top of the table, he jumped over it, placing it between himself and the undead horror. The mummy did not pause; it strode forward and closed its claws around the edge of the table. Effortlessly, the mummy flipped the heavy piece of furniture onto its side and swatted the obstruction from its path.

Brunner retreated once again. As he stepped back, his foot struck something lying on the floor. The bounty hunter glanced down to see Mahrun's blessed stake lying beside his boot. Quickly, he retrieved the weapon and held it dagger-like in his fist.

The mummy did not hesitate to surge forward, its claws lunging for the bounty hunter. Summoning up every ounce of his courage, Brunner met the monster's attack, and braved the clutch of its skeletal hands to plunge the stake deep into the mummy's chest. The undead monster did not seem affected by whatever holy power had been woven into the stake. With the wooden spike protruding from its breast, its hands now closed about Brunner's body.

The bounty hunter felt himself being lifted up by the monster, and swept up from the ground as though he were a rag doll. The mummy shifted its grip, holding Brunner over its head by his shoulder and thigh. The bounty hunter fumbled to free his axe from his belt. He had already driven Ursio's stiletto into the monster's palm as it clutched him –

with no effect. Every motion was a test of his will power. His mind began to darken, as pain surged where the mummy's crushing fingers bruised his bones. As Brunner struggled, he felt the first hint of pressure on his spine as the mummy began to bend his body.

Suddenly, the pressure lessened. The mummy's head turned, as though it had been distracted by a noise. Dismissively the mummy tossed Brunner aside, sending him crashing into the shelves again. Brunner lay in a heap on the splintered floor, as still as the other bodies lying about the room.

Nehb-ka-menthu paid the hired killer no further thought. It had sensed a familiar presence, a presence he had not encountered for thousands of years. After so many centuries, it would be interesting to renew his acquaintance and finish what had been left undone.

THE SUN WAS casting its dying rays across the derelict district. The lingering twilight highlighted a black coach that almost blocked the narrow street. A pair of coal-black stallions snorted agitatedly before the elegant carriage, resisting the best efforts of a pasty-faced coachman to calm them. A group of armed men, nearly a dozen strong, clustered about the carriage, staring at the door of the coach and at the red-roofed building behind them.

Contessa Carlotta de Villarias pulled aside the thick, veil-like black curtain that shrouded the windows of the carriage. She flinched from the fading orange light of the setting sun. Unlike many vampires, de Villarias was able to endure the rays of the sun, for a time, though she was weak during the bright hours of the day, and became filled with a sickness of stomach and heart. Her two devoted thralls were not so strong and they cringed in the coach, horrified at being outside before night had fully fallen.

De Villarias smiled, as she always did when she forced her slaves to endure fear and hardship. The power of command, the compelling force she could exert over others was one of the few remaining things that still gave her pleasure. It was another reason she would exact her own measure of

retribution on the bounty killer. In defying her, and refus-
ing to submit to her beguiling gaze, he had denied her the
satisfaction of dominating his will.

Very well, the vampire would just have to extract a different measure of satisfaction from him. De Villarias licked
her lips hungrily.

'Is this wise, my lady?' asked Torici, cringing as far into the
dark leather seat as he could. He was squinting distastefully
at the faint light. The Lahmian turned her face toward her
creature, irritation written on her features.

'I have to agree with the fop,' snarled Relotto. His hand
closed about the hilt of his duelling sabre, as though he
might brandish the weapon at the sun to hasten its with-
drawal. 'If the bounty killer has failed, it may be dangerous
here. My lady should not endanger herself so.' Relotto
smiled, showing his fangs. 'Leave this to me, my lady. I can
deal with a mere mortal.'

De Villarias considered her creature's words. Why *was* she
here? If the bounty hunter had failed, if the withered husk of
Nehb-ka-menthu contained even a fraction of that madman's hideous soul, then this was the last place she should
be. The vampiress stroked the sleeping cat curled in her lap,
seeking to dispel some of her doubt and fear in the comfort
of the animal's fur.

She was here because she needed to know. She needed to
know if the bounty hunter had succeeded, if the deed had
been done. She needed to know if that awful thing had been
destroyed at last, whether the shadow that had haunted her
through the centuries was no more. She could not sit idly
within her decrepit palazzo and await word of the bounty
hunter's fate – she had to see for herself, run her hands
through the ashes of her ancient tormentor.

But Relotto was right. What if the bounty hunter had
failed? What if the foolish necromancer had awoken that
dread carrion husk, to make even a vampire know fear? De
Villarias shuddered at the image of that dry cadaverous
shape swathed in the funeral wrappings. Of a tomb king
clutching at her, bearing her back to the sandy wastes of
Khareops, and resuming his vile experiments upon her. She

pushed aside the curtain once more, watching the last rays of light fade.

'You are right,' she said, staring out the window. 'Relotto, take the mortals and see what has transpired in the house.' She turned her piercing gaze on the thrall. 'If the bounty hunter is still alive, bring him to me.' She let her voice slip into a menacing undertone. 'Bring him to me alive, Relotto,' she warned. The duellist twisted his face as though he had swallowed something unpleasant, but nodded his head.

'And the mummy?' asked Torici, hoping to unnerve his rival by suggesting that Relotto might have to deal with the abomination as well.

De Villarias struggled to keep fear from her voice. 'See that it has been destroyed,' she answered after a pause. 'Whatever has happened, see that it has been destroyed!'

RELOTTO LED THE contessa's human guards toward the ramshackle palazzo of the necromancer. They were a motley group of bewitched mercenary vermin, the sort of trash Relotto had cut open in countless street duels. True, they were devoted to the contessa, bound to her by supernaturally enforced chains of devotion and adoration. In the service of their mistress, these men would break before no enemy, no matter how terrible. Still, the vampire considered the mortal warriors with contempt as he addressed them. He was more than capable of dealing with the bounty hunter, and a shambling, stiff pile of bones. He would cut the head from that thing and present it to his mistress. He would show her that he alone was worthy of her attentions.

'When we get inside, spread out and search every room,' the vampire ordered. 'If you find the bounty hunter, call out.' A cunning smile crossed the duellist's face. He had seen the way de Villarias had looked at the mortal. Did she really think that he had not seen her intentions toward him? Did she really think he would allow her to replace him with that scum? He tolerated Torici as he would a small, yappy dog, but the bounty hunter was another matter. 'I will deal with him myself,' the vampire hissed.

Suddenly the wall of the house exploded in a shower of wood splinters and dust. Relotto and his warriors flinched from the violent display, covering their faces to ward away the flying debris. Striding from the wreckage was a tall, wiry figure, a cadaverous giant with glowing green eyes. The mummy did not pause; it advanced like an unstoppable juggernaut. It closed upon the nearest of Relotto's men, grabbing the warrior's sword arm and ripping it from its socket as a man might pull a drumstick from a cooked chicken. The mutilated warrior screamed wretchedly and fell, blood spurting in a crimson torrent from his mangled shoulder. While the man toppled, the withered corpse was in motion, chopping its hand into the face of a second swordsman, pulverising the front of the man's skull, leaving him trying to scream through the crimson puddle that had replaced his face.

The mummy turned from the ruin of the two warriors, finding its path blocked by the vampire Relotto. The duellist feinted toward the creature with the long dagger clenched in his right hand. For an instant, the green witch-fires burning in the monster's face focused on the weapon. The vampire struck, driving his sword into the mouldering wrappings that shrouded its emaciated remains. The fang of steel penetrated deep, its point emerging from the other side. The mummy, however, was not as easily disposed of as the vampire's usual prey. A powerful fist crashed down on the sword, snapping the blade.

Relotto backed away, staring in momentary horror at the useless hilt he now held. Before him, the mummy clawed at the transfixing length of steel, pulling it back out of its body.

The cold, emotionless movements of the mummy infuriated Relotto more than any amount of bravado could have done. He gripped his dagger in both hands, bared his fangs and leapt at the ancient cadaver with the full fury of his supernatural strength. It was an attack that the vampire had resorted to in the past when overcome by anger and red rage. In such a frenzy, he had once torn apart a bear with no more than his bare hands and unholy might. How much easier would the rotten remains of the priest-king crumble apart under his mangling claws?

Relotto fell away from the mummy, his berserk leap transformed into an agonising fall. The vampire pawed at his chest where the mummy had driven the snapped steel of his own blade. Relotto tried to draw it from his cold, blood-ridden heart. The vampire paused in his labour to look up, to stare at the shadow that had fallen upon him. The mummy of Nehb-ka-menthu was tossing aside the torso of an axe-wielder it had torn in two when the man had tried to come to the vampire's aid. It did not look down as it raised its cloth-wrapped foot and brought it crashing down upon Relotto's head, grinding the vampire's skull as a man might grind a beetle under his heel.

Torici and the contessa had emerged from the black carriage. They watched as the mummy massacred the vampiress's minions with a contemptuous ease. Fear had driven out all thought in the undead noblewoman's mind. She watched the mummy's relentless advance with the same mute horror she had seen on the faces of the countless people she had fed upon through the ages. Nehb-ka-menthu walked again! Could any horror in all the world fill de Villarias with the same mortal terror? The mummy glanced away from the headless body of a valiant spearman. Again a blade was removed from the monster's dried out body. Its ghostly green fires fixed upon the woman beside the coach. The terror filling the vampiress increased a thousandfold as she saw the skull beneath the funeral wrappings smile at her.

The few remaining retainers noted their mistress's terror and renewed their desperate attack on the monster, throwing away all caution in their frantic attempt to protect their beloved contessa. But it was like setting terriers against a lion. The lives of the reckless men would quickly be spent.

Torici quickly roared for the coachman to remove the kerosene-filled lamps from the sides of the driver's box. The vampire and the coachman soon had the lamps removed, the lanterns still burning inside, the hot metal singeing the hands of the coachman. The last of the contessa's defenders raced toward the murdering mummy.

The green witch-fires of the mummy's eyes considered the improvised flame bombs with contempt. It extended its clawed hand, pointing imperiously at the coachman.

A dry hiss, like the whisper of sand falling through an hourglass, emerged from the cadaverous skull of the priest-king. As the thin tones of the ancient incantation were uttered, the lantern clutched in the hands of the coachman exploded, bathing the man in flame. The enflamed servant uttered a long wail of torment. He became a walking torch that staggered blindly away from the coach, collapsing at last in the muddy trench of the nearby canal.

Torici gave vent to a shout of rage as he saw the mummy dispose of the coachman. It was now left to him alone to protect his mistress. He lunged forward, casting the remaining lantern at the undead horror.

The glass facing of the metal cage shattered on impact, as did the bowl of the lantern, bathing the dry brittle shape of the priest-king in kerosene. But even as the lantern impacted, its effectiveness as a bomb expired; the taper had blown out as it was thrown. The mummy cast its malevolent gaze on the vampire, advancing on the coach with great strides.

'Run!' urged Torici, staring at his mistress. The vampire thrall reached past de Villarias and wrenched a wooden spoke free from the front wheel of the coach.

Snarling like a wild beast, the vampire fop flung himself at the mummy, smashing the creature's head with the side of the spoke. The wood burst like a rotten forest log upon impact with the mummy's supernaturally strong bones. Torici did not ponder his thwarted attack, but jabbed the splintered end of the improvised weapon into the monster's face. The vampire gouged the wood into the skull-like countenance, grinding away at the mummy's features.

Torici was flung back as the mummy's fist punched through his breast. Nehb-ka-menthu lifted the black, gleaming slab of the vampire's diseased heart and tossed the ruptured organ at the feet of de Villarias. Once again, the withered features of the ancient priest-king seemed to twist into a mocking smile of triumph and sadistic anticipation.

* * *

CARLOTTA DE VILLARIAS stared at the discarded heart of Torici, viewing her minion's gruesome demise as nothing compared to what her ancient foe would do to her if she did not free herself from her nameless dread. She, who had walked the paths of darkness for centuries, who had outlasted the gods of Nehekhara, who had watched from the shadows as the history of the Old World took shape and form – all that she was would end here, in a filthy, forgotten Miragliano slum. It was a demise fit for an animal, not an aristocrat of the night. Yet such would be her fate unless she were to act. Nehb-ka-menthu had butchered all her servants; the only thing left standing was de Villarias herself.

The horses screamed in terror as the smell of the mummy reached them. The animals strained and pulled at their yoke, threatening to snap the sturdy wood. The mummy paid the panicked animals no heed, but strode resolutely toward its immortal prey. As it did so, a small, lithe shape launched itself at the walking corpse, scratching at the layers of grey, mouldering funeral wrappings with sharp claws and savage fangs. The mummy was quick to pull the clawing cat from its chest, crushing its body in its powerful grip, and casting the limp, broken remains aside.

The sight of her familiar's death, the shock of its mental scream as Nehb-ka-menthu destroyed it, broke the terrible spell of fear that had conquered the vampiress. The contessa spat at her adversary like a desert asp. She hissed her wrath at the monster. The vampiress did not simply remove a spoke from the coach, she ripped the entire wheel free, and hurled the heavy missile at her enemy. It smashed into the mummy, hurling the creature back, and knocking it to the ground.

Talons grew from de Villarias's hands, transforming them into the claws of some great jungle cat. The fangs in her mouth extended into great ivory sabres. The feral sound that rolled over those fangs was unlike any human could have made. De Villarias pounced upon the cadaverous shape of Nehb-ka-menthu as the undead creature began to rise and slammed the desiccated mass back against the hard surface of the street.

De Villarias pawed at the monster, her claws tearing at the funeral wrappings. Bits of ancient cloth and brittle flesh were thrown into the air with every sweep of her hands. Lost in the frenzy of her attack, her mind little better than a beast's, de Villarias sank her fangs into the withered neck of the mummy. She began sucking uncontrollably at the empty collapsed veins of the shrivelled corpse.

The tomb king of Khareops did not long suffer such abuse. Its claw grabbed hold of the vampiress and hurled her away. De Villarias struck the ground a good dozen feet away and slid across the stones as though dragged by stallions – such was the awesome strength in the withered corpse's arm.

The vampiress turned the slide into a roll, nimbly coming to her feet after the violent rebuff. Some of the red rage had left her now and she began to watch the mummy rise with trepidation. She knew what this being had been capable of in life, and now she had felt its infernal might in death.

Nehb-ka-menthu regarded the vampiress for a moment, then strode toward the coach once more. Not for her a destruction brought about by some spell plundered from the books of Nagash. No, the priest-king would end her unnatural life with his own hands.

De Villarias backed away from the mummy, and rounded the carriage. She needed to keep its mass between herself and her enemy while she worked out some way of fighting the undead horror. Nehb-ka-menthu kept up with her, trying to catch the vampiress as she went round the coach. De Villarias had looked with loathing on those of her kind who shed their beautiful shapes for the cruder forms of bats and wolves, but now how she wished that she had learned such arcane secrets.

At last, the horses could tolerate the presence of the mummy no longer. With a scream of fright, the stallions broke loose from the carriage, snapping their traces and galloping away into the darkened, deserted night. The already unbalanced coach groaned and shuddered before turning onto its side, catching Nehb-ka-menthu beneath it. The mummy was lost to sight as the heavy framework of iron and ponderous panels and seats of wood crashed down upon it.

For a moment, de Villarias thought that the weight of the coach had accomplished what her slaves had been unable to do. She dared to hope that the carriage had crushed the old bones of the priest-king; that it had pulverised to dust the withered corpse of her ancient adversary. But her hopes were short-lived.

The mummy rose again, lifting the carriage as it freed itself. It let the heavy coach crash back onto the street after it had cleared the wreck. Nehb-ka-menthu glared at the contessa with eyes of green witch-fire, then grasped the upper railing of the coach, ripping a great length of it loose. The mummy hefted its improvised spear of wood and turned towards the vampiress.

SUDDENLY, THE MUMMY's upper body jerked as it was struck repeatedly from behind. Four steel darts exploded from the monster's chest and tore through its rotten husk. Nehb-ka-menthu paused as the force of the missiles upset its balance. The unliving tomb king was quick to recover, however, and resumed its steady march.

Brunner cursed as he witnessed the ineffectiveness of his attack. The priest-king's powerful assault had left him dazed, but the wiry bounty hunter had recovered quickly, pulling free two of his knives. He was determined to combat this supernatural foe with his every breath. But he was surprised that the monster was no longer interested in him. He had watched the mummy's rampage after it had burst through the laboratory wall. He had considered his options as he reloaded his weapons. Watching Relotto and Torici's impossibly swift movements, the bounty hunter had come to realise that there was something unnatural about his patroness, but even he had been shocked when the woman had grown claws and fangs and leapt upon the mummy with the fury of a feral wolf. Legends and rumours filtered their way up into the bounty killer's consciousness: tales of unholy things that stalked the night, and feasted on the blood of the living to prolong a profane existence. Contessa

Carlotta de Villarias was such a fiend, a vampire, a creature of the dark.

Brunner's first instinct had been to walk away, to leave the undead creatures to destroy one another, to let these abominations from beyond the grave fare as they would. But a colder, more cunning part of his mind caused him to linger. The bounty hunter emerged from the building just as the mummy freed itself from the coach. He had taken aim with the reloaded skaven crossbow, placing all four bolts into the monster's desiccated flesh. The deadly missiles had been as effective as pebbles thrown at a giant, their passing not even meriting the notice of the monster.

Nehb-ka-menthu closed upon the vampiress. He raised the splintered shaft of wood like an over-sized javelin. De Villarias coiled her body, preparing to lunge. Escape was not an option, the priest-king would track her down. He would find her in whatever nameless hole she might slink to. But perhaps she could cause some damage to the blighted thing before it could bring about her second, permanent death. Over the mummy's shoulder, de Villarias could see the bounty hunter racing forward. It puzzled her somewhat that the man had lingered, that he had chosen to involve himself in this struggle of beings that had been ancient before the lands of his birth were founded. The sight of the mortal charging toward his death made the vampiress pause. She had to admit that his was a powerful and fearless will. It would almost be a tragedy to see his life spent so uselessly.

Brunner swung Drakesmalice in a great sweeping arc. The sword dug deeply into the mummy's side, crunching through ribs and withered organs. This time, the mummy did pay attention to the warrior's assault; he turned on the man as he withdrew his sword. The green witch-fires in the sockets of the monster's skull-like face seemed to burn even more brightly. Powerful clutching claws swept the air in front of the bounty hunter, narrowly missing the man. Brunner stepped back, drawing the recharged pistol from its belly holster. He had smelled the kerosene dripping from the dried-out mummy's rags, and a new plan had occurred to him. As Nehb-ka-menthu took another step towards him,

Brunner pulled the trigger of the blackpowder weapon. There was a flash of flame and thunder as the pistol discharged. The bullet tore harmlessly through the monster's chest. The fiery muzzle flash was another matter.

Fire licked about the grey-green figure of the walking mummy, transforming it into a pillar of flame. Brunner allowed himself a smile of triumph as he holstered the pistol. But his smile faded as the mummy reached out to him, its fire-engulfed claw scraping across the front of his breastplate.

The bounty hunter fell back before the undead horror as the tomb king shambled forward, fire swirling about its figure. The dark shape of the monster's body could be dimly seen within the flames. Upon the undamaged funeral wrappings, eldritch writing began glowing with an amber light. The faded picture-writing of Nehekhara's liche priests was blazing into life, revealing figures of primordial gods, wards of ancient and terrible potency. Though fire clung to its form, the mummy of Nehb-ka-menthu did not burn. The protective spells its priests had carefully inked upon every layer of cloth that encased their lord still defended the tomb king. The pillar of fire reached out once more, seeking to draw the bounty hunter into a crushing, fiery embrace.

Suddenly, the mummy was struck from behind, as a great shaft of wood ruptured its belly. De Villarias snarled and drove the spear still deeper, the angle of the weapon causing its tip to sink deep into the gap between the broken stones of the street. The vampiress had been quick to exploit the bounty hunter's distraction of Nehb-ka-menthu. She had taken up the makeshift stake the mummy had dropped. Now she drove the weapon her enemy had thought to destroy her with through its shrivelled flesh.

De Villarias and Brunner both stood back as the fiery mummy struggled to free itself from the impaling length of wood, like a boar stuck upon a hunting spear. For a moment it seemed as if the monster might not be able to pull itself from the long shaft of wood. Then it lifted its blazing paw and struck the portion of shaft that had emerged from its belly. The wood shattered under the blow as through it were glass. The tomb king straightened, to face the vampiress once more. There was no mistaking the ghastly, inhuman malevolence behind its masks of cloth and fire.

The monster took a few steps, then stopped. Its withered skull craned downward, to stare at its fire-shrouded body. The shaft of wood that had pierced its body was now on fire, burning like a bright finger of flame. Part of that fiery finger was inside the mummy's dry, withered flesh, underneath the guard of the warding glyphs that covered its outer wrappings. Black smoke began to billow from the mummy's form as its innards were quickly devoured by the consuming flame that spilled from every cut and wound that had been dealt to its body.

Nehb-ka-menthu did not feel any pain as the fire devoured him from within. He was too close to the truly dead to feel such a sensation. The mummy knew it was being destroyed, that the flames would feed off the nitrates used to preserve and embalm its desiccated flesh. The mummy strode forward once again. If it were to pass into the realm of Ualatp, the vulture-headed god of the dead, then it would not do so alone.

Faster than even de Villarias could have imagined, the mummy was on her. A desperation gripped the monster, a shadow of urgency. It knew that its ancient essence would soon be banished, that it had only moments now to perpetrate one last act of destruction. Nehb-ka-menthu's claw gripped the front of the vampire's dress, causing the cloth to smoulder beneath its fiery touch. Foul smoke was now pouring from the tomb king's body, shrouding it almost as completely as the flames. Little fingers of fire licked outward from the rents and cuts in the mummy's wrappings. Yet through it all, de Villarias could see the grinning face of Nehb-ka-menthu, wresting a small victory even in his moment of defeat. The mummy's grasp tightened and it began to pull the vampire towards its burning body and the wooden stake that still protruded from beneath its ribs.

Before Nehb-ka-menthu could impale the vampiress, gleaming steel struck downwards in a cleaving arc. The burning paw of the mummy was severed from the its arm. The monster glared at Brunner as he readied Drakesmalice for another blow. But it would not be needed. The mummy's belly and chest crumbled, reduced at last to an ash-like state that even Nehb-ka-menthu's tremendous will could not force to retain its shape. The mummy collapsed in upon itself, its shoulders falling to rise impossibly from its hips.

With the decay begun, the rest of the mummy's body quickly followed, crumbling into ash. Now, where the almost unstoppable tomb king had stood, there now sprawled a mass of blazing bandages, the ancient hieroglyphs written on the grey-green cloth still glowing with sorcerous energy.

BRUNNER REGARDED HIS patroness coldly as he stepped back from the remains of the mummy. She swatted at the smoking cloth of her dress. The vampire fixed her red-rimmed eyes on the flaming pile of rags, then turned toward the bounty hunter. Her face slipped from an expression of relief into the stern, arrogant superiority she had shown in the black room of her palazzo.

'Well done,' the vampire said. She noted with a faint alarm that the bounty hunter still held his sword at the ready. In his other hand, his gloved fingers clutched a rounded wooden stake. De Villarias could sense the stake's purpose.

'Don't you think you have strained the limits of your luck enough tonight?' she asked. 'You won't find me as easy to vanquish as some story-book monster.'

'I won't have to,' the bounty hunter's icy voice retorted. 'Not if I'm paid.'

De Villarias's eyes burned with smouldering anger. The audacity of this filthy hired sword! The sheer gall of him to speak to her, to suggest that he would destroy her if his vile blood money were not given to him! The vampiress had killed men for lesser affronts, and she had taken great pleasure in each one of their deaths. De Villarias's fangs elongated, protruding over her lower lip. But the caution born of her centuries of unlife made her hesitate. Perhaps this man truly was a menace and a threat. Had he not held his own against Nehb-ka-menthu? Had he not helped to destroy that ancient and potent tomb lord?

The eyes of the contessa grew soft once more. From behind the visor of his helm, the bounty hunter did not flinch from her gaze.

Her voice was soft and silky when she spoke. 'Why settle for crude gold when you can have so much more?' The vampiress let her unnatural guile filter through her words. She stabbed into the bounty hunter's soul with her gaze. 'You are a powerful man, a strong man. Impressive even to me. Lay down your weapons and come to me. Let me embrace you. You will be my lover and we shall share the long nights together, force the world to give us all that we might desire.'

For a moment, Brunner's hold on his sword faltered, and he took a step toward the expectant vampiress. But just as quickly, he regained control of himself, and clenched his weapons more firmly.

'All I want from you is my gold, bloodworm,' he said. De Villarias drew herself back, scowling at the defiant hireling.

'Mortals with such willpower as yours are dangerous!' she hissed, fangs bared.

'Not when they are paid,' Brunner replied.

De Villarias considered the armed killer for a moment, weighing up her chances against the man. She should be able to destroy him quite easily – she had ripped such men apart with her bare hands many times before. But there was something different about this one. The bounty hunter had killed a tomb king of Nehekhara; he might be able to do the same to a vampiress as well. And there was that simple-looking wooden stake he held so firmly in his left hand. De Villarias could sense the energy that swirled about that fang of wood, the power that had been imbued into it, the baneful force that was more than capable of eradicating one of her kind.

The vampiress turned away, pointing a pale finger at the corpse of her former thrall Torici. Already the years had reclaimed him, reducing him to a crumbling skeleton in elegant clothes.

'You will find your money there,' de Villarias said coldly. 'And more besides.' The vampire watched as Brunner walked over to the skeleton, keeping his eyes on the woman. 'You can have it all, bounty hunter,' she said as Brunner set his sword down on the ground and removed a heavy money belt from around the skeleton's hips.

'Thanks,' Brunner said, weighing the belt in his hand, to determine how much wealth such a weight might represent. 'I'll take the extra as compensation for some of the things you neglected to tell me about this job.' There was a tone of threat in his voice. De Villarias chose to ignore it.

'I will be returning to Estalia,' the vampiress said as she slipped into the dark. 'I would suggest that you stay far from that land. It would be unfortunate if you were to cross my path again.'

Brunner threw the money belt over his shoulder and retrieved his sword. He stared into the shadows where the vampiress had vanished.

'Perhaps for both of us,' he told the dark, as he tucked the engraved stake under his belt. Without a second glance at the carnage all around him, the bounty hunter made his own way into the shadows.

THE MORNING LIGHT revealed the aftermath of the battle. Rats scuttled back into their holes, fat from their night of gruesome feasting. Crows and vultures descended to take their place, their hatchet-like beaks slicing flesh from the stiffening bodies scattered about the lane.

But there was one area that vermin and carrion birds alike avoided: a pile of still-smoking grey-green rags. The ancient evil of the remains kept even such fell creatures at bay. And yet one creature dared to crawl across the broken stones, undeterred by the aura of menace. A five-limbed rat-sized thing crawled onto the pile of rags. Like a bird returning to its roost, the severed hand of Nehb-ka-menthu settled down amongst the funeral wrappings, and burrowed its way beneath them to escape the growing light of the sun.

WHERE WALKS THE MARDAGG

I

THE ROOM WAS dark, lit only by pairs of pot-like oil jars set at either end of the chamber. What the flickering, dancing light cast by the flames did reveal was expensively furnished. The table that dominated the room was massive, stained cherry-wood imported from across the sea, its claw-footed legs tipped in silver, a great slab of polished black marble set into its surface. Stern-visaged portraits glowered down from the dimly illuminated walls, secure in their gilded frames. The polished wood-floor was barely visible, much of its surface strewn with expensive fur rugs, the gleaming black hide of the Arabyan jackal, the dun hues of the Ebonian lion and the pristine white of the Norscan ice bear.

Seated behind the table in this room of wealth was a non-descript man of advancing age. He held his hands folded before him, the silver-threaded cuffs of his robes drooping from his wrists. An immense gold medallion hung from a heavy chain about the man's neck. His name was Masario, chamberlain to the powerful Merchant Prince of Pavona, Bensario. He regarded the armoured figure standing before him in silence for some time, studying the man with an experienced eye. In his role as chamberlain, Masario had often been called upon to engage the mercenaries who would fight Pavona's wars, years of such duties making him a keen judge of character. The chamberlain could, at a glance, see the limits of a man's courage, the depths of his greed, the shallowness of his loyalty.

Masario nodded in satisfaction. He could see the determination and ruthlessness in the man before him. Such qualities were, in the chamberlain's mind, much more dependable than lofty ideals and foolish notions of honour and chivalry.

'I am pleased that you answered my summons,' the chamberlain spoke, his voice resonating with the authority of his position. He made a pretence of looking at some of the sheets of parchment strewn about the table. 'You are highly spoken of,' he added. 'Apparently yours is a most fearsome reputation.'

The bounty hunter shifted his stance. 'What's the job?' he asked, in a cold tone of voice.

The chamberlain leaned back in his chair. 'I had heard that you were a no-nonsense sort.' Masario leaned forward once more, the subtly amused quality dropping instantly from him. Like the bounty hunter, he too was now all business.

'I wish to hire you to find a murderer, Brunner,' the chamberlain stated. 'I am certain that you have done this sort of thing often before. I wish to employ you, on behalf of his highness, the Prince of Pavona, to find this despicable creature and kill him.'

'Who and how much?' Brunner asked the question without a hint of emotion in his voice.

'Ten thousand gold ducats,' Masario pronounced. The bounty hunter inclined his head slightly, a gesture that indicated the money was good, though he wondered what made the job worth such a price. The chamberlain easily read the gesture. 'You will find the "who" a bit more difficult. You see, we do not know the identity of the murderer.'

'Would you care to explain that?' Brunner asked.

Masario rose from his seat and paced behind his desk. 'There was a murder recently in the household of Prince Bensario, a most vicious murder. It occurred two weeks past. The victim was a mere serving maid, one of Prince Bensario's household, but that is not what is of concern to His Excellency. It is the senseless, savage brutality of the crime that alarms him, the fact that this atrocity was committed under his very roof. The murder could have been no more foul had some blood-mad Badlands orc been smuggled into the palace. And the fact that the murderer is from Remas – the only thing we know about him – has also earned Prince Bensario's ire.

'The prince's eldest daughter, Princess Juliana, has been betrothed to Prince Gambini of Remas. Prince Gambini sent a delegation from his city to conduct his bride back to his palace in Remas.'

'And the killer was one of the members of this delegation,' stated Brunner.

Masario nodded his head. 'Indeed. He was observed by one of the servants as he was finishing his crime. The man was speaking to himself as he butchered his victim's body, in the accent of Remas. Unfortunately, it took the servant several days to work up enough courage to report what she had seen. The investigation held at the time turned up no clue as to the fiend's identity, and it is only this witness who points the way to the killer. By that time, the delegation had already left Pavona, conducting Princess Juliana to her wedding.'

'How many men were in this delegation?' Brunner inquired.

'Thirty men, including the soldiers sent to protect them on the road. The others included Prince Gambini's nephew, a priest from the prince's household and a few retainers to attend them on the road.' Masario seated himself once more, staring intently at the bounty hunter.

'The witness to the crime only saw the murderer's back. He had bared himself, no doubt to prevent any blood from staining his clothes, and the servant had a clear look at a tattoo on his back, which she described as being a black serpent rearing backwards to strike.'

'That won't make finding him easy if the tattoo is the only means to identify him,' commented Brunner. 'Unless you propose that I force my way into Prince Gambini's palace and start forcing his retainers to remove their shirts.'

'No, you'll have to be more discreet than that,' Masario said. 'This matter must be handled carefully. Prince Bensario hopes to form an alliance with the marriage of his daughter. The support of the Republic of Remas would be of great benefit in quashing once and for all the foolish ambitions of the princes of Trantio. Prince Gambini holds a great deal of influence with the other ruling families in the Republic, and with him on Pavona's side, Prince Bensario thinks he may just be able to gain Remas as an ally in any forthcoming campaign against Trantio. Obviously, Prince Gambini will not smile too fondly on us should we accuse him of harbouring a maniac in his household. Nor can we simply ignore the danger to the princess by letting such a creature go on living. I mean, such a madman might be capable of anything, even attacking a princess. If the princess were to die in Remas, it would destroy at once Prince Bensario's ambitions.'

'Alright,' Brunner's cold voice spoke. 'It won't be as easy as I had hoped, but I'll find your murderer. What proof do you want me to bring back?'

Cruel, hungry anticipation filled Masario's face. 'Bring back the tattoo,' the chamberlain answered, his voice dropping into a low hiss. 'The priests at the Temple of Morr have their ways of verifying that the skin truly came from the man I seek.' An almost maniacal gleam shone in the chamberlain's eyes.

Masario noticed the curious look the bounty hunter gave him, and quickly strove to compose himself. 'Just the tattoo,' he repeated. Brunner nodded his head again and quietly made his exit from the chamber.

MASARIO WAITED UNTIL he could no longer hear the footfalls of the bounty hunter retreating down the corridor outside, then rose and made his way to a small table set against the wall. He removed the crystal stopper from a fat-bodied bottle of smoky glass and poured a measure of dark Pavonan wine into a glass. The chamberlain's face became worried for a moment, but quickly some of the fire he had shown at the conclusion of his meeting with the bounty hunter returned.

It had not been a mere serving maid who had fallen prey to the murderer from Remas, it had been Masario's own daughter. It was not the concern of the prince that motivated his hiring of Brunner, but the chamberlain's own need for justice. The prince had told Masario to forget the matter, as if the loss of his daughter was of no greater import than the loss of a few hundred ducats at the card table. Prince Bensario was not about to let anything jeopardise his alliance with the Republic of Remas. It was instrumental in his aspirations to be the ruler who finally defeated Pavona's age-long rival city-state of Trantio, to expand the coffers of Pavona as had no prince before him, swelling them with the plunder of conquest. Trantio had suffered greatly from their defeats by Borgio the Besieger of Miragliano, there would be no better time to strike at them. The alliance would be forged, and nothing would stop it. Prince Bensario was not worried about his daughter's safety, he had haughtily declared that even a madman would have sense enough to seek out his victims among the lower classes.

The chamberlain downed his wine in a single swallow, his hand tightening about the glass. He would not forget his daughter, would not forgive the atrocities that had been done to her. Prince Bensario might well have Masario's head if he were to learn what his chamberlain had done. But if that was the price of avenging his daughter, then Masario was willing to pay it.

BRUNNER EMERGED FROM the palazzo of Prince Bensario into the narrow, winding streets of the town. Pavona was the easternmost of the Tilean city states. The streets were haphazardly laid out, the better to confuse and disorient any enemy who managed to force their way through the city's thick walls. Overhead, numerous bridges arched above the cobbled streets, connecting the palazzos of the ruling elite, enabling the merchants and nobles to avoid the throngs of soldiers, peasants, labourers and servants that filled the lanes as they hurried about their own petty affairs. Located almost at the middle of Tilea, south of the Trantine Hills, on the fertile plains between the River Remo and the Apuccini Mountains, Pavona was blessed by a much milder climate than the lands of the Empire, enjoying almost year round the kindly favours of the warm Tilean sun. Although small, Pavona was a wealthy city, ever at odds with its neighbour Trantio for control of the eastern trade, all seeking to monopolise the market with the dwarfs and the few hardy caravans bearing goods along the famed Silk Road from legendary Cathay. Above the reek of the bodies packed within the streets, there rose the smell of riches and the ambition to secure still greater wealth.

As the bounty hunter made his way through the narrow lanes, pushing aside those slow in clearing his path, he considered his most recent patron. Prince Bensario was a very powerful man in Pavona, second only to the ruling Princess Lucrezzia Belladonna. Indeed, it was rumoured that Bensario entertained hopes to become the famous beauty's fifth husband, an aspiration which no doubt made Bensario's current wife both furious and nervous. Brunner suspected that Bensario's hopes for an alliance with the Republic of Remas were married in some way to his ambitions for the hand of Princess Belladonna. With such lofty pursuits in the balance, it did not surprise the bounty hunter that Bensario would offer such a generous reward for quietly eliminating a possible foil to his plans.

Brunner found the stables where he had left his warhorse, Fiend, and packhorse, a trusty grey he called Paychest. The bounty hunter tossed a few silver coins to the stable master and took charge of his animals. Mounted upon the back of his warhorse, leading the packhorse behind him, he found his progress through the bustle of Pavona's slender avenues much easier, though he was often forced to bend forward when passing beneath a particularly low bridge. Despite the crowds and his slow advance through them, Pavona was a small city and Brunner soon found himself approaching the massive stone gatehouse that loomed over the city's western gate.

As the bounty hunter drew closer to the gate, he could see the scraggly rows of mendicants and beggars squatting beside the tower. The guardsmen tolerated the wretches in exchange for a portion of their alms, another way of supplementing their wages in addition to their skim of the modest tax charged on all those seeking entry to Pavona. Yet poor and miserable as they were, sporting deformity, mutilation and the ugly sores left by the red pox and other noxious ailments, all the beggars knew better than to beseech succour from the grim horseman who marched his steed past their line. For his part, Brunner cast a perfunctory glance over the dregs, keeping his eyes peeled for any remarkable feature lurking beneath the filth and rags, something that would put a name to one of them.

The bounty hunter was somewhat surprised when one of the miserable creatures rose to its feet and stepped toward his horse. Brunner's hand reflexively closed about the grip of his pistol, inching it slightly from its holster. If the scraggly white-headed beggar noticed the action, he was not dissuaded by it.

The man's age was hard to guess, but he looked immensely old, his limbs thin, his hair long and matted, his beard hanging down to his belly. When he opened his mouth, he displayed a collection of blackened stumps. Foul, stinking breath escaped along with his words, increasing the wretch's offensive smell dramatically.

'Let me tell your fortune, sire!' the old beggar asked in a scratchy voice. Brunner nudged Fiend away from the mendicant, seeking to pass him.

'Sell your lies to someone stupid enough to put merit in them,' Brunner snarled. The mendicant was determined however, stepping once more into the path of the horse.

'Only a copper coin, master,' the beggar said, peering up at the bounty hunter's helm. 'When you undertake a journey, you should see what the gods have planned. Oh yes, you should do that, yes!' The old man fumbled at his ragged robe and removed a number of animal bones and small pond stones. With a sharp laugh, the beggar tossed the collection into the road, dropping to all fours and scrambling to where each object had fallen. The other traffic coming through the gate drew away from the deranged fortune teller, trying to give him a wide berth. In this they failed, the hooves of mules and the boots of drovers crushing many of the wretch's divining stones into the dust. Brunner seized the opening and the man's momentary absence to hurry his animals toward the portal.

The beggar, however, was soon trotting beside Brunner's horse again, his face a look of imbecilic glee.

'You set upon paths most dark, noble sire,' the beggar declared. 'Where you go, distrust splendour and suspect piety. Suspicion, yes! Dark things await you,' the beggar's voice dropped to a low whisper, 'in Remas.' The last word caused Brunner to turn in his saddle, meeting the old man's gaze for the first time.

'What did you say?' he asked. Despite himself, the mention of Remas had intrigued him. Now he wanted to hear what else the ragged prophet might have to say.

'You are caught in a web, bounty killer,' the beggar hissed. 'A web woven from darkness and Chaos. Darkness, yes! Chaos, yes! Woven by a mad spider. The spider sits at centre of his web. He feels every step those caught in the strands make. Everything caught, yes! Everything he watches, everything he draws into his plan. Oh yes, yes!' The beggar gave voice to a short cackling laugh. 'You're caught in the web now, Reiklander, the spider knows you now!'

'Who is this spider you speak of, old man?' Brunner felt uneasy. It was possible that the old beggar had heard of him, he was certainly well known enough among the thieves and gutter trash of Tilea to be recognised as the infamous bounty hunter Brunner. But how had the man so expertly guessed the realm of his birth? Most Tileans would not know a Reikland accent from that of Talabecland, and in any event, Brunner had long ago lost the tones of his birthplace.

The beggar laughed again. 'Ahhh, that would be telling. Telling, yes! The gods favour not humble fortune tellers revealing all before the unfolding. You need only know the spider is mad, thinks it can shape the Chaos-web of its creation to its own design. Mad little spider, yes! Thinks it can trick the Dark Gods to do its bidding.' The old man's voice trembled slightly as he spoke of Chaos and Dark Gods, but Brunner sensed that his faltering voice was due to excitement rather than dread. 'Worry not, bounty killer, you will find the mad spider where you are going.' The old man broke off into another cackle. 'Or the spider will find you,' he laughed.

Brunner dug a small piece of copper from a pouch on his belt and threw it down to the hoary old man. 'Thanks for the oracle, grey one,' he said. 'Now I know that both spiders and snakes are in my future.' With a contemptuous snort, Brunner edged his horse away from the fortune teller, but the beggar staggered forward once more, the copper coin forgotten in the dirt at his feet.

'Something more. Much more, yes! A warning,' the old man said, and this time there was a note of fear in his voice. 'Where you go,' the man's voice fell into a low whisper, 'tempt not the Mardagg.'

Brunner's horse began to snort in alarm when the beggar whispered the final word of his prophecy, as if the animal had nearly trodden upon a serpent. It took the bounty hunter a full minute to calm his mount. When he turned about to question the beggar further, the old man was gone. Brunner cast his gaze over the ranks of the other mendicants, but the white-bearded prophet was not to be found among them.

The bounty hunter's thoughts dwelled on the strange old beggar as he passed out from the walls of Pavona. Doomsayers and prophets were commonplace in the great cities of the Old World, deluded and crazed beggars even more so. Still, there had been something unsettling about the wretch, something that made Brunner wonder who and what the man might once have been.

The walls of Pavona began to diminish in the distance as Brunner rode through the farmlands and peasant villages that crowded outside the city, yet his thoughts were still on the old man's strange words. What would he find in Remas, Brunner wondered?

* * *

THE BOUNTY HUNTER had a fair distance to travel. Remas lay to the north and east of Pavona, nearly a hundred and fifty miles as the crow might fly. But it was a much longer distance on the ground, for the roads were few and progressively more ill-tended the further from Pavona they became, marks that the land itself was no longer firmly under the domination of man. Just two days' ride from Pavona and the only traces of civilisation were the dirt road upon which the bounty hunter travelled and the occasional ruined traces of some villa or farm house lurking just off the path. The days of peace and tranquillity had deserted Tilea, forcing the wealthy merchants from their country villas and back into the overcrowded cities. The wilds were still not quite so hazardous as those of the Empire, but there were enough unnatural things prowling the countryside to make them not so devoid of danger as they had been in ages past.

Late in the afternoon of his fifth day from Pavona, Brunner chanced upon stark evidence of the dangers presented by the Tilean country. Smoke rose lazily from a mass of charred wood and canvas strewn about the road. It soon became apparent that the wreckage was the remains of a dozen or so wagons, their cargo of sailcloth and timber consumed along with the wagons themselves. Scattered amid the wreckage were a number of rotting bodies, the wagon masters and their guards.

Brunner dismounted and inspected one of the bodies, rolling it onto its back with his steel-toed boot. The purple-faced corpse that stared up at him crawled with maggots, big black corpse-flies flitting from the body's mouth. The skin of the slain guard was blackening, sloughing from his bones. Brunner could see a great gash in the man's mail shirt, and it seemed to him that where the cut had been made, the metal was corroded. By the evidence of the smoke rising from the charred remains of the wagons, these men had been slain not more than a day ago. Yet the body he looked upon had the rotted look of a man weeks in the grave.

The bounty hunter stalked away from the corpse and remounted his horse. Brunner had seen such remains before, and he knew that the agents of such death were far fouler and more loathsome than orcs or beastmen. He did not look forward to running into such degenerates on his own.

As Brunner rode away from the scene of carnage, his eyes chanced to fall upon a body that certainly did not belong among the slaughtered men of the caravan. Clearly the murderers had not been able to enact their butchery with complete impunity; the slaughtered men of the caravan had evidently brought down at least one of their attackers. It was a bulky form in grey plate armour, great rusty chains lashed about its shoulder pads and interconnected across its chest. Gruesome, rotting trophies dangled from the chains: severed hands, tongues and even less pleasant organs. Great fat worms writhed in the decaying tissue of the trophies, filthy black things that looked like animated veins.

The warrior's head was enclosed in a great helm fashioned like the head of a scavenger bird. The corpse flies were even thicker around the dead warrior, and rose in an irritated cloud as the bounty hunter rode nearer. As the flies took wing, Brunner could see the crude sign that was emblazoned upon the breast of the dead raider's armour, and he felt a wave of revulsion seize his gut. It was a simple sign, three interconnected circles, each radiating a single arrow, but its power was not in its complexity, but in what it represented. It was the mark of one of the great powers of Chaos; Brunner had seen it before, in a plague-stricken district near Miragliano some time past.

The bounty hunter fought down his revulsion, spitting a blob of bilious phlegm on the dead warrior's armour. His wary gaze considered the surrounding countryside more closely than before. Deciding at last that no lurking ambushers had remained behind, Brunner urged his animals onward, his pace slightly faster now. Knowing for certain now that there were Chaos-worshippers prowling the vicinity, and in numbers great enough to strike down an armed caravan, the bounty hunter was even more eager to put the wilds behind him.

A FEW HOURS later, as the sun began to set, the bounty hunter came upon a second caravan. The terrain had become even closer, stands of trees with thin trunks and small leaves spreading to either side of the narrow road, permitting only a limited view of whatever might lie just off the road. Brunner was eyeing the woods with great suspicion, knowing that a location such as this would be a prime site to spring another ambush. This caravan, however, was no cluster of burning wreckage and rotting corpses; instead, Brunner found himself gazing upon a half-dozen wagons, laden down with bundles of dyed wool from the north, barrels of olives from the Trantine Hills, and other, less readily identifiable goods.

The caravan was just making camp for the evening, the wagons arranged into a barricade across either end of the road. Brunner could see several of the drovers bustling about tending their horses while other men prepared a fire at the centre of the camp. The bounty hunter could also see a number of armoured figures prowling about between the wagons, inspecting the makeshift barricade.

It would be easy to bypass the encamped caravan, but Brunner considered once more the unpleasant nature of the dead raider he had discovered on the site of the massacre. There were some decidedly nasty things about, and it would pay to be cautious until he was safely arrived in Remas. His decision made, the bounty hunter slowly rode toward the camp, one hand casually resting on the grip of his pistol.

'That's far enough!' a hard voice called out from the line of wagons when Brunner had come within fifty feet of them. The bounty hunter could see three men aiming weapons in his direction, two crossbows and a bulky-looking handgun. Brunner could see at least another dozen men peering over and beneath the beds of the wagons, some of them drawing blades from their scabbards. He also caught a faint motion from the side of the camp and soon heard the furtive rustle of a body moving stealthily through the trees.

Brunner reined in his horse, staring for a moment at the speaker. He was an older man, tending toward fat, wearing a gaudy red coat of some heavy cloth, an outrageously plumed hat scrunched onto his head. The man's full-featured face bore an air of command, but also a suggestion of fear.

Indeed, now that Brunner considered it, he saw the same nervousness on almost all of the other faces he could see, drovers and mercenaries. Apparently the bounty hunter wasn't the only one who had come upon the massacre site.

'Who are you?' the plump man demanded. 'Speak quickly or my men will shoot!'

'Just a traveller,' Brunner replied, keeping his voice as even and pleasant as he could manage. When he saw the doubtful look on the merchant's face, Brunner straightened his position in his saddle. He smiled grimly as he noted the three marksmen adjust their aim slightly to account for his movement. 'You must think I'm a ten-fold fool. I can see that you have me in check. Even if your men there miss me, I know you have another fellow flanking me in the woods just to my right.' A low curse rose from the bounty hunter's right. Brunner stared out the corner of his helm to see a wiry man wearing black leather armour come stalking out of the trees, a crossbow gripped in his hands. The look on the sneaking marksman's sharp-featured face was murderous. He lifted his weapon, keeping it trained on the bounty hunter.

'A traveller, eh?' the merchant said. 'And how do we know that's all you are? How do we know that you're not in league with the scum that hacked down the caravan we passed this afternoon?' As the merchant spoke, there were sombre nods from some of his men.

Brunner was preparing a retort when a voice called out from within the camp.

'He's what he says he is, Emiliano,' said a loud voice in a Reiklander accent. Brunner watched the speaker emerge from the cover of the wagons. The man wore an elaborately engraved breastplate over a bright blue shirt. A brace of pistols and a slender longsword dangled from a brass-studded belt about the man's waist while steel armour covered much of his upper legs. Black leather cavalry boots completed his costume, save for the dull steel helm that guarded his skull. The face of the rounded helm was open, exposing a countenance that had seen too much of the world to still be considered young. The skin was dark and leathery, weathered by years of exposure to the hot sun of the south.

The man's blond moustache and keen blue eyes betrayed his northern origin however, every bit as much as the rampant griffon upon his breastplate and the accent in his voice.

'I met him in Miragliano shortly after we arrived,' the mercenary said, turning away from his employer and walking away from the barricade. 'Apparently, he is a bounty hunter of some note.' As the captain made this statement, the marksman in the trees gave a disgusted, hateful hiss. 'An unpleasant sort, but not a follower of the Ruinous Powers.'

The mercenary captain strode towards Brunner, stopping when he was only ten feet away. Brunner focused his attention on the man. He remembered only too clearly their last meeting. This time, the man was not drunk, and backed by more than a few besotted companions as he had been in the Black Boar. More, Brunner could see by the way the mercenary carried himself that he was a man who knew his business, who knew how to handle a sword and had depended upon it for his livelihood for quite some time. The bounty hunter considered his options, not liking the conclusions he was drawing. Even if he was able to best the mercenary in a fair combat, he knew that the waiting marksmen would quickly avenge their captain's loss.

'I see you still carry the sword,' the mercenary declared, pointing a gloved finger at the dragon-hilted shape against Brunner's left thigh. The bounty hunter did not speak, fixing his eyes upon those of the sell-sword. The mercenary met Brunner's gaze. 'Tell me,' he asked in a sombre voice, 'that story you told me about how you came by the sword, was it the truth?'

Brunner sneered at the mercenary. 'Lies are what we tell those we fear,' he said. He cast a furtive glance at the black-garbed marksman as the man moved to complete his flanking of the bounty hunter, then returned his attention to the man before him.

The mercenary captain was quiet for a moment, his face unreadable. Then he nodded, reaching a decision. He lifted one of his gloved hands, waving his fingers. Ahead of him, Brunner could see the other mercenaries relax, the marksmen withdrawing their weapons. Brunner looked back to the blond-haired captain and nodded. The Reiklander returned the gesture.

'If you would share our camp,' the mercenary said, 'I would hear a more complete account of Albrecht Yorck's demise.'

'That is a small enough thing,' the bounty hunter replied. 'But why should it interest you? Of what matter is this sword and a slaughtered pig to you?'

'My father was a soldier in the service of the man to whom that sword rightfully belonged,' the mercenary said, indicating the dragon-hilted weapon once more. He turned to make his way back to the camp.

'What was his name?' Brunner called after the mercenary.

'Zelten,' the mercenary said, turning around once more. 'Karl Zelten, Rittmeister to the Baron von Drakenburg.' There was a swelling pride in the mercenary's voice as he spoke of his father and his position with the deposed baron. 'I am his eldest son, Manfred Zelten,' the mercenary concluded with equal pride, turning on his heel and resuming his march back to the encampment.

THE SHADOWS HAD grown long by the time Brunner had finished relating his story to the mercenary captain. Manfred Zelten had listened with marked interest from the folding camp chair he had removed from one of the wagons. Around him, a number of his sell-swords had gathered, eager to hear this tale which so interested their captain, among them the heavy, bear-like warrior who had risen to the defence of Zelten in the Black Boar and the wiry marksman who had tried to flank the bounty hunter during the earlier stand-off.

The story Brunner told was simple enough. He had been hired by the down-trodden people of Yorckweg, a miserable little town in the Border Princes, to remove their despotic ruler, a usurper named Albrecht Yorck. The bounty hunter had infiltrated the town and found the tyrant, feeding Yorck's belly the full length of his sword before kicking the expiring man down into his fighting arena to be torn apart by his own wardogs. As a way of supplementing the meagre funds offered by the peasants, Brunner had relieved Yorck of his magnificent sword before knocking him down into the pit to meet a well-deserved end.

The relating of Yorck's gruesome demise brought a look of shock and horror to the face of the merchant, Emiliano Tacca, perhaps more due to the cold, emotionless tones in which it was recounted than anything else. Several of the listening mercenaries chuckled however, applauding the ruthless act with their grim humour. Zelten himself wore a broad smile, clearly pleased by what he had heard.

'Nothing less than the swine deserved,' the Reiklander spat. 'You did the Empire a service removing that scum from the ranks of the living.'

'I gather you knew this Albrecht Yorck,' Brunner stated, crouching beside the fire.

'Indeed, he was seneschal to Baron von Drakenburg, second in command of his soldiers, among other duties.' Zelten's face grew hard as he recalled the man. 'It is because of his treachery that my father and many other brave warriors are dead.'

'I suspect that you have your own tale to tell,' the bounty hunter observed.

Zelten looked over at the heavily-muscled bear-like man. 'Horst, ensure that the rotation schedule for the sentries is maintained. Two in camp, one in the trees at either side of the road. I want no tired eyes watching over us when Chaos is abroad.' The bear-like Horst Brendle nodded, muttering a curse on all those who would bow before the Dark Gods, and strode away to carry out his captain's orders.

'I fear that my own story has a less pleasing finish than yours,' Zelten admitted when he returned his attention to the bounty hunter. 'As I mentioned, my father was captain of cavalry to the Baron von Drakenburg, a noble house whose lands lie upon the Reikland side of the Grey Mountains. He was a very wealthy man, as his domain included Iron Pass, a slender finger through a break in the Grey Mountains which allowed passage between the Empire and Bretonnia. Unfortunately, the Baron's Bretonnian neighbour was a very ambitious man, a villain named de Chegney, a viscount with less honour and decency about him than an orc.'

The bounty hunter's gaze became even harder as he heard the treacherous Bretonnian lord mentioned. 'Much of the baron's wealth was poured into building forts and arming soldiers to protect his lands from the viscount's numerous and unrelenting attempts to expand his domain eastward. It is a testament to the baron's tactical acumen and the quality of his soldiers that the Viscount de Chegney was repulsed every time, sent back to Bretonnia to lick his wounds.'

Zelten snapped his fingers and an elderly looking soldier advanced. The old veteran wore a suit of often-mended plate mail about his lean yet-powerful frame, the faded outline of a laurel-wreathed skull visible on his greaves and breast-plate. The veteran cast a dubious look at his captain, his wrinkled face further disfigured by a worried scowl. The mercenary handed his captain a lead flask which Zelten took from him without a word. The younger man took a long pull from the bottle, then stared at the flask for a moment before handing it back to the veteran. There was something akin to relief in the older man's face as he returned the flask to a pouch on his belt and withdrew.

Fortified by whatever he had imbibed, Zelten continued to speak. 'For many years this went on, until at last, the viscount himself proposed an end to the fighting. He proposed a treaty with Baron von Drakenburg, a treaty that would be sealed with blood. The viscount's son would marry the baron's daughter, thus uniting their houses and fortifying the peace with a bond stronger than mere words. After much thought and consultation with his advisors, the baron at last agreed to the marriage and the treaty.' Brunner listened to Zelten speak, clenching and unclenching his swordhand, as though eager to grip the hilt of his blade. The mercenary did not notice the gesture and continued with his tale. 'Although no coward, the baron had grown weary of the constant skirmishes and raiding, and this proposed alliance seemed the only chance for bringing peace to his realm. The marriage was announced, to be held on neutral ground, a glade located along Iron Pass, mid-way between the two realms.

The two factions would each bring however many soldiers they desired and the ceremony would be conducted by both a priest of our most Holy Sigmar and a cleric of Bretonnia's Lady of the Lake.

'The wedding itself passed without incident. Indeed, even the most sceptical of the baron's men had to admit that it seemed that at last his troubled realm would know peace. How could they have imagined the black-hearted deceit that was the true intention of the viscount? How could the baron have imagined how deep the Bretonnian's foul reach had stretched into his own barony? Riding back from the wedding, with his loyal,' the mercenary fairly sneered the word, 'seneschal Albrecht Yorck by his side, the baron dared to hope that the security and happiness of his land had been secured, that it would know no more the sound of battle, at least in his time. But the wedding feast had been long, and the hour had grown late. At the suggestion of Yorck, the baron's party did not head back toward the massive walls of the Schloss von Drakenburg, but instead diverted their path toward a small border fort. It seemed a most reasonable thing to do, with the sun long faded from the sky and many hours' travel before reaching the warm halls of the Schloss.

'But it was not comfort the baron found, but darkest treachery. The fort had been betrayed. While the viscount had toasted the peace and prosperity of both their realms, mercenaries in his employ had taken over the fort, sneaking past its defences by means of an escape tunnel whose location had been told to them. They had put the baron's garrison to the sword, then had awaited the baron's coming. As the baron's party reached the keep, the mercenaries sprung their ambush. First they dropped the portcullis, cutting the baron's forces in half. Then their archers opened fire, both on the men within the keep's courtyard and those without. Surprised, their reflexes and wits dulled by the excesses of the wedding feast, the baron's company were easy prey. Only three of his horsemen escaped the ambush, riding off to alert the castle and summon aid.

'One of these men was my father. Mortally wounded by one of the viscount's archers, he reached the castle nevertheless. He told of the treacherous ambush, and of what he had seen through the keep's gate ere he had ridden off, the loyal seneschal Albrecht Yorck with his sword at the throat of the man he had professed to serve. He said these things, before his wound finished him, another victim of the viscount's plotting and Yorck's betrayal.'

Zelten clenched his own fist as he recalled these memories and Brunner could imagine the man's knuckles whitening beneath his gloves. 'I took up my father's sword and marched out with the soldiers who had remained at the castle. We thought that if we could reinforce the keep that held the pass, we might yet force the viscount to undo his villainy. But the wily Bretonnian had been swifter. His men had not removed themselves very far from the site of the wedding feast and were much closer to the mouth of the pass than we. Worse, the viscount's traitor had been at work on the fort's garrison. Fully half of the men were in his pay, and the faithless curs wasted no time in murdering their still loyal comrades when Yorck gave the order. We found the pass held against us, and the viscount's knights ready to take full advantage of a foe tired from having marched since dawn. If ten men escaped the ensuing slaughter, then Morr was cheated his due. It is to my shame that I was among those who did not die that day.'

'The only shame in this world is spending your life on a useless cause,' the bounty hunter interrupted, his voice chill and grim. 'You and the other men at the castle should have taken service with one of the neighbouring barons rather than spending your lives needlessly on a fallen lord.'

The mercenary captain took to his feet, bristling with outrage. 'Indeed yours is an honourless breed!' he snapped. 'I should have taken service with the likes of them? That princely scum? They were as much traitors to the baron as that vermin Yorck! Each one of them had been bought off by de Chegney, told that they might partition the holdings of the von Drakenburgs in exchange for their complacency. Had they stood against him, the viscount would never have dared to move so boldly and treacherously. Instead, they had stood aside and allowed the viscount to overthrow their fellow noble lord, hiding behind the marriage of de Chegney's son to the baron's only child as a moral excuse to not interfere. I've served many masters since making my way south, since taking up the profession of the sell-sword, but never have I served men so vile!'

Brunner smiled at the mercenary. 'Cling to your high ground while you may,' he said. 'Go on thinking there is some honour to be found in this dirty world we live in. You should have learned from the story you've told me. Trust is a fatal flaw for a man to have, and loyalty is just as foolish a notion to nurture in your heart. No man, no cause is worth dying for.' The bounty hunter patted the sword at his side with a leather-covered hand. 'This is the only friend you can count on.' He stared hard at the mercenary, his eyes like chips of ice behind the visor of his helm. 'If your baron had understood that, he wouldn't be dead now.' Brunner rose from his crouch and strode away. Zelten and those around him watched the hardened killer walk toward the far end of the encampment, near where his animals were tethered. The bounty hunter removed a blanket from one of the bundles he had earlier taken from the packhorse. Casting the blanket to the ground, the bounty hunter settled himself for the night.

'That sort of man makes even my blood turn sour,' commented Schtafel, the wiry marksman who had been caught flanking the bounty hunter. He was one of Zelten's best men, and had been with Zelten throughout the long march south through the Empire. For all of that, he knew little about the man. Whatever secrets were in his past, Schtafel kept to himself. Truth be told, Zelten had been quietly impressed that the bounty hunter had noticed Schtafel's stealthy approach. He'd seen the crossbowman sneak up on even orcs and beastmen without the monsters noticing.

'I'll second that,' shuddered a tall mercenary, his face framed by the close-fitting cheek-guards of his Tilean-style barbute helm. 'I've drunk with ogres that were better company.'

Zelten considered his fellow mercenaries for a moment, then rose from his camp chair. 'If that Chaos warband is still about, you'll be glad to number him with us,' he stated. 'That caravan we passed today was twice our size. If fortune betrays us and we run afoul of those marauders, you'll be glad of every sword.' So saying, Zelten departed, to seek his own bed. Schtafel watched his captain go.

'The captain can think what he likes,' the marksman confided to his companions. 'But I'll feel better the further I am from that bastard.'

II

BEHIND THE THICK stone walls of Remas, among the clustered warehouses, tenements, inns, taverns, shops, palazzos, temples and barracks, innumerable shadowy, hidden places existed, forlorn refuges for thieves, murderers and men guilty of still darker crimes. In one of these secret places, a single candle burned, its flame dancing in the pitch black all around it.

A figure moved within the tiny circle of light cast by the lone candle. Soft hands, their fingers long and thin, worked within the light, moving with an almost inhuman grace. The hands performed long sweeps above the floor, with each movement allowing a trickle of dark powder to fall upon the rough stones. As the hands continued to weave their invisible, intangible pattern, the trickle of dust described the movements upon the stones. By degrees, the shape of an octagon began to form. When the shape had become firmly established, when the last trace of the powder had fallen from the cupped fists of the hands the figure drew away from the light. The crinkle of rustling cloth sounded within the dark, secret place as the shadow rummaged about in the blackness. Soon the opening and closing of some box with a ponderous wooden lid added to the rustle of the garments. Then the hands appeared once more in the flickering candlelight.

Now the hands did not hold something so insubstantial as powder. The left was closed about the hilt of a wavy-bladed copper dagger, the blade defaced by a gruesome skull totem set close to the guard of the knife. The other was closed about something even more unsettling: a tiny, struggling grey-furred form. It might have been a field mouse once, before corruption had settled into its flesh and bone. Now it was a disgusting thing, two scaly heads squirming against the fingers that held it, a long tail bearing suckers like an octopus curling about the wrist of the hand. The mutant thing had no voice and continued its struggles in silence. Those struggles ceased entirely when the copper dagger slashed through both its throats in one swift motion.

The dead aberration spilled its corrupt sapphire-hued blood into the centre of the octagon. Instantly the steaming blue liquid began to disperse, running in straight lines to each point of the octagon. Where bare stone had been before, now a crude arrow had formed. The blood of the slain mutant began to glow, shifting colours as it grew in brilliance, fading from red to green then to blue once more.

Steam began to rise from the unnatural blood, forming into a cloud of weirdly glowing smoke. As the smoke changed colours, a hazy image began to form within it, a small caravan encampment somewhere in the wilderness of Tilea's countryside. The conjurer could see that the wagons had been formed into a barricade to protect the wagon masters, their beasts and their wares from the night. Mercenary soldiers patrolled the perimeter of the camp, wary eyes studying the dark for any sign of danger. Yes, there was danger here. The caravan was destined for Remas. There was a man in the camp who could prove dangerous if he were to reach the city, dangerous to the magic-maker's schemes. He should have dealt with him before, but had always hesitated to do so. Now there would be no more doubt, and no more delay.

A pale hand swiped at the swirling smoke. The image faded, the smoke bubbled like boiling soup as it congealed to show a new scene, the shape of an immense armoured warrior, slumped against a rotting log. The magic-maker's head nodded as the image took form, pleased by what had been revealed. From the darkness, soft words whispered. The warrior stirred slightly as the words intruded upon his dreams. The magic-maker spoke again, the words becoming more forceful. The armoured warrior shook his head, the grotesque insect-like helm shaking as the conjurer's words consumed and supplanted his dreams. The words stopped flowing and the caster smiled once more. All that had been needed to be done this night had been accomplished.

The pale hands moved within the yellow glimmer of the candle once more. This time they moved only twice above the octagon and the glowing cloud hovering above it. Then the left hand dropped a silver coin into the centre of the octagon. Instantly, the mist vanished, as though it had never been. A terrible chill filled the dark chamber, blowing out the feeble candle. It was the icy cold of unclean, fathomless reaches, of places beyond the confines of time and substance, the chill of ancient and inhuman evil. The conjurer paid the chill no notice, for many times had he felt its touch. He relit the candle, and bore it away as he made his way through the silent, benighted passages that led away from this secret, profane place.

THE CARAVAN DECAMPED in the small hours before dawn. By first light the wagons were once more under way, their mercenary guards walking alongside. Ahead of the wagons, the few mounted members of the mercenary band rode ahead of the column. Beside them rode Brunner, though his inclusion in the marching order had drawn a number of complaints from some of the mercenaries, chiefly the cross-bowman Schtafel, but the protests had been overruled by Zelten. Again, the captain pointed out to his men that they would appreciate every sword if they were set upon by raiders. However, the captain's words were not enough to keep suspicious eyes from glaring at the bounty hunter, nor nervous fingers from staying close to the hilts of knives and swords.

Zelten rode beside Brunner, as much to forestall any impetuous act on the part of one of his men as to assure his soldiers that he was keeping a watchful eye on the bounty hunter. For his part, Brunner seemed to pay no notice to the quiet hostility around him, his keen eyes scanning the stands of trees, patches of thick brush and piles of boulders that dotted the landscape.

'You expect trouble?' the mercenary asked, trying to follow the direction of the bounty hunter's ever shifting gaze.

'I always expect trouble,' Brunner replied, not looking at Zelten. 'It's what keeps me alive.'

Zelten smiled, clearly having expected such a response from the hired killer. 'We made a thorough search of the site of the massacre. One of my men used to be a game warden on the estates of Count Capritti of Luccini. He reckons there were about fifty in the warband that hit the other caravan.'

Brunner nodded his head, eyes still scanning the trees. Zelten noticed that the bounty hunter's hand lay upon the grip of his pistol, gloved fingers slowly drumming on the polished wooden frame of the gun. 'That sounds about right. It would take at least that many to hit a caravan of that size and prevent anyone from escaping.'

'Fifty,' Zelten said, as if considering the number. 'We have about that many among us.' The mercenary snorted a humourless laugh. 'Of course, that includes the labourers and wagon masters. Our actual fighting strength is nearer to thirty-five.' Zelten laughed again. 'Of course, a few of my men are worth more than most I've fought beside. Horst, for instance, is worth five men on his own.'

'That might count for something,' Brunner replied, his voice grim, 'if we were worried about fighting men. But what destroyed that other caravan long ago abandoned any right to call themselves human.'

'I've fought the servants of the Dark Gods before,' Zelten commented, his tone somewhat defensive. 'I know all too well what to expect from their kind.'

Brunner faced the mercenary for the first time. 'I've dealt with their kind as well, often enough to know one thing. Where Chaos has extended its hand, you can never know what to expect.'

IT WAS AN hour after sunrise when they saw the raiders. The keen eyes of the bounty hunter noticed them just as the foremost of Zelten's riders did, the swarthy former game warden Guglielmo. The Tilean turned around in his saddle shouting a warning to the rest of the column. The mercenaries began hastily readying themselves for conflict, breaking into small groups of four: three men armed with spears or swords providing support and protection for a fourth man armed with either a crossbow or a long-barrelled black powder weapon. The wagons tried to manoeuvre themselves into a defensive wedge behind the groupings of mercenaries, but it was taking the wagoners time to force their animals to obey, despite the orders and curses being shouted by the merchant Emiliano Tacca.

Ahead of the column, at the top of a small rise, a cluster of armed shapes could be seen, numbering at least a score. They had been hidden from view until the caravan had rounded the last rock pile, yet they were still far enough away for Zelten's marksmen to knock down their numbers before the raiders would be able to reach the formation. Or perhaps not, the bounty hunter reconsidered as he noticed the nature of their foes. Most of them wore armour, and lots of it, though Brunner knew from experience that even the thickest armour was no proof against a bullet, nor certain protection from a close-fired crossbow bolt. And he suspected, these were no normal men, but vile followers of corruption and pestilence. Their flesh would be bloated, puffy with disease and corruption. Followers of the plague god were almost immune to pain, even more so than orcs and their ilk. Their necrotic flesh was largely eaten away by disease, there was little left of them that could be injured or hurt. The fire of Zelten's marksmen would have to be very good, for only a kill-shot would bring one of these degenerates down.

'Prepare to repel attackers!' Zelten called out in strong, harsh tones. The mercenary captain brandished his sword overhead, waving it like a standard. 'Let's make them regret taking on Zelten's Dragons!' The officer's words were greeted with whooping war cries from his men. The other horsemen readied their own weapons, forming a line before the infantry. Zelten gave orders to the other cavalry to stand their

ground until the raiders had come half-way across the gap
between them. The idea was to give the marksmen as much
time as possible to whittle down the numbers of their
attackers. Then the cavalry would strike the weakened
enemy, holding them back for the marksmen to gain still a
few more opportunistic shots before their enemies could
reach the small infantry formations.

Brunner watched as the armoured warriors upon the rise
began to advance, setting up a fierce howl of devotion to
their profane god. The keen eyes of the bounty hunter studied the ranks of the hideous Chaos warriors.

'I count thirty-two,' the bounty hunter observed.

Zelten nodded his head as the first volley of fire struck the
armoured raiders. Four of the warriors were hit, one of them
dropping his halberd as a bullet exploded his unarmoured
shoulder, another falling with a bolt through his neck. The
other two just shrugged off the attack; whether the bolts had
failed to penetrate their armour or whether they had simply
failed to hit a vital area, it was impossible to say. The crippled warrior tossed his heavy shield aside and retrieved his
weapon from the ground, gripping it in his other hand.

'They seem to be taking their own time about getting over
here too,' commented Zelten. The mercenary shouted at one
of the other horsemen. 'They're baiting us!' he told the
horseman, the same old veteran who had produced the flask
the previous evening. 'Leave Horst here with me and take the
rest of the horse to the rear. Be ready for an ambush!'

The veteran saluted with a sharp, precise gesture more
befitting one of the Empire's knightly orders than some rag-
tag Tilean mercenary company. The old warrior barked
orders to the other horsemen and at once they were racing
to the rear of the column. Left behind, the bear-like Horst
swung his heavy flail back and forth beside his horse, clearly
eager to crack an enemy's skull with the brutal weapon.
Zelten watched them go, then turned his attention forward.
He was slightly surprised to notice that the bounty hunter
was still at his side.

'Not joining the rearguard?' he asked. Brunner continued
to watch the plague warriors advance as another volley

struck their ranks. Once again, only one of the armoured warriors fell, though this time the other warriors struck seemed to notice their injuries a bit more. The marksmen had learned where to place their shots after the first barrage.

'I think the real action is going to be up here,' Brunner commented, drawing his pistol. 'Even if your bearded bear is worth five men, I think you'll need me here.'

'You don't think the rest of them are planning an ambush?' Zelten asked, a worried note in his voice. There were any number of reasons why the number of their enemies was so low. The rest of the warband might be watching another part of the road, lying in reserve, or perhaps they had simply overestimated how many of them there could be. However, the deliberate hesitance of the raiders' advance could only be evidence of some subterfuge.

'Oh, they are going to spring something on us,' Brunner commented as a third salvo struck the plague warriors, this time felling two of the diseased madmen. 'But this is where the main assault is going to be.' Brunner nodded his head toward the slowly advancing ranks of armoured reavers. 'I suspect these are his good troops. The ambush is a double-bluff to draw your best troops elsewhere. The real attack is going to be here.'

Zelten cursed, the hand gripping the reins of his steed slapping his leg in frustration. 'Damn it man, why didn't you say so before I sent the cavalry back!'

'Because if you hadn't, we won't be able to draw out their leader,' replied Brunner in a cold voice. 'Bringing him down is going to be the only way to rout this vermin. Do that...' the bounty hunter's words trailed off as he noted a horseman appear at the top of the rise.

The horseman was surrounded by a cloud of flies, leaving no doubt as to his allegiance. The horse itself looked like something that had been rotting in a field for upwards of a week. Clumps of fur had fallen out, exposing sickly green skin. Great pustules clumped about its neck, trailing off towards its belly, open sores wept yellow filth from each of its legs. Leather barding studded with spikes of rusting steel and bronze covered the diseased animal, a mask of leather enclosing its entire head, save for its drooling, black-toothed mouth and rheumy eyes.

Atop the plague steed was an even more disordered apparition, a huge shape in a grimy suit of plate armour, the green, corroding metal covering every inch of the rider, baring not the slightest portion of the form within. The armour itself was green with corrosion, grimy rust-like crust dripping from every edge or join upon the pieces of steel plate, as though the metal had become contaminated by whatever disease the vile plague god had seen fit to gift his servant. Visible between the rotting trophies that dangled from thick leather cords fastened to studs on the warrior's shoulder guards, the interlinked circle symbol of the Grandfather of Pestilence could be seen etched across the breastplate of the armour.

The helmet that rose above the breastplate was fashioned in the shape of some noxious insect, numerous tiny holes in the bulging eyes of the insect mask allowing the warrior within to see the world upon which he preyed. Gripped in the gauntlet of the bloated Chaos champion was a huge sword, its blade pitted with decay, clotted encrustations of blood and brain staining the length of the giant weapon.

Brunner saw the rider, swearing under his breath. 'Pulstlitz!' he snarled. Zelten glanced over at the bounty hunter as he heard Brunner name the Chaos rider. It had been nearly a year since Brunner had crossed swords with the filthy plague knight. The bounty hunter was not looking forward to repeating the experience.

Zelten roared an order back at his men. 'Concentrate your fire on the leader!'

'Keep firing on the foot soldiers!' Brunner snarled, his voice riding the echo of Zelten's order. 'Foul magics watch over that bastard, don't waste your shots on him!' After a moment of indecision, the marksmen opened fire again, still directing their shots at the slowly advancing plague warriors. Zelten cast a suspicious look at the bounty hunter, but did not protest his countermand of his orders.

Pulstlitz stared down at the battlefield for a moment, then lifted his sword overhead, swiping it through the air and the cloud of flies hovering about him. Then the plague knight charged, barrelling down the slope of the rise. As he did so, the slowly advancing foot soldiers broke into a run, roaring their profane war cries. The war cries were answered from a large pile of rocks behind and a few score yards to the right of the caravan. A motley mob of enraged, howling creatures scrambled out from the cover of the rocks. They wore little armour, many of them were just scrawny, sickly peasants with rusted swords and axes, but mixed among their numbers were a half-dozen or so larger loping shapes, filthy fur hanging in mangy strips from their twisted bodies, massive horns rising above their bestial heads. In all, the ambushers added another thirty to the numbers of the caravan's attackers.

The spirits of the mercenaries faltered as they saw the diseased mob sprinting toward them. Many of the wagoners gave cries of horror and despair, leaping down from their seats and racing to escape the beset convoy. The mercenaries watched them flee with contempt. They were not any more hopeful about their chances, but to a man they would prefer to die standing their ground and smiting their enemies rather than cringing in the woods to be hunted down and slaughtered like an animal once the battle was over.

'Sigmar watch over us!' grunted the bear-like Horst, making the sign of the hammer with the hand that gripped his horse's reins.

Brunner shook his head. 'He may watch, but expect nothing more.' The bearded mercenary glared at the bounty hunter's impious remark. 'Look to your steel, that is the only thing that will see you through to the day's end!'

Then the time for talk and prayer was at an end as the Chaos warriors struck the mercenaries' line.

THE MARKSMEN HAD accounted for eight of the armoured Chaos warriors by the time the degenerate plague worshippers closed with Zelten's front line. There was more than enough to go around for Zelten, Horst, Brunner, and the half-dozen foot-troops who had advanced to support them. Half of the other mercenaries had fallen back to support the rearguard, taking two of the marksmen with them, leaving only Schtafel and another crossbowman to continue to pick at the raiders attacking their front. The fighting was brutal and savage, with no quarter asked or given by the combatants of either side. The plague worshippers fought to honour their diseased god, throwing themselves into combat with a reckless abandon, giving no thought to defence as they slashed and hewed at their foes. The mercenaries fought with just as great a determination, knowing that their lives and possibly their souls would be forfeit if they failed to repel their awful adversaries. But the mercenaries fought more defensively than the plague warriors, and they fought as soldiers, not frenzied beasts, each man acting as a part of a whole, supporting and assisting their comrades. The plague warriors fought as individuals, pushing one another aside to reach their foes, giving no thought to helping their fellows, only to rending the clean, unblemished flesh of their enemies. For every one of the mercenaries who fell, two of the plague warriors spilled their life from pierced bellies and split skulls.

Yet they were losses that could be ill afforded. The weight of numbers was in the favour of the plague warriors. Brunner swore as he slashed the edge of Drakesmalice through the helm of a Chaos warrior, removing the top of the degenerate's skull. It was the third such to fall to his sword, yet still it was not enough. Four of the mercenaries were down, and the last two were hard-pressed by four of the remaining plague warriors. Two more of the armoured scum were sprinting toward the wagons, determined to end the sporadic fire coming from the remaining marksmen.

Zelten was down, his horse gutted by a plague warrior's axe, and the mercenary captain was now trying to finish off the raider who had killed his mount. Horst was still in his saddle, his flail clotted with blood and brains. Brunner could see perhaps a half dozen plague warriors strewn around the man, their helms crushed out of shape by the mercenary's violent blows. Horst's eyes cast a vacant, empty glance across the battlefield, unsettling even to the bounty hunter in their homicidal intensity. Foam dripped from the man's beard as he gave voice to a loud war cry and rode toward the embattled swordsmen.

Brunner took in the state of the battle around him quickly, then his eyes watered as an unspeakably vile stench filled his lungs. Fiend reared beneath him, threatening to toss him from the saddle. Brunner fought to restrain the warhorse. He could not fault the animal its reaction, he had himself hoped to never endure that smell again. A black buzzing host of flies swirled about Brunner as a huge monster charged toward him, the hooves of its diseased horse crushing the bodies of mercenary and plague warrior alike as it surged forward.

'Brunner!' the droning echo that served Pulstlitz as voice buzzed from the Chaos champion's helm. 'Zhiz zhime you die!'

The bounty hunter watched as the plague knight rode toward him. With a smooth, fluid motion, Brunner released Fiend's reins and drew his pistol. He'd known as soon as he'd recognised Pulstlitz that this moment would come and had prepared for it as best he could. Yet he had not counted on Fiend's violent agitation to the plague champion's aura of filth and pestilence. If the horse reared now, he'd be thrown.

The pistol exploded as Brunner pulled back the trigger. The steel ball hurtled into the avalanche of corroded steel and diseased flesh that was Pulstlitz and his loathsome steed. The rheumy ball of pus that served the plague steed as an eye burst like a squashed grape, spattering mucus-like phlegm across its barding as it ruptured. The ball tore through the decaying substance of the infested animal's skull, ripping apart its brain. The plague horse gave a low, painful neigh, rearing away from the discharge, arresting its advance. Then the horse fell, slamming onto its side, pinning its diseased rider beneath it.

Brunner breathed a sigh of relief as he dropped the pistol from his gloved hand and reclaimed the reins. As if sensing its master's danger, Fiend had quieted the moment he had released his grip. The bounty hunter muttered a few words of gratitude, then urged his horse toward Pulstlitz's slain mount. He found the loathsome plague champion trying to wriggle out from underneath the dead mass of his steed. The insect-shaped helm shifted, glaring at Brunner as he advanced. Pulstlitz grasped for where his sword had come to rest after his fall, but the diseased warrior was unable to reach the blade.

'This time you don't walk away,' declared Brunner. Pulstlitz snarled up at his enemy, the sound rumbling from deep within his armour. Suddenly, Brunner was struck from behind, falling from his saddle to crash down on the top of Pulstlitz's slain horse.

The bounty hunter found himself lying on his belly, his lungs filled with the rotten stink of the diseased horse. Brunner lashed out blindly with Drakesmalice to fend off whatever had attacked him, sweeping the sword behind his back. He rolled his body, facing upward just in time to ward off the blunt knobby head of a massive iron mace.

The shape behind the crude weapon could no longer be called human, if it could ever have been. It was a hulking mass of lice-ridden fur and boil-blemished flesh, its huge chest rippling with muscle despite the sickly green that coloured fur and flesh alike. The beastman roared, its goat-like head lifted in feral anticipation of crushing the skull of its defiant foe.

Brunner tried to stab his sword through the Chaos monster's unprotected belly, but found that he was unable to rise. Powerful steel-clothed hands had closed about his shoulders, holding him down. From beneath the carcass of the horse, Pulstlitz laughed in the bounty hunter's ear. 'Zhiz zhime, you donz walk away,' the droning sound of the Chaos champion buzzed.

Brunner struggled against the plague champion's clutch, his eyes locked on those of the diseased beastman as it raised its weapon. The pestigor's inhuman features split into an expression of supreme confidence and triumph.

A moment later, its expression was one of shock and horror as the beastman's foul blood cascaded down its face from the wound in its forehead where a crossbow bolt had ripped through its skull. The knobby mace fell from the pestigor's suddenly lax claws and a moment later the monster crashed to the ground beside its weapon.

The grip of the plague champion grew slack for a moment as Pulstlitz watched his warrior fall, as surprised as the pestigor by its sudden demise. Brunner exploited the diseased marauder's moment of inattention to break away from his grasp. The bounty hunter quickly regained his feet, staring down at the trapped Pulstlitz. He brandished Drakesmalice before the struggling Chaos knight. The metal of Brunner's sword seemed to blaze with orange flame, reacting dramatically to the overpowering taint of the Chaos champion. Despite himself, Pulstlitz recoiled from the magic blade as a spasm of fear wormed its way into his diseased frame. The Chaos champion, with a superhuman effort stretched his trapped body, his hand closing on the hilt of his fallen sword. As Brunner swung Drakesmalice downward, Pulstlitz swept his rotted blade upward, its infected metal crashing against the blazing edge of Drakesmalice.

The two swords groaned as they met, Drakesmalice burning yet more brightly as it came into contact with the plague champion's blade. There was a bright flash of light, then the shriek of tearing steel as Pulstlitz's sword was shorn in two. Unimpeded, Drakesmalice drove downward into the arm behind the broken blade, tearing through the plague knight's armour.

The droning tones of Pulstlitz's voice echoed in a mad scream as his arm fell away. From the ruptured, penetrated armour, hundreds of shiny black bodies crawled forth, scattering across the battlefield. Brunner smashed one of the fleeing cockroaches under his steel boot as it fled, then lifted Drakesmalice once more.

'Now you meet your filthy god!' the bounty hunter snarled, swinging Drakesmalice into the neck of the Chaos champion. The insect-like helm flew away, clattering across the ground. A fountain of vermin exploded from the hole at the top of Pulstlitz's body armour, the insects spilling to the ground in a crawling flood. Brunner could see that more of the disgusting insects were also creeping from the empty helm of the Chaos champion. He smashed several more underfoot and walked over to the helmet. Brunner kicked it over, gazing at the now empty steel. Long in the service of the Chaos Lord of Decay and Corruption, Pulstlitz's body had been consumed by the evil he worshipped, until at last he wore not one body, but thousands. Now, with the controlling spirit of the Chaos champion gone, the vermin were evacuating the armour that had contained them and given the plague knight form and substance, crawling back to the filthy holes from which they had once been summoned.

Brunner lifted Pulstlitz's helmet high over his head then set up a loud cry, hurling the empty helm at the closest of the Chaos warriors. The diseased raiders set up a cry of agony and horror as they saw the evidence of their champion's defeat, at once abandoning their fight with the mercenaries. News of Pulstlitz's death quickly spread to the rabble and pestigors attacking the rear of the column and the ambushers quickly turned tail and ran. Their flight was hastened by the frenzied one-man charge of the mercenary Horst, who rode down and slaughtered as many of the degenerates as he could catch before they reached the security of a nearby patch of forest.

The bounty hunter turned away from the empty armour of Pulstlitz, sheathing Drakesmalice and clutching at the spot on his side where the pestigor had struck him from Fiend's back. The armour had absorbed most of the force of the blow, and Brunner could detect no broken bones beneath the skin, yet such knowledge did little to offset the numbing pain. Still, he had little time to spare for his own hurt, and made his way about the battlefield to reclaim his horse. He leaned upon Fiend, resting his weight on the warhorse as his eyes swept the area for any sign of his pack horse. He was still in such circumstances when Manfred Zelten strode towards him, the old veteran Mietz and the wiry marksman Schtafel at his side.

'How'd we do?' the bounty hunter asked Zelten as he came near. The mercenary's expression was grim, but not entirely without an air of triumph.

'We lost ten, and I have another four wounded that probably won't make it to Remas,' Zelten stated. 'Especially since their wounds are certain to become infected. The magic of these plague worshippers is potent, and fast.' Zelten shook his head. 'Still, we took nearly three times as many of them. Though I have to confess that if you hadn't taken their leader and broken their resolve, it might have gone the other way.'

'You should thank your man there,' Brunner said, pointing a gloved finger at Schtafel. 'If he hadn't finished that brute who was preparing to brain me, I wouldn't have had my chance at their leader.'

The marksman looked away, somewhat unnerved by the statement. When he looked back, his eyes were just as suspicious and wary as before. 'Sometimes a man has to decide between two evils.'

Brunner's eyes were just as cold as he returned Schtafel's stare. 'Then I am glad the decision went my way,' he said.

It took an hour before the caravan was under way again. The wounded had to be made secure in the wagons and Zelten insisted on burying their own casualties, though the swiftly decomposing bodies of the plague worshippers were left to rot where they had fallen. In that time, a few of the wagoners emerged from the trees to rejoin the convoy. Emiliano Tacca overrode any talk of waiting for the other men to return, decrying them as miserable cowards, though the stout merchant had spent the battle cringing under the bed of one of his wagons. It was noted that the merchant seemed especially wary of the trees and rocks, and it was the return of the raiders, not his men that so agitated the man.

There were now only five riders to form the vanguard of the column, the other two claimed by the diseased spears of the pestigors, and Brunner took his place among them.

III

THE SUN WAS just dropping into afternoon as the caravan drew within sight of Remas. The road had been long, but after the attack by the plague warriors, there had been no further attacks. Seated on their horses, Brunner, Zelten and the other mercenaries gazed upon the mighty city. Built upon the tip of a vast peninsula, nearly one hundred miles

in length and almost half as broad, the city completely surrounded a giant lagoon, a body of water almost perfectly
round in shape. Long had been the speculation that the
lagoon was no natural formation, but some vast undertak-
ing constructed by the long departed elves. Great blocks of
masonry stabbing upward from the lagoon like fangs of
stone and other ruins lying just beneath the water certainly
gave evidence that the elves had exploited this place, even if
they had not created it.

Whatever its origins, the elves were gone now, and where
their outpost may once have stood, men had reared a still
greater city. The tiled roofs and plastered walls of Remas
spread across either side of the lagoon, surrounding it completely on its landward edges. The mouth of the lagoon was
also claimed by the city, a colossal bridge spanning the
entire length of the lagoon's narrow mouth, rising high
above the water on mighty stone piers, allowing the swift,
sleek warships of Remas easy access to the sea. Upon the
bridge, grand palazzos stood, their balconies facing outward
toward lagoon and sea. These were the houses of the wealthiest of Remas's merchant princes, those who made up the
ruling council of fifty and the triumvirate who was elected
from those ranks to decide how that rule would be directed
and enforced. On either end of the bridge, great towers
stood, leaning away from the bridge at impossible angles, as
though at any moment they might escape the support of
their many buttresses and crash into the sea.

On either side of the bridge, the vast sprawl of the main
city stretched. An inner wall of massive stone blocks enclosed
the oldest portion of the city, hugging the coastline in places.
This eventually met a second wall, larger and thicker than its
predecessor, which likewise hugged the coast before sweeping inland to enclose a still larger amount of the peninsula.
Along the coast, this second wall met and joined with an
equally enormous wall of much later construction and even
more impressive proportions. Twenty men standing one atop
the other should not have been able to reach the top of the
outer wall, and the thickness of the barrier was such that two
companies of double-ranked pikemen could pass one

another without disturbing their formations. Towers and guardhouses rose from this wall every hundred feet or so, crossbowmen keeping a wary watch as they patrolled the battlements. Like the older walls, the outer wall hugged the coastline for much of its distance before turning inward and bisecting the peninsula, forming an unbroken barrier of stone from shore to shore, completely enclosing the lagoon and the city built around it.

Between the first two walls, on a great rise of land, the skeletal remains of the mighty fortress of Remas yet stood. It was a relic of older, darker times, when tyrannical despots lorded over the city, long before the enlightened rule of the republic. The fortress had been largely cannibalised by the citizens of Remas in the centuries after the founding of the republic, the stones from its walls used to build the palazzos of the city's leading families upon the giant bridge at the mouth of the lagoon, for it was felt that the very presence of such a castle in the city would feed the ambition of some future tyrant and no man could be trusted with ownership of the place. The fortress had briefly risen from the rubble into which it had fallen during the short despotic rule of Omilo Mondo as the self proclaimed Prince of Remas tried to repair the castle and so fortify his rule. But with Mondo's death, the reconstruction of the fortress was once again prohibited and it now languished as a forlorn pile of rubble overlooking the inner city.

Much more impressive was a mammoth structure located in the outer city, overlooking the sea. Its spire reaching nearly two hundred feet into the sky, the Temple of Solkan had taken nearly three hundred years to complete. A vast, megalithic building, giant columns of flawless white limestone imported from Araby fronted the plaster-covered walls that enclosed the shrine to the grim god of vengeance and order. Nowhere else in the Old World had the worship of harsh Solkan, the Fist of Retribution, found so firm a hold as it had in Remas, and such a gigantic shrine to the Master of Vengeance was unique to the city. Even from the distance at which they gazed upon the city, Brunner could see the giant golden fist topping the spire of the temple gleaming in the sunlight, as though it would reach up and drag down the sun should that celestial body offend the pitiless deity.

'Remas,' muttered Zelten as they slowly began to descend toward the peninsula. 'Never thought I would ever think of such a place as being home.' He smiled and stared over at Brunner. 'I imagine a man like you has travelled widely?'

'No,' Brunner replied, his eyes still fixed on the familiar symbol of Solkan. He'd had an unfavourable experience with an Estalian bounty hunter named Osorio, a fanatic worshipper of the Fist of Retribution, a few years past in the city of Tobarao, an event that had coloured his attitude toward Solkan and his followers. 'I've been to many places, but never Remas.'

Zelten's expression grew somewhat severe. 'You should stay with us for a time,' he commented. 'When in Remas, it is best to be in the service of one of the merchant princes. Very unwise to be independent.'

'I've always depended on no one but myself,' the bounty hunter stated.

'Let me put it this way,' sighed Zelten. 'In Remas, you need friends, and the more powerful the better. A man on his own could find himself in very bad trouble. The kind that you don't walk away from.'

UPON REACHING ONE of the three massive gates that provided entry through the outer wall, the caravan was forced to halt. The gateway was teeming with activity, no less than three other caravans vying for entry into the city. The mules and horses of the other traders snorted and stomped at the rancid city smell wafting outward from the gateway even as their drovers tried to quiet them. Mercenary guards in the armour of a half dozen lands glowered at one another, their already foul moods turned still more sullen by this last delay to their journey's end, this final obstacle between themselves and the taverns and brothels of Remas. In the gateway, the merchant owners of the caravans haggled with the guards at the gate, trying to reduce the custom the soldiers expected to exact on their wares. The raised voices of the merchants drifted back to Brunner as Emiliano Tacca climbed down from his wagon and made his way toward the gate. Tacca spoke a few quick words to one of the guards, imposing himself between the soldier and one of the other caravan masters. The man's angry glare became somewhat homicidal as the soldier nodded his head and waved Tacca's caravan forward. The other trains parted before the caravan, the muleskinners and mercenaries glaring at Brunner and his companions as they passed by.

Beyond the gates was a wide square, large numbers of burly-looking men sitting in the shadow of one of the walls. As they saw Tacca, representatives from each gang hurried forward, loudly offering their services to unload the wagons for the merchant. Tacca dismissed the men, and the imposing sight of Horst and several of the other mercenaries did much to silence the protests of the draftsmen. They settled back into the shadow to await the next caravan. Other individuals hastened forward as the draftsmen retreated, peddlers and street sellers offering sips from jugs of water and dried fruits to the newly arrived travellers. These fared a little better than the draftsmen had, and several of Zelten's soldiers and Tacca's drovers parted with their silver for such welcome refreshment.

Brunner took in the city he now found himself within. The walls at his back were high, imposing things, casting their shadow across much of the square, yet the buildings in the immediate vicinity were much less imposing, most of them no more than two storeys tall. There were a number of inns and stables fronting on the square, each sign swaying before their doors promising better service and lower prices than that of their neighbours. The street leading away toward the south was wide, and Brunner could see quite a bit of foot traffic trailing away in the direction. Toward the north, the street ended in a small plaza surrounded by inns. A number of streets snaked their way toward the west, but unlike the wide lane leading south, these were narrow and Brunner could see no one walking them.

Tacca's wagons and several of the mercenaries turned south, destined for the warehouses where the merchant would store the goods they had brought back from

Miragliano. Zelten shared a few words with the merchant, then brought his horse around.

'I've left Mietz in charge of things here,' Zelten told Brunner. 'We're going to go ahead of him and let Prince Gambini know that we're back.'

'Prince Gambini?' Brunner asked, his eyes suddenly narrowing with suspicion.

'Oh, yes,' Zelten said. 'He is our employer. He charged us to accompany Tacca up to Miragliano. Apparently Emiliano Tacca has some hopes of arranging a new trade agreement with Prince Borgio. I'm certain that he will be most anxious to know that we have returned.'

The bounty hunter remained silent as he followed the mercenary captain into the narrow streets of the city. Once away from the teeming press of bodies near the outer wall, and the traffic passing to and from the city, the numbers of people began to diminish, falling off drastically the further the two men rode away from the wall. Soon, only a few furtive figures were visible on the street ahead: fearful, downcast citizens hurrying along the streets, eager to reach their destinations. Compared to the din of hawkers, travellers, and beggars that filled the air in the other cities Brunner had been in, the silence that filled the streets of Remas was eerie and unnatural.

'This place is like a graveyard,' the bounty hunter commented as they made their way along yet another deserted stretch of road. Zelten favoured Brunner with a grim look.

'It is much more lively the closer you get to the docks and the tavern district,' Zelten said. 'But up here, the people keep to themselves.'

Brunner shook his head. 'Keep to themselves? I've smelled fear before, and I can tell you that it is thick enough here to choke the life from a man.' Brunner looked around, watching as a swarthy face hastily withdrew behind the edge of a window. A moment later a thick wooden shutter slammed close. 'What I don't understand is what these people fear. I see no soldiers about, and by all accounts the rulers of this city are fair-minded and even-handed in their policies, no worse than any other and better than most.'

'Better not to ask, my friend,' Zelten advised. 'Those who get too curious don't prosper very well in Remas.'

Suddenly a sharp scream broke the silence. Brunner and Zelten at once grasped their weapons and the bounty hunter spurred Fiend ahead, eager to find the source of the sound. Ordinarily, he was much more cautious about minding his own affairs, but the almost tangible dread in the city had set him on edge and it was with an amount of eagerness that Brunner anticipated confronting whatever trouble lay ahead. Zelten hesitated a moment, then spurred his own horse to keep up with that of the bounty hunter.

The screams had died down into frightened, choking sobs and a harsh voice, shouting. The sounds came from directly ahead of the two riders and soon the source of the trouble became all too clear. Brunner's gloved hand slowly worked his pistol from its holster and he noted Zelten's grip on his sword tighten.

The two men found themselves at the mouth of a small plaza, a large, ornate fountain bubbling in the centre, depicting some impossible mixture of man and fish spitting water into a great stone clam shell. The buildings opening upon the plaza had the look of shops, but their doors and windows were closed tight, shutters drawn. There was but a single exception, a small baker's shop. The door to this establishment had been knocked from its hinges and was lying in a splintered pile just within the threshold.

In the centre of the square, in the very shadow of the fountain, a group of men stood. They were dressed alike, white cloaks thrown over leather tunics and breeches, their faces covered in plain, featureless masks of polished white wood. Though featureless, the faces of the masks were not without expression, locked as firmly into a single emotion as the classic tragedy and comedy masks employed by the playhouses of the Empire. The expression so firmly stamped upon the wooden masks was that of an angry, judgmental disdain. Upon the left breast of each of the men's cloaks was worked the symbol of a golden fist.

Two of the men struggled to hold onto a squirming woman, her clothing drenched and in disarray, her long black hair hanging about her face in long dripping strands. A third cloaked man had a grip on her head, the eyes behind the mask that hid his features fixed upon a fourth cloaked figure. This masked man stood slightly distant from the fountain, shouting in a loud, stern voice, turning his head frequently that he might address each of the buildings fronting the plaza, clearly intending his words for those citizens cowering behind their locked doors and shutters.

'Know that this foul creature, this harlot and speaker of falsehoods has blasphemed against you!' the speaker stabbed a bloodied finger at the sobbing woman. 'She has profaned the marriage bed, deceived her husband and lord!' The masked man pointed his finger upward, indicating a badly beaten, water-logged shape dangling from a noose cast across the outstretched arm of the fountain's central statue. 'She has drawn him to wretchedness and iniquity, to value her vile flesh more than the honour of obeying and serving Mighty Solkan, he whose justice is certain, whose retribution is swift!' The speaker inclined his head slightly and the man holding the woman's head savagely forced her face into the pool of the fountain.

'Know that this woman, through her profane lusts has been seduced by those powers righteously called ruinous! Through her lusts, she has nurtured Chaos within this most exalted city, this temple to our divine protector! She has profaned and defiled the immortal spirit of her own husband and cast him screaming from the grace of Mighty Solkan!' The masked speaker nodded his head again and the woman was withdrawn from the pool, gasping and spitting water from her lungs. 'She shall confess her evils, Mighty Solkan, before your swift retribution shall bear her to the black pit of atonement that is the reward for all who would hearken to the lures of Chaos!' The zealot glared at the sputtering, gasping prisoner and nodded his head again. Once more, the woman's head was plunged into the pool.

Brunner watched the scene unfolding before him with a mixture of loathing and anger. The pistol gripped in his hand began to rise as his cold gaze locked upon that of the shouting zealot. Almost instantly, a gloved hand reached over and arrested the bounty hunter's action.

'Don't,' warned Zelten, his voice almost lowered to a whisper. 'There is nothing you can do. This sort of thing happens all the time in Remas. The cult of Solkan is powerful here, and its followers most zealous.' Zelten released Brunner's hand and turned his horse's head. 'Come, we'd best find another path to the palazzo.'

'Too late,' commented the bounty hunter. As Brunner said the words, the temple militia began to detach themselves from the fountain, leaving only one of their number to restrain the woman. Zelten groaned as he saw them walking forward, each of the white-garbed zealots drawing a heavy wooden cudgel from beneath his robes. They seemed almost unreal as they advanced, phantom forms without shape, their white wooden masks stern and uncompromising.

'For Sigmar's sake,' Zelten addressed Brunner through the corner of his mouth. 'Don't kill any of them!'

The bounty hunter's face twisted into a feral smile. 'That depends entirely on them,' he told the mercenary. The foremost of the Solkanites was just rounding Fiend's head, the brown eyes staring out from behind the wooden mask fixed upon Brunner. A second zealot strode toward Zelten, while the third maintained a position in front of both riders, clearly thinking to grab the reins of the animals should the two men think to flee.

The militiaman near Brunner looked the bounty hunter over from head to toe, then looked to the other zealots. 'More foreign scum!' he declared. 'Mercenary swine brought from lands where they know not the light and the glory of Mighty Solkan!' The ringleader of the zealots glared into Brunner's icy eyes. 'How long must we suffer such filth to profane the streets of our holy city with their...'

Whatever words the Solkanite thought to conclude his diatribe with were knocked back down his throat as Brunner smashed the heavy wooden butt of his pistol into the man's mask, cracking both the white wood face, and the jaw beneath it. The zealot fell into a heap, coughing and spitting blood and teeth through the splintered mask. At the same time, Brunner drove his spurs into his horse. Fiend reared up, front legs kicking forward. The zealot before the animals fell back, alarmed by the sudden eruption of violence from the animal and the man who rode it. But he did not withdraw far or quick enough, one of Fiend's flailing hooves crunched against the side of the man's skull, tearing the white cloak and throwing the stunned militiaman to the ground.

Zelten reacted to Brunner's attack far more quickly, kicking his foot into the midsection of the Solkanite beside his horse before the man had time to even begin raising his cudgel to strike the mercenary. Air exploded from the zealot and the man doubled over, clutching his chest and trying to gulp air back into his lungs.

Brunner had some satisfaction watching the last standing zealot in the plaza release his hold on the woman and race off down the street. But what satisfaction he felt was quickly vanquished as a second group of white-cloaked men strode into the square from one of the side streets. This time, there were ten of the masked men, many of them carrying swords or axes instead of clubs. Still more intimidating, however, was the towering apparition who led them. Nearly seven feet tall, his body encased in a suit of blackened plate armour, a black hooded cloak cast about his shoulders, the face of the leader was hidden behind a mask similar to those worn by the zealots, but made of gold rather than wood.

The sight of the huge warrior made Zelten curse colourfully under his breath.

'An inquisitor of Solkan!' the mercenary swore. 'Now we're in the fire!'

The towering warrior Zelten had identified as an inquisitor strode forward, well ahead of the white-garbed temple militia. As he did so, the huge warrior drew an enormous hand-and-half sword from its scabbard, the polished metal of the blade gleaming in the sun. Brunner could see the fiery, fanatic gleam in the eyes watching him from behind the golden mask, could see that here was a foe who would show no quarter, who was as prepared to die as he was certain that no man would best him in battle. The bounty hunter began to raise the pistol still gripped in his hand, then noticed that in smashing the zealot's face, he had dislodged the firing cap.

With a disgusted motion, Brunner holstered the weapon and drew Drakesmalice from its sheath. The bounty hunter was an excellent judge of a man's combat prowess, able to ascertain from the way a warrior moved, the way he gripped his sword, the look in his eyes, how proficient with the blade he was. The man he now faced displayed the qualities of a master duellist, with the build of an ogre to support his skill. Even if Brunner might hope to match the inquisitor's ability, he knew there would be no way to match his prodigious strength.

The inquisitor halted several paces away from the horses, his gaze encompassing both the riders and the injured militiamen strewn about them. When the armoured giant spoke, it was with a voice of steel and thunder. 'You have laid hands upon servants of Mighty Solkan engaged in their holy duties,' the inquisitor stated, his rumbling voice surprisingly level for all the fire in his eyes. 'To do so is to forfeit one's life.' The zealots filed to either side of the inquisitor, their weapons held before them.

'Prepare to taste holy vengeance!' the inquisitor snarled. He took a step towards Brunner, his gigantic sword raised. Then the sound of numerous hooves clattering upon the cobbles caused the huge man to step back. Brunner and Zelten each risked a glance behind them. Racing toward them was a group of five riders.

Zelten's face broke into a wide smile as he recognised the features of Horst and some of his other men. The mercenaries rode straight toward their captain, falling in line between himself and Brunner.

The huge inquisitor cast his stern gaze across the figures of the mounted mercenaries, then stared at the masked militia to either side of him. Brunner could almost read the hulking war-priest's thoughts. The men he faced were hardened, professional warriors, the men with him were untrained fanatic rabble. He might have been willing to confront two warriors with such a force as he had, but he was less sure of his chances against seven. With a snarl, the inquisitor slammed his sword back into its sheath and slowly stalked to the side of the plaza. The zealots followed suit, some of them scuttling forward to assist their stricken comrades. When the last of the masked fanatics was out of the way, Zelten urged his horse forward at a careful, wary trot. Brunner and the other mercenaries followed close behind the Reiklander.

As he passed the huge inquisitor, the armoured giant's steel voice addressed Zelten. 'The memory of Mighty Solkan is long, blasphemer! When you no longer cringe beneath the skirts of your decadent nobles, you shall answer for this day! The Master of Vengeance is not to be denied!'

Zelten spat onto the cobbles after the inquisitor spoke, maintaining his steed's trot. Soon, the plaza was behind the riders, the glowering temple militia and the huge priest-warrior lost to view. Brunner rode up on the mercenary captain's left while Horst fell in on the man's right.

'That went well,' the bounty hunter commented dryly.

'We were lucky to ride away from that,' said Zelten. He looked over at the wild-haired Horst. 'If you hadn't chanced to take the same path back to the palazzo, I wouldn't like to think about what might have happened.'

Horst cast a sullen look at Brunner. 'Actually, we followed you. When Meitz told us you had ridden off alone with the bounty hunter, none of us felt too good about it.'

Brunner gave a short chuckle as he fixed a new firing cap to his pistol. 'In my line of work, I get pretty used to profiting by people's fear.' Satisfied that the firing cap was firmly in place, the bounty hunter holstered the weapon. 'But I never thought I'd do so in quite that way.'

IV

THE GAMBINI PALAZZO was located mid-way along the enormous Great Reman Bridge. As Zelten's party drew near the massive structure, Brunner found himself impressed by the massive dimensions of the bridge. It was nearly two miles long and almost a quarter of a mile wide, constructed entirely of polished granite, the heavy grey rock supported from below by gigantic stone piers. It was construction on a scale that should have even impressed a dwarf, though there seemed no trace of the influence of demi-human engineers in the simple architecture that bolstered the span.

Both sides of the bridge were entirely covered by massive, elegant palazzos, each of the opulent dwellings trying to outdo the other in the richness of their adornment and the majesty of their facades. The palazzos reached upwards three, four, even five storeys, their structures leaning far beyond the foundations of the bridge itself, supported by their own piers of steel and wood.

Gigantic columns and statuary dominated the fronts of each palazzo, while colourful banners and flags depicting the heraldry of Remas and that of each of the noble houses snapped in the cool sea breeze from every tower and spire rising above the palazzos. In addition to the heraldry, the pennants of numerous mercenary companies flew above the palazzos, a silent reminder to the enemies of a particular house of which band of hired soldiers protected the family and its interests.

The surface of the bridge itself was alive with the traffic of those who had business with the merchant princes, those who would petition the noble houses about some matter of government, servants hurrying about their masters' needs and anxious tradesmen hoping to peddle their wares to the inmates of one of the palazzos, be they master or servant. It was a completely different world from that of the silent, subdued streets where the fearsome cult of Solkan held sway.

Each end of the bridge was protected by a massive iron gate, supported on either side by a pair of towers. Soldiers, elements of the Republican Guard engaged by the Council of Remas for the protection of all the noble houses and ostensibly for every citizen of the city, carefully monitored the traffic passing onto the bridge, turning back any who looked too ragged to have any proper business to conduct. The towers to either side of the gate were enormous, rising high above the bridge, twice the height of even the tallest of the palazzos and leaning out over the water at insane gravity-defying angles that seemed impossible even with the many stone buttresses that rose from the water to support them.

As the small group of riders passed through the gates, they were examined by the guards. However, it was obvious that Zelten and his men were known to the sentries and though they cast a few lingering looks at Brunner, the riders were passed with only a cursory inspection.

Making their way along the bridge, Brunner could see that each of the palazzos was very sturdily built, a small fortress in its own right, despite the ostentatious extravagance that clothed the structures. The windows of the lower floors were narrow, far too small for even a goblin to wriggle through. Only the upper floors were given to great stained-glass panels and enormous skylights, yet even these were less prevalent than Brunner had seen in similar wealthy districts in Luccini and Miragliano.

Between the rich palazzos, at regular intervals, squat grey forts stood, small two storey structures. One of the mercenaries riding beside him mentioned that each of the forts held a battery of cannon. It appeared that many centuries past, the Great Reman Bridge had been sacked by a fleet of elf corsairs, an event that had never been forgotten or forgiven. If such a fleet were ever to dare such an attack again, they would rue the decision.

At length, very near the centre of the bridge, the palazzo of Prince Gambini loomed before the riders. It was one of the larger palaces on the bridge, its plaster walls decorated with extravagant murals and tile mosaics. Before the gates that led into the courtyard of the palace was set a giant stone statue, a leering gargoyle-lion from legendary Cathay. Four halberdiers in heavy steel armour, their helms rising into a short sharp spike, stood at attention before the gate. Zelten broke away from the other riders and saluted Prince Gambini's guards. The sergeant in command of the detail returned the salute, then stepped forward to talk with the mercenary.

'The prince has been very eager to hear of your return,' the sergeant stated. 'You have news for him?'

Zelten shrugged his shoulders. 'Tacca is seeing about getting his trade goods secured for the night. He will be better able to tell his lordship the details of his meeting.' The sergeant nodded as he considered Zelten's words. The guard seemed most sympathetic; the workings of merchants were something far beyond his understanding as well. Then the guard noticed the new man among Zelten's troop.

'New recruit?' he asked, some of the suspicion of a trained sentry slipping into his voice. Brunner met the sergeant's gaze, keeping his own face expressionless and indifferent to the man's interest in him.

'We ran into some trouble on the road back,' Zelten confessed. 'I fear that his won't be the only new face I'll be bringing here.' The sergeant nodded his head, then snapped orders to his men to open the gates. Zelten favoured the man with another salute and made his way into the courtyard, the other mercenaries following behind him. Brunner came last of all, leading Paychest after his own steed. The bounty hunter stared at the walls of the courtyard, at the massive doors of the palazzo itself. He was near his prey now, the bounty hunter could sense it. Now he just had to figure out how he would get his target to reveal himself.

THE OLD WARRIOR loomed above the long table, his keen eyes considering the charts and maps strewn across its surface. The man's grizzled, powerful features wore a look of intense study, a wrinkled finger slowly tapping against a waterway shown on one of the maps. The ring that adorned the finger was huge, depicting a lion's head with a large red ruby stuffed between its jaws. It was as much a symbol of position and authority as the bronze pectoral that hung from a thick gold chain about his broad neck. They were the emblems of rank belonging to a man who had once commanded the army of Remas, the most powerful soldier in all the city.

The general lifted his hand, scratching at his thick grey eyebrow as he considered the map again. It was an old map, dating back many centuries, and he wondered how much accuracy he could allow in the antique document. None of the newer maps showed the canal that had arrested his interest. Had it ever been there? Or perhaps it had been filled, perhaps simply blocked up? Mandalari considered that point. The city of Miragliano had destroyed a good number of their canals after the plague had stricken their city and they had forced back the hordes of the verminous skaven. Tradition held that many of these canals had not been filled in, only bricked over. If this old canal had indeed been simply covered rather than filled, it might be of value to him. He would have to have his next batch of spies check on it, determine what its current state was.

Mandalari stood, stretching his once powerful frame. He was still far from an infirm man, he had not allowed the stamp of age to wither his body, but had fought its approach through a brutal regimen of exercise and the painful ministrations of a waterfront witch purportedly crafted to extend his vitality. Yet the general had to admit that he was but a poor shadow of the man he had once been. Once he had led victorious armies through the still burning streets of half the great cities of Tilea, he had taken his part in the fighting, seeking out the staunchest resistance his enemies could muster and crushing them with his own hands. The general's craggy features split into a stern smile. That had been the life, those moments in the midst of the fray, lungs filled with the smell of blood and fire, ears filled with the war cries of the valiant and the screams of the slain.

But that life was no more, only a mocking shadow of all that he had been now remained. Mandalari limped away from the table, making his way across the cedar-wood floor toward a tall mahogany cabinet. As he walked, his crimson robe swirled about him, exposing the dark wooden post that completed his left leg below the knee. The base of the post was fashioned in the shape of a dragon's paw, and upon its surface had been etched depictions of the general's past victories.

As Mandalari hobbled his way to the cabinet and began to rummage about for yet another folio of maps, the general grimly pondered his artificial leg. The real limb had been crushed by a stone cast down from the walls of Miragliano twelve years past, when Remas had been handed a humiliating defeat by Prince Borgio.

Mandalari smashed the palm of his hand against the side of the cabinet as he recalled the ignominy of his wound. It had turned the tide of the battle, he knew in his heart that had he not been struck down, he would have seen through Borgio's ploy and it would have been Mandalari the Magnificent not Borgio the Besieger who would have carried the day. Instead, the surgeons in his camp had taken his ruined leg and the great mercenary army of Remas had taken to its heels, routed by the timely counter-assault of the Miraglianan host.

The old general savagely pulled the desired folio from among the numerous leather-bound folders within the cabinet and turned to hobble his way back toward the table. But as he turned, Mandalari froze, startled to find that he was not alone. Recognition of his visitor calmed the general's initial surprise and the soldier continued toward the table.

'You should announce yourself before intruding upon your betters,' the general observed. He set the folio down on the table and looked up at his visitor.

The man he addressed idly considered a marble bust resting atop a pedestal near the door leading into the general's bed chamber, a slim hand running along the cold jaw line of the sculpture. Casually, and in his own time, the visitor returned the general's gaze.

'I apologise,' the visitor said at last. 'I did not realise you wanted our arrangement to be better known in the palazzo. I had thought that you wanted me to see and hear and report.' The man smiled, a mocking, snide expression. 'I was unaware that I was to be seen and be heard. I was unaware that a spy should be noisy in his comings and goings. Shall I seek out some of the ogres engaged at the Old Tower and see if one of them might teach me a few things about subtlety and silence?'

Mandalari glared at his agent, his eyes hardening to a sharp edge. 'Do not make light of me,' he warned. 'I am still a general and I will be respected.'

'Indeed,' sighed the visitor, voice heavy with sympathy. 'I sometimes forget that you are a man of such distinction, easily capable of standing on your own.'

The general's mouth twisted into a snarl. 'One day your wit will be the death of you,' he said.

'But not so long as I have such interesting things to say,' the agent winked at Mandalari. 'Isn't that so. I hear and see so many things. There are so many places I can go that you can't. Up steps, for instance.'

'Make your report,' Mandalari growled, face reddening from his agent's scornful abuse. When he once more commanded the armies of Remas, he would take great pleasure in rewarding his spy for the humiliation and indignity of his mocking tongue. Perhaps he would even hand the villain over to the Temple of Solkan. Their inquisitors had a way of making a man regret every breath he had ever drawn before they were finished exacting their god's cruel definition of retribution. For now, however, he would have to continue to endure the spy's flippant bearing.

'Tacca has returned from Miragliano,' the spy said. 'Is that not good news? Does it not do your heart good to see the tensions between our two cities healed by the search for ever bigger markets, ever higher profits? Is not greed the mightiest peace maker of them all?'

Mandalari grew pensive for a moment, then stared hard at his agent. 'Did they... did they meet with any trouble on the way back?' he asked at last.

'Some,' the spy favoured his master with a knowing smile. 'They have lost some men.' The agent's smile broadened into one of condescension and mockery. 'Manfred Zelten was not among those who perished on the road.'

The general smashed his hands against the surface of the table. 'Ulric and Myrmidia!' he roared. 'Everything I have built is threatened by that foreign filth!' Mandalari pointed a thick hand at his agent. 'You will keep your eyes and ears upon this Reiklander! I will not permit this scum to threaten my plans with Prince Gambini! I have worked too hard to set my plans into motion to have them denied by a mere captain of a rag-tag band of brigands!'

'Of course not, general,' the man near the door said, brushing a strand of hair from his face. 'This man will not endanger your ambitions.'

'No, he will not,' the general declared, the thunder of his enraged outburst lurking within his quiet tones. He pointed again at his agent. 'Keep an eye on him. See where he goes and what he does. And report his activities to me.'

'Is that not what I always do?' asked the spy as he turned and slipped away. Mandalari watched him go, then turned his attention back to the table, his eyes burning into the cluttered maps.

There would be war with Miragliano, he would have his revenge upon the city. And no man, be he prince or peasant, would stand in his way.

WITHIN THE GAMBINI palazzo there was a room as bright as the white sands of Araby's shore, as cool as the summer breeze across the plains of Bretonnia. Thick matting of soft pristine fabric covered the floors, vibrant murals depicting quiet pastures alive with wild flowers graced the walls. The furnishings were slender and graceful, crafted of some pale wood from the slopes of the Abasko Mountains, the legs of the dainty tables and chairs forming the downward curves of swan necks, the heads of the birds forming the feet. Upon the tables reposed slender-waisted vases, intricately painted vessels from far Cathay, each worth more than even a modest nobleman in the Empire could brag his fortune into amounting. Each of the vases was filled with fragrant bouquets of fresh white roses, seemingly chosen for their ability to match the trim of the walls, the hue of the furnishings and the dye of the rugs.

The room had been appointed many months ago by Prince Umberto Gambini. In previous weeks it had been alive with the noise of decorators, the protests of artists angered at the hurrying of their trade, and the glowering sentries who ensured that the expensive accoutrements of the chamber did not stray from it.

Now the room held but one occupant, a tall, slender woman with lustrous black hair and milky skin. She wore a long dress of soft velvet, the luxurious fabric hugging her with just a trace of immodest tightness about the waist and bosom. She sat lounging upon a small couch, gazing up at a small delicate cage in which a small black songbird trilled its dainty notes. The lady's eyes were hooded in the half-sleep of idle contemplation, her thoughts far beyond the room, as though carried away by the bird's warbling lyrics. Her comely features held breeding and power in them, and her mouth was pinched into the quiet, secret smile that often heralds the ruin of men.

The sound of light footfalls intruded upon the woman's thoughts and she looked away from the caged bird. Rising to her feet, she seemed almost to glide across the room, so effortless were her movements. As she neared the outer door to the sitting room, the sound of tiny bells jingling overcame the light footsteps she had heard. The lady paused before the door as the portal began to open. For a second, a brief glimmer of worry clouded her fine features, but as she saw who her visitor was, the cloud passed and her face wore a look of excitement and anticipation.

'My lady,' the visitor said, as he bowed deeply before the woman. 'Manfred Zelten has returned.'

BRUNNER HAD TO admit that the Gambinis had indeed found ways to make the most of the reduced space that dwelling upon the bridge had forced them to accept. The stable to which Zelten and the other mercenaries had led their horses was three storeys high, a wooden ramp within the building allowing the animals to be led to the upper tiers and berthed directly above their fellows. Brunner was also surprised to see that the animals on the ground level were not elegant, light-limbed riding horses, nor heavy, plodding carriage horses. Instead, he found himself looking at a motley collection of scarred, thick boned warhorses. Zelten seemed to read the bounty hunter's thoughts as he made the observation.

'The good horseflesh is kept up top, well beyond the muck and the smell,' the mercenary laughed as he handed the reins of his steed to a haggard-looking groom. 'Actually, old Mandalari, the man in charge of Prince Gambini's guard, gave the order to keep all cavalry horses on the lower level where they would be ready if they were to be needed at short notice.'

'Pretty sound reasoning,' commented Brunner as he removed a crossbow and a large leather bag from his packhorse. He nodded to one of the waiting stablehands and the young boy came forward to lead the animal away.

'I understand that he served as general of Remas's army before he lost his leg in battle with Miragliano,' Zelten shook his head. 'Still, if his body is weaker, his mind is still sharp and displays some good tactical sense. Prince Gambini listens to him too. I don't think any other palazzo on the Great Reman Bridge is more ready for another insurrection if such a thing were to come to pass.'

Brunner faced the mercenary, seeming to study him closely. 'That sounds almost like a street hawker's pitch,' the bounty hunter said. Zelten nodded his head.

'You could do worse than hire on with Prince Gambini,' Zelten said. 'Trust me, he's a lot better than most I've taken service with. He actually understands that he doesn't know everything about everything and listens to those around him when they have advice to give. He's not the sort to throw away his men on some mad scheme to retake the Badlands, and that means a lot to a mercenary.'

'That might be why it means little to me,' commented Brunner, unfastening his long-barrelled handgun from the side of Fiend's saddle. 'I'm not one of your mercenaries.'

Zelten reached forward and gripped Brunner's shoulder. 'You could be,' he said. 'I saw you fight, you're good, probably better than me. I could use you. I'm short ten men after the fight with the plague warriors. Recruiting you would go far to filling out that shortfall.'

Brunner shook his head. 'I agreed to come here with you. There was mention that Prince Gambini might be prepared to offer some reward as recompense for my part in defeating Pulstlitz and his mob. That's why I'm here.'

'Don't you get tired of it?' Zelten asked. 'Always on the move, calling no man friend or comrade? Always having to keep one eye open for that knife at your back?'

Another groom came forward and led Brunner's bay towards the stall in which Paychest had been placed. The bounty hunter looked back at Zelten. 'I've done pretty well on my own,' he said. 'I don't think I'd do so well splitting the money.'

Whatever retort Zelten was preparing was lost as the noise of jingling bells sounded from the entrance to the stables. The mercenary and the bounty hunter both turned around. Brunner expected the noise to have originated from some expensive and outrageous harness on some equally expensive and outrageous horse. Instead he found himself looking at one of the oddest creatures he had ever seen.

The man was tall, his arms and legs on the thin side and seemed too long for his body. His face was sharp, the nose upturned slightly, like the bent bill of a finch, the cheekbones high and his skin somewhat pallid, despite the Tilean cast of his features. The man wore a checkered tunic and matching checkered breeches, pale-blue against bright grey. A matching rounded cap sporting an enormous red feather perched atop the man's head of lengthy black hair. The man's thin hands sported a number of gaudy rings and gripped a tall staff of dark wood. Topping the staff was a bronze head, fashioned to resemble a grinning goblin, a pair of silver bells dangling from each side of the head. The eyes that regarded the stables were bright and friendly and his long face was spread by a broad smile.

'I am pleased to be the first to greet you, captain,' the tall man said, bowing slightly at the waist. Zelten strode forward quickly. Brunner noted the haste in his companion's steps and discreetly fingered the grip of his pistol. He relaxed slightly, however, when he noted the bright, eager look in Zelten's eyes. Clearly whatever this foppish shape represented, the mercenary did not regard him as a menace.

'Corvino!' the mercenary shouted. The foppish man bowed his head once more as the mercenary addressed him. Before Zelten could add anything to his greeting, Corvino spoke again.

'I was here to give you a message,' he said, 'and to conduct you to the palazzo with all haste.'

Zelten nodded to the tall man, then looked over at Brunner. 'This may take some time,' he apologised, his words rapidly spoken. 'Please consider my offer again. When Tacca arrives, I'll present you to Prince Gambini.' Having said his piece, the mercenary turned and was led away by the garishly costumed Corvino.

'And who exactly was that?' Brunner asked, directing his question at Horst. The large, wild-haired soldier was leaning against the wall support of the stall in which his horse stood.

'Corvino, Prince Gambini's fool,' replied the warrior, casting a sour look after the departed men.

'You don't sound like one of his admirers,' the bounty hunter said. Horst detached himself from the wall and strode toward Brunner.

'Let's just say I don't share his sense of humour,' the bearded man said, sucking at his teeth. 'Manfred's had some dealings with him, the fool is always bringing him messages at all hours of the day. I'm sure he's gotten Manfred involved in some matter he'd be better off not being entangled with.'

'So, all is not quite as idyllic in the Gambini household as your captain would paint it,' commented Brunner. The bounty hunter rolled his shoulders, resetting the weapons and bags he had removed from his horses. 'Perhaps you might show me where you men are billeted. This gear isn't getting any lighter.'

Horst nodded his head. 'Come along, I'll show you where our barracks are.' Brunner began to follow the warrior out of the stables.

'Once I'm situated, perhaps you might also suggest a good tavern in the vicinity,' Brunner said. 'I imagine that Tacca will be some time ensuring the safe storage of his goods. Long enough that I might have a chance to wash the taste of the road from my mouth.'

Horst chuckled as Brunner spoke. It was the first sign of anything approaching human feeling the bearded mercenary had heard the bounty hunter give voice to. He did not know that the bounty hunter was not looking for ale and wine. His desire to find a drinking hole was not to find drink, but to fish for information. It had been the bounty hunter's experience that taverns gathered as much lore within their walls as any library, you just had to know how to ferret it out. If the soldiers of Prince Gambini frequented a particular establishment, there might be some useful information that the seemingly indifferent bar keeps and serving wenches might have heard and remembered.

BRUNNER WAS LED past the towers on the edge of the bridge, before turning left, toward the lagoon and the waterfront. The bounty hunter knew that Horst's reasons for escorting him were based on suspicion rather than any concern for the bounty hunter's safety, but he was also realistic enough to know that it would save him considerable time having a guide in the unfamiliar city, whatever the man's motives might be. If he decided that he did not want the bearded mercenary looking over his shoulder, it would be easy enough for him to lose the big man.

The streets leading from the Great Reman Bridge to the waterfront were a marked contrast to the blighted, fear-haunted lanes Brunner and Zelten had travelled before. Instead of dour, silent buildings, here thrived all manner of businesses. Alehouses, wine shops, taverns and grog shops were in abundance, their wooden signs displaying names often as creative as they were vulgar. Brothels, fighting pits, gambling houses and weirdroot dens openly enticed their patrons from the street with vividly painted depictions of the vices they offered to sate. Remas was a prosperous city, thriving upon both the mercantile goods brought to the port from lands as near as Luccini to as distant as Marienburg, and as exotic as the cities of Araby. It was not unknown for a trading ship of the elves of Ulthuan or one of the great steam-powered ironclads from the dwarf port of Barak Varr to visit the city. Beyond such trade, the city of Remas boasted the most prosperous fishing fleets in the Old World, their fishermen pulling catches from the surrounding waters and the inland lagoon itself that were unrivalled in any other land. Indeed, much of the vast catch was preserved in salt and shipped across the length and breadth of Tilea, drawing still more gold into the coffers of the city.

The salty tang of the sea was heavy here, the occasional grey-feathered gull circling overhead, its squawking cry adding to the din of the street. Though the close streets denied him any view of the lagoon, evidence of its nearness

was everywhere. The streets were filled with men from
dozens of lands. Brunner could see sailors from Tobaro in
their stripped, loose pantaloons rubbing shoulders with
scar-faced mariners in the blue and gold of Marienburg.
Dusky skinned Arabyan traders, their heads encased in
wound turbans, jostled against black moustached ship cap-
tains from Estalia, croaking, cawing birds perched upon
the shoulders of their crimson tunics. Sometimes a common fisherman would push his way through the crowd, a
net filled with wriggling scaly shapes dripping from his
back, destined for the larder of some nearby grog shop or
tavern.

Interspersed between the houses of entertainment were
crammed all manner of stalls and shops, virtually any ware
imaginable presented to entice the custom of passers-by.
Here, the bounty hunter's progress was hindered by larger
crowds of people and animals, the air a constant murmur of
voices speaking in a dozen dialects and nearly as many lan-
guages. He could see hawkers peddling everything from
dried fish to rusty old pieces of armour to trained, swan-
necked fisher-birds wherever a bare patch of wall gave them
a place to stand.

Entertainers blocked the mouths of alley ways, small
crowds gathered about them, watching with rapt attention
as they performed, sometimes tossing copper, or more rarely
silver, into the upturned hat or bowl set before them.
Brunner saw an Arabyan snake charmer carefully taunting a
fell-looking hooded serpent, swaying its body in time with
the Arabyan's movements, the dusky skinned man sometimes leaning forward to tap the reptile's head with his
finger, much to the thrill of the crowd. Just a few yards away,
across the narrow street, a pretty Strigany woman danced
before a cheering crowd of sailors and soldiers, her shapely
hip batting against the tambourine held in her hand as she
whirled before them.

Brunner was just considering that obviously the stern,
unrelenting discipline of the cult of Solkan must not apply
to this district, that the disciplinarian temple must confine
its activities to the outer reaches of the city, when he noticed

a pair of white-cloaked figures stalking through the crowd, their faces hidden behind their wooden masks. The bounty hunter tensed, hand falling automatically to the hilt of his gigantic knife. Normally, he thought of the Headsman more as a tool than a weapon, but in the thick press of bodies around him, a sword would be unwieldy. What was coming would be work for a knife.

Horst noted Brunner's action and chuckled. 'No reason to be worried about them,' he laughed. 'Not here, anyway. The temple knows better than to try and push the people here. It would be bad for business, and the council wouldn't look too favourably on that.' The bearded mercenary laughed again. 'Besides, the people around here would push back! No, those fanatics prowl around here just to remind people that they're around, to remind the credulous that their heathen god is always watching.'

'I'm surprised that the rulers of Remas tolerate them at all,' commented Brunner as he watched the crowd swallow up the two zealots. Horst shook his head.

'This isn't the Empire,' he said. 'They have strange ideas down here in the south. Odd ways of waging war and odd ways of governing their cities. Remas, for instance, is a republic. No single ruler, but a council of fifty elected and appointed by the good people of Remas, with a triumvirate of their choosing above them. In theory, any citizen could sit on that council, though in practice only the richest of the merchant princes ever do. But even so, they have to be very careful about just how much power they exhibit. There have been numerous wars here, uprisings when some ambitious triumvir decided to try and seize control from the council and the other triumvirs, or when the council itself grew too corrupt and self-serving. Insurrection is probably the biggest thing the inhabitants of this city fear.'

The two men continued to make their way through the crowd. Brunner noticed a few soldiers in the colours of the republican guard walking past them, clearly headed back toward the bridge. What made them noticeable to the bounty hunter was the fact that they were the first soldiers he had seen since leaving the towers behind. As if picking up on his thoughts, Horst continued to explain the state of things in the city.

'Above all, the people feel that they control the government, even if they do nothing more than change which faces fill the council every few years. They don't like any show of force, don't tolerate a large army within their walls, an army that could be used against them.' Horst paused before a man selling small iron bucklers, inspecting one of the small shields before handing it back to the trader and continuing. 'That is where the Temple of Solkan comes in. While the people won't tolerate the council sending companies of soldiers through the streets, who are they to question a god? When the temple was first founded, they were just another cult, just another pack of priests preying on the gullible.'

Brunner caught a note of resentment and scorn in the mercenary's voice as he spoke of the gullible. 'But slowly the council began to see a way that they might turn the cult's fanaticism to their advantage. They began to turn a blind eye to the temple's witch hunts, to their often violent excesses of faith. Those who protested the actions of the temple to the council somehow were found out by the cult and exposed as daemon-worshippers and heretics. Naturally, very soon there was no one willing to stand up against the temple. Where an army of soldiers could not be used to keep the people in their place, an army of religious fanatics has. So long as they don't interfere with the mercantile interests of the city and don't bother the nobles, the temple is allowed to conduct itself pretty much as it pleases.'

Brunner shook his head, marvelling at the ruthless politics of the city. Better a tyrant secure in his position than a gathering of politicos frightened about maintaining their own status.

The two men continued to walk along the busy street, the light of day slowly giving way to the long shadows of the night. Lamplighters began to appear, igniting the numerous oil lanterns fastened to the walls of the buildings that lined the street. Ahead, Brunner could see that the street made a sharp turn. Set in the angle of that turn was a small wooden stage. The bounty hunter could see a pair of the white-cloaked followers of Solkan flanking the structure, though their presence did not seem to deter a small crowd from gathering to watch the performance.

Drawing nearer, Brunner saw that what was going on was a puppet show. A number of robed puppeteers stood above the stage, manipulating several wooden dolls by means of numerous strings leading from the dolls to the wooden handles held by the entertainers. Brunner paused for a moment, watching the curious performance. A number of tiny wooden figures in small cloth costumes pranced about the stage, in what was clearly intended to be fright. A much larger puppet dominated the centre of the stage. It was clothed in a long black cloak, its face that of a grinning skull. In its hands it held a huge scythe. As the deathly puppet swung its scythe, several of the other puppets dropped as though they had been slain.

'I did not realise that the cult of Solkan had dealings with the cult of Morr,' Brunner observed, indicating the puppet show. Like the masked men flanking the stage, the puppeteers also wore white cloaks. Clearly the performance was intended as some sort of passion play, a disguised sermon to minister to the wayward souls of the Reman waterfront.

'No, that's not meant to be Morr,' replied Horst. 'Though I thought so myself. It is some sort of daemon, some fell creature that supposedly nearly destroyed Remas long ago, just after the elves had gone away. According to the cult of Solkan, the daemon was only stopped when Solkan sent a good spirit to do battle with it. They fought, so the cult says, for a year and a day before the good spirit overcame the daemon and imprisoned its soul in a bottle.' Horst allowed himself a short laugh. 'The cult says the spirit sent by Solkan was called a Viydagg, though an elf ship captain I once talked to said that such spirits are associated with a goddess called Arianka, not Solkan. All heathen nonsense if you ask me.'

A feeling of dread began to crawl up Brunner's spine as he watched the puppet daemon continue to cut down the little wooden people on the stage. 'What about the daemon?' he asked. 'Does it have a name?'

'Yes,' Horst answered. 'They call it the Mardagg.'

V

HE LAY RIDGED in his bed, every muscle tensed. The man's skin seemed to crawl where it touched the blanket, as though it was alive with thousands of lice. The man slammed his fists against the mattress, trying to will the sensation away. There was nothing in his bedding, the man knew this, he knew that it was impossible for anything to be crawling across his skin. He boiled his bed clothes every night, accepting the warm dampness in exchange for the possibility of any six-legged thing scuttling across his flesh.

The man gritted his teeth against the tormenting sensation, knowing that he had to overcome it before it grew worse, knowing that he would not. The smell of burning flesh filled his nose and the man groaned. He knew that it was not a real odour, that it was some phantom of his mind, but still its sickly stink made his stomach turn. He fought against the bile rising in his throat. He smashed his fists against the bedding once more, trying to force his senses to obey.

Next would come the sounds. He moaned, praying, begging any god that would listen to spare him the sounds. But no god, it seemed, cared to hear him. First the rattle of chains slithered into the man's ears. Then the sound of harsh, brutal voices, voices snarling and laughing, cruel and wicked in their tones. Then the screams, such screams, echoing through his brain. Louder, louder, and louder still they grew. Why could they not just kill him? Why would the screams refuse to end? The tormented man folded the edge of his blanket and bit down upon it to keep from repeating the shrieks pounding upon the inside of his skull.

He spat it out with disgust. It tasted like blood and filth, the flesh of a rat, raw and salty, its excrement staining its rancid fur. The man moaned again, fighting to keep the sound from rising into a scream.

What would happen if he opened his eyes, he wondered? Would he see anything? Would there be anything to see? Oh

please, let there be something to see! Let there be light in his
cell! Let his captors have had that much pity! But he knew it
would be dark, he knew that his captors were without mercy.
If he opened his eyes, he would see nothing, only the blackness of his prison.

The skin upon the man's back began to crawl. It felt as if
it was trying to rip itself free from his body. The agony built
and built, like a red-hot iron slowly pressed against his
naked flesh. The tortured man clenched his teeth against the
pain. He must not give in, he must not submit!

The man's eyes snapped open as his scream filled the
room. His body shook as he felt the agony wash away. No,
it was still there, like a dull ache in the back of his skull, just
waiting to rise up and devour him once more. The man
looked around him. He was still in the palazzo of Prince
Gambini, as he knew he must be. He had endured the terror
many times, yet he was always shocked to find himself
somewhere other than the Caliph of Martek's dungeons. He
sometimes wondered if his escape from that place and all
that had happened after was nothing more than some
dream concocted by his tortured mind. Had he ever really
left that blighted place?

The man shook his head, cradling it in his hands. Yes, he
had escaped the dungeons of Martek, and he had brought
their evil with him. He could still feel the sensation of the
skin on his back crawling. The evil was there, waiting, hun-
gering. Soon it would need to be fed.

The man cried softly, pulling his knees to his chest and
slowly rocking upon his bed. Soon he would have to allow
the evil to feed.

It was quite late when Brunner at last returned to the
Gambini palace. He had spent some time in the tavern Horst
had led him to, an establishment named the Red Horse. As
Brunner had suspected, the mercenary was a prodigious
drinker, and he found it not too difficult to slip from the
man's company once he was in his cups.

Unfortunately, there was little to be learned in the tavern.
Many of the Gambini soldiers did indeed frequent the Red

Horse, but if the man he was after was among them, he had left no clues among the serving wenches and bar keeps. A few pieces of gossip and rumour about the Gambinis were related to Brunner, the eccentricities of Prince Gambini's uncle, the elderly Remaro (none would be so bold as to call the old aristocrat mad) and the peculiarities of Remaro's son, the decadent Alfredo Gambini. But there was little of real value to Brunner's hunt. Certainly a few of the soldiers who had been involved in escorting Princess Juliana down from Pavona had spoken of their important duty, but the few names Brunner was able to pry from the serving wenches' addled memories hardly accounted for all of them. Still, it was a start.

The bounty hunter helped a drunken Horst back to the palace, placing him in the custody of the gate sentries as soon as the guards had allowed the two men back into the courtyard. Brunner paid no attention to their demands that the bounty hunter conduct the nearly insensible mercenary back to the barracks. He had carried the hulking soldier far enough, he reasoned. If he had been certain that the sentries would have allowed him back into the palace without him, Brunner would have left the man to sleep it off in the tavern, to be robbed or rolled into the street as the tavern keepers decided.

Brunner made his way into the darkened palace, picking his path through the marble-floored halls, past the fluted columns that supported the high arching ceilings. He knew his way well enough from earlier to find his way back to the mercenary barracks, though he would feel better once he knew the layout of the rest of the palazzo. It always paid to know the lay of the land.

As Brunner made his way through the dark, quiet halls, his footsteps echoing only slightly on the polished marble tiles, he suddenly saw a light ahead. Instinctively, the bounty hunter stopped, pressing his back against the wall. Most likely it was just some servant getting an early start on the day's duties, but the bounty killer's cautious habits were something that were second nature to him and he had no mind to put them in check.

Brunner watched and saw that the light emanated from a half open doorway just ahead. He could see two figures framed in the doorway, illuminated by a candle in an ornate brass holder, held by a hand that was elegant and smooth, its milky skin as flawless as the marble upon the floor. The woman holding the candle was clad in a thin shift of pale, gossamer-thin cloth, possibly even silk from distant Cathay. The thin garment did nothing to conceal the shapely curves of the woman's figure, displaying her charms as readily as if it had been absent. The woman turned her head at some faint sound from elsewhere in the palace and Brunner could make out her pretty face in its frame of lustrous dark hair. The woman turned back toward her companion, accepting a heavy fur wrap with her free hand and casting it about her shoulders. She leaned forward, kissing the man beside her, then turned and stealthily made her way down the hall.

Brunner waited until the light of the candle had vanished, then continued down the passage toward the barracks. His stride was slower now, his pace careful and measured. When the woman had leaned forward, he had seen the face of the man she had kissed. The bounty hunter had no great desire to alarm Manfred Zelten by catching up with the mercenary as he was stealing away from his midnight rendezvous.

BRUNNER ROSE EARLY the next day, long before most of the mercenaries who shared the hall-like barracks. Horst had said that there were five of these rooms, each given over to a separate mercenary company. After the losses incurred by the warband of Pulstlitz, the chamber held more empty beds than sleeping bodies. Brunner armed himself and marched past the sleeping soldiers, pausing for a moment before Horst's loudly snoring body. Apparently the sentries at the gate had decided to carry him back to his billet after all rather than leaving him to sleep it off in the courtyard.

Near the door to the room, Brunner could see the wiry form of Schtafel sitting in the corner, a blanket thrown about his dozing body, his crossbow lying across his waist. The bounty hunter studied the man for a moment. Clearly he was still extremely nervous about Brunner's presence. The mercenary must have noted his return sometime in the night and decided to stand guard against the bounty hunter. Brunner hoped that the marksman was ready for many such nights of discomfort. He had no idea how long it might take him to sniff out his target, and he had no intention of leaving the Gambini palazzo until he had his prey.

In the hall outside the barracks, Brunner was somewhat surprised to see Zelten emerging from his room. All of the mercenary commanders had their own private quarters, as befitted men of their position. After the man's late night, the bounty hunter had assumed that Zelten would be much later in rising. The mercenary smiled as he sighted Brunner and walked toward him.

'I have spoken with Prince Gambini,' he said. 'He is most anxious to meet the man who saved his caravan. I think I can easily talk him into engaging you if you were to take a position in my company.'

'Perhaps,' Brunner said, noncommittally. 'I'd like to get the feel of the place better before I make any decision.'

'Of course, of course,' beamed Zelten, pleased that the bounty hunter had not flat-out rejected his proposal as he had the previous day. If the truth be told, Zelten was not entirely certain why he was so pleasantly disposed toward the grim warrior. Perhaps it was simply the sword that he wore, a symbolic link to Zelten's destroyed past. Or perhaps it was simply his way of showing gratitude to the man for killing the traitor Albrecht Yorck. Whatever his reasons, and despite the short time he had known him, Zelten wanted to number the bounty hunter among his friends. 'The prince is arranging a feast tonight in celebration of his coming marriage to Princess Juliana Bensario. All of his officers are invited to intend. As a gesture of his gratitude, he has asked that you attend also.'

Brunner was quiet for a moment as the two warriors strode down the marble halls. At last he nodded his head. 'Yes, I think that might prove rather instructive. You may tell the prince that I will accept his invitation.'

Zelten clapped Brunner's shoulder. The bounty hunter winced slightly at the hearty slap, feeling once again a slight sting from the old wound he had been dealt by the orc warlord, Gnashrak. 'I am certain the prince will be pleased to be informed that you will be attending the feast.' The mercenary suddenly looked up. Their steps had carried them toward the main hall, where a large flight of stairs rose toward the upper floors of the palazzo. Descending the stairs were two regal-looking figures. The first was a broadshouldered, handsome featured man wearing a red tunic embroidered with silver braid, sporting tight breeches and polished leather shoes adorned with large bejewelled buckles. He was holding the hand of a young woman. Despite the long, heavy dress of dark green fabric she now wore, Brunner recognised her instantly.

'Ah, you can tell him yourself,' Zelten said. 'There is Prince Gambini now.' The mercenary was surprised when Brunner's gloved hand closed about the front of his tunic and the bounty hunter pulled him back out of the hall.

'What do you mean by this?' demanded Zelten, his voice indignant.

'Tell me who that woman is!' demanded Brunner, speaking in a low snarl.

'That is the Princess Juliana Bensario,' the mercenary replied. Brunner released his grip on Zelten and pushed him away.

'Are you insane, or just an idiot?' demanded the bounty hunter, keeping his voice low.

'Explain yourself!' hissed Zelten, hands balling into fists at his side.

'I saw you last night,' Brunner said. 'Leaving a storeroom. You weren't alone.' He watched as the colour drained from Zelten's face. 'The question remains, are you insane, dallying with a princess, and the betrothed of your master, no less?'

Zelten tried to voice some explanation, but the words caught in his throat several times. Brunner waited for the younger man to collect his thoughts. 'I… I met her when the prince was trying to arrange his marriage with her. My men were charged with protecting Prince Gambini's representatives on the road to and from Pavona. We… we were attracted at once. I don't know how it happened, it just did.'

'They might be saying the same thing when they find your throat slit,' snapped the bounty hunter, his voice tinged with disgust at the mercenary's recklessness.

'You... you won't say anything?' asked Zelten. Brunner shook his head.

'No,' he said, 'I have few enough friends in this world to go around arranging their murders.' Brunner paused for a moment, staring hard into Zelten's eyes. 'I won't tell anybody, but I suggest you show a little more care in your meetings with her, if you are so stupid as to continue them.' The bounty hunter's voice changed suddenly, becoming less emotional, more calculating. 'I won't say anything, but I want to meet with your mistress. There are some things I'd like to ask her.'

Inwardly, a part of Brunner felt disgusted by his exploitation of Zelten's reckless dalliance, but the bounty hunter quickly dismissed the feeling. He had done far worse things than exploiting a friend's misjudgement, things he had never felt any regret for having done. Indeed, this would provide him his best chance at tracking down his prey. The princess was the only person who had left Pavona who he could be certain was not the murderer, and as such was the only one who had made that journey he could make inquiries of without risking alerting his target that someone was on his trail. With knowledge of her activities with the dashing mercenary captain, Brunner would be able to get all the information he needed from the woman. Then it would only be a matter of time before he would be filling his pockets with Prince Bensario's ducats.

PRINCE GAMBINI SMILED at his bride as they descended the wide staircase. They had spent the morning discussing petty arrangements for their wedding, simple things such as the colour scheme that would be used to decorate the small chapel of Shallya that was the venue for the ceremony, the seating arrangement for the guests who would be arriving from Pavona, and a host of other equally small matters. Umberto Gambini was surprised to find that he did not begrudge the time spent on such trivial things. He did not deceive himself that the coming wedding was anything more than a political alliance, a business arrangement to strengthen the ties between Remas and Pavona, designed to cultivate more favourable trade agreements between the two cities. But the fact that his intended bride was such a beautiful and charming lady did not distress Umberto in the slightest. He even considered that he might break off relations with his mistresses once they were wedded.

Umberto laughed at some witty remark Juliana made, squeezing her hand slightly. She made him feel young, as though the weight of position and power were not heavy upon his shoulders, crushing his vigour long before its time. In her presence, it seemed like all the trade agreements and political manoeuvres he found himself dealing with every day were meaningless, as trivial as any of the hundreds of colour schemes and seating plans they had discussed that morning.

The sight of two men climbing the stairs made the smile die on Umberto's face. He had hoped that the day might remain light and somewhat carefree, yet already, it was destined to turn unpleasant.

The foremost of the two men was dressed in a long yellow robe, stylised sirens and sea monsters embroidered upon the fabric in blacks and reds. The man wearing the robe was old, his head worn down to a thin, fleshless shadow of what it had once been. Scraggly wisps of hair were plastered upon the top of his head in a vain attempt to cover it. The old man strode forward, his eyes darting from the prince to his bride with every step he took. Behind the old man, the garishly dressed figure of Corvino followed, looking almost like a devoted puppy, were it not for the sneering, superior look he favoured the old man's back with.

'Uncle Remaro,' the prince greeted the old man. 'You should be in bed,' Umberto cast a chastising look at Corvino. 'The morning chill is not good for your old bones.'

The old man stared at the prince for a moment, then reached out a withered claw. He gripped the princess's dainty hand, pulling it toward him. Juliana smiled nervously, clearly disliking the clammy touch of the old man's cold skin. Umberto, however, remained unmoving, hoping that what he was observing was some sign that his uncle had at last accepted his bride. There had been several instances already where the half-mad Remaro had upset Juliana.

Remaro studied Juliana's hand for a moment, patting it as though it was some small pet. Juliana cast a pleading look at Umberto. Before the prince could react, however, a strange look came over Remaro's face. The old man's hairy nostrils sniffed at the air. With surprising quickness, he lifted the woman's hand to his nose, sniffing at it like a hound. Juliana removed her hand from the old man's feeble grasp, staring at him in open disgust.

'Smells like man's hands,' the old man cackled. 'Have you been touched by a man? Man's hands been touching you? Eh? Hmmm?' Remaro cackled again, climbing past the shocked prince and his bride. Umberto glared down at Corvino as the fool started to follow after the old man.

'I told you to keep him in his rooms,' the prince growled. 'I do not want my uncle upsetting Juliana.'

'I apologise, my lord,' said the fool, bowing his head. 'I thought that it would be safe to take him for a walk while you were busy discussing the wedding arrangements in the sunroom. I did not think you would be about until your uncle was back in his own rooms. I certainly did not intend any discomfort for her ladyship.'

'See that it doesn't happen again,' Umberto said, his voice surly. 'And keep my uncle out of his cups. He has little enough of his wit remaining, I don't want him further put out of sorts by drinking too much.'

'Only a little wine, my lord,' Corvino explained. 'The physicians say it will help strengthen his blood.'

'More than a little, I trust,' sighed Umberto. 'So far as sneaking bottles from the cellar, my uncle's mind is still as sharp as a knife.' He returned his gaze to the fool. 'Keep a better watch on him,' he said.

Corvino bowed again, then hurried up the rest of the stairs, the bells upon his staff jingling madly as he raced to catch up with the elderly nobleman.

* * *

GENERAL MANDALARI SETTLED his body into a leather-backed chair, his clawed wooden leg stretched before him on a small stool. The general slowly swirled the dark brown liquid around in the crystal goblet he held. Then he looked away from his contemplation of the thick Estalian brandy and stared at his guest.

'I am disappointed in you, inquisitor,' the general confessed, unspoken menace lurking in his voice. 'My contacts with the temple recommended you very highly. They said that Gualtiero Bocca was one of the most zealous of the sacred warriors of Solkan.' The general gave a contemptuous snort. 'In my army, I would have had a man like you chopped up and fed to the ogres.'

The man he addressed stood like a black shadow across the room from the seated general, one armoured hand resting on the top of the map-strewn table. Whatever expression Inquisitor Bocca wore, it was hidden behind the cold, judgmental expression of his golden mask. When the inquisitor spoke, however, his voice was anything but cowed.

'The mercenary has only delayed the inevitable,' the priest's words rumbled from behind the mask. 'Those who evoke the wrath of Solkan will find his justice in due time. The Fist of Retribution is as inevitable as the rise of the sun and the turn of the tide.'

'Then your god had best act swiftly,' the general commented impiously. 'Every hour that worm draws breath threatens my plans.' Mandalari sipped at his drink, then set the glass aside. 'If someone else discovers his affair with Princess Juliana, my hold over the woman will crumble. I have worked too long and too hard to allow that to happen.' The general gestured with his hand to indicate the map-strewn table.

'I've urged the council to pursue a new war with Miragliano for five years now. I have the support of one of the triumvirs, but I need two of them to make my campaign a reality. I can bring Prince Gambini to my view, but not if that scheming harpy from Pavona is whispering in his ear every night. She stood against my plans as soon as I revealed them to her.'

'So you use blackmail to keep the tramp in line,' observed Bocca with scorn. The inquisitor was disgusted by the wanton ways of the nobility, but especially by this display of infidelity even as preparations were underway for the woman to be wed to one of the most powerful men in Remas. Once again, the inquisitor thought how much better the city would be without any of the merchant princes, how much nobler the people of Remas would become under the stern discipline of the Temple of Solkan alone.

'Yes,' admitted Mandalari with a laugh, 'I use her own infidelities to ensure her loyalty.' He gave the inquisitor a hard look. 'You should approve of anything that furthers my plans, Bocca. Your temple stands to gain much when my army marches on Miragliano.'

Indeed, the cult of Solkan had been promised a piece of the plunder. Not in gold and treasure, but in power. Mandalari's army would help the cult gain a foothold in Miragliano, help them establish themselves in the conquered city as the cult had established itself in Remas. The high priests of the temple were eager to expand the dominion of their faith in such a manner, to bring the discipline and vengeance of Solkan to the godless scum of the northern city. And from there, who could say. Perhaps every corner of Tilea might yet recognise the supreme authority of the Fist of Retribution.

'You place far too much value on the mercenary,' said the room's third occupant. Bocca and Mandalari both looked over at the general's spy. 'Prince Gambini would not trust rumour and suggestion, he would need evidence. He is deeply in love with his princess, something which you did not account for when you suggested the marriage. It will be hard to convince him of anything that besmirches Princess Juliana's character.' The spy shook his head. 'No, better to forget the mercenary. The pressure that the inquisitor's friends can put upon the council should be enough to sway Prince Gambini. This blackmail of his wife is a useless sideshow that can only hurt your ambitions in the end.'

The spy's face widened into a smile. 'Besides, there is a more immediate problem. You are aware of this mysterious

benefactor who aided Zelten's mercenaries in the ambush?'
Mandalari nodded his head. He had been alarmed when his
spy had informed him that the ambush had failed, especially after he had likewise assured the general that the
expedition to Miragliano would never return to Remas alive.

'I have learned that his name is Brunner,' the agent said. 'A
notorious bounty hunter, who often operates out of
Miragliano.' The spy paused, enjoying the puzzled and
slightly uneasy look of Mandalari's face. 'I understand that
he assassinated some petty baron in the Border Princes not
too long ago. I also understand it is not the first time he has
plied the assassin's trade.'

'You think he may have been sent here to kill me?' asked
Mandalari guardedly.

'It seems rather a coincidence, does it not?' replied the spy
with a smugness in his words. 'An assassin-for-hire leaves
Miragliano and arrives in Remas, conveniently managing to
gain entry to the very house in which the guiding force
behind a plan to overthrow the ruler of Miragliano is
dwelling. I think it would be very dangerous to assume that
Prince Borgio has either forgotten you, or would underesti-
mate your desire to avenge your defeat.'

'He'll not see another sunrise!' roared the general, clum-
sily lifting himself to his feet. 'I'll send the head of this
bastard back to Borgio in a box!'

'Do not worry, general,' soothed the spy. 'I shall deal with
the bounty hunter. I would never allow any harm to threaten
you. Leave it in my hands.'

The spy turned to depart, then faced the general once
again, shifting his gaze from the wooden-legged soldier to
the masked inquisitor. 'If you feel you should kill Captain
Zelten, do so. He may be working with the bounty hunter.
But forget this scheme to coerce the princess. It will only
hurt our plans in the long run.'

VI

BRUNNER HAD TO admit that when Prince Gambini held a
feast, he held a feast, and spared no expense. He could not
even name half of the delicacies offered to Gambini's guests.

Of those that he did recognise, there were Arabyan dates and figs, Estalian duck basted in the hot chilli peppers favoured in that land. A massive marlin, easily nine feet long from tail fin to the point of its sword-like nose, formed the centrepiece of the table. Brunner was surprised at the variety of wines presented to the prince's guests, even including the fabulously expensive yellow-white wine of Lustria among the selections from the prince's cellar.

Despite his usually cautious nature, Brunner was tempted to let himself relax and enjoy himself. Manfred Zelten certainly showed no qualms about doing so, delving into his food with a boisterous gusto which the courtiers seated around him found alternately offensive and amusing. But any inclination to let his guard down was pushed aside when a hulking man in black armour entered the dining hall. His face was hard and craggy, nose and mouth conspiring to form a perpetual scowl. He might not be wearing his golden mask, but Brunner knew he was the warrior who had led the ambush in the streets the previous day. A hush spread amongst the diners as the inquisitor strode past them, making his way to the head of the table and sitting down beside an intense old officer with one leg who Brunner had learned was General Mandalari, commander of Prince Gambini's soldiers and mercenaries.

The murmur of conversation began once more, this time focusing on the inquisitor, whose name was Bocca. It appeared that the Solkanite had been invited by Mandalari, as a way of including the temple of Solkan in Gambini's celebration. It was a political move, but one, it was generally felt, which was in poor taste.

To invite a priest of Solkan might have been understandable, to invite one of the grim inquisitors was not. They were a cheerless, stern and unrelenting sort, suspicious of anyone who did not devote themselves to the temple, seeing heretics and followers of the Ruinous Powers in every face. The inquisitors, the guests whispered, never removed their armour, or their swords, save perhaps within the Temple of Solkan itself. It was a constant reminder to everyone seated at the table that the inquisitor suspected the presence of corruption even at a dinner such as this, and that he was ready to confront it.

Prince Gambini sat at the head of the enormous table, his bride on his left, his uncle, the elderly Remaro, on his right. Beside Remaro was the old man's son, Alfredo Gambini, a rakish youth with a calculating glint in his eye. Seated beside the two Gambinis were the merchant Emiliano Tacca and a black-robed priest of Morr named Scurio.

Scurio was the personal priest of the Gambinis, attending to daily services devoted to honouring the ancestors of the house, as well as performing last rites whenever tragedy might rear its head in the palazzo. On the opposite side of the table, General Mandalari and Inquisitor Bocca took the places to the left of Princess Juliana. It seemed that even the high and mighty were disconcerted by the presence of the inquisitor, even Mandalari, who had apparently invited the man.

The only exception to this trend appeared to be Alfredo Gambini. Bocca took only small portions of the most plebeian of the dishes set before him, causing those around him to rather self-consciously limit the amount of food they placed before themselves. Alfredo Gambini, however, attacked the dishes with gusto, heaping his plate high, openly relishing every bite, sometimes directing a haughty sneer at the grim Solkanite.

Two incidents intruded upon this quietly tense situation, both of which drew Brunner's rapt attention. The first followed close on the performance of Prince Gambini's fool, Corvino. The fool had just recited a particularly ribald bit of prose for the enjoyment of the diners, bringing colour to the faces of the ladies present, laughter from the men and a look of condemnation from Bocca. As Corvino rose from bowing before his audience, he noticed a servant hurrying past him. With a deft manoeuvre, the fool caught the servant's tray with the end of his staff, knocking it from the man's arms.

The servant bit back a curse, bending to retrieve the platter. Corvino, however, pinned it in place with his staff, then began to slide it about the floor, moving it just as the man would bend down to retrieve it, forcing him to chase the platter about the dining room. The fool's antics brought fresh laughter from the diners. Prince Gambini's laugh trailed off in a fit of coughing and the aristocrat fumbled for his wineglass.

'Careful, my prince,' Mandalari laughed. 'You don't want your young lady thinking that you are some sickly, bedridden wretch!'

'I am quite certain of my betrothed's vigour,' Juliana replied, smiling at the prince.

'He gave us some scares when he was born,' the general retorted. 'His mother died bringing him into this world,' he explained, seeing Juliana's questioning look. Prince Gambini grew somewhat sombre as Mandalari recounted the tragedy. 'It looked certain that he would follow her, but his father was not about to lose his entire family. He stayed with the infant all night, keeping him warm with his own hands, telling him over and over again that he would not die, that he would live and be strong.'

'Yes,' muttered Remaro from across the table. The old man's hand was shaky as he spilled some wine onto his lips. 'I stayed with him that night, all through that long night. It was by your father's will alone that you survived.' The old man shook his head, sagging into his seat. 'Would that my own son had been so fortunate.' Remaro began to weep.

Prince Gambini smiled awkwardly at his bride. 'My eldest cousin, Giovanni, was born two months before me. He died shortly after I was born.'

'My son,' Remaro sobbed. Alfredo reached toward him to calm the old man while the others looked away, embarrassed by the dotard's drunken melancholy. As Alfredo touched the old man's arm, Remaro drew away from him, staring at his son as though he were some sort of verminous reptile. Alfredo shook his head with disgust and returned to his meal.

'My son, my son,' Remaro continued to cry. Prince Gambini looked over at Corvino, indicating that the fool should take his uncle back to the old man's room. Even as he was led from the room, the old man's sobbing calls for his infant son echoed across the dining hall. It took several minutes before anything resembling the previous murmur of conversation was restored.

THE SECOND INCIDENT began when Princess Juliana asked a question of the inquisitor. The cult of Solkan was all but unknown in Pavona, the city's experience with the cult limited to a few wandering witch hunters in that grim god's service, and she was naturally curious about this strange religion that held such power in her new home.

'Tell me, inquisitor, do you burn all of the heretics you uncover?' she asked.

Bocca turned his face towards her, his craggy features displaying the first trace of pleasure since he had seated himself at the table. 'When we are able, lady,' he replied, his voice a deep rumble. 'Sometimes the heretics are so steeped in their wickedness that they will not submit to the righteous judgement of Solkan. When that happens,' the inquisitor spread his hands in a gesture of helplessness, 'we must force them to see reason, with whatever means we may muster.'

'Is that true?' Alfredo interrupted from across the table, sucking a shred of marlin from between his teeth. 'I had thought that even the most degenerate follower of the unnamed powers would just shrivel up and die as soon as you mentioned the name of your god.' Alfredo laughed at the remark, though those around him did not seem to find the flippant comment particularly humorous.

'You would do well not to mention such powers aloud,' warned Bocca. 'They are more real and dreadful than you imagine. Than any here imagine, else they should discard these trappings of power and wealth and take up the mantle of the temple. For it is the strength of Solkan that keeps the Dark Gods from devouring us all, body and soul.'

'Are you an expert on the Dark Gods, inquisitor?' Alfredo sneered. 'I would have thought such knowledge would be heresy.' Alfredo's voice dropped into a grave tone. 'You aren't a heretic, are you, inquisitor?'

Bocca's eyes were like daggers, stabbing the baiting nobleman across the table, his hands balled into fists where they lay upon the table. 'I know their signs, how to find their vile

followers. That is all the lore of the Ruinous Powers which it
is safe for a man to know, and even that little must be given
only to those strong enough of mind and spirit to remain
steadfast before such foul forces.'

'Men such as you, inquisitor?' Alfredo asked. 'Tell me,
would you not be better able to recognise the followers of
these powers you call ruinous if you had first been one of
them? Like setting a half-wolf cur to sniff out the lair of a
wolf pack?'

'Those that ally themselves with the Dark are forever
tainted,' Bocca stated, a tone of threat within his voice. 'Be
they great or small, long in the service of the Dark or newly
converted to blasphemy and wickedness, they are likewise
unclean. Only the fire can redeem them, only flame can
purge their evil from the land.'

'No!' interrupted the priest seated beside Tacca. 'That is
not so, inquisitor.' Bocca turned his gaze to the dour cleric,
some of the hostility he had been directing at Alfredo passing from his eyes. 'With all due respect to your temple, and
your position, inquisitor, I believe that the Ruinous Powers
are more insidious than you give them credit for. There are
entire nations that bow before them in the north, beyond
the Sea of Claws and the Troll Country. In every dark place
in the Empire, and even here in the valleys of Tilea, twisted,
malformed things cry out to them from their filthy lairs.
Why then, with so many, do these Powers relentlessly try to
seduce men from civilised lands to their vile worship?'

Scurio paused, letting his question linger. 'It is because we
know what evil is,' he stated. 'What does a Norse reaver
know of evil? He has been born into the profane worship of
the Dark Gods, taught from the cradle to honour and respect
them, to pray to them and serve them. It is all that he knows,
he has never known any other way. But a man from Luccini,
or Tobaro, or Pavona, such a man knows what good is, and
has been taught to recognise evil. Because he must be
brought into the service of the Dark Gods from without, he
sees them for what they are, he has a greater understanding
of what they represent. He knows what good is, what
decency and humanity are, and he rejects them in exchange

for the dark promises of the Ruinous Powers. And because
he has made this choice, because he has polluted his soul
with his own hands, he has greater value to them.'

Alfredo shook his head, laughing slightly as he returned to
his meal. Prince Gambini and the other courtiers nearby
continued to regard the priest, considering his words. Bocca
turned away, rising to his feet.

'Whatever has put the taint upon them,' he told Scurio,
'their fate is still the same. Heretics burn.' Bocca strode from
the dining hall, his black cloak billowing about him.

HE HURRIED HIS way along the corridors, the skin writhing on
his back, as though it were trying to rip itself from his bones.
It had been agony to remain at the feast, to sit quiet and
polite, nodding his head at the inane prattle of the prince
and his guests. The nature of good and evil indeed! There was
only one thing that mattered, and that was the cessation of
pain! Anything that could accomplish that was the greatest
good in all the world, nothing was higher and mightier than
that which would provide relief from his suffering.

The man tried to control himself, pausing beside a column as a pair of servants hurried past, hands knotted into
fists at his sides. He wanted to scream, to cry out, but he
knew that if he opened his mouth, he would never stop
screaming. Because they would call him mad and throw
chains about him and toss him into some pit where the pain
would devour him like a hungry beast until not even his
bones would remain. He watched as more servants passed
him, their arms laden down by the soiled plates and bowls
from the prince's table. It would be an easy thing to fall
upon someone who was encumbered in such a manner. The
easiest thing in all the world. Before they would even be able
to react, it would be too late for them.

The man clenched his eyes shut, his breathing growing
rapid and heavy, like a hound that has just run a hare to
ground. He fought to steady his breath, fought to keep the
desperate, reckless thoughts from gaining a foothold in his
mind. He would be found out, he kept telling himself. He
had to wait, had to wait until it was safe.

'Feeling well?' a voice asked. The man opened his eyes, almost sobbing with relief as he saw the man who spoke to him.

'Help me,' he gasped. The man he addressed smiled, uttering a disapproving chuckle.

'So soon after the last one?' the jovial voice spoke. 'You should try and get some control of yourself. After all, one can't indulge the flesh all of the time, or so the priests say.' He laughed again, a withering, punishing sound.

The tortured man fell to his knees, reaching up with pleading hands. His pained mouth moaned a single word. 'Please.'

The laughter stopped and a soft hand reached down, patting the man's head. 'Just wait a little longer. I'll bring you something very soon.' The speaker detached himself from the pleading man's embrace, ignoring the muttered thanks that trailed after him as he continued on his way down the gleaming marble hall.

THERE WAS A single sharp rap on the door of Manfred Zelten's room, then the portal began to swing inward. Quickly, a figure dressed in black and red checks slipped inside, closing the door behind him. Corvino leaned on his staff, staring at the man seated on the bed that dominated the small room.

'The prince is occupied with Emiliano Tacca,' the fool told Zelten. 'He will be quite some time going over the details of Tacca's audience with Prince Borgio's chamberlain. If you insist on seeing her ladyship this evening, you must do so now.'

'*He* didn't insist, jester,' a cold voice spoke from the corner of the room, just to the right of the door. Brunner stepped into the light cast by the lantern beside Zelten's bed. Corvino recoiled before the sudden appearance of the grim, armoured killer. '*I* did,' Brunner stated.

'Brunner has learned of the matter between Princess Juliana and myself,' confessed Zelten, his voice heavy with guilt. Corvino fixed the mercenary with an outraged, accusing glare. 'He has agreed not to speak to Prince Gambini, but only if he is allowed an audience with the princess.'

Corvino stood for a moment, eyes hooded in a glower of suspicion. At last he nodded his head. 'If such is the agreement you have reached,' his voice was sullen, and there was a tone of menace in it, a quality of barely restrained anger, 'then I must conduct you to her ladyship.' The fool turned to open the door once more. But before reaching outward for the handle, he stabbed the end of his staff against the floor, causing the bells attached to the brass head to jingle madly. 'But if any treachery is plotted by either of you towards the princess...' Corvino left the threat lingering in the room as he opened the door and stalked out into the corridor.

ONCE MORE, BRUNNER entered the crowded streets of the Reman waterfront, guided by a grumbling Horst Brendle. His interrogation of Princess Juliana had been a tense, but necessary affair. Having spent days upon the road with the entourage, she was easily able to recall who had made the journey from Pavona to Remas, though she did not, of course, know the names of each soldier and servant. She did recall that the captain of the soldiers was a man named Giordano, and that he had ten men under his command. There had also been Alfredo Gambini, representing the interests of his cousin, the prince, and the dour priest of Morr, Scurio, as well as three servants to attend Alfredo's needs.

Brunner decided to start with the soldiers, as both Scurio and Alfredo, given their positions within the Gambini household, would prove more troublesome if one of them turned out to be the man he was after. The bounty hunter preferred to start his search with much more easily eliminated possibilities. The captain, Giordano, would be a good start. Even if he was not the man he was after, Giordano would know the names of the other soldiers.

It took only a few words of inquiry on Zelten's part to discover that his fellow mercenary captain was not in the palazzo, but had rather boisterously stated his intention to spend a two-day leave at a bordello called the Pink Rose. Zelten detailed Horst to show the bounty hunter the way. Intent on sleeping off the imported Stirland beer Zelten's men had been given as recompense for not being invited to share in the feast, the bearded warrior was as surly as the animal he resembled. Brunner was not entirely off-set by Horst's bear-like mood. Should any of those zealots of Solkan get in their way this night, they would be leaving with more damage than broken noses and bruised bones. The presence of the inquisitor at the feast had removed any doubts in the bounty hunter's mind as to whether the attack on himself and Zelten upon their arrival had been coincidence or a planned ambush.

After a half-hour of pushing their way through the late-night crowd of revellers, the Pink Rose stood before the two men. It was a large building, standing almost as tall as the Gambini palazzo, but its opulence was a façade, the white plaster covering its walls were chipped in places to expose the stonework beneath, the paint upon the wooden balcony that fronted the structure flaking away. Yet, for all its somewhat decayed exterior, the building certainly had a large amount of traffic passing through its front door. A young man in a brightly-coloured tunic, an outrageous ruffled hat scrunched on his head, stood before the building, his loud voice extolling the delights to be had within in rapid, quickly spoken words. Horst and Brunner pushed their way past the bawd and entered the main parlour of the brothel.

Horst gave a delighted gasp as his eyes took in the lavishly appointed chamber, his surly humour instantly clearing. The room was large, dominating much of the ground floor, filled with cushioned divans, large, potted ferns and palms from Araby, vases of flowers in every shape and colour imaginable, and an ornate fountain with a centrepiece that depicted something Brunner considered to be physically impossible. As rich as the furnishings were, they were but a setting for the smiling faces that regarded the two men as they entered the room. There were at least twenty women lounging upon the divans or sitting beside the fountain, each more lovely than the next, and each in such a state of undress that it seemed to be a competition to see who could display the most flesh without exposing her charms entirely.

Horst let his eyes linger over the company, his face broadening into a grin. 'I take it back, bounty killer,' his words came from the corner of his mouth. 'This was worth crawling out of a beer keg.' Without a further word, the mercenary strolled toward one of the divans, striking up a conversation with a seated woman with the blond hair and pale skin of the Empire while slipping his thick arm about the waif-like waist of a dusky Tilean wench standing beside the couch.

Brunner removed his helmet and strode further into the chamber. He was still for a moment, his practiced gaze studying the room, lingering for a moment on the hulking brutes who sat on chairs against one wall, big Arabyan-style scimitars propped against the wall beside them. The bounty hunter raised his eyebrows. A bullet might not even stop one of those brutes. Brunner hoped that he could accomplish what he needed without attracting the attention of the guards.

'See anything you like?' a soft voice inquired from beside him. Brunner turned his head, finding himself looking at a dark-skinned Tilean woman wearing a loose gown of bright red silk, her generous cleavage straining against the web of white lace that fronted the garment. The woman's heart-shaped face was marked by a knowing smile, a lock of her dark brown hair dangling down against her cheek.

'Actually, I was hoping to speak with the owner of this establishment,' Brunner said, smiling back. 'I have a business proposition for him.'

'Indeed,' the woman commented, shaking her head slightly. 'And what sort of proposal would this be?'

'The sort of proposal that involves gold,' Brunner stated, tossing a small cloth pouch in his gloved hand. The woman's face brightened noticeably as she heard the sound of jingling coins.

'In that case, I think she might be very interested in your proposal,' she said. 'So long as it is within reason,' she added with a wink. She extended her hand toward Brunner with a gesture that mocked the grace of queens and duchesses. 'Madame Rosa, owner of this house of entertainments,' she introduced herself.

Brunner nodded his head, kissing the woman's slender hand. 'I am certain that it will be a pleasure doing business with you, madame.'

GIORDANO PROPPED HIMSELF up on the pillow, staring at the door of the small room, a smug look of pleasure on his face. This was indeed a good way to work off his frustration. He had needed to get away from the Gambini palazzo for a few days, at least until all the unwarranted attention being given to Zelten and his mob of rabble died down. It was woefully unfair, Giordano and his men had escorted the princess herself to Remas, an event of vast import to the future of Prince Gambini. Yet Prince Gambini had thrown only a minor feast in honour of their return, a peasant's supper compared to the event he had arranged for Zelten. All because the cursed foreigner had butchered a mob of starving, pox-ridden bandits! Giordano shook his head at the inequality of it all.

The mercenary's face brightened as the door opened and his supple bedmate of the last few hours slipped into the room. He always liked coming to the Pink Rose. Rosa kept the cleanest girls in Remas, and every one of them was learned in tricks that would shame a sultan's harem. Giordano smiled again as the long-legged girl strode across the room. Then he noticed the heavy iron manacles clutched in her tiny hands. Giordano chuckled.

'Are those for me, or for you?' the soldier laughed.

'They are for you,' a cold voice said. Giordano tore his eyes away from the strumpet. A tall man had followed the girl into the room. He had the look of the Empire about him, his brown hair cropped short, his piercing blue eyes fixed upon Giordano. It was the pistol clutched in the man's gloved hand, however, which drew Giordano's attention. The girl touched his wrist with her dainty hand, causing the mercenary to flinch away. The mercenary froze when he heard the hammer of the pistol draw back.

'Just let her do her job, if you please,' Brunner advised the soldier. Giordano snarled at the bounty hunter, but did not resist as the harlot locked the manacles about his hands after working their chain through the iron bedstead. Her task done, the girl hastily left the room. Brunner strode forward.

'I have a few questions for you,' the bounty hunter said.

'I'll tell you nothing, Morr rot your bones!' Giordano spat.

Brunner sighed and holstered his firearm. 'I had hoped that we could do this the easy way.' Giordano's eyes grew wide with terror as he saw the bounty hunter remove the massive knife from his belt, the serrated edge of the blade gleaming in the dim light cast by the candles in the room.

'Wait!' he cried.

'I'm glad you have decided to be reasonable,' Brunner stated, making no move to return Headsman to its sheath. He had already found out from the girl that Giordano was not the man he was after, there was no tattoo, of a snake or anything else, on his back. But he could still provide the names of the men under his command who were a part of the entourage that was in Pavona.

A few minutes later, the bounty hunter had learned all he needed to know. As he walked toward the door, Giordano struggled against the manacles.

'I think it best if I leave you here while I finish my work in Remas,' Brunner told the man. 'Keep you out of the way. It shouldn't take more than a few days. I suggest you make the best of it.' The bounty hunter closed the door on the stream of curses and obscenities the mercenary hurled at him.

'You found out what you needed to know?' Rosa asked Brunner as he exited the room. Brunner nodded his head.

'At least all he could tell me,' he said. Brunner looked at the door, then back at the shapely Tilean madam. 'You'll keep him here for three or four days?'

Madam Rosa smiled. 'We'll see that he's well taken care of.' Her eyes lingered on the bounty hunter, looking him over from head to foot. 'You know, I don't really think that was worth what you paid me,' she said. 'I feel rather bad about taking your money for such a small thing.'

'Then I suppose we should figure a way to work out the difference,' Brunner commented, allowing Rosa to lead him away.

* * *

NIGHT HUNG HEAVY on Remas when Brunner emerged from the Pink Rose. The streets in the waterfront district were not quite deserted at this hour, certainly more lively than the lanes of the inner city in late afternoon when Brunner had first arrived, sailors staggering back to their ships or else trying to figure out which taverns they had yet to be thrown out of, a handful of street walkers trying to earn a few extra silvers before the custom died away completely, even the odd armed watchman, ensuring that no enterprising souls took it upon themselves to open any of the shops without the knowledge of the shopkeepers.

The bounty hunter was alone, not having waited for Horst to emerge from whatever diversion he had discovered in the Pink Rose. Having been led to the brothel, he could easily find his way back to the bridge and the Gambini palazzo. Brunner adopted his customarily cautious manner as he made his way through the shadowy streets. There might not be many people about, but he knew well enough that it only took one man to slip a knife in someone's ribs.

By degrees, the bounty hunter's wary senses paid off. He could detect furtive footfalls trailing him, stopping when he stopped, mirroring his own pace. Brunner smiled grimly at the inexpert shadower and continued on, a gloved hand resting on the grip of his pistol. He saw a small alleyway ahead and strode towards it. The bounty hunter was not one to ignore a menace, however slight, and the time to deal with this one was at hand.

Brunner slipped into the alley, proceeding down it a few steps. As he had anticipated, the sudden move caused his shadow to hasten his pace, trying to get the bounty hunter back in his sight. Brunner saw his pursuer turn into the alley, his lean frame illuminated by the flickering light cast by the lamps on the street. The bounty hunter strode forward, raising his pistol, letting the cold metal barrel gleam in the lamplight. He was certain that his pursuer would not fail to notice that the weapon was aimed at his face.

'You should find a new line of work,' Brunner snarled. 'You're no good at this one.'

The bounty hunter had expected the supposed thief to retreat before the threat of his gun, or else fall to his knees and plead for mercy. The last thing he expected was for the man to charge at him. With a bestial howl, the lean figure lunged forward. Brunner's reflexes were instant, the pistol's flash exploding in the darkness as he sent the steel ball crashing into his attacker's face.

In that brief flash, the face of his attacker was revealed to Brunner, and it was not human. The face was almost hairless, only a cluster of wispy strands standing out in ragged patches upon its scabby scalp. The features of the visage were sharp and angular, a knife-blade nose with distended nostrils, slanted eyes that bulged wildly from their sockets. The gash-like mouth was filled with pointed fangs, a long snake-like tongue darting in and out between them.

Brunner braced himself for impact even as he heard the ball rip its way through flesh and bone. The lean body ploughed into him, causing the bounty hunter to lose his footing and fall to the ground, the body of his attacker crushed against his chest.

Brunner gagged at the sickly sweet odour of the thing as he strove to push its weight aside. As soon as he began to shift the creature, however, it sprang into life once more. Brunner felt powerful hands pressing down against his chest, as his attacker pushed himself back to its feet. As the monster loomed over him, the bounty hunter could see the light from the street shining through the savage wound that had replaced the left side of its face.

Brunner tore one of his knives from its sheath and hacked at the monster's wrist. Hot blood gushed from the wound and the monster uttered a shrill cry of pain. The powerful hands clawed at his armour, pulling Brunner to his feet. No sooner had the bounty hunter been lifted from the ground than the enraged creature tossed him aside like a sack of rubbish. Brunner hit the floor of the alleyway, rolling on his shoulder back into the street.

His shoulder pained him, the bounty hunter could feel blood trickling down his arm. His violent fall had probably torn open the scar tissue clothing the injury he had been dealt by the orc Gnashrak. Brunner forced the affected arm to move, pulling a throwing knife from the bandoleer across his chest while his right arm pulled Drakesmalice from its scabbard, the metal of the blade rippling with flame. Carefully, Brunner backed away from the darkened alley, eyes focused on the shadowy corridor. The few people on the street paused to watch, eager to witness whatever violent confrontation was going to unfold before them. Yet these would-be spectators gave voice to screams of terror as they saw the bounty hunter's adversary emerge into the street.

It was the same size and shape as a man, perhaps it even had been a man at some point in its existence. But now, through magic or mutation, it bore only a trace of humanity. The thing's body was twisted, almost curled over in a perpetual stoop, its legs somehow too short for its body. The rough cloak that covered the creature bulged at the centre of its chest, speaking of some horrible malformity beneath the cloth. The face was more loathsome than before, the left eye-socket blasted into ruin, greasy brain tissue and the pulp of its eye dangling from the wound. Even for a mutant, such a wound should have been final, there was something even more unclean about this creature and a chill swept up his spine as Brunner put a label upon his thoughts: *daemonic*.

The possessed creature gave voice to a shrill snarl and lunged once more at Brunner, leaping ten feet in a single hop. The bounty hunter lashed out with both weapons, Drakesmalice slashing across its leg, his knife digging at its belly. He was gratified to hear the thing cry out in pain, even more pleased to see it hobble away. The wound in its belly wept a dark mixture of blood and bile, the gash on its leg bubbled and sizzled like bacon in a pan. Brunner could sense the monster's alarm. Blades and bullets of steel might injure the creature, ruin its host body, but the enchanted blade of Drakesmalice could attack the thing itself. The sword might even be able to kill it, if such a creature as this could ever be truly killed.

Cries of alarm sounded nearby. Brunner risked a glance and saw three white-robed men rushing forward, heavy wooden cudgels in their hands. The bounty hunter cursed.

Alone against the daemon-creature, he would be pressed hard enough. Having to deal with it and three of the Solkan fanatics, he wasn't so certain of his chances. However, as they ran forward, the white-robed fanatics paid no attention to the bounty hunter, converging on the daemon-thing instead.

The monster grabbed the first zealot by the hood, tossing him aside. The man crashed into the wall with a shuddering impact, howling in agony as he clutched at broken ribs. The second and third brought their clubs smashing into the daemon-thing's body, punishing it brutally. The daemon recoiled for an instant from the attack, the pain inflicted on its physical host momentarily stunning it. Brunner saw the cloak fall away from the monster's body, exposing the single tear-shaped breast that rose from the centre of its chest. The sight of the monster's grotesque body caused the militiamen to pause in their attack, allowing their daemonic adversary a chance to recover and regain the initiative.

Or so it might have, had the bounty hunter not charged forward. The creature's injured head swung around to glare at him, snarling its shrill growl. Drakesmalice swept outward in a fiery arc, crunching through the monstrosity's neck. The head fell away, the wound bubbling as though it had been bathed in corrosive troll vomit. A pale light rose from the body as it slumped to the ground, and the sickly sweet stench of the monster intensified for a moment, almost overcoming the zealots and the bounty hunter. Then there was a high-pitched, almost human scream and the light flickered away, the smell vanishing with it.

Brunner breathed heavily, leaning over the body. On the corpse, just below the unnatural mammary growth, the bounty hunter could see a sign branded into the flesh. The bounty hunter knew little of arcane matters, but he had taken enough jobs for religious officials in the Empire to recognise this one. A full moon, a downward pointing crescent and an upturned sickle-shape moon, all united by a thick shaft. The sign of the most seductive of the Ruinous Powers, the perverse Lord of Pleasures.

Brunner strode away from the quickly putrefying body. It would be easy to dismiss the attack as coincidence. The ways of the Chaos gods and their creatures had no pattern or reason to them. Yet somehow, the bounty hunter felt that the horrible daemon-thing had been sent especially to kill him. It seemed that more than one man in Remas wanted him dead. Unless there was some schemer wily enough to manipulate both the powers of Chaos and the fanatic worshippers of the gods of Law.

'WHY DO YOU bring your suspicions to me?'

The room was dark, its cheerless grey stone walls laid bare, unadorned by either tapestry or portrait. The only furnishings were a pair of bronze braziers, a large dais with five high-backed chairs and an iron ring set into the floor just before the dais. It was a room designed to crush the warmth within a man, to remind him that life was a trial, and that it would be judged at its end. Or perhaps just before.

Only one of the chairs was occupied now, the one on the rightmost side. A tall, powerful figure in black armour sat there, his golden mask resting beside him on one of the armrests. Inquisitor Bocca's face was suspicious as he spoke his question. There was the usual hint of threat and menace in his tones, the promise that the answer had best meet up to his expectations.

The man standing below the dais bowed his head once more. 'If my suspicions are correct, who else would I turn to?'

Bocca uttered a short, doubtful laugh. 'I find it difficult to believe a man of your sort would do anything if he did not stand to profit by it. If General Mandalari is, as you say, playing false with the temple, I doubt any pious concern would cause you to bear such tidings to me.'

The informer fell silent, staring at the floor for a moment before lifting his eyes once more. 'You are right, inquisitor, it is not piety that makes me warn you. It is fear.' A look of interest filled Bocca's eyes for the first time since granting the man his audience with him. The informer hastily continued. 'I was not certain until I heard him talking after the feast. I am certain that he has hatched some sort of plot with

Alfredo Gambini.' The man paused as a look of intense hate filled Bocca's face. 'I am also certain that Alfredo Gambini,' the informer's voice dropped into a frightened whisper, 'is a servant of the Dark Gods.'

'Indeed,' commented the inquisitor. 'And how reliable should I hold your information?'

'There is to be some manner of profane ceremony soon. This much I have learned. Perhaps in only a few days. I could follow Alfredo, discover where his filthy coven is to hold their ceremony. Then you would be able to arrest them all!'

Inquisitor Bocca was silent as he considered the possibility. To capture Alfredo Gambini, cousin to the most powerful merchant prince in the city, in the midst of some ritual to the Ruinous Powers! Such an event would shake the very structure of the city. The temple would be able to prove its suspicions that corruption had wormed its way into the houses of the rich and the powerful. It would be able to insist that the families of the council submit themselves to the investigations of the inquisition of Solkan. No longer would the decadent nobility be above the justice of Solkan. The filthy waterfront district could be razed, its thieves, drunkards and whores put to the torch. Bocca looked aside, glancing at the centre chair upon the dais. The man who brought about such things would be great in the eyes of Mighty Solkan, he might even aspire to inheriting the position of grand inquisitor when the time came.

Bocca leaned forward, his armoured finger stabbing at the informer below. 'Return to the palazzo then. Keep your eyes and ears open. If this is true, if we discover that Alfredo Gambini is indeed a worshipper of the Dark Gods, you will be richly rewarded.' The inquisitor's voice slipped into a rumbling growl. 'But if you lie to me, I shall take great pleasure in making you confess your falsehoods!'

VII

THE RED HORSE was swarming with patrons as the sun sank into the sea. Many were merchants and shop keepers relieving throats dried out by the day's haggling and cheating. Others were sailors and dockhands, simply trying to drown their bodies in enough drink to make them forget their tired muscles and fatigued frames. A few were none of these things, however. They were of an even harder stock, flint-eyed men who wore armour and weapons, the worn condition of their equipment letting all in the tavern know that they had had cause before to use them, and had been skilled enough to walk away afterwards. These were the mercenaries, drinking their wages as often as their masters would let them slip their leash. One such group of six hardened sell-swords had taken over one of the large round tables that cluttered the main floor of the tavern.

Manfred Zelten stood amidst his men, saluting each in turn with his beer stein. The old veteran Meitz nodded his head and returned the captain's salute. The wiry marksman Schtafel smiled and made a show of tossing the stein from one hand to the other without spilling a drop of its nearly overflowing contents. The tracker Guglielmo, having no taste for the drink of his cohorts from the Empire, had to employ the clay cup he was drinking dark Reman wine from to return Zelten's salute. The thick-bearded Horst Brendle managed a semi-articulate grunt from behind his stein as he guzzled down its contents.

'And let us not forget our friend,' Zelten said, turning to regard Brunner. The bounty hunter sat beside the mercenary captain, quietly nursing an expensive glass of imported schnapps from Marienburg. 'Even if he should be back at the palazzo resting his wounds.' There was more than a suggestion of reproach in the look Zelten gave Brunner.

'I've suffered worse,' Brunner stated. The truth of it was that his old injury was still stinging his shoulder, reopened by the daemon-creature's powerful assault, but the bounty hunter was not one to let a little thing like injury interfere with his hunt. There was also a nagging sense of danger tugging at the back of Brunner's mind. He wasn't entirely certain what it might portend, but he did know that if it heralded another attack such as he had faced the night before, he would prefer not to meet it alone.

As if sensing the bounty hunter's thoughts, Guglielmo spoke. 'You shouldna let old Horst sleep himself off in the

Pink Rose. He would be good fellow to have with you with
a monster at your throat.' Horst grunted his assent through
the foam of his fifth tankard of the night.

'I've already heard,' Brunner commented. 'He's worth any
five men.'

'He certainly can drink like any five,' laughed Zelten.

'And eat like five,' complained Mietz, rolling his eyes.

'And wench like five,' chimed in Schtafel, his voice bubbling with amusement. He looked over at the bear-like man.
'Horst ever tell you he was the best pit fighter in
Middenheim?' the crossbowman asked, redirecting his gaze
at Brunner's helmet-shrouded face. 'Oh yes, he was
renowned in all the big fighting arenas. He used to draw
more people into the Baiting Pit than it could hold. There
was a saying on the streets of the city that Horst Brendle had
killed more men in Middenheim than the red pox.'

'So what happened?' Brunner asked, sensing that Schtafel
would go on and on extolling the exploits of his comrade
until dawn if left on his own.

'Ah, that is a story in itself,' the wiry marksman laughed.
Horst shot a sullen, warning look over at Schtafel, but the
man continued to speak anyway. 'One day, Horst is walking down the street and he comes across a preacher, a
missionary of Sigmar! In the bastion of Ulric no less!
Anyway, Horst is attracted by the mob shouting down the
preacher, tossing stones and vegetables at him. Just as he is
about to join in however, Horst starts listening to the priest
and his words start making sense to him. The preacher is
talking about how the people of Middenheim must repent
their ways, must cease putting the White Wolf ahead of
Most Holy Sigmar. He says that the Day of Doom is soon,
and that the people must scour themselves, that through
their pain they might atone for their heathen ways and
spare their souls being devoured by the Dark Gods when
they consume the world.' Schtafel nodded his head toward
Horst and grinned. 'This idiot bought the whole rigmarole,
gave away all his belongings and put on a sack cloth robe,
joining the mob of flagellants trailing this preacher across
half the Empire.'

'He was a crackpot, a deluded madman profaning Sigmar's holy name!' growled Horst, slamming his stein against the table.

'I was getting to that,' grinned Schtafel. 'So, Horst here follows this lunatic to every pigsty and peasant shack between the Middle Mountains and Mootland for five years. Five years, living on unleavened bread, water and boiled cabbage! No drink, no meat, and no women!'

'That's why he indulges himself so much now,' commented Guglielmo. 'He's making up for lost time!'

'Anyway,' Schtafel continued, ignoring the Tilean's interruption, 'after five years of this, Horst suddenly realises that the world still hasn't come to an end. The Dark Gods haven't eaten the sun, the rocks haven't started to bleed, orcs aren't singing in Altdorf opera houses, in short, there is nothing to indicate that everything this nutjob has been prophesying is coming to pass.'

'So I strangled him in the middle of another of his heretical prophecies,' Horst finished the story, his voice cold and murderous. 'The others he had deceived didn't understand what I had done, so I was forced to defend myself against them.'

'His wits might have been a bit addled after five years of living as a crazed wandering mendicant, but Horst still had sense enough to put as much distance as he could between himself and twenty corpses rotting beside the Talabheim-Altdorf road.' Schtafel added, draining his own stein. The other mercenaries muttered their own grim chuckles at the recounting of the impressive, if murderous, feat.

Brunner did not share in the merriment of his companions. While Schtafel had been speaking, he had been watching a lean man wearing a leather tunic and an expensive-looking ruffled hat talking to a large, scar-faced warrior with the weathered look of an Estalian about him. The bounty hunter had caught the man in the hat looking over at their table several times over the course of the night. In turn, he had kept an eye on the furtive character. Now he saw the man turn away from the Estalian. The soldier moved toward another table, speaking with a number of armed men sitting there. Brunner watched as the men rose.

'Trouble,' he warned his comrades from the corner of his mouth. At once, the laughter and conversation died. Each of the mercenaries stared at the bounty hunter.

'Where?' asked Zelten.

'Ten men, heading our way,' Brunner answered, not moving. 'There's an ugly-looking rogue wearing an Estalian helmet and breastplate at their head.' The mercenaries looked away, easily spotting the warriors making a path through the crowded tavern. Brunner turned his head and stared at Schtafel.

'These men were paid,' the bounty hunter said. 'There's a man in a ruffled black hat standing beside the bar.' Schtafel nodded as he spotted the man Brunner indicated. 'Whatever else happens, don't let him get away.' Once again, Schtafel nodded his understanding.

The warriors had closed almost to Zelten's table now. The crowd had drawn away from the warriors, as if sensing the coming violence, allowing the hired killers to advance more quickly. Other patrons drew away from the proximity of Zelten's table, clearing some room for the coming violence to unfold. Closer now, it was obviously apparent that, like Zelten's crew, these men were mercenaries, displaying a motley collection of races and nations between them.

One by one, Zelten and his men drew their swords, Horst producing the massive chain flail he had employed in the battle with the plague warriors. Brunner rose slowly, dragging Drakesmalice from its sheath. The metal was cold and lustreless, which the bounty hunter took as a good sign. At least these were foes unmarked by the Chaos powers. In his other hand, Brunner held his pistol, drawing concerned looks from the rival mercenaries. At this range, the bounty hunter's bullet could not help but hit a target.

FOR SEVERAL MINUTES, the two groups stood, glowering at one another in silence. Then a hulking, swarthy man with the bristly moustache and beard of an Arabyan fixed his glaring gaze on Zelten. 'Sigmar was a drinker of his own piss,' the Arabyan spat.

With a roar of maniacal fury, Horst up-ended the table, hurling it at the rival mercenaries. So sudden and intense was the bearded man's rage that even the goading Arabyan was taken by surprise as Horst exploded into violence. The table smashed against the foremost of the warriors, smashing two of them to the floor. Even as the table was coming to rest, Horst was lungeing on top of it, swinging his flail in a brutal arc that crushed a slow-moving swordsman's jaw, showering the man beside him with blood and teeth.

Brunner fired his pistol as Horst leapt forward, the shot ripping through the throat of a pale-eyed Tilean bearing a cutlass and a duellist's dagger. The man collapsed into the arms of his nearest comrade, leaving the man exposed to Zelten's blade. The Reiklander stabbed past the body of the man Brunner had shot, puncturing the other mercenary's lung. Guglielmo and Meitz moved forward to support their commander, trading sword strokes with a pair of flint-eyed Tileans. In only a few short, vicious moments, the attackers had lost their numerical advantage. That knowledge did not rest easy on their minds, and they fought defensively, with one eye peeled for any chance of escape.

The patrons of the Red Horse were no strangers to violence, many of them practiced mercenaries themselves. Immediately wagers began to sound from several quarters, even as swords, axes and virtually any other weapon conceived by man found their way into callused hands, in the event that the combat were to expand beyond the space the onlookers had allowed it. Behind the bar, the scarred proprietor studied the tide of battle, trying to determine if the potential for damage to his establishment would outweigh the value of whatever loot could be plundered from the bodies of the losers. A handful of more timid patrons trickled out onto the street, suddenly deciding that perhaps it was time to retire for the evening.

Brunner found himself matched with a leather-faced man who looked to be at least partially Estalian, reluctantly conceding that the man was indeed quite capable with the large,

notched sword he wielded. The bounty hunter caught a
motion out of the corner of his eye and decided that he had
no time to play with the swordsman. Brunner let his oppo-
nent crush Drakesmalice downward, seeking to trap the
blade against the floor. As he did so, the mercenary left himself exposed to Brunner's left hand. The man sneered as he
saw the bounty hunter swing his seemingly empty hand,
more than willing to trade a punch for the chance to disarm
his enemy. But as Brunner swung, he depressed the catch on
the spring mechanism concealed beneath his tunic. The
short, sharp blade he had claimed from the body of the kid-
napper Ursio shot from underneath Brunner's sleeve and
into his hand, and from there into the soft jelly of the mercenary's eye.

Brunner turned away from his dying enemy and looked
for Zelten. He saw the Reiklander fighting a fair-faced man
with the look of Marienburg about his clothes and armour.
The two swordsmen were fairly evenly matched, though
Brunner could see that the Marienburger was tiring far more
quickly than Zelten, putting too much of himself in each
strike. A mistake of inexperience rather than skill. Then
Brunner saw the swarthy figure closing on Zelten from
behind and realised that perhaps the Marienburger had no
need of conserving his strength. The Estalian drew his arm
back for a stabbing blow to Zelten's kidneys. The first Zelten
knew of the man's presence was when he screamed, one of
Brunner's throwing knives piercing his neck.

The death of their captain decided the fight. The remaining members of his mob hastily removed themselves from
their adversaries, turning and fleeing out of the tavern's side
door. As they left, Brunner took stock of their situation.
Mietz was being helped into a chair by Guglielmo, one of
the old veteran's arms covered in bright blood. Horst was
crouched over the Arabyan, smashing the man's face into the
floor and snarling into his ruined features to recant his blasphemy before slamming his head once more into the floor.

Zelten wiped the blood from his sword with a rag torn
from the sash about the dead Estalian's waist. The captain
looked about the carnage.

'Schtafel?' he asked. Brunner nodded to a man quickly making his way through the spectators.

'Did you get him?' Brunner asked when Schtafel emerged from the crowd. The wiry man nodded.

'He made it to the street, but he won't get far,' the marksman reported, sheathing his dagger.

Brunner turned toward Zelten. 'I doubt if our friend with the hat was the mastermind of this attack,' he said. 'You can be sure that whoever wants you dead will try again.'

Zelten looked over the dead and dying men strewn about them.

'Let us hope then that we fare as well next time.'

THE DYING MAN stared up into the pale face of the man who stood over him. He reached toward the stranger, but his hand was bloody and the man standing above him drew away, not desiring to stain his long black cloak. The wounded man gurgled a supplication to the black-cloaked figure, but his plea fell on deaf ears. The stranger in the black cloak strode away even as the man with the ruffled hat bled out into the gutter.

He had recognised the dying man, had seen him several times before in the Gambini palazzo. He was General Mandalari's valet. Briefly the black-cloaked man wondered how the valet had come to meet such a dismal end, then he saw the band of warriors emerging from the Red Horse. They were helping a wounded man into the street. The observer at once recognised Manfred Zelten. That answered his question, then. Clearly Mandalari was moving ahead with his plans. The man in the black cloak considered the fact for a moment then sighed.

He had other friends to help this night. The general would have to wait. The man in the black cloak was careful to walk in the opposite direction to that taken by Zelten and his men. It did not matter, really, there were harlots to be had on any street near the waterfront, and he had yet to meet one that did not become agreeable at the sight of gold.

Not that the woman he engaged this night would ever be spending whatever she was given.

* * *

VIII

THE MAN IN black released his hold on the harlot's hand. He reached forward and opened the door that stood before them. By secret paths and hidden doors had he brought the woman here, deep within the Gambini palazzo. No one had remarked their coming.

'In there,' the man said, noting the girl's hesitancy. 'Do not worry, my master will pay you very well, even if the room is dark.' The mention of money seemed to dispel much of the girl's fear. Firming herself, she stepped into the darkened room. No sooner had she crossed the threshold, than the man in the black cloak slammed the door shut. The woman turned, rushing at the door, beating on it with her fists. Outside, in the hall, the dark man held the portal closed, his ear pressed to the panels. He did not want to miss the sound of what would soon transpire.

The harlot beat on the door, trying to escape the trap she had been led into. But it was already too late. There would be no escape. Powerful hands closed about her waist, pulling her away from the door. She screamed, but the sound did not penetrate the thick stone walls of the room. Savagely, she was thrown to the floor. The woman rolled onto her side, slightly dazed from having struck her head against the unyielding floor. Then she felt the deep gash in her side, where the hands had clutched at her, felt the warm blood seeping through her fingers and she screamed again.

In the darkness, her attacker licked the blood from his knife. The taste washed away the torment racing through his body, stilling the skin on his back as it tried to tear itself free from his body. He knew that he would need more, much more to satisfy the agony, to spare him its attentions for a few more days. But there was more blood in the woman, much more. And he would spill every drop.

OUTSIDE, THE MAN in dark clothes listened to the sounds of butchery within the room. His friend was indeed insatiable tonight. It would take quite a bit of effort to clean up after him this time. It was just as well that the usefulness of his friend was almost at its end, there were only so many times they could get away with these offerings to the evil within him. With every taste of blood, the darkness grew still stronger within his friend's soul. Much longer, and it would manifest itself of its own accord. And that would not do anybody any good, least of all himself.

The eavesdropper let a light giggle pass his lips as he heard the slaughter within the room grow still more frenzied. The hour would soon come when sounds such as these would echo across all of Remas.

SOME TIME LATER, the man in the black cloak crept along shadowy halls. He paused before one door in particular, his pale hand emerging from the dark folds of his garment to softly rap upon the portal. The dark man smiled as he heard sounds of movement within the room. Presently the door opened, revealing the bleary features of Alfredo Gambini.

'What do you mean, disturbing me at such an hour?' the nobleman snarled when he recognised his visitor. By way of explanation, the dark man dropped a large sack onto the floor of the corridor. Alfredo swore. 'Again?'

'Quite so, quite so,' the dark man smiled. 'It was necessary to make a special offering to our lord,' he explained. 'The possessed brother you sent to dispose of the bounty hunter was itself destroyed.'

Alfredo's face grew ashen. 'Destroyed? How?'

'I warned you that the bounty hunter was here to assist the temple of thrice-damned Solkan,' reminded the aristocrat's visitor. 'How else would he be prepared to confront a true believer who had married his soul with that of a daemon?'

'But he was attacked by the followers of Solkan when he first arrived,' protested Alfredo Gambini.

'You should be used to the deceits and tricks of the Solkanites by now,' chided the dark man. He directed a sour look at the aristocrat. 'But perhaps we can discuss the whys of it later, when you do not have an offering sitting on your threshold.' The reminder of just what it was that his visitor's sack contained evoked a haunted look in Alfredo as the nobleman considered how dire events would become were such a thing discovered here.

'What is it you wish me to do?' he asked.

'Take the offering to the temple, and gather the true believers,' the dark man said. 'Prepare the ceremony. We must apologise to our lord for the death of his servant.' The man's pale hand flipped toward Alfredo in a dismissive gesture. Alfredo hastily withdrew into his room, quickly dressing himself. He reappeared minutes later, stooping to retrieve the heavy sack from the floor.

'Stay at the temple and make sure that all of the preparations are in order,' the man in the black cloak stated. 'I will join you when the ceremony is to begin.' He paused, smiling once more. 'I shall be bringing a new initiate to our faith with me.' The dark man waved his hand again, shooing away the burdened nobleman as he might ward off an annoying dog. Alfredo Gambini scuttled off into the dark, the heavy sack slung over his shoulder.

The dark man watched Alfredo go, then reached beneath his cloak. He withdrew a scrap of cloth from a pocket in his tunic. The cloth was stained by the still wet blood of the murdered harlot. He considered the rag for a moment, then wiped it against the handle on the door to Alfredo's room. Once he was satisfied that enough blood had been smeared onto the bronze fastening, the man replaced the rag in his pocket. Whistling a morbid dirge in a high, jaunty note, the man slipped away into the darkness.

PRINCESS JULIANA BENSARIO could not sleep. For the past four hours she had paced the floors of her sitting room, trying to decide how she could escape her current dilemma. She had passed the crippled General Mandalari shortly before retiring. As she had walked past the old warmonger, he had slipped her a piece of paper. It was the contents of that paper that had occupied her mind so completely. The general had not veiled his words in flowery script, nor couched them in suggestion and innuendo. No, with the brutal straight-forwardness of a soldier, he had stated quite plainly what he knew, and what he expected of Juliana. In exchange for the general's silence, Juliana would support the general's war plans. Otherwise, Prince Gambini would be informed of his bride's dalliance, the wedding would be called off and Juliana would have to return to Pavona in shame to face the scorn of her city.

So lost in her troubled thoughts was the princess, that she did not hear the hall door of the sitting room open.

'Princess?' a familiar voice spoke. 'I saw your light from the hall. Are you well?' Princess Juliana looked up to see the concerned features of Corvino staring down at her.

More than any other soul in the Gambini household, Juliana had formed a bond with the fool, attracted by his pleasant manner and sympathetic ear. Perhaps, in her own home in Pavona, she might not have trusted someone so much, but in the still unfamiliar setting of Remas, she had needed a confidant. Had Corvino not aided her in her affair with Manfred? Knowing that the fool was privy to half her problem, she handed him the note from Mandalari, that he might learn the other half.

Corvino quickly read the letter. Juliana watched as the fool's expression faded from worry to anger and finally to rage. His soft hand clenched into a fist, crumpling the letter, then tearing it into ribbons with both hands.

'That scoundrel dares threaten you!' he hissed. The fool's face had twisted into an animalistic snarl. His eyes met those of the princess and his expression softened. He stepped forward, cradling one of her hands in his own.

'I shall teach that scheming swine the price for such roguish audacity!' he declared. He saw the confusion in Juliana's face.

'How can you do anything to help me, Corvino?' she said. 'You are only a jester. He is a general.'

'I shall, you will see,' asserted the fool. 'I would do anything for you, my lady.' Corvino dropped to one knee, staring up at the noblewoman with wide, watery eyes. 'There is nothing a man would not dare for love.'

Juliana recoiled from Corvino, pulling her hand away. She retreated a few paces, as though the fool were a noxious serpent.

Corvino saw the emotions play across her beautiful features. Shock, disbelief, then disgust. It was the last emotion, however, that thrust into the fool's breast as though it were a dagger. The final feeling that won control of Juliana's face. Pity.

Corvino rose to his feet, a tear sliding down his gaunt face. 'I do not presume that you could ever return my affection,' he confessed. 'I am no grand prince, worthy of your hand. I am not even a dashing young mercenary captain to win your eye. As you have said, my lady, I am only a fool. All I can expect, all I can ask, is the joy of serving you. That is my honour, that is my reward.'

Juliana tried to compos herself as Corvino spoke. She stepped forward to speak, but the tall fool lifted his hand, motioning for her to remain silent.

'Let me serve, my lady,' Corvino begged as he backed away, moving toward the door. 'That is all I can ask.' Juliana watched the sorry spectacle of the man trying to recover the scraps of dignity he had worn before entering her sitting room. 'Allow me to remain near you.' He reached behind him and opened the door.

'But, know this,' Corvino said before slipping back into the hall. 'The man who troubles you, will not trouble you again.'

MANDALARI AWOKE, STARING upward at the canopy of his bed. The old soldier rolled his head, trying to focus on whatever had disturbed his sleep. By degrees, as his eyes grew accustomed to the dark, he began to detect a man's figure standing beside his bed. The general acted at once, dragging a long knife from beneath the mass of pillows that supported his aged frame.

'Forgive the intrusion,' the calm, modulated tones of Mandalari's spy addressed him, their suggestion of scorn just a bit more pronounced than usual. 'I have learned things that are of great importance.'

Mandalari relaxed his grip on the knife, staring at the dark silhouette of his agent. 'Indeed,' he grumbled. 'Of such importance that it could not wait until a decent hour?'

'I fear not,' the spy stated gravely. 'I have learned that someone is going to try and kill you.'

General Mandalari's face betrayed the shock that his spy's report caused, but quickly the bluster of a man who had faced death on dozens of battlefields rose once more to the fore. 'Indeed,' Mandalari snarled. 'And what is the name of this gallow's bait that seeks my life?'

'Someone very close to you,' the spy replied. The arm of the silhouette swept towards the old general and the mauling force of heavy cold-wrought iron smashed into his chest. The old man was knocked from his bed by the blow, crashing against the floor in a crumpled heap. He moaned, trying to disentangle himself from the bed clothes twisted about his body. His attacker circled the bed, standing over him once more, blood dripping from the iron mace he gripped. The spy smiled down, watching the general's frantic efforts.

'It appears you got up on the wrong side,' the spy said. The general howled in agony as his attacker swung the heavy iron mace at his leg, sending it crunching into the man's remaining leg with a loud crack. The general turned his shriek into a snarl of rage, clawing at the assassin, who swiftly stepped away. Mandalari tried to twist around, to reach toward the knife lying on the floor near where he had fallen. As he exerted himself, however, he screamed again, his body wracked by frenzied spasms in its attempts to free itself from the twisted sheets that were wound about him like some insect's cocoon.

'Now you don't have a leg to stand on,' the assassin sighed, watching Mandalari struggle to reach the knife once more. 'But let's make certain of that, shall we?' He brought the mace crashing downward once more, pulverising the already maimed limb once more.

'Gods' pity!' howled Mandalari between screams, his outstretched hand forsaking the knife to clutch at his broken limb. 'Have mercy, Corvino!'

The fool smiled down at his former patron, the mocking sneer more pronounced than ever before. He sent the mace crashing down again, cracking the general's ribs. Mandalari howled, bright red drops exploding from his mouth.

'I warned you about pursuing your plans regarding Princess Juliana,' Corvino said regretfully. 'But you wouldn't

listen.' He swung the mace into Mandalari's side again. 'I
trust you know better now.' Corvino let the mace break the
general's arm as the old soldier roared at him and tried once
more to gain the knife lying on the floor, then he tossed the
weapon away. He walked toward the headboard of
Mandalari's bed, lifting a large object propped against the
wall there.

On the floor, the general writhed in torment, his mouth
muttering garbled words between groans of agony. Corvino
looked down at Mandalari. 'It is no good calling for your
valet,' he said. 'I saw him earlier, bleeding his life away in the
gutter.' Corvino snorted with contempt. 'You couldn't even
manage to kill that mercenary without botching it.'
Mandalari's eyes grew still wider with horror as he saw what
his former spy held.

He lamely reached his hand upward, muttering through
his pain-wracked lips.

'Now now,' chided Corvino, lifting the heavy wooden leg
high over his head. 'None of that please, I detest long good-
byes.' The fool brought the claw-footed leg down, smashing
into the general's head. And again. And again… Only when
the sound of babbling voices began to drift into the bed
chamber from the outer door of his sitting room did
Corvino tear himself away from his gory distraction, slamming the wooden limb one last time into the puddle that
had been Mandalari's face.

The fool quickly made his way to the small concealed
door he had used to visit Mandalari in his capacity as the
general's spy. Just before slipping into the hidden passage,
he glanced back at the general's mangled body, a mad giggle
rasping from his throat.

'I always said you knew how to put your foot down,' he
laughed, before disappearing into the darkness.

It was two hours after the fight in the Red Horse before
Brunner and his companions returned to the Gambini
palace. The men had taken the injured Meitz to a doctor
dwelling in the district, forcing the leech out of a sound
sleep to attend the old veteran. Zelten had refused to leave

until he was satisfied that Meitz was past any immediate danger, though the doctor made it a point to remind the mercenary captain of the possibility of infection setting into his man's wounds.

Meitz had been left to rest in the doctor's parlour, the Tilean tracker Guglielmo remaining with him to ensure that infection was the only thing that would arise to hinder the warrior's recovery. The others had left to return to the palazzo, and investigate something Schtafel had observed about the mysterious man who had hired their assailants. The marksman was almost certain that he had seen the man at the palazzo before, attending the crippled General Mandalari.

But whatever confrontation Zelten had been planning between himself and the old general was at once put aside by the scene outside the general's room. Half the household seemed to be gathered in the corridor, Prince Gambini and Princess Juliana among them. A number of the household guards were forming a barrier between the servants and lesser courtiers and the doorway itself. They made to bar the way for the mercenaries as well, but one look at the grim visages of Zelten and his companions made the men think better of getting in their way.

A small cluster of people were gathered about a shrouded form lying upon the floor. Standing over the body was the dour-faced priest Scurio, his black robe drawn tight about his body. The priest bore a look of solemn detachment, those others around him who had seen the corpse were ashen faced, some showing signs of sickness about their mouths.

'Poor Mandalari,' Prince Gambini commented. 'Whatever could you have done to make someone do this to you?' The merchant prince shook his head.

'He is not going to answer you,' observed the elderly Remaro, leaning against the tall slender figure of Corvino. For once, the fool's smile was absent from his face, and he was clad only in a long white night shirt, instead of his normally extravagant attire. Corvino patted the old man's shoulder, trying to soothe him into silence.

'If my lord will allow,' Scurio said, bowing before Prince
Gambini. 'It is within my ability to attempt to speak with
the spirit of the departed.' The priest's dirge-like voice
became still more grave. 'Perhaps he may be able to reveal
the identity of his killer. If I could remove the body to the
chapel, I have everything I need to perform the necessary rituals there.'

Prince Gambini waved his hand, giving Scurio permission
to attempt his ritual. Brunner noted a quick fearful glance
that Juliana directed first at Corvino, then at Zelten. The
mercenary captain shook his head, trying to assure the
princess that he had not been involved in the general's
demise. Corvino's face, however, remained impassive, even
after the frightened, accusing glance the princess had given
him. The bounty hunter wondered about this, filing the fact
away in his steely mind.

'I shall perform the ritual at once,' the priest stated.

Scurio gave instructions to two of the soldiers standing
near him to gather up the body. The two warriors walked
toward the bed, removing a heavy blanket that had not fallen
to the floor along with Mandalari. The mercenaries laid the
blanket on the floor beside the dead general and rolled his
ruined body onto it. Juliana hid her face as the full extent of
the man's injuries was revealed. Even Brunner was impressed,
at once recalling Masario's description of the slain serving
wench in Pavona, a murder that looked like the handiwork
of a blood-mad orc. Suddenly the murder of the old general
assumed a professional interest for the bounty hunter.

The soldiers each took two corners of the blanket, lifting it
and the messy remains of Mandalari from the floor. The
prince and the other onlookers parted as the two soldiers
followed Scurio from the room.

Prince Gambini looked over at the nearest of his palace
guards. 'I want all the sentries doubled,' he stated. 'I want the
whereabouts of everyone in this house accounted for. I will
find the murdering swine who dared this outrage within my
house!'

The prince's tirade was interrupted as a guard forced his
way into the room.

'My lord,' the man called out. 'Your cousin is not within his rooms. We went there to ensure that he was safe, as you ordered, but he was not to be found.' The guard paused, then added, 'There was blood on his door!'

This report caused the room to fall silent once more. It was Corvino who broke the quiet. 'Can it be?' he asked in a horrified voice. 'Can it be that Alfredo committed this hideous crime?'

The fool looked over at his master as he voiced the thought, then shifted his gaze to Juliana, favouring her with a knowing look. Brunner noticed the sudden pallor that crept into the woman's face, the frightened widening of her eyes. There was something here that wasn't being spoken, something that might prove of profound interest to the bounty hunter.

Prince Gambini considered the fool's accusation for a moment, then faced his guards once more. 'Search the palace from gable to cellar! Find Alfredo and bring him to me!'

The soldiers hastened to obey the prince, Zelten and his men departing with them. Brunner stood in the room a moment longer, considering the body for a moment before jogging after Zelten.

'Well,' he said as he caught up with Zelten in the corridor, 'if Mandalari was trying to kill you, he certainly isn't now.'

Zelten shook his head. 'Assassins I can deal with. Searching every dark corner of this palace looking for a madman is another matter entirely.' The Reiklander laughed grimly. 'This is no work for honest sell-swords and bounty hunters.'

Brunner considered for a moment the look that had passed between Corvino and Juliana, then decided that perhaps it was something entirely unrelated to the murder. Perhaps the princess numbered men other than Zelten among her lovers. After all, he was certain that Corvino had been in Remas when Masario's serving wench had been butchered. That fact decided him. 'On the contrary,' Brunner corrected him. 'I believe I may have been looking for this man ever since I arrived.'

* * *

IN THE CORRIDOR outside the small chapel of Morr within the Gambini palazzo, the once more gaudily dressed Corvino looked down at the young servant standing beside him in the corridor. The fool explained what he wanted in a soft, almost conspiratorial voice.

'You must take it straight away,' Corvino said, thrusting a rolled slip of parchment into the boy's hand. 'Don't let anything stop you. It is very important,' he emphasised, tousling the boy's short black hair with his pale hand. 'After all, you wouldn't want the inquisitor to be angry with you.' With the warning spoken, Corvino dismissed the boy, watching as his messenger raced along the hall. Nearly every soldier in the palace was hunting for Alfredo; they wouldn't pay a lone youth too much notice. The awful terror that the Temple of Solkan inspired in the common people of Remas would ensure that even if he were questioned, the boy would say nothing of Corvino's letter to Inquisitor Bocca.

The fool smiled, whistling a funeral dirge in a disrespectfully jaunty fashion. As he strode toward the chapel, the bells on his staff jingling with his every step, Corvino considered how very quickly everything was falling into line. Poor Mandalari. If the idiot had just taken his advice, the general might have died in a more pleasant manner. A simple knife across the throat, or perhaps a dagger in his heart. But the man simply had to try and threaten Juliana despite everything his valued spy Corvino had warned him of. That had made things a bit less professional between them.

Corvino had already decided that Mandalari had to die, of course. He needed to have some victim for 'Alfredo's' murderous rampage and the general had been the obvious choice. The failed attack on Manfred Zelten had only firmed Corvino's decision, the crude attempt to blackmail Princess Juliana had made that decision personal. Of course, the general had long ago outlived his usefulness to Corvino's plans. He no longer needed the general's contacts and wealth to support his own ambitions. Everything was prepared now, all the pieces in their places. All except for one, the fool corrected himself.

Corvino opened the heavy oak door, stepping into the dark, musty chapel. The room was only dimly lit by the flickering candles set about the altar. Corvino watched for a few moments as the black-robed priest moved around the carcass strewn atop the altar, old piles of rag and canvas sopping up the blood dripping from Mandalari's ruined head. The priest of Morr was muttering the secret incantations of his order, those sacred mixtures of words and tones that would place Scurio into contact with the soul of the slain man. As he chanted and circled the altar, Corvino could see the priest casting a mixture of grave dust and salt upon the body. There were few people who had the nerve to stand by and watch a priest of Morr conducting his strange, sinister rituals. It was almost like watching a necromancer working his spells. As the fool stood just within the doorway, he could feel the room growing cold, as though all the warmth and life was being drained to power Scurio's incantation. It was little wonder then that the guards who had brought Mandalari's body here had not lingered to watch Scurio work his magic.

The fool could see the black-robed priest suddenly stop in his circling of the altar. The candles flickered as their fires began to dim. Scurio stood stock still, staring down at what once was Mandalari's face. A faint, pale light seemed to be glowing from the corpse. Corvino's smile broadened as he imagined what the old general might have to tell the priest. Somehow, however, he didn't think the dead man's knowledge would be leaving the chapel. Indeed, as fascinating as Scurio's ritual was, Corvino had little time to waste.

A sharp shrill note echoed through the chapel as Corvino whistled through his fingers. As soon as the sound intruded upon the ceremony, the blue corpse-light vanished, the chill began to lessen and the candles returned to their normal level of illumination. Corvino saw the black-robed figure of Scurio hurry around the altar and come toward him. The fool grinned as he saw the look of fear and disgust in the priest's eyes.

'A splendid performance,' Corvino congratulated Scurio, clapping his hands softly. 'You should have been a tragedian instead of,' he paused to allow his face to slip into a mask of mockery and derision, 'what you are.'

'Why did you kill him?' Scurio demanded in a low, harsh whisper, the calm, rigid demeanour of a priest of Morr absent from his voice now.

'I had nothing better to do with my evening,' the fool replied. 'I don't understand why you are so upset, I didn't leave nearly so much a mess as *you*, my friend.' Corvino put a warning emphasis on his last words.

Scurio looked at the marble floor, fighting against the remorse and guilt welling up within him. Corvino left him to his self-reproach for a moment, then spoke again.

'I have news that should lift your spirits,' again, he put a twisted emphasis on the word. 'All is in readiness for the ritual.' Scurio looked up, his face lifted into an expression of rapturous joy.

'When?' he asked, hands closing about Corvino's arms. 'When is it to be? When am I to be free of this daemon that torments me?' Corvino brushed the priest's hands from his body.

'Soon,' the fool said. 'This very night! Would you like to go there now?' Corvino listened for a moment to the pleading, grovelling entreaties streaming from Scurio's lips, then held his hand up, motioning the man to be silent. 'I thought you might feel that way. Follow me.'

The fool strode from the chapel, down the marble halls, watching as Prince Gambini's soldiers continued their search, smiling at their fool's errand. These men would never see Alfredo Gambini, not on this side of the veil, in any event.

Alfredo Gambini was already where he needed to be, as were all the other pieces in the puzzle Corvino had carefully put together. But the cornerstone of that enigma, the key to the entire plot, that piece of the puzzle, Corvino would put into its place himself.

The fool looked over his shoulder at the dark-garbed priest following after him. Poor Scurio, he thought, he can't even begin to understand what an important man he is.

BRUNNER STRODE TOWARD the gate leading out onto the Great Reman Bridge from the Gambini palazzo, Horst and Schtafel close behind. Brunner had informed Zelten of his suspicions, and had asked that he be given the use of the mercenary's two soldiers. Zelten himself had insisted on remaining behind, ostensibly just in case Brunner was wrong, but the bounty hunter suspected that concern for the safety of his beloved Juliana was more to blame for the Reiklander's reluctance to leave the palazzo.

'And why aren't we helping search the palazzo for the killer?' Schtafel asked in a snide voice. 'I know there was a reason, but it seems too slippery to keep hold of.' The crossbowman's flippant attitude faded as Brunner rounded on him, fixing him with his icy stare.

'Because if he has half a mind,' the bounty hunter said, 'he isn't in there. He had enough time to slip away before anybody thought to go looking for him?'

'But how does that help us?' Horst questioned. 'I mean, how do we know where to even start looking for him.'

'I've been trying to fit things together ever since I arrived in this mixed-up city,' Brunner said. 'I have a feeling that Alfredo may have some connection to the thing that attacked me outside the Pink Rose.' The bounty hunter drummed his fingers on the grip of his pistol. 'I think it might not have been mere coincidence that the creature I fought was lurking near the brothel.'

'So that's where we start our search?' Horst asked.

'That's where we start,' the bounty hunter stated. 'I have a feeling that where we wind up won't be anywhere so pleasant as Madam Rosa's establishment.'

IX

FOR MANY CENTURIES it had stood, just within the innermost wall of Remas, overlooking the cliffs and the sea below. The great Temple of Morr had served the funerary rites of the people of Remas for as long as the citizens could remember, consecrating the bodies of the deceased before dumping them over the wall and into the sea. It was said that the spirits of the dead would guide fish back towards the city, that it

was by this custom that the fishing fleets of the city pros-
pered, that their nets were always full. None considered that
perhaps the fish were drawn by the free meals each funeral
provided them.

There had been times in the past, often when Remas
found itself at war with the southern city-state of Luccini,
where the Great Mausoleum of Morr was located, when the
priesthood of Morr had fallen out of favour in the city. But
in the last decades, with the hold of the Temple of Solkan
tightening about the city, the worship of the other gods, even
of Morr, had become dangerous. Zealous militia in the
white robes of Solkan had set fire to the temple, killing most
of the priests. In the aftermath of the atrocity, which was
publicly condemned by the priests of Solkan, the funeral
rites of Remas had been taken over by the Solkanites, alter-
ing the rituals to include cremation before casting the ashes
into the sea, thereby preventing any impurity in the flesh
from tainting the waters which supported the life of the city.
The Temple of Morr was never repaired, but was abandoned
and forgotten, left to rot beside the wall. Those priests of
Morr who escaped the purge sought sanctuary with the
houses of the rich and powerful, men who would gladly
continue the old traditions if only to flaunt their disdain
before the inquisitors.

But if the priesthood of Morr no longer had any use for
their temple, there were others who did. Over the course of
long years of furtive excavation and laborious nocturnal
construction, another temple had been built within the cel-
lars of the first.

It was this undertemple that was now alive and vibrant.
Several scores of people danced and cavorted within a massive chamber, hundreds of feet long, its ceiling formed by
the stones of the floor fifty feet above their heads. Heavy
stone columns flanked the chamber, arching overhead into
supports from which dangled colourful pennants and
streamers of fur and feather and silk. Upon some of these
had been daubed profane symbols, upon others had been
painted the outlines of human figures in all manner of poses
and lascivious activities. Great bronze pots, filled with oil,

were spaced about the chamber, casting a diabolic light about the capering congregation.

The celebrants wore long white robes, their faces masked in parody of the servants of Solkan. But where the robes of the Solkanites covered them almost completely, those of the cultists were loose, slit down the front and sides to expose the sweating bodies beneath. The masks were not just of wood, but of leather and fur and paper, adorned with sequins and feathers and lace. Each suggested an emotion, but all were more passionate and wanton than the faces of stern judgement the Solkanites hid behind. Amidst the dancing celebrants there were some who wove their way among them swinging large censers. From some of these instruments exuded the fumes of an exotic perfume, from others came the stench of animal dung, for fair or foul, both odours excited the cultists equally. From one side of the undertemple, a drummer and a pipe player set a raucous, discordant tune snaking about the columns, exciting the senses of the Slaanesh coven still further.

At the very centre of the chamber, upon a great altar of blackened, burned wood, stood the profane shrine to the power which the gathered throng prayed to. It was a great statue carved from the same light, white wood the Temple of Solkan constructed the masks of its devotees from. But this was no stern-faced god of vengeance: it was something else entirely. Standing nearly eight feet tall, it was the lithe figure of a woman, her belly swollen with life, her hips tilted in sensuous suggestion, wooden breasts drooping about her chest. Yet the head of this vision of depraved lust was not that of a beautiful seductress, but the bovine face of a cow, pointed antelope horns arcing from its brow. It was the Mother of Mystery, a foul relic carved by a madman in Tobaro five hundred years earlier. Now it once more stood before those who gazed upon it with adoration, wantonness, and despair.

Standing before the statue was a man, his face bared before the inhuman idol. He lifted the butchered portions of a human body, smearing the blood from each scrap about the statue's feet before tossing the meat to the closest of the capering cultists. Like wild beasts, the Chaos worshippers fell upon the discarded offerings, savaging the meat with their teeth, eager to savour the taste of their loathsome repast.

Alfredo Gambini did not linger to watch the ghoulish display, but turned back toward the shrine, continuing to make his offering to the Dark Prince of Chaos, drawing yet another scrap of flesh from the heavy brown sack.

INTO THE CELEBRANT throng, a tall, sinister figure strode, clad in a costume of red and black checks, the bells upon his staff jingling with every step. Corvino paid no attention to the startled, curious looks the cultists gave him and the man following at his heels. The fool had eyes only for the shrine at the centre of the undertemple and the cult leader standing before it.

Alfredo Gambini met the fool's stare, then looked past him at the nervous Scurio. The leader smiled. 'I understood that you had a new initiate to the circle,' he chuckled. 'But I did not imagine you would bring us a priest!'

'Is all in readiness?' Corvino demanded, his tone short and hurried. 'You have completed the ritual?'

'Fear not,' Alfredo assured the fool. 'All is in readiness for his initiation. I have just completed the offering to the Mother of Mystery which you were gracious enough to provide me with.'

It was Corvino's turn to smile now, his face spreading into a corpse-like rictus. He ignored the cultists who drifted forward to remove Scurio's black priest's habit from his body, his eyes instead locked upon those of the cult leader. Despite all the hideous rites he had presided over, despite calling daemons from the very pits of the Realm of Chaos, Alfredo felt his pulse quicken as he met the fool's insane gaze.

'Excellent,' Corvino laughed. 'Now it is time for the game to truly begin!'

THREE SETS OF eyes watched the wanton ceremony of self-indulgence unfold within the great hall beneath the abandoned Temple of Morr. The observers were concealed behind one of the huge stone urns scattered about the undertemple, a sickly sweet perfume rising from the urns' smouldering contents. None of the men placed much trust in the defensibility of their position should they be discovered. Fortunately, the cultists seemed entirely lost in their own perverse acts, so there was little risk of discovery from that quarter.

'Now, if temple was a bit more like this, they might have made a Sigmarite out of me,' joked Schtafel, though there was little humour in his voice. Horst ignored the marksman's irreverent comment and stared at the bounty hunter.

'Looks like you were right,' the bearded warrior growled, stabbing a finger outward, pointing at the altar. 'That's Alfredo Gambini lording over this sacrilege.'

Brunner just nodded his head. It had actually taken surprisingly little time for them to find this place, for all that it was supposed to be a secret. The bounty hunter had been certain that there were devotees of Slaanesh in the city, and that Alfredo Gambini was in all likelihood one of them. He also knew that such degenerates were constantly seeking ever deeper levels of depravity to experience, craving new sensations to expose themselves to with the same consuming passion of a weirdroot addict.

He guessed that such human fiends would not be unknown to a place like the Pink Rose, in fact, he supposed that they would be rather notorious. Madam Rosa had been extremely forthcoming when Brunner had told her what sort of individual he was looking for. Exposing the patron to the Temple of Solkan might have given her house a bad name, turning him over to the bounty hunter seemed a more respectable venture, especially since the man wouldn't be saying anything afterwards. A bit of gold smoothed over the lingering traces of reluctance on her part to point Brunner in the right direction.

The bounty hunter had found the man in an upstairs room, 'fortifying' himself before a meeting of his decadent cult. For a man whose doctrine would have him look forward to pain as just another experience to be savoured, it had taken the bounty hunter surprisingly little time to drag the location of the cult's meeting place from the man's bleeding lips.

One thing Brunner had neglected to ask the man before he had allowed Schtafel to finish him, had been how many were in his vile little congregation. The bounty hunter had never guessed that there might be so many. Even with the threat of a gruesome execution at the hands of the Solkanites, the lure of Slaanesh was still attractive to the people of Remas.

Brunner looked over at his two comrades.

'Now that we know he's here,' Brunner said, 'I think it's time we sent for reinforcements.' Schtafel eagerly nodded his head at the suggestion, but Horst just continued to glare at the Chaos worshippers, a burning frenzy growing in his eyes. Brunner tugged at his arm. 'Even if you think you're Magnus reborn, there's too many for you,' he informed the warrior. Then he saw two new figures stride into the unhallowed ritual.

Brunner watched in silence as Corvino led the dark-robed Scurio to the altar. The fool traded words with Alfredo Gambini for a moment, as several cultists detached themselves from the celebration and busied themselves with stripping Scurio of his robe. As they did so, Brunner became stock still, his vision narrowing to include nothing except his view of the priest's back.

There, in black ink, the long, sinuous length of a fat-bodied serpent had been applied to Scurio's flesh. The mark of the killer from Pavona. The serpent was the hooded adder of Araby's great deserts, the style of tattoo clearly the crude and painful needle-work of that southern land.

Brunner watched as the cultists continued to tug Scurio from his robes. The bounty hunter lifted his pistol from its holster.

'What are you doing?' hissed Schtafel, eyes wide with alarm.

'Change of plans,' Brunner told him. 'We're staying.' Horst Brendle looked over at the bounty hunter and grinned a murderous smile.

Then the undertemple exploded into confusion and carnage.

INQUISITOR BOCCA STORMED into the chamber, his gigantic sword gripped in one hand, the severed heads of the two cultists who had been left as sentries in the ruin above dangling by the hair from his other fist. Around him, dozens of temple militia swarmed into the vast hall. Bocca tossed his gruesome trophies into the midst of the shocked cultists as they faced the intruders.

'Cleanse this place in the blood of the corrupt!' roared the inquisitor's bellowing voice. 'The Day of Judgement is at hand!'

The cultists were scrambling for weapons or trying to dodge their way around the temple militia as the white-robed fanatics fell upon them, hewing and cudgelling the armed and the defenceless with equal zeal, sparing neither the aged nor the young their righteous rage. Through the carnage, Bocca stormed towards the altar, his sword cutting down any cultist who either in flight or in attack chanced to cross his path.

None of these scum would escape this place. Bocca would present their bodies and the filthy altar before which they worshipped to the temple fathers and the grand inquisitor. It would be a fitting tribute to Solkan, and a momentous note in the inquisitor's career. Only one thing would make his victory any greater. Bocca turned his gold-masked face from side to side, searching for the one man he would bring before the grand inquisitor alive. Death was too good an end for Alfredo Gambini. At least a quick death.

BRUNNER OBSERVED THE Solkanite militia crash into the Slaaneshi cultists like leopards falling upon sheep. The slaughter was horrible, but no better than the depraved cultists deserved. He was disturbed to see the hulking figure of Inquisitor Bocca among the zealots, wondering how coincidental it was that the inquisitor should happen to discover this place only now. There had been entirely too much coincidence occurring in this city since he had arrived.

The bounty hunter swore as he saw three men racing towards the back of the temple. Brunner was not interested over much in what fate might befall two of the men, Corvino and Alfredo Gambini were of no import to him. But the third man, clutching his black cloak about his midsection as he ran, he was of importance to the bounty killer. Brunner leapt from his cover, intent on cutting off Scurio's escape. Horst followed the bounty hunter's example, dashing forward to join the zealots in their attack. Schtafel called out after his friend, scrambling out from behind the urn in an attempt to stop Horst's reckless charge at the Chaos cultists.

Brunner looked over at Schtafel. 'Watch Horst's back!' he told the wiry marksman. 'I'm going after Scurio!' Brunner did not give the mercenary a chance to object, racing off into the midst of the swirling battle, trying to keep the fast retreating shape of his prey in sight. A white-robed figure loomed before Brunner and he discharged his pistol into its mask, heedless of whether his shot bore through wood or leather. Neither side in this frantic melee could be considered friendly to the bounty hunter. He replaced the pistol in its holster, relying upon Drakesmalice's sharp edge to fend off any others that got in his way.

Soon, Brunner was clear of the melee. He could see Corvino leading the other two men down a small stairway at the back of the undertemple, beyond the rear wall, whose opening closed up behind them, leaving only a flat surface of pitted black stone, as though the door in the wall had never been. The bounty hunter swore under his breath, not looking forward to trying to find whatever mechanism controlled the hidden door, still less happy with the time such a delay would give his quarry to escape.

Such thoughts were put aside as a hulking shape in black armour turned toward Brunner. The inquisitor had forsaken the melee, seeking instead to destroy the profane idol of the cultists. But now the war-priest stalked out from behind the altar and its hideous icon, intent on a more personal form of retribution. Bocca's golden mask silently condemned the bounty hunter as it came around to face him. The cloaked inquisitor's eyes were like fire behind his mask.

'You!' Bocca roared as he saw the bounty hunter. He had not expected to find the man who had escaped him in the plaza only a few days ago here in the Slaaneshi temple, but now that he had, Bocca would only be too happy to visit the vengeance of Solkan upon the wretch. The inquisitor lifted his huge sword in anticipation of what he was certain would be a swiftly decided struggle.

Brunner watched the hulking giant advance upon him from the right, firming his own grip upon Drakesmalice. So intent had he been on Scurio's fleeing shape, he had not seen the inquisitor straining at the Mother of Mystery, trying to knock it from its altar. Now there was nothing to do but face the imposing priest. He would hardly be able to find the hidden door with an inquisitor of Solkan hacking at him with five feet of steel. It seemed that he should have saved his pistol shot. It looked like he was going to need it.

'WHERE ARE WE?' Alfredo demanded as Corvino lit the only candle in the small, cell-like room to which the fool had led them. Alfredo took quick note of as much of the room as the candle revealed, seeing a dark opening in the far wall that might indicate a passageway. The sounds of battle sounded from overhead, clearly indicating that they were only a few feet below the undertemple. Upon the floor, daubed in dried, crusty blood, was the eight pointed symbol of Chaos.

'You might think of this as an "under undertemple",' Corvino laughed. 'I had it constructed shortly after I led your cult to this place,' the fool added, removing a wavy-bladed copper dagger from a pocket within his tunic.

'Why?' the cult leader asked, not understanding.

'We must all have our secrets, must we not?' Corvino said. He looked past the cult leader to Scurio. The priest had recovered his robe, once more garbed in his black priest's habit. 'Scurio, be so kind as to take hold of Alfredo's arms,' he calmly ordered the priest. Alfredo struggled in Scurio's grip, but found the hold upon him surprisingly strong and unyielding.

'You see,' smiled the sorcerer, speaking with the superior tone of a lecturer, 'this is a very special temple. The priests of Morr never desanctified this place, it was still devoted to Morr when your cult profaned it with your first ritual to the Lord of Pleasure. And now I shall doubly profane this place by making an offering which I am certain Slaanesh would find most disturbing.'

Corvino stepped closer, showing Alfredo the skull rune inscribed upon the blade. The Slaaneshi cultist paled as he saw the loathsome symbol of that other power.

'My friend here, Scurio, is rather unique too,' continued Corvino. 'You see, he really is a priest of Morr. He was captured by Arabyan corsairs many years ago, tortured and tormented by them night and day for months on end. He should have died, but in his despair, he called out to any power that would heed him. And one did, though Scurio did not expect the price that power would demand.'

'Please,' Scurio moaned, 'you said tonight was the night! You said tonight I would be free of this evil inside me!' Scurio could feel the hideous thing that had been inked into his back writhing, crawling under his skin, striving to be released.

'Quite so,' stated Corvino. With no further warning, he reached up and ran the dagger across Alfredo's throat. 'Blood for the Blood God,' he snarled into the man's face. The cultist gargled on his own blood as the crimson liquid bubbled from the wound in a river of red. Corvino observed the blood for a moment, ensuring that most of it dripped into the Chaos star daubed upon the floor. Then the fool turned away, striding over to an iron-bound wooden chest that formed the only visible furnishing in the room. He lifted the heavy lid and removed a small clay jar from within.

Scurio let the dying Alfredo fall to the floor as Corvino returned. 'You said you would free me!' he shouted. 'I can feel the evil swelling within me! You must hurry!'

Corvino smiled at the frantic priest. 'I shall free you of the evil that has haunted you these many years,' he said. He directed Scurio to step forward and stand at the centre of the eight-arrow symbol, and the expanding pool of Alfredo's blood, then the fool handed the priest the clay jar. It was an artefact of great antiquity, discovered in Araby during some long ago crusade and brought back to the Imperial capital of Altdorf. Through General Mandalari's contacts, Corvino had arranged to have the artefact stolen and smuggled into Remas. Now he would put the object to the use for which it had waited throughout the ages.

Corvino smacked the dagger's hilt against the lead seal of the jar, each time speaking the Blood God's name. Scurio's eyes were wide with horror as he heard the vile sound issue from the fool's lips. The priest trembled as he held the jar, struggling to keep from dropping the ancient clay vessel. All his hopes depended upon this ritual.

When the dagger struck the lead seal for the eighth time, the old metal crumbled away, falling to the floor in a crusty black ash. The stench of rancid, ancient blood issued from within the jar. Corvino waved his hand at Scurio, instructing the priest to inhale the fumes issuing from the mouth of the clay jar.

'That's it!' crowed the fool, as Scurio breathed deeply of the filthy vapour. 'You must breathe in as much as you can if we are to solve your little affliction.' Corvino laughed as he watched the priest struggle to keep from vomiting as the stench filled his lungs. The priest's trembling grip at last faltered and the old clay jar fell to the floor, shattering within the eight-pointed star drawn upon the floor. A black mist rose from the shards, quickly dispersing.

'The pain!' screamed Scurio, clutching at his chest. Blood sprayed from his mouth as he shouted, sizzling as it struck the floor. Corvino continued to smile as he watched the priest's body convulse in agony.

'Of course there is pain,' the fool said. 'No new life is born without a lot of pain, and much blood.' Corvino leaned down to stare into Scurio's face. The man's eyes were pools of crimson now, sanguine tears rolling down his face. The priest opened his mouth to speak but no sound issued, only a great bubble of black blood. Corvino patted the stricken man's head, as if consoling a frightened puppy.

'Poor Scurio,' the sorcerer said, his voice laden with regret. 'You can't imagine how hard it was, finding you, recognising what had made a home within you. Compared to that, finding the old Arabyan jar was a mere conjurer's trick. Think of it, for the first time since it was vanquished, the spirit of the Mardagg has come into contact with the vessel that holds its essence!' the fool laughed loudly, paying no heed to Scurio's hacking cough, or the blood spilling from his mouth. Corvino looked at the shattered clay fragments. 'Or perhaps I should say the vessel that held the Mardagg's essence? Seems that it isn't holding much of anything now.'

Scurio doubled over, crouching on his hands and knees over the ruinous symbol drawn upon the floor. His blood was pouring from him now, as though he was trying to vomit every drop from his body. As the crimson liquid fell on the floor, it steamed, gnawing at the stones like acid. In response, the dried blood that had been used by Corvino to create the eight-arrow symbol began to glow with a hellish light.

'So very many things to do this right!' he called down at Scurio, oblivious to the fact that the priest was so far gone in his pain to hear anything the fool was saying. 'This place, for instance, twice profaned. I don't think you really appreciate the power of that. And poor Alfredo, a devoted servant of Slaanesh! What better sacrificial offering to attract the attention of Khorne the Blood God than a priest of his most despised rival? Why, even yourself, my dear Scurio, you too were a priest of a rival deity. The spirit of the Mardagg did well when it chose you.' The fool laughed again. 'But, then, even before it made a home within your mangy skin, you had ever so much in common. I mean, you both were very interested in death.' Corvino paused for a moment, deep in thought. 'Actually, I think that is about all you have in common.'

Scurio reached out, his hand gripping Corvino's shoe. With an extreme effort, he looked up into the sorcerer's face. Though no words emerged from his mouth, Corvino could easily understand the word the priest's dripping face mouthed. It was a last, desperate plea for help. The fool shook his head.

'I'm afraid that it is much easier to free the evil of you rather than you of the evil,' the fool explained. Scurio groaned, falling onto his face within the eight-pointed symbol. 'You did a very nice job of feeding it all these years, fattening it upon blood. Your filthy evil little body is just the thing to house a daemon after it has been locked up in a nasty old jar for a thousand years or so.'

Corvino watched with eager eyes as the blood gurgling from Scurio's wound began to thicken and darken. Soon the priest's body began to twitch beneath its cloak upon the floor.

The fool leaned down, reaching toward the hand clutching his shoe. The skin was already beginning split, cracking open like the fabric of a moth's chrysalis. The flesh beneath was wet and gleaming, withering even as the bones beneath began to swell. Corvino brought the dagger raking across one of the fingers, cutting it free. He gripped the digit and cackled at the mutating body at his feet.

'Now I shall lead and you must follow,' he told the growing shape on the floor. Corvino dashed towards the passage at the rear of his sanctum. The daemon was now bound to its host body, all of its host body. Even removed from Scurio, the finger was still a part of him, and the daemon a part of it. The Mardagg would be drawn after the severed digit, tracking it like some loathsome hound, compelled to find it by an all-consuming compulsion. Of course, the daemon would need blood to keep it from decaying while it hunted down its finger. But in a city as large as Remas, Corvino did not think it would have any trouble satisfying that need.

'I shall lead and you must follow,' he laughed again, before slipping into the dark tunnel. The passage came out very near the Great Reman Bridge, he would be back inside the Gambini palazzo within only a score or so minutes. The daemon, however, would use a different route. After a thousand years of cold captivity, its spirit wandering from one madman to another, Corvino knew that it would be in no mood to hide and slink in the shadows. It would find a route that would allow it to appease its hunger. And where it walked, so too would walk death and destruction on a scale the city had never seen.

Corvino considered this to be a rather wonderful bonus to all his plans. Oh yes, the fool thought as he ran down the subterranean tunnel, there would most assuredly be a hot time in old Remas tonight.

X

OLD REMARO GAMBINI sat within his bed chamber on one of the upper floors of the palazzo. The elderly man stared at the wall, not seeing it. After being led to this room, his mind had deserted his surroundings, focusing instead, as they had so often in the last few years, upon his son. He had known the secret since the beginning, and had borne it stoically for decades. But now, as his life began to ebb from his tired old bones, Remaro found that the secret was crushing him, squashing him like an insect under the hoof of an ox. It was choking him, robbing the air that filled his lungs of its sweetness. He should never have agreed, should never have allowed it to happen. But he had, and it was far too late to try and undo what had been done.

Still, to have his son gaze upon him, looking upon him as a son should look at his father, now that seemed to be the only thing he wanted out of his life, the only thing that could allow him to rest easy in his grave.

'Are they still looking for Alfredo?' a quiet voice asked. Remaro swung his head around, watching as the red and black clothed Corvino emerged from the depths of his wardrobe. There was a secret door in that closet; Remaro wondered how the fool had come to learn of it. The old man smiled at Corvino, the only man in the palazzo who seemed to listen to him any more.

'I'm afraid they won't find him,' the fool sighed, flopping down into a chair. As he did so, Remaro noticed that there was blood on Corvino's clothing. Seeing the old man's reaction, the fool realised what he'd seen. 'I apologise, uncle, I must present such a sight.' The fool pointed at his sleeve, the red fabric stained a darker hue. 'That, I believe, is Scurio.' He pointed to a large splotch across his chest. 'This, I'm afraid, is Alfredo.' The old man stared at him stupidly, as though wondering why he should be concerned by the death of Alfredo. 'I might still have some Mandalari on my shoes,' he quipped, hopping to his feet.

All at once, something Corvino had said registered within Remaro's addled mind. The old man's eyes bulged with horror, as if seeing the fool for the very first time, seeing him for what he truly was. Corvino's smile spread into the grinning rictus of a skull.

'Very good,' he hissed. 'I was wondering when you'd come around.' Remaro turned to scurry to the door, but Corvino was on him in an instant, tossing him to the floor with contemptuous ease. The fool brought the edge of his staff cracking into the old man's head, opening a gash in his scalp. Remaro's trembling hand patted the flowing crimson.

'I must insist that you stay, dear uncle,' Corvino snarled. 'There is a reckoning between you and I. It can't be delayed any longer, dear brother of my father.' The fool lashed out again with his staff, cracking the old man in his ribs. 'Usurper!' he spat.

'It was the only way,' Remaro gasped. 'You were born…'

'I know what I was born!' shouted Corvino. 'Do you think you need to tell me of my deformity, of the stamp of ruin upon my body? How my father must have cursed all the gods when he saw me! So proud to have sired a son, an heir, until he saw that clawed foot at the end of my left leg!'

'He killed your mother before I could stop him!' Remaro exclaimed. 'But you I saved! You were only a babe, I couldn't allow him to kill you.'

'So you proposed a trade? Your son for my father's?' Corvino sneered maliciously as he saw the pained look on Remaro's face. 'Ah, I see, it was he who proposed the substitution. It must have seemed such a good deal, one mutant whelp for the security of your son, for letting little Giovanni inherit the title, the property, the position! How that must have pained you, dear uncle, to in one instant make your line the future of the house Gambini.'

'Do you think it has been easy?' Remaro asked. 'To see my son every day, to watch him grow before my very eyes and never be able to acknowledge him as my son?'

'You could have kept me,' Corvino pointed out. 'But, no, what would the Temple of Solkan say if one of our enemies were to tell them that a Gambini had sired a mutant? We couldn't risk that, any more than we could risk my ever learning who I was. Ever discovering that I am Umberto Gambini!'

'He wanted you destroyed,' Remaro said, reaching toward Corvino. 'It was I who sold you to a travelling band of Strigany entertainers. It was I who got you away from your father's bloodlust.'

Corvino smiled down at the old man. 'Then I have much to thank you for,' he said. 'The Strigany sold me in their turn. They saw my... disability... and sold me to a sorcerer. He reared me as his apprentice, but he was more deserving of the title "fool" than I have ever been. Through his dark arts, he learned who I was. Through his stupidity, I learned who I was. When I had learned enough from him, I left, stealing what I would need to work my vengeance.' Corvino lifted Remaro back to his feet. 'You see, I've come home to claim my kingdom!'

Corvino looked down at the front of his tunic. The cloth was moving, as something within one of the inner pockets wriggled against his shirt. He looked back at Remaro, this time his smile was neither cruel nor mocking, but apologetic. 'It was a very potent ritual I stole from my teacher, uncle, a spell that even he did not dare contemplate. Sadly, it is well under way now, and I have much to do before my guest arrives.' Corvino suddenly whipped the length of his staff against the floor in a savage, one-handed motion, snapping it in half. He lifted the upper portion, staring at the goblin head and its jingling bells. 'If I don't want the daemon to cheat me, I have to finish this now!'

'Not my son!' wailed Remaro as Corvino drove the bronzed head of his staff against the old man's head. For a minute or so, Remaro struggled against the fool's assault, but at last he choked, slumping to the floor.

'Oh, most certainly your son,' the fool told the corpse as he walked away. 'He presumes that everything that belongs to me, belongs to him. I simply have to correct that delusion.' Corvino paused as he opened the door, tapping his chin contemplatively.

'But first I think I'll go claim my bride.'

BRUNNER STAGGERED BACK as the inquisitor's sword struck his blocking blade. The bounty hunter snarled, feinting an overhand return, then swiping low toward the inquisitor's knees. Bocca second-guessed his adversary, and once more Drakesmalice crashed against the man's intercepting steel. Brunner stepped away to recover and instantly Bocca was following through with his own attack. Brunner barely managed to avoid the murderous downswing of the inquisitor's blade, dancing backward just as the priest's steel flashed past his face. The bounty hunter did not have time to consider this latest in a series of narrow escapes, for Bocca was already swinging at him once more.

He had expected Bocca to be no mean hand with a sword, but Brunner found himself woefully outclassed by the fanatic. The bounty hunter had fought all manner of swordsmen in his time, from the most skilled to men who would have been better off using a farm tool to defend themselves. Generally, the more practiced swordsmen were cool, calculating men, taking the measure of their foe and awaiting their chance to strike at some opening in their defence. Bocca was a different sort of creature entirely. He had the knowledge and instincts of a fencing master, but these skills were suborned to his fanatic lust to spill the blood of heretics. The inquisitor threw himself completely into the attack, trusting to his thick black armour to guard his body from any attacks that an enemy might manage to strike at him.

It was a deadly combination, Brunner could only think of a trained bear from Kislev he had seen once that some lunatic had taught actual wrestling moves, filling the brute mind of the animal with the knowledge that would allow it to exploit its bulk and strength to its best advantage. Bocca was no less a monster than the bear had been, a blood-crazed animal devoting its learning toward one solitary goal, restraint and self-preservation cast aside in a fit of bloodlust. He was just the sort of man Brunner would never have chosen to face in close combat. If ever there had been a man meant for a crossbow bolt or a pistol shot, that man was Bocca. Brunner would have laughed if he had enough wind to do so. The way things were looking, the inquisitor might not have gone down if Brunner had fired a cannon ball into him.

The bounty hunter had already attempted several times to tip the odds back into his favour. He had stabbed at the inquisitor's knee with one of his knives early in the fight, but the war-priest's thick armour had deflected the thrust, causing Brunner's knife to sink into Bocca's calf rather than the vulnerable tendons of his knee. Later, exploiting a brief opening, Brunner had driven the slender stiletto concealed within the sleeve of his tunic into the inquisitor's neck, but the slim blade had again missed the intended target, striking the edge of Bocca's armour and snapping like a twig.

The inquisitor showed no sign that he was becoming fatigued by the long battle, nor any trace of concern or impairment from his leg wound. The bounty hunter only wished that he could say the same. It was becoming an effort for him to maintain the speed and strength required to meet and match the fanatic's blows. Brunner cursed whatever unnatural power kept the inquisitor from tiring like any normal man.

The gold mask of the zealot considered Brunner with its unmoving, disapproving face, the eyes staring from behind it burning with a feral fury. There was triumph in that mad gaze, and Brunner knew that unless he thought of something to upset the tide of the contest soon, that triumph would not be long in coming.

Suddenly both of the combatants staggered as the ground beneath their feet shuddered. Brunner recovered first, but even as he lashed out at the inquisitor, the floor rumbled again, nearly knocking the bounty hunter from his feet. It was as if a giant steam-hammer was pounding on the floor from below. Bocca stared at the floor for a moment, then tried to steady himself as it shuddered yet again.

Brunner began to warily back away from the disturbance, eyes locked on the black-garbed inquisitor. Bocca saw his enemy withdrawing and began to follow, his huge sword held upward at his side. Yet the gold-masked priest had taken no more than a few steps when an even greater tremor rocked the undertemple. The sound of tearing stone screamed across the vast hall, dust and chunks of rubble exploding from a great rupture in the floor.

A thick, sanguinary stench billowed upward from below, causing many of the surviving cultists and temple militia to retch, all thoughts of battle momentarily slipping from their minds. A dark shape loomed up through the hole, a black silhouette within the stone dust. A miasma of dread rolled across the chamber like a tide of terror. Moans of despair and screams of fright sounded, echoing from the walls and the ceiling high above.

Brunner watched as a shape strode forward from the dust. The bounty hunter could make out little more than a shadow within the murk, but what he could see added to the air of dread that suddenly filled the hall. The shape was huge, looming up at least twelve feet above the floor, its frame gaunt and scrawny for such an imposing height.

It had been some time since the bounty hunter had known fear. He had never known terror such as gripped him now, as the monster emerged from the shadows and the daemon's ancient aura of merciless evil washed over his soul.

JULIANA CONSIDERED THE chaotic turn events had taken in the last few hours. Mandalari was dead, and the prince's cousin appeared to be the killer. Things were happening much too fast for her to handle. She was used to politicking and double-dealing from her life in the Bensario palace, but all those years of learning how and who to manipulate had never prepared her for this!

The princess tore at the cloth clenched in her delicate hands, trying to work the tension from her body into the tortured rag. The thought that a madman might even now be prowling the halls of the palazzo made her skin crawl. Prince Gambini had posted five men outside her door, however. Even a madman would have a hard time getting to her through that many guards.

'You look ravishing this evening,' a familiar voice spoke from behind the princess. Juliana spun around, shocked by the unexpected voice. She was greeted by the sight of a smiling Corvino emerging from a panel in the wall, a secret door whose existence Juliana had never even guessed. There was blood on his checkered clothes, and an ugly glimmer in his eyes. The princess gasped, licking her suddenly dry mouth. She'd been upset enough pondering her own private suspicions regarding who had killed the old general. Now the subject of those thoughts stood before her. She began to tremble as she saw the mad gleam in Corvino's eyes. It was like facing some rabid animal, a deranged, unpredictable beast that might pounce at any instant.

Juliana tried to control the trembling in her limbs, tried to calm her breath, lest her agitation disturb the lunatic. Slowly, carefully, Juliana backed away from the fool.

'But, then, brides always look beautiful on their wedding day,' Corvino said, walking around the divan upon which Juliana had been sitting.

'What do you want?' the princess demanded, though somehow she could not quite force any real measure of authority into her voice. She continued to back away as the fool advanced.

'Why, I have come for you, my love,' he said, reaching his pale hand out to her. There was blood on his wrist, blood on his sleeve. 'You do intend to marry Prince Gambini, do you not?' Juliana cringed away from the mad gleam in his eyes, and only then realised her mistake. She had allowed herself to be backed into a corner, away from the outer door, where the guards were positioned.

'Prince Umberto Gambini? That is the man you are going to marry?'

'Please, Corvino,' she sobbed, wondering if she dared provoke the man by screaming for help.

'Corvino?' the fool asked, touching his hand to his breast. 'Why, there is no one of that name! There never was! I am Prince Gambini, Prince Umberto Gambini! I am the real prince! That man you thought to marry was but an impostor, a usurper! I am the man you want!'

Juliana tried to run towards the door, but the fool was quicker, grabbing her wrist in a vice-like grip.

'Oh yes, it is true,' Corvino assured her. 'I've just spoken to my treacherous uncle about it at some length.'

Juliana started to scream, but Corvino's other hand closed upon her mouth. With her free hand, the princess tried to rake her attacker's eyes, but Corvino leaned away from her clutch, causing her hand to tear at his tunic instead. Something fell on the floor, wriggling upon the rug. Juliana stared at it in horror, too frightened even to scream when Corvino removed his hand from her mouth.

It was a severed finger, enormous and skeleton-thin, the bone-like length of it a dark red, like old blood. And it was alive, wriggling on the floor like some hideous worm. It struggled in Corvino's grip as the fool retrieved it.

'We really must hurry,' Corvino told Juliana as she passed out. The fool stepped forward, catching her body as she swooned. He stared down at her, patting a lock of hair away from her face. 'You see,' he added as he replaced the loathsome finger within one of his pockets, 'the priest is already on his way.'

IT STOOD TWICE the height of a man, shrouded in what looked like the black hooded habit of a priest of Morr. The long garment only reached to its waist, the legs beneath it standing bare. They were thin, little more than bones, as were the long arms that extended from the sleeves of the robe. The skeletally thin limbs were the colour of blood, seemingly composed of a slimy sheen of gore. The face that stared from beneath the cowl of the priest's habit was that of a skull, though it was no such skull as any clean creature had ever been born to. The jaw was long, the teeth pointed fangs each three inches long. Bony growths resembling hound-like ears rose to either side of the skull, disappearing into the depths of the cowl. Like the rest of the apparition, the skull too was red, composed of a glistening, writhing sheen of blood.

The daemon turned its head slowly, causing drops of blood to fall from its face, sizzling upon the stone floor. The sockets of its eyes were empty, filled only by a black vacancy, yet Brunner could feel the homicidal hatred of the daemon's stare surging from those dark, empty pits.

The daemon uttered no sound as it inspected the under-temple. Solkanite zealots and Slaaneshi cultists alike stood in a horrified silence, eyes locked upon the ghastly shape, terror numbing legs that wanted nothing more than to flee, to run until the walls of Remas were many leagues in the distance.

The daemon took a step forward, sizzling blood dripping from its body. The sight of the monster moving dispelled the paralysis gripping the onlookers, and as it stepped forward, they took a collective step back. The abomination seemed to notice their reaction, and it extended its bony arm. Gleaming blood began to boil around its hand, extending in either direction from the skeletal claw. The blood began to solidify, to take on a shape of its own. Soon, a gleaming scythe composed of the daemon's otherworldly substance was gripped firmly in its claw.

Screams sounded once more and the onlookers fled as the daemon resumed its unhurried advance. Cultists scrambled alongside militia, forgetting their mutual hatred in their desperation to escape the nightmarish being. Only one man retained his courage in the face of the baleful manifestation. Inquisitor Bocca firmed his grip on his sword, stepping into the path of the skeletal daemon.

'Test my faith, filth!' Bocca cried up at the horror. 'I shall let the city of Mighty Solkan be profaned by neither man nor hell-sent abomination!'

Brunner had to admit it was a display of bravery as immense as any lie he had ever heard recorded in legend and song. The bounty hunter turned, hurrying toward the stairs that led to the abandoned Temple of Morr high above. Unlike the legends, he didn't think Bocca's heroic stand was going to fare very well.

The Mardagg stared down for a moment at the defiant mortal who stood in its path. The daemon gave Bocca no more thought than a steer swatting flies with its tail. The sickle-bladed scythe of the Mardagg descended in a swift, murderous arc. Bocca did not even have time to understand that he had been killed as the daemon's weapon clove through his thick steel armour as neatly as a knife through cheese.

The upper half of the inquisitor was hurled across the chamber by the force of the blow, crashing against the wooden altar, causing the Mother of Mystery to splinter, such was the intensity of his impact. A stream of blood sprayed upward from his severed waist for a moment, like some macabre fountain, before his muscles relaxed and the dead man's legs fell to the floor.

The Mardagg strode onward, crossing the hall of the undertemple. Like all creatures of the Blood God, it was attracted to the sounds of conflict, to the smell of blood. It had been unable to resist the combat unfolding just above its head as it consumed Scurio's body, once more manifesting itself in flesh. But now, it felt another pull, something else drawing it onward.

The daemon's claw flexed, feeling the absence of its severed digit.

It would reclaim its flesh from the fool who had called it into being. And then it would complete the task it had started long ago, offering the lives of all upon the peninsula to Khorne.

BRUNNER WAS ASTONISHED to find Schtafel and Horst waiting for him in the street just outside the ruined temple. The bearded mercenary was injured, a gash running along one side of his face, courtesy of a temple militia man. Schtafel supported his friend. Both mercenaries gave a sigh of relief when they saw the bounty hunter emerge.

'Praise be Myrmidia!' exclaimed Schtafel. The wiry marksman was pale as a corpse, his hands trembling. Brunner considered that it would probably take such a shock to make the warrior show a religious streak.

'What are you two doing here?' demanded Brunner.

'Horst wouldn't leave without you,' explained Schtafel. 'What the hell is that thing?'

'Some devil from the very heart of Chaos!' Brunner answered. He reflected upon the black cloak the daemon had worn, and where he had seen that garment last.

'Get Horst somewhere safe,' Brunner told the crossbow-man. Schtafel started to scuttle off down the street.

'What about you?' Schtafel asked, looking back.

'That thing isn't going to stay down there,' Brunner stated in a grim voice. 'I think I know where it is heading, and if I'm right, somebody had better go and tell Zelten!'

The mercenaries might have pressed him further, but the sound of stone crashing within the ruins of the temple brought a renewed look of terror to Schtafel's pale features and the marksman began to hurry away with all the speed the cumbersome weight of Horst would allow.

Brunner looked over at the temple. The sounds of destruction continued. The bounty hunter could easily guess their origin, as the daemon kicked the rubble from its path. He could feel its intense aura of evil, of bloodlust emanating from the ruins. In his hand, Drakesmalice could sense the immense Chaos energies of the monster as well, the blade glowing red-hot. Brunner knew that the ancient sword had been forged for the Great War against Chaos, that upon it had been worked potent spells to smite the creations of the Ruinous Powers. But a sword was only as good as the hand that held it, and against such a monstrous, unnatural foe, the bounty hunter did not trust his own resolve.

People were starting to appear in the street now, wondering what had caused so many temple militia and masked revellers to race past their homes. They murmured amongst themselves in whispers of wonder as a dark shadow began to move within the temple. A few, the smartest, began to back away. Brunner did not linger to wait for the Mardagg to emerge onto the street, but began to sprint along the street, dodging past the citizens who now cluttered it. He did not know how long he would have to reach the bridge and the Gambini palazzo, but he felt that it would not be long.

Behind him, as if to confirm his suspicions, screams began to echo from around the old temple.

PRINCE UMBERTO GAMBINI stormed down the wide staircase, a dozen of his guards behind him. The aristocrat's face was one of sullen rage. Things had been going so well only the previous day. Now his military advisor and commander of his household guard was dead; his own cousin, the apparent killer, missing, possibly hiding somewhere within his own house. Now a messenger had arrived from the garrison at the bridge gate informing him that sentries standing watch in the tower had reported what appeared to be some sort of riot spreading from the old Temple of Morr, and advancing toward the bridge. The prince was not sure which god had decided to heap misfortune upon him, but he swore that he would have the faith proscribed within the walls of the city.

Prince Gambini was almost at the base of the stairs when a low, solemn note echoed along the marble halls. The nobleman and his soldiers looked down the passage, wondering if they had indeed heard what they thought they had heard. The note sounded again, confirming their first impression.

'I'll wring the neck of whatever dolt is ringing the alarm gong!' snarled Prince Gambini, racing off down the hall, all thoughts of riots and bridge guards momentarily pushed aside.

The alarm gong was located within the palazzo's great hall, the room in which the prince held court and strove to impress petitioners and enemies alike with his wealth and authority. The floors were covered in expensive Arabyan rugs, the walls covered in tapestries depicting great moments in the history of the Gambini line. At the centre of the chamber, upon a small dais, stood a throne of dark wood, supposedly brought from the forests of Ulthuan, the scrollwork upon the carved armrests and back detailed in silver. Beside the throne, the heavy bronze gong was still vibrating from the final blow struck against it.

Others had heard the sound and when Prince Gambini arrived, he found a large number of servants and mercenaries already gathered there. He also saw the smiling figure seated upon the throne, one leg dangling over the armrest, swinging in the air, one hand idly toying with the hammer with which the gong had been struck. Seeing the beautiful woman sprawled at the base of the chair, the outraged nobleman surged forward, only stopping when a powerful grip took hold of his arm and restrained him.

'No, my lord,' Manfred Zelten spoke into the prince's ear. 'He'll kill her if you try to approach him.' The prince stared angrily into the mercenary's face, then tore his arm free of Zelten's grip, but did not try to advance toward the throne.

'Ah, there you are!' crowed Corvino, tossing the hammer away over his shoulder as he sighted the nobleman. 'I was beginning to think you'd never get here!' The fool shook his head. 'I don't think we'll be able to make anything of someone with such poor notions of time-keeping. I don't think you'd even make a good fool!' Corvino laughed, a soulless, grating sound devoid of reason and humanity.

'You scum!' bellowed Prince Gambini, drawing his sword and once more advancing on the throne. With a speed even an elf might have envied, Corvino whipped out a long copper dagger, aiming its point downward at the throat of Juliana, lying sprawled and unconscious at his feet.

'Don't force me to do something I'll regret later,' Corvino threatened. 'I have other plans for the princess, I'd hate to have to change them.' Prince Gambini lowered his sword, meeting the mad gaze of the fool.

'What do you want?' he asked, his voice filled with defeat.

'What do I want?' repeated Corvino. He looked around the room, then back at the prince. 'Why, everything, right down to the fleas in the kennel.' The fool's jovial tone slipped into a murderous growl. 'But for now, all I want is for everybody to just stay where they are, like nice little statues.' The death's head grin spread across Corvino's face once more. 'I am expecting company.'

At that instant, a soldier from the gate rushed into the chamber. The man stopped short when he saw the curious scene, but soon recovered from his surprise. Putting his questions aside, he ran to the prince.

'Prince Gambini!' the man exclaimed. 'There is a daemon loose in the streets! It is herding the people towards the bridge, cutting them down like wheat!' The man's voice dropped into a frightened whisper. 'My lord, they say it is the Mardagg!'

BRUNNER RUSHED TOWARD the gate of the Great Reman Bridge. The sounds of horror, madness and death rising from the streets behind him had been growing louder and more terrible the farther he had run. Ironically, the sounds were drawing more and more people from their homes and onto the streets. A single scream might not disturb the people of Remas, but this sort of clamour was entirely unique in a city where the Solkanites kept things peaceful and quiet. And because it was so unique, curiosity, not fear took hold of the people, at least until they saw the source of the panic for themselves.

At first, the crowds had kept ahead of the daemon quite easily, and its slow, steady gait had been easy to distance. But as the crowd fled, they increasingly came into the unyielding bodies of other citizens, ones who had not seen the monster and wondered what the commotion was about. They stubbornly refused to move, and in their desperation to get past, the frightened crowd had come to blows with those who stood in their way. The flight had degenerated into a desperate brawl. And as the conflict grew in violence and vigour, the daemon had hastened its steps. The Mardagg struck the rear of the terrified herd of human cattle, lashing out with its scythe, cutting men in half with every sweep of its weapon. The image was like some diabolic parody of a farmer harvesting his crop as the Mardagg cut its way through the field of struggling bodies filling the street before it.

Those who by chance or design managed to get out of the line of the Mardagg's path did not entirely escape the daemon's horrible presence. Many were driven mad by such close proximity to a being of such timeless malevolence and terror. Others suffered an even more virulent madness, as drops of sizzling blood fell from the daemon's body, burning into their flesh. All who were so marked became ravening beasts, falling upon those around them with clawing hands and gnashing teeth, only the urge to kill left within their maimed minds. In the wake of the daemon, mobs of crazed killers loped off into the streets of Remas to spread terror and death throughout the city.

Brunner was certain that he knew where the hideous abomination was heading. The stairs the bounty hunter had seen the three cult leaders escape by had led downward, the very direction from which this nightmare horror had emerged. Brunner suspected that it was one of them, in a desperate effort to destroy Bocca's men, who had summoned the daemon. And if a creature summoned by any of those men was now heading toward the bridge, there could be only one place its destination could be. Perhaps it was even, in a twisted sense, going home. The black robe hanging about the monster's upper body was all too similar to the robe of a priest of Morr. That seemed to confirm Brunner's suspicions as to what the daemon had once been. The prospect of bringing Scurio to Pavona did not look very feasible now.

Brunner rushed to the iron bars of the gate between the towers that blocked the entrance to the bridge. The fleeing mob was not so far from him now, only a few dozen yards. The guards at the gate were barring the portals against the seeming riot. The bounty hunter hastened his gait, slipping through just as it was closing. The guards on the other side closed upon him, spears aimed at his chest.

'I bring a report on the cause of the riot for Prince Gambini!' Brunner declared as he recovered his breath. The guard captain cast him a suspicious look, but at that instant the foremost of the fleeing citizens crashed into the gate, clawing at it and screaming for entrance. The captain was too busy snarling demands at the frightened wretches and orders to his men to trouble himself any further with the bounty hunter. As Brunner resumed his sprint, he could hear new screams sounding from behind him. The captain, fearing that the panicked citizens would topple the gate by sheer weight of numbers, had ordered his spearmen to begin stabbing their weapons through the bars. If the Mardagg had hastened its stride to indulge in the violence of a duel, Brunner did not want to consider how much more eager it would be to reach the site of this atrocity.

THE BOUNTY HUNTER sprinted across the bridge, trying to ignore the sounds of death and terror rising from the distance. The bridge was alive with activity. Soldiers were pouring out of several of the palazzos, some hurrying toward the towers and the iron gate, others forming up around the families of their noble lords as the merchant princes hurried toward the opposite side of the bridge. Dozens of servants, their arms burdened with chests, sacks, and all manner of other containers filled to bursting with the valuables of their masters scuttled across the bridge, sometimes beside the entourage of their masters, other times doing their best to put distance between themselves and some shouting nobleman.

Brunner saw a dozen men trying to run towards the far shore while straining to carry a massive bronze sculpture, some art treasure their master was not willing to leave behind, even with a horrible daemon stalking ever nearer his door.

Other palazzos were being sealed shut, armed soldiers forming up within the gates, marksmen leaning from every window. At least some of the rulers of Remas were not going to abandon their homes without a fight. A small band of mercenaries was even removing a small cannon from one of the guard houses scattered across the bridge, moving it into the centre of the span, in anticipation of the monster's breakthrough at the gate.

The gunners did not have long to wait. The screams had risen to a hellish din, wailing sobs of mortal terror that could be heard even on the opposite side. Then the screams faded and in their place there came a dull, echoing thump, a tremendous blow struck against the iron gate. Brunner could hear the frenzied shouts of the guards at the gate and the mercenaries who had run to their position to support them. Every back was straining to hold the gates before that

which knocked upon them, the mortal strength of scores of
men pitted against the power of the daemon.

It was not enough. The thunderous boom sounded once
more as the Mardagg beat upon the metal portal with its
bony, club-like fist. The soldiers were pushed back as the
gates sagged inward. The men desperately reasserted themselves, pushing the portals back, stark terror now giving
them an impossible strength. Still it was not enough. When
the daemon knocked a third time, the gates broke open,
spilling soldiers onto the flagstones of the bridge. The
Mardagg stood for a moment framed in the gateway
between the two towers. The guards and mercenaries stared
up at it, every man shuddering with horror.

Then the daemon ducked its hooded head and stepped
onto the bridge.

Some of the soldiers tried to fight, jabbing at the Mardagg
with spears, pikes, halberds and swords. A small group of
hackbut men fired on the abomination with their rifles,
though more of their shakily aimed shots struck fellow mercenaries than found the unnatural flesh of the daemon.
Other soldiers ran at all speed away from the monster, cutting breastplates free of their bodies with knives and daggers
as they fled, that they might run all the faster. Some dove
from the bridge, all but a few of them sinking like stones to
the bottom of the lagoon in their armour. Still others simply
cringed before the daemon, sobbing and crying, their minds
broken by the Mardagg's aura of death and blood.

The daemon was pierced in dozens of places by bullet and
pike, yet it gave no sign that it had felt any of the injuries.
Before the horrified eyes of the soldiers, the Mardagg's red,
bubbling hide closed up behind each wound shortly after it
was inflicted. Then the daemon swung its scythe, hewing
down ten of its adversaries in a single sweep. What resistance
remained broke at once, the surviving mercenaries fled
before the skeletal apparition. The Mardagg pursued, cutting
down any that were too slow to escape its lengthy stride.

BRUNNER FOUND THE gate before Prince Gambini's palazzo
standing open, several soldiers standing outside it on the

main path of the bridge to observe the scene unfolding
between the towers, still undecided as to whether they
should try to secure the palazzo's gate or simply join the
frightened exodus fleeing the bridge. The sound of the cannon crew firing on the daemon boomed across the waters as
the bounty hunter entered the courtyard. Brunner grabbed
one of the sentries, a man he recognised as belonging to
Zelten's regiment.

'Where is your captain?' the bounty hunter demanded.
The mercenary, taken aback by Brunner's fierce tone, simply
pointed back at the palazzo. The bounty hunter relieved the
man of his crossbow and hurried across the courtyard.
Within the palazzo seemed to be deserted, at least until
Brunner heard raised voices sounding from the direction of
Prince Gambini's throne room. He hurried in that direc-
tion.

'It seems my friend is quite near now,' Brunner heard the
laughing voice of Corvino boast. 'You did not think you were
the only one with powerful friends, did you?'

Brunner stopped at the entrance to the great hall, spying
out the scene within.

At an instant, he observed the stand-off: Corvino leaning
before the throne, crouched above the prone form of Princess
Juliana, a wavy-bladed dagger in his hand. Prince Gambini,
Zelten and a large number of servants and guards stood in a
circle around the madman, chafing at their helplessness.
From behind him, Brunner could hear shouts and screams,
much nearer now than before.

'You're insane, Corvino,' Prince Gambini stated. 'Give this
up now and I promise no harm will come to you.' The
nobleman couldn't quite manage to get enough anger out of
his voice to make the offer sound convincing.

'I have told you already!' roared the fool. '*I* am Umberto
Gambini! And why would I trust the word of a man who
treated his own father like a pariah, who turned against his
own brother?' Corvino began to giggle, a weird, unnerving
sound. 'Mad? Perhaps, but in the land of the blind, the madman is king!' He puffed out his chest proudly as he made his
declaration.

Horrified screams sounded from outside the palazzo, perhaps originating from as near as the courtyard. All heads within the great hall turned toward the sound. Upon the dais, Corvino stood, laughing once more. 'My friend is here!' he cackled. 'I called him up from the abyss and now he is here!'

'That's all I needed to hear,' a cold voice said from the shadows near the doorway. Corvino turned his head toward the voice. As he did so, a steel crossbow bolt punched into his chest, throwing him from the dais.

Brunner stepped into the light, dropping the crossbow. 'You cost me ten thousand gold ducats,' he spat.

Zelten and Prince Gambini rushed the dais, both men reaching the unconscious form of Juliana at the same time. While the mercenary supported her, the prince slapped her face, trying to rouse her from her stupor.

'You might want to wait on that, gentlemen,' Brunner called to them. 'There's a damn big daemon heading this way!'

Screams erupted from the gathered servants and many of the soldiers and for an instant, Brunner wondered at the reaction to his words. Then the unforgettable stench of spilled blood, the chilling aura of dread and death washed over him. The bounty hunter turned his head, leaping further into the room as the hulking shape of the Mardagg lumbered down the corridor. The daemon's blood-scythe lashed out, cleaving through the marble wall and missing the bounty hunter by the merest fraction.

Brunner drew Drakesmalice, the sword blazing white hot in the proximity of a being so steeped in the ruinous energies of Chaos. The daemon seemed to take note of Brunner's weapon, turning from its path to glare at him with its eyeless sockets. Now, closer to the monster, Brunner could see that where before the daemon's flesh had simply resembled running blood, now there were tiny faces within the monster's liquid skin, small screaming images of those who had fallen beneath its scythe. The Mardagg was not merely killing its victims, it was collecting them, gathering them to present before its master, Khorne. Brunner froze as he considered the enormity of the horror the daemon represented. Then the murderous scythe was lashing toward him once more, the daemonic weapon glistening in the light.

It was instinct, not thought, that saved the bounty hunter's life. As the gore-hued blade swept toward him, he lifted Drakesmalice upward to block the blow. Indeed, had Brunner considered the action, he might have remembered the ease with which the Mardagg had sliced through Inquisitor Bocca's plate armour and never have trusted his own steel against the daemon's might. But Bocca's armour had not been guarded against the dire energies of Chaos, and the blade of Drakesmalice held against the Mardagg's scythe. But even if the cleaving blow was thwarted, the awesome strength of the daemon was not. Brunner was lifted from the floor by the sweep of the Mardagg's weapon and cast aside like a gnat. The bounty hunter crashed against one of the walls, the heavy tapestry cushioning the impact.

The daemon stared for an instant at the bounty hunter lying on the floor, then its skull-like face came around to regard the other occupants of the chamber once more. The daemon glared at them with its empty sockets and slowly began to advance again, drawn to the wriggling finger hidden within the slain fool's tunic.

Manfred Zelten was the first to react to the monster's steady, silent advance. Ripping his pistols from their holsters, the mercenary stepped away from Prince Gambini and his unconscious bride.

'Get her out of here!' the mercenary snapped at his master. 'We'll try and hold this abomination while you escape!'

Umberto Gambini did not need any further encouragement, rising to his feet and hurrying toward the far door of the chamber, Juliana draped across his arms. Those servants who had still not fled hastened after their master.

The Mardagg lumbered closer, the murderous scythe held in its bony clutch. Zelten stood in its path, casting a sidewise glance at the soldiers to either side of him. There were a half dozen of them whose loyalty to Prince Gambini had overcome their inclination to flee. Many of them held hatchet-headed halberds in their hands, and grim fatalistic expressions on their faces.

Zelten gave voice to what he hoped was a stirring war cry and fired one of his pistols at the daemon. The shot blasted into the skull-like face, disrupting the oozing, bloody substance, until it flowed back into place a few seconds later, filling the wound as though it had never been struck. At the same time, the halberdiers rushed at the daemon, thrusting and slashing at it with their weapons. As the Mardagg reacted to the men slashing at its legs, Zelten ran forward, firing his last pistol into the monster's bony chest. Once again, the bubbling, oozing substance closed over the wound almost as soon as it had been dealt. The skull-face of the Mardagg glared down at the Reiklander. Zelten dodged back as it swept the scythe in his direction.

'Pistols aren't going to work,' a cold voice informed Zelten. The mercenary was somewhat surprised to see Brunner on his feet again.

'I noticed,' Zelten snarled, hurling the discharged pistol at the monster's head and drawing his sword. The Mardagg paid the futile gesture no notice, busy trying to fend off the attacks of the halberdiers. Two of the men were forced to retreat as the daemon's weapon cut through the wooden shafts of their halberds, their remaining comrades trying to distract the daemon away from their now unarmed fellows.

'Any ideas?' Zelten asked the bounty hunter.

'Maybe,' Brunner replied, eyes focused intently on the daemon. Was it his imagination, or was the creature slower? Clumsier? He'd never heard of a daemon becoming fatigued, yet this monster, after its brutal march across Remas, was showing signs of tiring. Perhaps they might actually have a chance against it.

The bounty hunter lunged forward, striking at the daemon's flank. Drakesmalice impacted against the gleaming, screaming skin of the Mardagg, scouring its unnatural flesh. The Mardagg spun about, but too slowly to catch the bounty hunter before he dodged away. Where Drakesmalice had struck it, the oozing flesh had taken on a ridged, dark quality, almost as if the sword had caused the flowing blood to coagulate. Brunner grimly shook his head. The sword had certainly done something to the creature, but perhaps nothing more injurious than a scratch. Slow as it might be, Brunner knew firsthand the awful power within that skeletal frame, and knew that it would take only a slight slip, the merest fraction of slowness on his own part to give the monster another chance at him.

Brunner fell back to where Zelten stood. 'Well, I guess we now know that it can be hurt,' he commented between panting breaths. Zelten didn't respond, instead staring not at the Mardagg but at the glowing blade gripped in Brunner's hand. A scream of mortal terror brought the mercenary out of his thoughts and back to the situation at hand. One of the soldiers, emboldened by Brunner's attack, had lunged at the Mardagg, slashing at it with his sword. Unlike Brunner's blow, however, the sword had failed to injure the monster. Nor had the soldier been quick enough to avoid the Mardagg's return. Pausing for an instant, gaping at the ineffectiveness of his attack, the guard had waited too long to leap away. The Mardagg's scythe ripped through his back, exposing a fist-deep section of his spine.

There was no mistaking the effect the man's death had upon the daemon. At once its movements began to quicken, the speed of its scythe increase. The Mardagg swept the scythe low, coming in under the guard of the halberdiers, killing one of its opponents, strewing the bleeding halves of the man on the ground before it. A second died as Brunner charged towards it, the man's body flung across the hall by the immense scythe, smashing into a brazier of coals set against the far wall. The Mardagg turned on its last enemy as the man's halberd ineffectually hacked into the daemon's side. The man turned to flee, leaving his halberd still lodged in the Mardagg's side.

'It feeds on death and slaughter!' the bounty hunter shouted to the remaining soldiers. 'Every man it cuts down makes it stronger!' Brunner slashed at the daemon's back once more, Drakesmalice tearing through its glistening flesh. Once again, the skin seemed to harden and took on a darker hue. The Mardagg spun about, and this time Brunner missed the daemon's retaliation by a hair's length, the heat of the daemon's weapon washing over his face as it swept past. 'Get out of here!' he shouted to the last soldiers. There was a slim chance if the daemon could be denied its grisly nourishment that it would die. The already terrified men did not need much encouragement, taking to their heels. As they fled Brunner noted that the tapestries and rugs near the brazier overturned by the Mardagg were burning. Brunner could see that if the flames were left unchecked, it would not take long for the entire room to become engulfed in flame.

The Mardagg's scythe swept forward once more. Again, Brunner barely missed being cut by the deadly blade, jumping back at the last instant. The cold, empty sockets of the Mardagg stared down at him, and Brunner had the unpleasant sensation that the daemon was enjoying their deadly game, like a cat toying with a mouse. Unfortunately, in this game, Brunner had no illusions as to who was the cat.

Brunner started to retreat before the Mardagg, finding that he was being pushed deeper into the chamber by the daemon. He understood its intention now, as the heat and smoke began to grow behind him. Perhaps Drakesmalice had taught the daemon to be a bit more cautious. It was herding him, pushing the bounty hunter toward the flames. Fire might not harm the daemon, but it knew that its adversary could not boast such an immunity.

Suddenly the Mardagg spun around once more, swiping at something behind it. Brunner saw Zelten stabbing at the daemon's already injured flank. The mercenary intercepted the Mardagg's descending scythe with his sword. It was an expert parry, one that should have turned even that murderous blade. But the daemon's weapon was anything but normal. The scythe slashed through Zelten's sword, and continued on into the man's side, ripping through his flesh. Entrails erupted from the wound just below Zelten's ribs and the Reiklander fell in a mass of gore.

Brunner seized the moment it took the Mardagg to recover from its slaughter of his friend. Fuelled by hate and rage, the bounty hunter slashed at the back of the daemon's skeletal leg, cutting it just behind the knee. The skeletal limb bubbled and steamed where the enchanted sword struck it, cleaving halfway through the monster's leg. The daemon turned toward Brunner, its skull-like face as emotionless as ever. A wave of blistering heat billowed about Brunner as he firmed his grip upon Drakesmalice. The Mardagg's empty sockets stared down at him for a moment, as though savouring the man's hopeless defiance. Then the daemon's gaze shifted, staring at something beyond the bounty hunter.

For a moment, Brunner considered attacking the daemon as it stalked past him, seemingly oblivious now to his very existence. But he quickly dispelled the thought. Somehow, he had been granted a reprieve. He'd stared at death, and it had let him slip from its fingers. Only a fool would tempt its attention once more. The bounty hunter hurried towards the corridor, away from the intense heat and smoke surging outward from the blazing ruin of Prince Gambini's throne room. He looked back into the chamber, seeing that much of it was engulfed in crackling, snarling sheets of fire.

At the very centre of the room, through the leaping flames, Brunner could just make out the dais. He was surprised to see that Corvino was seated once more in the throne, having dragged his body back up the steps of the dais. The fool kept one hand around the crossbow bolt protruding from his chest, while pulling his body forward with the other. The madman was holding something that to Brunner's eyes looked to be a large, skeletal finger. Then a massive shape loomed above the dais. The black cloak about the Mardagg's shoulders was on fire, flaming scraps of cloth dropping from the burning garment, but the daemon was oblivious. Its skull-face glared down at the dying madman, its skeletal hand reaching out toward Corvino.

What more there was to see was obscured by the collapse of the supports for the floor above, fiery timbers and marble blocks raining down into the room. The bounty hunter retreated before the flames, heading back down the hallway. As he did so, he noted a mangled form lying upon the floor. Brunner paused and crouched over the ravaged frame, recognising it as Manfred Zelten. There was still some life in the mercenary and his eyes opened as Brunner knelt over him.

'Juliana?' he asked in a hoarse whisper. Dark blood bubbled from his mouth as he spoke.

'Safe,' Brunner assured him, seeing the man's body relax as he heard the news. 'Prince Gambini got her out.' The bounty hunter removed his helmet, staring down at the dying man. The roar and crackle of the flames was growing louder, smoke was filling the air, yet Brunner paid them little notice. There was something he had to know.

'Why didn't you go with them?' he asked. For a moment, he thought he had voiced his question to a corpse. Then Zelten's eyes focused on him once more. A faint smile twisted on the dying man's face.

'Dra... mali...' Zelten coughed. 'Only one... who can... use it.' The mercenary's gaze grew intense. 'He's... not... dead...' The words trailed off into a strangled gargle.

'No,' Brunner told the corpse as he stood. 'No, not dead. The bounty hunter's gloved hand closed into a fist. 'Waiting.'

The room was engulfed in flames now, the rear half of the chamber a veritable firestorm as the musty old tapestries burned. The bounty hunter paused in the doorway a moment, staring back into the conflagration. He could not see either the dais or the daemon through the fire and smoke, but just for a moment, he thought he heard a sound rise above the roar of the flames. The sharp, cutting, maniacal laughter of the lunatic Corvino.

BRUNNER SLOWLY RODE out the gates of Remas, his packhorse trailing after him, attached by a rope to Fiend's saddle. Brunner left behind him a city in turmoil. Hundreds had died in the Mardagg's brief rampage, and hundreds more had been killed by those the daemon's madness had infected. In the aftermath of the riots and turmoil of that night, the long suffering people of Remas had collectively and loudly risen up against the brutal Temple of Solkan, blaming them for not protecting the city from the manifestation of Chaos. It would be some time before the Solkanites regained their hold over the people again, some time before their white-robed militia would be able to walk the streets instilling fear.

The power and prestige of Prince Gambini had been severely crippled. The fire that had started in the throne room had raged out of control for much of the night, devouring the support timbers within the palazzo. As a result, two-thirds of the structure had toppled off the bridge and into the sea. Ambitious political enemies had taken the opportunity to undermine Gambini's position within the government, placing blame for the unrest on his shoulders. It was doubtful if Gambini would remain a triumvir after the next election, doubtful even if he would still sit on the Council of Fifty.

With the failing fortunes of Prince Umberto Gambini, Princess Juliana Bensario was summoned back to Pavona by her father. Among her entourage, the princess engaged the remains of Manfred Zelten's mercenary command. Brunner was certain that Schtafel and Meitz would find the smaller, quieter city more to their liking. Horst would probably sign up with the next expedition to reinforce the Border Princes after a few weeks of such surroundings.

The bounty hunter might have ridden with them, to take safety in numbers on his own journey back to Pavona, but he had no stomach for the woman's company. She had played no small part in the death of Manfred Zelten, it had been to cover her escape that the mercenary had stayed behind to fight the daemon. If not for her, Zelten might yet be alive. Brunner did not number so many among his friends that he could dismiss the death of one lightly. And there was another reason the bounty hunter had for wishing to remain alone. He glanced over his shoulder, staring for a moment at the leather bag lashed across Paychest's back.

The Temple of Morr would be a shunned place for decades, if not centuries. Not lightly would the people of Remas enter its dilapidated walls, recalling all too clearly the frightful abomination that had emerged from within. The place's dire reputation would grown until every dark imagining of the citizens would come to haunt its abandoned halls. Eventually, perhaps in a few hundred years, some prince would decide to prove to his people that he was above their superstitions and have the ruins razed, but until

then, the shadow of the Mardagg would continue to linger
on the city.

The bounty hunter, however, was too practical for such
imaginings. The daemon had left the structure, and he
doubted if, so soon after its dissolution, it would be able to
exert any great influence over the place of its summoning.
And there had been a chance, albeit however slight, that
Brunner might have been wrong in his assumption, that the
body of Scurio might yet lie beneath the Slaaneshi cult's
undertemple. It had taken him two hours to find the secret
to unlocking the concealed door that led to Corvino's sanctum. Within, he found a small chamber, the body of Alfredo
Gambini lying upon the floor. But he had also discovered
something else.

It was a strange and horrible thing, lying just beyond
Gambini's body, draped across the floor like a flat man, thin
as parchment, lying on the stones like some flesh-coloured
shadow. Brunner stared down at the thing, studying it for a
moment before he understood what it was. The flesh-shadow
was Scurio's skin, shed by the daemon like a serpent sloughing its scaly hide. It was split down the centre, almost like a
suit of clothing. Brunner turned the macabre skin over with
his foot, flipping the light, leathery husk onto its belly. The
face below the brim of Brunner's helm parted in a grim smile.
Staring up at him, almost perfect, was the hooded asp tattoo.

The bounty hunter had lost no time, rolling up the morbid skin like a blanket and stuffing it into a leather sack.
Masario had wanted proof that the murderer was dead, had
wanted the tell-tale mark of the killer brought to him.
Brunner only hoped that whatever spell his wizard
employed to verify that Scurio had been the killer didn't
draw the attention of that which had consumed the murderer's body.

Masario's gold would go far to lightening the heavy spirits
that had settled upon Brunner. The bounty hunter caressed
the hilt of Drakesmalice. Too many reminders of the past
had beset him during this hunt, too many old wounds had
opened up again. Manfred Zelten had reminded him of
much that he had put aside.

Brunner considered the young mercenary captain for a moment. There were too many men like Zelten and his father whose lives had been destroyed through treachery. Perhaps the time was coming for them to be avenged. Yes, perhaps Brunner would leave the squabbling politics of Tilea behind him for awhile, and ply his trade in the Empire or Bretonnia for a time…

THE BOUNTY HUNTER was lost in thoughts of faraway places and long ago times as he rode out the great gates of Remas. He did not notice the scraggly old beggar with the long white beard who watched him depart. Had he done so, he would have been surprised to recognise the same mendicant who had cast bones to tell his fortune in the streets of Pavona.

The old beggar cackled to himself as he watched the bounty hunter ride away. The hired killer had been a useful pawn, just as his foundling apprentice Corvino had been. It was always wise to get someone else to cast the most dangerous spells. One did not last long in the service of the wily Changer of Ways without learning never to put one's own neck on the chopping block. The spell to free the Mardagg was almost certainly lethal to the one who invoked it; removing its spirit from its human host was an even more certain form of death. Fortunately, Corvino had thought he would be able to control the daemon. If he had only paid attention, perhaps the little fool might have seen how he was being used, that his ambitions were nothing to the Dark Gods. All his schemes had been used solely to return one of Khorne's prized servants to the Realm of Chaos, nothing more. Poor Corvino, he had never understood that no man uses Chaos; it uses him.

The sorcerer looked again at the diminishing figure of the bounty hunter. He hoped that the man would fare well wherever his trail led him.

'The Ruinous Powers,' he prophesied, 'may yet have a use for you.'

ABOUT THE AUTHOR

C. L. Werner has written a number of Lovecraftian pastiches and pulp-style horror stories for assorted small press publications. More recently the prestigious pages of *Inferno!* have been infiltrated by the dark imaginings of the writer's mind.
Currently living in the American south-west, he continues to write stories of mayhem and madness in the Warhammer World.